10/2

ANUMAL EMPIRE

Book One

LAZARBALL

By
David Ayres
&
Darren Jacobs

CHAPTER ONE

INTO THE PLAINS.

Raindrops beat against the desert ground. The moon slipped out from behind the clouds, reflecting silvery light off the dirt-filled puddles. The cold, denning night air grated against Clinton's throat as he raced through the Great Plains of Nomica. His leg muscles burned. Adrenalin surged through his body, powering his flight. He could smell his pursuer's breath, dank and rancid, and chanced a peek over his shoulder.

His attacker leaped.

A paw slammed into Clinton's ribs, swatting him like a knat. He crashed to the ground, yet rolled to the side, extending his clawed fingertips. Digging into the soft earth he tried to scrabble away, but the scavenger skidded to a halt next to him, churning up mud and grit with its sickle-clawed feet. Something smashed into Clinton with the force of a hammer, beating him down again. He struggled, gasping for breath, but the scavenger cuffed him again. The swipe flipped him onto his back. A leathery paw suddenly pressed against Clinton's chest, pinning him under its weight. The scavenger's face loomed above. It sniffed. A strand of saliva trickled from its mouth while a meaty tongue slid along its teeth in anticipation.

"Grack!" groaned Clinton, recognizing the breed of scavenger. The young lion shoved against its leg. He sunk his teeth into the grack's hide and raked its flank with his claws, yet he barely left a mark.

"Get off!"

The pressure on Clinton's chest increased.

"Help me! Help…me!"

With every passing second, he felt the boulder-like slab of muscle squeezing the life from him. A tear slipped down his cheek as his struggles weakened. His vision started to fade, overwhelmed by sparks of light and approaching darkness.

Something whooshed over his head.

The beast glanced up before emitting a confused whine.

Framed by the moonlight, a shadow flipped through the air and landed on the grack's back. In one fluid movement a rope was lashed around its chunky neck, causing the scavenger to buck. Clinton felt the sudden release of pressure as the paw rose, and he gasped for air. His senses sharpened. Wasting no time, he shoved the beast off him and scrabbled to the side.

"Is he clear?" yelled a croaky voice behind Clinton.

"Yes!" shouted the shadow on the monster's back. "Now get a move on!"

With another whoosh, a spear streaked over Clinton's head and slammed into the grack's neck, squelching to a halt. The monster roared. Blood splattered. The scavenger shook its head from side to side, desperate to dislodge the weapon, while a steady stream of blood trickled from the wound. Slowly, the scavenger released a sickening gurgle. The figure on the grack dropped the makeshift reins and flipped from its back, landing neatly on his feet as the beast's legs buckled. With a final fluid-filled grunt, the grack crashed to the ground like a collapsing building, and rolled onto its side.

Clinton cringed. He felt an impulse to run, to flee as fast as he could, but remained rooted to the spot. The scavenger shuddered. Its chest rose and fell with each labored gasp. Every shred of ferocity it possessed seemed to melt away, reducing it from the fearsome predator and into the vulnerable prey. The shadowy figure stepped in front of the lion, blocking his view of the dying beast. It reached into its coat and slowly unsheathed a deadly hunting knife.

Clinton flinched.

The figure flipped the weapon around and presented the handle to Clinton. "So? What you waiting for? C'mon, stand up."

The young lion blinked away his tears as he climbed to his feet. "Dad, I—"

"How many times have I told you to never run from a grack? But you don't listen. You know you can't outrun them."

Clinton wiped his nose with his sleeve. "*You* could," he mumbled.

Clinton's father opened his mouth to snap a reply but then stopped himself. The rain plopped against his brimmed hat as he peered at the boy. Like Clinton, he had a strong feline physique and muscular legs and arms evolved specifically to hunt. Graying fur framed his narrowed eyes. He sighed. "That isn't the point, Clinton. You know what you should have done." He squeezed his son's arm. "Tell me! What do you do when a grack pins you down?"

Clinton's mouth floundered. A list of scavengers ran through his head, their primary defenses, their social structures, their territories, and most importantly their weak spots. His dad had drilled all of this knowledge into him over the seasons. And normally he would have answered. But now...

"I-I don't know," he finally admitted.

"Their belly, boy." His father shook him. "You could have kicked its lower belly and winded it. Look, if you don't know this stuff inside out, then...then you won't stand a chance out here."

"Aww, leave him be, Grayorr," chided the croaky voice. "You should be impressed. He's certainly got his dad's speed. Gotta hand him that."

Clinton turned around and saw Arkie, a small gecko, yank his spear from the grack's neck. "Me, though, I'm too old to be running round the desert in the middle of the bluggin' night. Sure hope I don't catch a cold, 'cause if I do, there's a certain young lion I'll be feeding to the scavengers myself."

Arkie winked at Clinton and smiled.

Grayorr huffed. "Hardly a time to break out in celebration when my son almost gets himself killed. At least he's in one piece though." He caught sight of the wound on Clinton's side. "Oh, for scrud's sake! Your mother is going to go crazy."

"What's he done, Gray?"

"It's his ribs. Pass me a bandage will you. I'm in serious trouble. Loretta is going to kill me."

Arkie began to fish around in his bag.

Grayorr glanced down at the grack as the beast continued to gasp for breath. "Still, no time like the present." He sighed. "Might as well get it over with tonight and make this your first kill. Clint, you ready?"

Clinton tensed. He looked at the knife in his hand, then back at the scavenger. "What? You mean now?"

"When do you think I mean?" chuckled Grayorr. "You gotta do it sooner or later. Put it out of its misery, son. Besides, the meat will fetch a nice price at the village."

"Five nugs a steak," added Arkie, tossing a bandage to the older lion before peering off into the darkness. "Won't be long before the rest of the pack arrives, Gray. We'd best hurry."

Clinton stared at the knife. "But I-I can't... Do I have to?"

Arkie rolled his eyes. "Of course you do, kid. Or do you think the humans are gonna magic themselves out of extinction an' do it for you, huh?"

"Look, Clint, he's right. We haven't got long."

"But I—"

"Do it, son. It's in pain."

Clinton shook his head. "But it's not right."

"Clinton Narfell! Do you think meat just appears from out of nowhere, huh? That your meals are conjured up from thin air? How are you ever supposed to hunt the Plains if a bit of scavenger blood gets your hackles up? Just do it!"

Howling cries echoed in the distance.

Grayorr peered off towards the mountains lining the horizon. "Damn it, they're nearer than I thought." He turned back to his son. "Come on, Clint. Let's get it over with, then I'll distract them while you two take it back to the village."

Clinton took a reluctant step closer to the scavenger. He raised the knife, but something seemed to freeze his actions. He felt hopeless and desperate, yet he knew the feelings were not his own; they appeared to radiate from the dying scavenger.

More tears slipped down his cheeks. His heart pounded. Everything around him seemed to be sucked into a bubble of silence. The scavenger locked its shiny, black eyes on Clinton. Too weak to move, it shuddered, aware of the advancing figure. Clinton pushed the uncomfortable emotions aside, trying to clear his mind.

He clenched his jaw and pressed the knife against the grack's neck, determined to prove his worth to his father, but however much he tried to slit the scavenger's throat, he could not do it. The feelings remained.

"I-I can't," he confessed, stepping away. "I just can't."

He dropped the knife and escaped into the darkness.

"Clint!" shouted Grayorr, over the sound of the rain. "What are you doing? Come back here!"

The young lion, however, continued to run, desperate to flee from the disappointment he had caused.

"I said get back here right now!" yelled Grayorr.

Clinton refused to listen. He charged ahead, running away from his father and from the expectations forced upon him. He vaulted the skeletal shell of an Olde-world car and sped off into the darkness. A long, moaning grack call wailed out along the horizon.

Traversing the edges of a huge, scrap-filled hole, Clinton's gaze remained fixed on the horizon when the ground suddenly fell away beneath him. He hit the dirt with a thud before skidding down a slope towards the scrapheap below. His body crashed into jutting boulders and half buried metal, while rocks and grit scraped his face. He yelped and grunted with every strike, until he eventually skidded to a stop.

"Clinton! CLINTON!" bellowed Grayorr, appearing at the top of the incline.

Clinton lifted himself onto his hands and knees. Cuts and gashes latticed his furry skin, and blood trickled down the side of his ribs. Climbing to his feet, he looked back up at his dad and Arkie.

"I'm alright," he muttered.

Something moved to his left.

Clinton snapped his attention onto the shape of a small figure stumbling towards him through the scrap. It swayed on its feet as if drunk on grain water.

The lion scrunched his eyes together, bringing the shadow into focus. "H-hello?"

The figure trundled closer, and with every step he could make out more of its details. It looked feline…and young, around the same age as him. It wore a long cloak, but he could not fully see the anumal's features underneath the hood. Desperation and sadness washed over Clinton again, soaking into him, making him feel empty and hollow. The smell of blood tinged the air.

He jumped as Grayorr placed a hand on his shoulder.

"Easy now, Clint," said his father. "Are you okay?"

Clinton nodded, but his gaze drifted back to the approaching figure.

Grayorr stepped in front of him. "Careful. We don't know who it is yet."

Arkie raised his spear. "Some kinda trap? Nomads? A feral tribe maybe?"

"Not this close to the village," replied Grayorr. "I'm not sure what's up."

The trio stared at the approaching figure for a moment, before Arkie finally called out, "Hey! You in trouble?"

The cloaked stranger did not respond. It continued onwards, swaying on its feet.

"What happened to you?" shouted Grayorr.

The figure coughed and stumbled against an oil drum before dropping to one knee and collapsing face first into a puddle of rainwater. No one hesitated. The group sped towards the figure, but Clinton got there first. Grabbing its shoulders, he turned it over. The wet hood clung to the stranger's face, obscuring his view, so he yanked it away…

A male tiger stared back at him. He looked a bit younger than Clinton, but his blood-covered fur gave him a grim appearance. Clinton's head cocked to the side, unable to tear his gaze from the pitiful sight before him.

"Help me," murmured the tiger, feebly, before his eyes rolled back in his head and he passed out.

CHAPTER TWO

HIDDEN AMONGST THE SHADOWS.

TEN YEARS LATER.

Hidden beneath the bleachers of Wooburn's lazarball stadium, Clinton studied the two players through a small gap between the seats. A glowing lazar plummeted into the submerged gamefield.

"Incoming!" shouted a warthog named Jed Medinka. He charged ahead, metal-clad boots clanking against the polished floor as he chased the ball of light. The warthog dove forwards, thrusting his arm out to catch it.

A stocky wolf suddenly ploughed into Jed's side, his rusty shoulder-guard ramming into the hog's stomach. The lazar sped past them both, bounced against the floor and rebounded through the stadium's open roof. It fizzled away to nothing while the two crashed down in a tangled mess.

"Scrud it, Keefer!" snapped the hog, heaving himself to his feet. He stepped over the wolf, managing to give him a swift dig in the ribs with his boot. "You dumb glux. Now I have to reset the generator."

Clinton winced at the jab and a dull pain flashed through his own ribs - the ghost of an injury he had picked up a decade ago in the Plains.

The midday sun had almost reached its peak, shining through the gaps in the rickety bleachers. He peeled his hunter robes away from his sweaty chest. Dust danced through the air in trance-inducing whirls. It amazed him how the old stadium was still standing. Above him, wooden posts reached up into the sky, supporting row upon row of seating and metal beams that sprouted from the ground like rusty trees, barely holding the structure together. He could not help but shake his head. What was once an inspiring building had slowly been beaten down by years of neglect. Now it sat disused and abandoned like a lame giant.

He closed his eyes. If he imagined hard enough he could almost hear the roar of the crowds, smell the blood and sweat in the air, and taste the pride and fear that every player had felt on the gamefield in the ancient days. Back then blood was spilled, bones broken, and determination tested as every player battled for clan honor.

"Come on, Jed. Stop scruddin' 'round an' fire another lazar!" yelled the wolf.

Clinton snapped back to the present and sighed. The reality of the building's decay betrayed its grandeur, and since the disbandment of Wooburn's team - the Plains Punishers - the stadium had festered. Padlocked and chained away from the villagers, the only anumals who used it now were ones like the fools in front of him.

"Okay, okay. I'm doing it, Keefer," replied the warthog. He ran up the side of the gamefield to a large black box positioned on the top of the sloping wall. The warthog grabbed a crank handle on its side and began to turn it. Lights flickered erratically on the box. Two exhausts juddered to life, spewing black smoke skywards. Attached to the box was a long funnel, angled in the direction of a giant crystal hanging above the center of the stadium. Jed wound the handle with more gusto, and the generator let out a whine. Sparks began to pop out of the heating vents. Clinton could see the wolf growing nervous as the noise increased.

"Come on, Jed! Fire the thing!"

The warthog huffed. "Reckon you can do it faster?"

"Yeah, but it's your turn, so shut up and get a move on before we get caught," growled the wolf.

Just as the generator began to emit a high-pitched wail, Jed slammed his hand against the release button. The box shuddered as a burst of light streaked out the side funnel and off towards the giant crystal. The noise faded as the lazar disappeared into the hanging jewel, only to be redirected out one of its many facets, randomly shooting it into the sunken gamefield again.

This time it headed straight for the wolf.

"Oh, scrud!" snorted the warthog, sliding down the sloped wall. He barged the wolf out of the way and stretched his arm out. The lazar slammed into his gauntlet, causing the glove to glow bright red, but the hog dithered, unsure of how to further press his advantage.

Clinton knew Jed Medinka had only a few seconds left before the ball of light would automatically be ejected, and he shook his head when the hog flung his arm towards the scoring targets at the other end of the field.

The lazar shot out.

Jed set off running.

"No you don't!" shouted Keefer. He grabbed Jed's back leg, sending him crashing to the ground.

Jed tried to scrabble back to his feet again, but the wolf would not yield, leaving them both squabbling on the floor like infants.

"Pathetic," Clinton muttered. He resisted the urge to show them exactly how the game was played, and took a small leather-bound book out from under his cloak. Using a nub of a pencil, below a long list of player's names and notes, he quickly scribbled:

Jed Medinka – Warthog (nephew of Kit Medinka)
Mid-Fielder
Physically strong – possible defender?
Bad at long-range

Keefer Jolt – Wolf
Defense
Bad at everything!

Clinton closed the book with a snap, but a folded piece of paper slipped free and fell to the ground. He picked it up. *Wooburn Biennial Solo Lazarball Tournament* was written across its top, while underneath was *Players Application Form*. He examined it for a moment before folding it up again and slipping it back amongst the other pages.

A burst of red suddenly exploded against the bleachers next to him, lighting up the darkness with a blinding flash. The lion jumped to his right as shards of tingly light sprayed through the hole and over him.

"Scrud!" shouted the warthog.

"You can't even shoot straight, you dumb pig!" laughed the wolf.

"Shut up a moment. I think I saw someone," snapped Jed

Clinton flinched.

"Where?"

The warthog's voice gained volume as he carefully approached. "Over here."

Clinton sank to his knees and scrabbled into a pool of shadow, pressing himself up against a wooden support. Footsteps thudded against the boards above, and grit dropped onto the dreadlocks of his sandy mane-like hair. He held his breath as the two anumals peered through the gap next to him.

The silence stretched out.

"You're seeing things, Jed," laughed the wolf, finally.

"No, I definitely saw someone." Jed snorted, his breath wafting Clinton's mane. "I thought you said we had the place to ourselves?"

"We do... I think."

"You think? We'll be banned from the tournament if we're caught here without permission."

Keefer sat down. "Oh, stop moaning. You sound like my mom."

Wooburn's clock tower suddenly began to clang.

"That the time already?" The warthog turned to look at the sun's position in the sky. "We'd better go."

"Eh? Nah, I reckon there's time enough for one more round," growled the wolf.

"Yeah, and risk getting caught by the guards after their break? I don't think so!"

The warthog pounded back down the bleachers and across the gamefield. The wolf sighed but followed after his friend.

"Jed? Jed, come on! We won't get caught. I swear..."

His promises slowly faded with his departure.

Clinton let out a deep breath. He picked up a large bag next to him, and chancing one last glance along the gamefield, fled from the underbelly of the bleachers. The lion ran out from the stadium's shade and into Wooburn's blistering heat. His thin robes flapped loosely around him, but they could not conceal the fact that he had grown up to have a lithe, athletic frame hidden beneath. He paused outside the entrance to catch a quick breath.

Market traders hollered from their stalls lining the street, selling Olde-world objects and human made items such as engine parts or refurbished mech. Others sold older artifacts and shiny stones excavated from the scrapheaps in the Plains. There was cloth for sale too, and spices, and herbs. Fires burned from the armorer's kilns, their hammers clanging a rhythm like a ticking clock over the bustle of voices. The smell of sizzling leece legs drifted in the air, mingling with the odor of bedpans and toilet pots emptied from the upper floors of the clay and brick built shacks.

Anumals swarmed outside the stadium as a procession of primates trundled towards the village's main entrance. Primates of every shape and size, from lumbering orangutans to scampering marmosets, surged in one huge tribe, dragging their scant personal possessions along with them.

"Good riddance to 'em is what I say," scoffed an elderly polecat standing in front of Clinton. Dressed in expensive looking clothes, she carried a leather parasol, shading herself from the sun. "The village is better off without 'em."

"Careful what you say there, dearie," replied a lizard next to her. She scratched her head, causing flakes of dry skin to sprinkle over her fine attire. "Who will you get to clean your house if they keep leaving the village like this?"

"Oh, I don't need to worry about that," snorted the polecat. "They're like scuttlers; they'll keep breeding, replenishing their stocks. Disgusting creatures."

Clinton barged past the old crones, jostling them out of their conversation, and ignored their indignant huffs and tuts. Pulling his hood up to hide his face, he grasped the bag tight, crossed the street, and disappeared from sight into a nearby alley.

* * *

11

Clinton Narfell hit Wooburn's back streets. He vaulted walls, skidded under fences, and flipped over low rooftops.

Dropping from a roof, he landed on all fours, and then took off again. The lion sprinted down a narrow alley and rounded a corner before skidding to a halt. Panic rose inside him. He quickly dodged behind a pile of broken boxes, squashing his body flat against the wall. After a moment, he poked his head out again and cursed to himself.

Two anumals loitered at the end of the alley. One of them, a large bear, swung a metal chain while sniffing the air. His smaller dingo companion paced back and forth as if on patrol. One of his floppy ears had been torn to pieces – the result of various 'work related incidents.' Wooburn's citizens parted around the pair like water breaking against rocks. Their voices cut above the crowd's din.

"I'm bored of waiting, Barn. Where's Snarg?" snapped the dingo. "Thought you said the wegg could hunt anything down?"

"He can," shrugged the bear. He snatched a flea from his fur and casually squashed it. "He's prob'ly found a fresh pile of dung to roll round in, that's all."

"I'll roll you in dung if he don't turn up soon. You do know we ain't gonna see any of that food again? However much the boss wants it back, it'll be hidden or eaten by now. I'm tellin' you."

Clinton gulped and looked down at the bag in his hands.

"Well, stealing from boss is bad. Get punished," sniffed Barn in his normal, blunt manner.

"You don't say," sneered Graff. "If you ask me, searching's a waste of time."

"Didn't—"

"'Cause we all know who took it. I mean, why we don't just go round to his house and smash his door down is beyond me."

"Smash who's door down?' Barn scratched the side of his head before his face lit up. "Ohhh, you think it could be—"

"Exactly," nodded the dingo. "Think about it, Barn. Monkeys start to leave, and food goes missing. It's a perfect opportunity for him to slip inside the store when everyone's back is turned. And where's he been all mornin', eh? He hasn't been working. I never saw him return from the first hunt. Did you?"

"Who?"

"Clinton Narfell, you dumb..." Graff huffed and turned in Clinton's direction, before turning back to Barn again. "Look, just keep them scruddin' eyes of yours peeled, alright? I'll bet you my wages he's behind this."

"Snarg'll get him," promised Barn. "Rip his legs right off."

Graff slapped Barn on the back and let out a cackle. "And hopefully his arms too."

Clinton's stomach churned. Lifting the bag over his shoulder, he turned and fled into the labyrinth of back streets. If he could ditch the bag at home and then head off to work before they saw him, no one would be any the wiser.

However, he would have to move fast.

The clock was ticking.

The race was on.

CHAPTER THREE

THE SABERS.

Even though a sound like rolling thunder barreled through Wooburn's bustling streets, not a single cloud lingered in the desert sky.

Ephraim's huge feet pounded against the ground as he charged into the market district.

"Watch it you dumb glux!" yelled a stall owner when the nine-foot elephant sped by, banging against his display and sending reams of material rolling across the ground.

Ephraim ignored the trader's cries. He chanced a quick glance over his shoulder. Through the crowds he could see silhouettes trailing after him on all fours, leaping over toppled stalls, skirting up the sides of walls, and flipping themselves over villagers in their chase. One of his pursuers let out a roar that echoed off the nearby buildings.

"You can't run forever, elephant! This ends today."

Ephraim pressed on harder. Sweat soaked his knee-length cargo shorts and trickled down his top, making it cling to his leathery, gray hide. His arm muscles bulged. Petrified anumals dove out of his way as the behemoth bolted past. He stumbled, yet managed to stop himself from falling into a butcher's stall. Glancing around, he saw an alley between two sun-baked buildings that led to the rear of a scrap metal shop. Snatching a lungful of air, he raced for the entrance. The temperature dropped as Ephraim plowed into the passageway lined with piles of precarious metal and trash.

"Scrud," he hissed, seeing only a dead end.

He juddered to a halt and spun around to retrace his steps, when the light at the end of the passage was suddenly blocked. Four phantom-like silhouettes lingered in the opening before slowly swaggering into the alley. Their shadows swamped the light on the ground like a creeping tide, and their panting breath seemed louder than the chug of the machines in the nearby yard. Ephraim inched deeper into the alley, darting glances everywhere, but the smooth walls loomed high, offering him no means of escape.

"What's up, fatso?" asked a voice. "Bet you wish you could fly now, huh?"

Behind the lead feline, two males and a female stepped into view. Each one wore scavenger skin jackets and utility belts containing a variety of knives. They all possessed an assortment of scars, torn tails, and bare patches of fur where it had been yanked out. On the back of their jackets were identical symbols: two fang-like knives crossing each other with blood trickling down each blade.

Ephraim retreated another step. "Look, Gizi. I don't know what you want, but—"

"But what?" he sneered. "Come on, spit it out."

The female barged her way past Gizi, knocking her comrade out of the way. "Thought you could run from us forever, didn't you? Thought the little pussycats'd give up and leave you alone?" She flicked her hand and sharp claws protracted from the ends of her fingers. "Well, think again, sugar."

Another fatter feline began to snigger. "Ha! You tell 'im, Hiro."

"Shut your mouth, Jakz!" she snapped. "You and Kayn watch our backs. Me and Gizi, well, we've got business to attend to."

"As you wish, sis," winked Kayn, a black patch of fur covering his right eye.

Ephraim could not catch his breath. Everything around him seemed to grind to a halt. The pounding of his heart echoed in his head, and for a moment all strength drained from his body. He clenched his hands into fists. "J-just stay away from me."

Gizi padded closer. "Now don't be doing anything stupid, elephant." He raised a hand and his claws sneaked slowly into view. "This won't hurt as much if you relax."

The feline charged.

Ephraim stumbled back and flattened himself against the wall. Realizing he had no other choice, he squeezed his eyes shut and bowed low like a battering ram. With the force of an explosion, he burst into a charge, not caring whom or what he slammed into.

Trashcans, boxes, and scrap metal erupted skywards in a storm of flying garbage.

"Gizi, look out!" Hiro yelled, diving out of Ephraim's way.

Catching the brunt of the attack, Gizi flew back through the air like a rag doll. Ephraim ignored the sound of the feline slamming against the wall, and ploughed on, his legs pumping away like a locomotive. An object suddenly clipped his feet, causing him to stumble. He glanced down and tripped over a garbage can that had been thrown in his path. The world spun as he careened into the wall.

"I got him!" hollered Kayn.

Ephraim toppled, crushing half the garbage can as if it was paper.

"He's down! Get him! Quick! He's down!" yelled Jakz.

"What about Gizi?" Kayn asked.

"Forget Gizi," snarled Hiro. "Concentrate on the fat mess."

Something shoved against Ephraim's chest. He looked up to see Hiro glaring down at him, pinning him under her weight, with a hand on each of his shoulders. She dug her claws into his wrinkly, gray skin, causing blood to trickle down the crevices of his muscles. Jakz and Kayn appeared by Hiro's side and stood on the elephant's arms.

Kayn waved a glass bottle in his face. "Now don't you even think about using that strength of yours," he panted. "One move and the sharp end of this will find your eye."

Elephant blood dripped onto the ground.

"I suppose you think this is all some kind of game, huh, fat boy?" Hiro snarled.

Ephraim swallowed, but his throat felt as dry as sand. "I-I haven't done anything wrong."

Hiro balked as she grabbed a handful of the elephant's ear, pulling the skin taut. "You know what you did." She flexed the fingers on her hand and her claws extended further. She licked her lips. "You may be big, but you sure are dumb. Oh, I'm gonna enjoy takin' you apart. Just try not to scream too loud. There's a good boy."

"Wait!" shouted a shaky voice.

Ephraim looked past Hiro and saw Gizi stumbling towards him, barely managing to stay on his feet. The feline jostled her out of the way and grabbed Ephraim by the throat.

"If anyone's gonna end this scrud, it's gonna be me."

CHAPTER FOUR

CURIOSITY KILLS.

Clinton ran effortlessly up a wall and flipped backwards. He twisted midair, and reaching out, grabbed a sign attached to the side of an adjacent building. Pulling himself up, he balanced on all fours and then padded along the narrow ledge until he came to its end. The lion stood up. Spreading his arms wide, he fell gracefully forwards, swan diving into the yard below. At the last moment he performed a flip…and landed on a line of washing strung across the alley. Clinton stumbled sideways, blinded by a pair of threadbare trousers that had wrapped around his face. He yanked them off, shook his head, and tried to regain his focus.

Mangled contraptions appeared before him. Metal girders stood propped against walls, and broken engine parts lay scattered across the ground, slowly rusting away with age. In the background a soft rumbling noise chugged and numerous machines spewed foul-smelling smoke into the muggy air. Clinton could not help but smile. He had ended up in the alley next to old Krog's scrap yard. He could not count the number of times he had been discovered taking this particular shortcut when he was younger, and could give an almost perfect rendition of what the grumpy scrap seller would yell at any trespassers. However, Krog was never the real danger in the equation; the real danger was something far worse.

Krog's Wife.

Named due to Krog never taking a mate and only ever showing affection towards his grumpy, old pet wegg, a familiar feeling of excited panic rushed through Clinton as he caught sight of the infamous beast. Piles of empty plant pots, a rocking chair, and some oil-smeared trashcans also framed the large, weather-beaten porch. A tall, metal fence, topped with rusted razor wire, surrounded the property, and a loose chain was left strewn across the center of the yard. Clinton padded closer to look through the gaps in the fence. His stomach dropped.

"Oh, scrud."

Krog's Wife lay sound asleep next to her iron kennel, sprawled flat on her back in the sun. Her long green tongue lolled lazily out the side of her mouth.

Clinton began to scale the fence. When he reached the top he hesitated and peered down into the yard. The mutt remained dead to the world. He shifted the heavy bag over the razor wire, but as he did so the top of the fence juddered and groaned. To his dismay, it slowly started to bow down into the yard. The links holding the railing jingled. Clinton gasped and leaned back towards the direction of the alley, intending to escape as quickly as possible, but the razor wire snagged onto his hunter's robes.

"Frag it."

Yanking his leg away, he ripped his robes free, but slipped and suddenly lost his grip. Spinning in midair, the lion landed with a thud inside the yard, only an arm's length away from Krog's Wife.

He froze.

Winded from the plummet, he struggled to control his breath while the metal fence sprang back into place with a metallic clang. The lion cringed, waiting for Krog's Wife to burst out of her slumber and attack, but the wegg merely let out a few sluggish snorts and twitched her clawed feet. Other than that, the hairless slab of muscle continued to sleep.

She must be going deaf in her old age, he thought.

Clinton climbed to his feet and padded towards the scrap yard's exit. He slipped out and quietly shut the gate behind him, but something made him pause. Voices echoed from the far end of the alley, hissing and laughing. A loud crash shook the ground. Fighting his curiosity, Clinton told himself to ignore the clamor, to leave the area and not look back, but something else inside also urged him to wait. An unexplainable feeling of pain and hurt overtook him, freezing the lion to the spot.

"Only a fool knowingly disturbs a kraggon's nest," he mumbled, quoting Arkie's words.

Nevertheless, Clinton felt drawn to the noise, and could not shake off the overwhelming need to stay and investigate. A panic rose within him that felt alien, but he dismissed it and took a few more hesitant steps...and then paused. He looked at the bag in his hands, and then back in the direction of the ruckus. The hissing intensified, accompanied by the cries of an anumal in distress. As quickly as he could, Clinton returned to the scrap yard and eased the bag into a small gap behind the wegg's kennel. When he was certain that it would not be discovered, he headed back to the alley again. Unable to ignore his curiosity, he boosted himself up to grab the top of the wall and slowly peered over.

"Sabers," he snarled. "I should've known."

The lion dove over the wall.

Clinton's shoulder collided with the Saber straddling an elephant. The feline tumbled to the side and his head bounced against the wall.

Gizi went down without saying a word.

Skidding to a stop in front of the elephant, Clinton bared his fangs and bellowed an ear-splitting roar. Jakz and Kayn hunched down defensively, hackles raised, while their claws shot out from their fingertips. In the near distance the sound of uncontrollable barking struck up as Krog's Wife was awakened from her slumber.

"Well, look who's decided to join the fun," jeered Hiro, slipping in between Kayn and Jakz. "Had a change of heart and decided to join the party, Narfell?"

Claws slid out from the end of Clinton's fingertips. "I'd rather rot in the Plains."

Jakz sidled closer to the elephant. "Oh, come off it. I'm sure we could do something to persuade you?" He smirked. "How long's it been since you've had a decent meal?"

"And what's that got to do with anything?"

"Come on, Narfell, it has gotta be ages since you've had a full belly? Tasted any fresh meat recently?" Jakz ran one of his claws playfully across the wall. "How do grain slops an' leftovers taste these days?"

Clinton snatched a glance at the elephant behind him. His clothes were torn, mud smeared his skin, and blood dripped from the gashes on his shoulders. "Shut up, Jakz. You've played your games, now leave him alone."

"Games?" replied Jakz. "Maybe scruds like you play games,

Narfell. But we're Sabers. We're above games. We're the prime anumals, y'see, the key species—"

"First to be created, leaders of the anumal army, blah, blah, blah," cut in Clinton. "Are you still spouting that same old supremacy rubbish? Aren't you bored of it yet?"

Hiro's jaw tightened. She stepped closer and pointed at the elephant. "Do you know what he did, Narfell?"

Clinton shrugged. "Probably looked at you the wrong way or something."

"He hurt Brox," Kayn answered.

Hiro came face to face with Clinton and stared straight in his eyes. "Intentionally or not, he killed my Brox. That heifer meddled in affairs that didn't concern him."

"T-they were attacking an innocent anumal," Ephraim stuttered. "He owed the Sabers credits, so five of them were going to attack him. I just tried to—"

"Shut up!" roared Jakz.

Ephraim flinched and closed his mouth.

"This gutter scum hurt and killed one of our number. So you know the rules, Narfell," Hiro hissed. "It's only fair."

"And you think you can just start carving him up as punishment? He's not a scavenger, he's an *anumal*: a thinker. You can't do that; it's against the law."

Jakz stepped forward. "He deserves it!"

"Frag the laws, bro," shouted Kayn. "It's time we reclaimed the natural order, hunter and prey, where only the strong survive."

Jakz rubbed his hands together. "Yeah, just like it used to be with mankind."

Hiro and Kayn spat on the ground at the mention of their predecessors.

"Exactly," hissed Hiro, wiping a stray globule from her lips. "That elephant is a second-rate species. That *thing* killed one of us."

"So allow the court to deal with it. Now let him go."

"Let him go?" Hiro chuckled. "This is a Saber matter, Narfell, we're above the law, and we'll deal with it our own way. Now if you aren't with us then get the skorr out of our way."

Clinton huffed and shook his head. "Listen to you. Stop trying to be something you aren't, Hiro."

"And what's that then, huh? Tell me, what am I trying to be?"

"Respected," answered Clinton. "You're trying to win the respect of Wooburn and everyone else in this village. But you'll never get any. Well, at least you won't get any from me."

An annoyed grimace flashed across her face. Kayn stepped past her, glass bottle gripped in hand. "C'mon, bro. Let's stop all this. Just reconsider our offer; join our number." He raised his arm to display the markings running across the back of his hand, up his forearm, and towards his elbow. A complex pattern of interweaving tribal markings had been burned into his flesh, stopping any hair from growing there. Hiro and Jakz revealed the same patterns on their arms too. "The Ocelot Brand is the key to everything you desire, Narfell. Become one of us and we'll have you out of the slums and living the high life before you know it."

Clinton laughed and stared at the back of Kayn's hand. He shoved his own unmarked arm out in front of his foes. "My fur may be dirty, but at least it isn't bloodstained. My father once told me the Sabers tried to recruit him into their ranks, but he told them where to shove their Ocelot Brand and made me swear I'd do the same."

"Easy for your father," shrugged Kayn. "He wasn't the one having to scratch around in the dirt to survive. He had a life, unlike the sons he left behind." Kayn looked at Hiro and then grinned back at Clinton. "Hey, maybe if we open up our invitation to your little bro, he might think differently."

The Sabers chuckled.

Clinton felt his heart begin to race. A flush of anger swept through him.

"Don't bring him into this."

Jakz danced about in front of Clinton's face, wiggling his chubby belly. "Ohhh, look at the big, bad kitty getting all angry with us."

The group laughed even harder.

Clinton's teeth clamped together. The urge to fly into them with his claws slashing built with every passing second, but then something made him stop. He caught sight of movement to his left; the elephant had climbed to his knees and was edging towards the exit. Clinton took a calming breath and backed up against the wall, keeping their attention fixed on him.

Kayn raised a claw and scratched behind his ear before licking the back of his hand. "Yeah, I reckon we're wasting our time on you, Narfell. But who knows, maybe we could save that little brother of yours, before Wooburn is landed with another pathetic scrud? We can only pray he's got more common sense." His smile slipped into a scowl. "I'm sure he'll be more pliable after he hears what we have to offer him."

Clinton fought to keep his anger in check. He leaned closer to Kayn and whispered calmly into his face. "Common sense, you say?" A smirk tickled the corners of his mouth. "Well, it looks like the elephant's got bundles of that."

At the mention of the elephant the Sabers spun on their heels, searching for him.

But Ephraim had vanished.

Swinging back to face Clinton again, Hiro's snarl twisted with fury. "You sneaky little..." She swung her claws at his face, but the lion blocked the strike. Ramming his shoulder into her chest, he shoved her towards the exit.

"I warned you to never mention my brother again!" He clenched his fists and slowly followed after her. "Now try that again and see what happens."

Hiro shook her head. "Y-you're gonna regret that, Narfell. I'm gonna make you pay."

Clinton rushed at her, but she sprinted away.

"The next time I see you, lion," she yelled, "I'll be laughing in your bust up face."

Without pause, she fled the alley.

Clinton ceased his pursuit. He wiped the sweat from his brow and turned to face the two remaining Sabers.

"Look, we don't want any more trouble." Jakz held his hands

up in submission. "Just...Just get out of here an' we'll forget any of this happened. Okay?"

"Jakz is right, bro." Kayn placed the bottle gently by his feet. "No need for violence. What did that ever solve?"

Clinton lowered his guard. "Are you kidding me?"

Kayn shrugged, before a triumphant smirk beamed across his face.

Claws suddenly dug into Clinton's shoulders as someone jumped onto his back. He yelped in pain.

"Attack me from behind, will you?" shouted Gizi, his teeth slicing into Clinton's ear, piercing the skin.

Clinton roared. He tried to shake off the feline and lashed out with his fists while spinning around in circles. He finally threw himself back with all his force he could muster and sandwiched Gizi between himself and the wall.

Gizi groaned and then slid slowly to the ground.

"Get him!" yelled Kayn.

Clinton flinched as a bottle swung at his head. It swept past his face and smashed against the wall, exploding in a shower of glass, leaving Kayn holding on to the broken bottleneck. Clinton grabbed a fistful of Kayn's fur, and pushing him to the ground, stamped on his hand. Pieces of glass fell from the feline's bloody fingers.

Jakz charged at Clinton, and a flurry of fists and claws rained down on the lion. Fur flew in clumps. Clinton threw himself away from the attack, towards the rear of the alley, while Kayn roared manically and sprang to his feet. He leapt at Clinton, claws ready to slice into skin and muscle, but Jakz lashed out first and kicked the lion in the face. Clinton's mouth filled with blood. Hot spikes of pain suddenly lanced the lion's leg as Kayn sunk his teeth into feline flesh.

Clinton slammed his foot against Jakz's chest, forcing the Saber away. With a quick swipe, he slashed his claws across Kayn's back and grabbed his neck. Letting out a defiant roar, he heaved Kayn off his feet and threw him at Jakz. The Sabers collided into the wall before falling to the ground in a motionless heap.

Clinton tried to catch his breath. He swayed on the spot and stumbled against a pile of trash as the adrenalin slowly ebbed from his muscles.

Then he remembered Ephraim.

"Elephant?" he gulped, stumbling for the exit. "Y-you still there?"

Clinton limped a bit further to see if Ephraim was nearby, but his vision seemed to drop in and out of focus. His head suddenly span and his body felt disjointed. The lion collapsed against the wall.

With every last ounce of willpower, he tried to get back to the scrap yard and retrieve his bag, but his energy had finally deserted him. His legs shook and he slumped to the ground, battered and bleeding from the slashes and bites to his arms, face, and chest.

Within seconds, darkness overtook him.

CHAPTER FIVE

OLD FRIENDS REUNITED.

An annoying dripping sound nagged at Clinton in his sleep. Opening an eye, a thin shaft of sunlight blazed onto his face through an iron grate in the ceiling. He lifted his pounding head from the stone floor.

"Damn it!" he cursed, taking in his surroundings. "Not again."

Stagnant water trickled down the walls in lazy rivulets, mixing with anumal urine to create small, smelly pools around him. Hay lay strewn in patches across the ground, clumped together with dried muck. Metal bars ran across the length of the room, stopping anyone from escaping into the subterranean, torch-lit passageway. Two open arches to the left and right of him linked his cell to other adjacent ones.

Clinton heaved himself to a sitting position, and letting out a pained moan, rested his back against the wall. His muscles screamed in agony, feeling like they had been tenderized. Squinting his eyes, he looked up through the grate to see that the sun had fallen low in the sky…and then his heart sank. The sun was not setting. It was only just rising.

He slouched down and sighed. "Raion, I'm sorry."

"What you say?" grunted a voice.

Clinton peered cautiously into the darkness but could not make out the owner of the voice.

"C'mon, speak up! What did you say?"

"Nothing," snapped the lion, tending to the bite on his leg. "Forget it."

A throaty laugh echoed around the cell. Something scraped against the floor and a few seconds later a scruffy-looking bear limped over to him. Clinton winced when he saw that the bear's eyes were welded together with brown gunk. The blind bear inhaled deeply, catching the lion's scent. His mouth suddenly tensed but then twisted into a satisfied smile, revealing brown teeth.

"Well, well, well. You've got some nerve coming back here."

Clinton shook his head. "I don't know what—"

"Don't play games with me. It's too late for that." The bear scratched his head, dislodging numerous fleas as he shuffled closer, leaving behind tufts of floating fur. "Swore, I did. Swore that if I ever got in front of you again, I'd take you apart piece by piece. And now here you are."

The bear grabbed the front of Clinton's robes. "You don't know how you've made my day."

"Who are you?" gasped Clinton, trying to break away from him.

"Who am I?" The bear pulled Clinton closer, continuously sniffing him. The pungent smell of burlico-sticks and grain water perfumed his breath. "Don't tell me you've forgotten your old pal Barak Burnjaw, huh? 'Cause I sure as skorr remember you...Grayorr Narfell."

The name hit Clinton like a kick to the teeth. "Grayorr? No, you've got it wrong. I'm—"

"Recognize that voice anywhere, and your scent." Burnjaw yanked him closer. "I don't know where you've been, lion, but you're crazy if you think you can just swagger back into Wooburn after all these years."

"I'm not... Look, I know your son Tanner."

Barak's grip tightened around Clinton's throat.

"You know what you cost us, eh? Do you *know* what you cost us? The Plains Punishers?"

"I am not Grayorr. I've no idea what you're—"

"You couldn't imagine, Narfell, what it was like that day. We all walked into the arena like gods, we did; warriors ready for battle. Oh, you should have seen how the crowd cheered and lapped up our glory. Picture a team in their prime and you'd be picturing us, ready to take on the champions and cut them down to size. And even though none of us cared to admit it, we all knew the cheers were for one anumal." Burnjaw hissed. "They were cheering for you, Narfell. They'd come to see you. Seven of us, *seven of us* stood on the gamefield that day. Waiting."

Clinton tried to breathe. His head began to spin.

27

"The crowd cheered, and we waited… Yet you never showed!" Barak yelled, spraying spittle in Clinton's face. "One more game. That's all you had to play, just one more game and the championship would've been ours for the taking. It was in our grasp, but you never showed. You…never…showed."

His grip tightened.

"They trounced us, Gray; the Thirstland Thunderers annihilated us because our so called 'hero' deserted us." Barak shook him as if he was weightless. "So now I'm going to destroy you, like you destroyed every last one of us."

Clinton's vision clouded over as a high-pitched ringing sang in his ears.

"You should never have returned, traitor. And now it'll be the last thing you ever do."

Barak's meaty fist drew back, ready to finish his attack.

"Let him go!" boomed a voice from the far side of the bars. "Let go of him right now, and get back, you dumb glux."

The bear flinched and instantly released his hold on the lion, allowing him to gulp down a lungful of air. Keys clanked, a lock clicked, and the cell door swung open as two giant figures approached with thudding footsteps. A flurry of movement erupted in the surrounding shadows. Criminals quickly dragged themselves off to the safety of the adjoining cells.

"What's the matter?" Clinton asked, watching everyone scarper. "What's going on?"

"You too, Burnjaw," snorted one of the figures. "Go on, get out of my sight!"

Barak Burnjaw bared his rotten teeth, but did as he was told and shuffled to a darkened corner of the cell. Clinton clambered on to his hands and knees to see a rhino and an ox looming over him.

Wearing the standard bottle green and black guard's uniform - with metal chest plates and shoulder pads, their helmets had been forged and hammered to fit their individual features.

The guards chuckled and parted to reveal another anumal casually leaning against the cell door. The glow from the passageway's torches could only pick out a few of his details, but it did not matter, Clinton knew exactly who his visitor was. The guards snapped to attention, their spears drawn regimentally to their sides.

"A-and what, what do you want?" stammered Clinton.

The figure did not reply.

"Look, if this is about the Sabers, then they were the ones who started it, not me."

The figure slowly strolled into the cell.

Emerging from the darkness appeared a tiger of immaculate appearance. Looking slightly younger than Clinton, the whites of the tiger's eyes sparkled, and torchlight bounced off the sheen of his fur. Suited in richly tailored clothes made from krimmel silk, the newcomer stood out like a diamond in the middle of a dung heap.

Clinton sighed. "I don't want any trouble with you."

The figure took another step. "Well, now, that would be a first," he replied, in a smooth voice.

Clinton fought to control his nerves and forced himself onto his feet. "What do you want, Dallas?"

"Oh, just going about my business, investigating a brutal attack that took place yesterday." The tiger smirked. "Would you happen to know anything about it?"

"I didn't start it. They didn't give me any choice."

"Ahh, here we go. As usual it is never your fault. Anyway, back to business."

"Business?"

"Yes. I just popped by to let you know that you forgot something."

The image of the stolen sack of food sprang to Clinton's mind. He ran a hand over his stubbly jaw, trying to maintain an air of innocence. "And what have I forgotten?"

"Why, this, of course."

Dallas lifted a hand and clicked his fingers.

The rhino guard pounded out of the cell for a moment before returning, dragging something large behind him. He flung it across the floor. Clinton stepped back in surprise as a cheetah skidded to a halt in front of him, unconscious and covered in blood.

Clinton shook his head, trying to comprehend what he was seeing. "W-what happened? What did you do to her?"

"This? Why this is merely an example."

"An example? Of *what*?"

"Cowardice." Dallas shrugged. "Hiro broke rank. She was a Saber, one of the elite, and she fled her duties to beg me for assistance. If a feline does not have the conviction to fight their own battles, then they are as much use to me as, well…as you are."

Clinton watched a trickle of blood drip from Hiro's nose.

"Now," sighed the tiger, "are you going to tell me what has been going on, or are we going to stand here all day playing guessing games?"

"Look, it's over, Dallas. Let's just leave it be."

The tiger stepped past the limp cheetah and strode into the center of the room, under the grate in the ceiling. He lifted his chin and sniffed the air. "I smell fear, Narfell, your fear. Now, I am going to ask you nicely. Tell me what happened…please."

The two guards fidgeted, tightening their grip on their spears.

Clinton shoulder's sagged. "I stopped the Sabers from hurting the elephant, okay?"

"Who?"

"The elephant. Ephraim. The one the Sabers were attacking."

"Ah, yes, the elephant. If I recall, he brutally assaulted a Saber trying to apprehend a criminal." Dallas protracted his claws to inspect them. "And such are the laws in Wooburn, and indeed Nomica, that the guilty deserve punishment. Etcetera. Etcetera."

"No, the elephant did nothing wrong. The Sabers weren't apprehending him; they were attacking him. This time, though, there'll be plenty of anumals to testify to what happened."

Dallas laughed. "The thing is, Clinton. No elephant… No case."

"What?"

"Yes, we searched and searched, but by all accounts he was spotted at the village gates weighed down by bags. One can only assume his intention was to flee into the Plains."

30

"Alone?" Clinton's forehead furrowed. "Without a caravan or travel gang?"

Dallas smirked. "Completely alone."

"But that's madness. He won't last more than a few days at best, then he'll—"

"Perish? Starve? Be eaten alive?" The tiger nonchalantly studied the room's shadows. "More than likely, yes. It is all incredibly tragic."

Clinton shook his head. He could not believe the elephant would be so stupid, or so desperate.

"Sorry, Clinton, but you often find that the guilty tend to act irrationally when they are exposed. I can only hope the Plains do not make him suffer too much. He might even be clever enough to find a junk mine in which to find refuge. Then again, if not, it serves him right for meddling in affairs that were none of his concern."

"Affairs?" Clinton barked. "Is that what you call mayor Ferris's dirty work?"

Dallas's smirk faltered. He gazed at Clinton for a moment before turning to the guards and nodding. The ox lunged and piled a fist into the lion's stomach. Clinton dropped to his knees, his breath gushing from him.

"You do not know what you are talking about," hissed Dallas.

Clinton slowly staggered to his feet and somehow managed to smile. "Come off it. Whenever you and the Sabers are involved it's usually Ferris pulling the strings. The 'mighty and supreme felines' are controlled by a fat, little—"

Dallas signaled again and the guard sent Clinton sprawling. As Clinton rolled onto his back, Dallas leaned over him. "Understand this, Narfell, I answer to no one."

"Oh, give it a rest. You're under his thumb all right. I wouldn't be surprised if he were looking for you right now with a long list of chores: muck out the cruzer pen, scrub his shoes, clean his bed pans..."

Dallas raised his foot, ready to stomp it down, but somehow managed to stop himself at the last second. He took a controlled breath, slowly lowered his leg, and pinched the bridge of his nose. "Clinton, do you know that you are only alive now because I enjoy seeing you wallow in your torment? It makes my own existence seem that much sweeter."

He extended his hand out for Clinton to grab, but the lion only glowered at it in response.

Dallas sighed. "Fair enough. Though think on this: however much you try and bring everyone down to your depths, you shall never succeed. The Narfell flames have been doused. Your family's name has fallen into shame. You are now the runts of Wooburn's pack. Take my advice, Clinton. Learn your place and stop with the heroics. You are, plain and simply, nothing."

Dallas turned and headed for the cell door. "Another few days in here should do the trick I think." He paused. "If it were up to me, though, I would throw away the key for good."

"You really think being in here a few more days is gonna keep me down? You know me better than that," spluttered Clinton, allowing his anger to grow. He dragged himself to his feet again. "I'm gonna show you, Dallas, and this whole village, exactly who the Narfells are."

Dallas let out a pitying laugh. "Clinton, short of becoming your father, I do not think you could ever do anything to endear yourself to the village. They hate you."

Clinton shrugged. "We'll see."

After a moment's silence, Dallas's calculating gaze relaxed as he began to chuckle. "Oh, please, say no more. You are so predictable."

"What? Scared I might win?"

"Scared? Of you?" The tiger stepped back into the cell and the guards automatically flanked his sides. "However much your death would be a waste of my time and energy, it does not mean that I would not take the utmost pleasure from carrying it out. I will say this only once to you though, so you had better listen and understand: stay away from the tournament. Erase it from your thoughts, forget it exists, Clinton, because you are not entering."

Clinton saw unease squirm across the tiger's face for the first time that day; the tiger's hackles had finally risen.

"And why's that, Dallas?"

"Because I am telling you so."

"Ohhh...what's wrong? You seem on edge."

"I am nothing of the sort. However, if you even go near the stadium you will wish you were never born."

"And what if I *accidentally* forget your warning?" he goaded, pushing the matter further. "What if I do? What then, huh?"

Dallas glared at Clinton before straightening his jacket and flicking a grain of dirt from his cuff. "Just you try it."

The tiger turned and clicked his fingers, exiting the cell as the guards quickly stomped into position behind him.

"I'm going to enter!" yelled Clinton, watching him stroll down the corridor and disappear out of sight. "You'll see. I'll take you all on."

One of the guards slammed the door shut behind him and locked it tight.

"I'm telling you, Dallas, I'll enter, and I'll embarrass you in front of the whole village. And you know I will!"

Clinton kicked a pile of hay across the floor before slumping down against the iron bars. He looked over at Hiro as she inhaled a shallow breath into her battered body. From the other side of the cell Barak Burnjaw rocked back and forth, chuckling quietly to himself while scratching his lice-ridden head. The lion calmed his anger, groaned, and then slowly started to bind the injuries he had sustained from the fight with the Sabers.

CHAPTER SIX

"That's it. End of the line. This is as far as I go." The canine jabbed the end of his stick into the ground and turned to his three companions. His cloak flapped in the wind while the rain lashed his face, making him squint. "I never signed up for any of this."

One of the travelers, an old panther dressed in black, faced the lead scout's canine companions. One of them shrugged as he unscrewed his water skin. Rain dripped from the rim of his hat like a leaky tap. "Hey, sorry, mate, he's the boss, mister...errr, what was your name again?"

"Wade," muttered the old panther. He hobbled forward, gripping his staff and scowling at the leader under his dark glasses. "And I say when it's the end of the line."

The lead scout yanked his stick out of the ground and threw his arms out wide. "Look at this! Scrudding look at it! It's wet and we're frozen. And I never agreed to travel this far inland." He bent down and stared into the panther's shades. "We're leaving."

The canine barged past Wade, heading back for the coast.

"I suggest you stay," croaked the panther, turning his head slightly. "The deal, if memory serves, was to accompany me to my destination of choice."

"Oh, indeed it was," laughed the lead scout. "Until your destination turned out to be Claw scrudding Point. You know what this place is, huh? What goes on here? What business does a cripple do somewhere like this anyway?"

Wade gritted his teeth and ignored the comment. "We had a deal."

"And I have a life!" yelled the canine. "And I'm not risking it in this skorr hole for one more second. So you either come with us now, or you stay alone. Your choice."

The lead scout shifted his heavy backpack into a more comfortable position and trundled away, his feet sloshing through the mud. The other scouts stared blankly at Wade, and then shrugged. One of them mumbled, "Sorry, mister Wade," before following after their boss.

The panther growled. He turned from the departing canines towards the battered terrain, judging whether he could continue on alone. Rain fell in heavy diagonal sheets from the ominous clouds. Nothing but dead trees cluttered the landscape, blowing erratically in the wind, their long needle-like branches thrashing through the turbulent air like greedy arms. The grass was a dark green, but black and gray spiky rocks poked up through the foliage like spires.

Wade rolled his neck. His long, black leather jacket felt heavy on his shoulders. He took a step forward, but his muscles flagged.

"Okay!" he shouted. "Okay, I'll double your payment."

The scouts paused.

"Triple it," replied one in a hungry voice.

"Shut up and keep moving," ordered the lead.

"And we get a cut of whatever you're taking back with you," added the third canine. "You *are* trading goods, aren't you?"

Wade scowled. "Something like that."

The lead canine grabbed his companions by their cloaks. "Are you two soft in the head? This is Claw Point! You know what they say about this place."

"Children's tales," dismissed Wade, his voice flat.

The two canines thought for a second, and then one shrugged. "Scary black shadows? Ghosts of a bloody war?" He chuckled. "I say it's a cover-up. It's probably just smugglers spreading tales to protect their loot. Isn't that right, mister Wade, huh?"

Wade nodded. "Something like that."

"Don't be fools," yelled the lead scout. "I don't trust him as far as I can throw him. Who's to say he'll even pay you when-*if* you ever return?"

"You have my word," promised Wade, "that when this is all over, you will be taken care of for your services."

"I do need the credits," mumbled a scout to his leader. "It's just too good an opportunity to pass up."

"You'll regret it," was his reply. "I've a feeling you won't be leaving this place alive."

The other scout rolled his eyes. "Superstitious old mutt."

A small, but triumphant, smirk shadowed Wade's face, and he set off walking again, heading inland with the two scouts by his side.

Uncountable hours drifted along. Dark clouds systematically plunged the land around the party into a dismal, gray setting. Continuous rain fell, dragging Wade's mood even deeper, sucking at the panther's determination and wearing down his stamina. Yet no matter how crooked his once lithe body stooped, or how gray his sleek, black fur had become, he knew he had no choice but to make the journey. For a time the two canines sang songs as they walked, or recalled the odd Journey Tale or two, but mostly they traveled in silence. They lit a small fire, and Wade sat on a rock while the two canines skinned a thicket louse. Cutting chunks from the scuttler's body, they stabbed the meat onto the end of sharp sticks and toasted it over the flames. A scout held out a chunk of blackened thigh for the panther.

"You...errrr...you want some, mister Wade? It's a nice piece."

Wade sniffed the scavenger meat. He reached under his coat and unscrewed the lid off a small hip flask.

"No, thank you."

He took a quick swig of the liquid. It burnt his throat, but then a warm sensation swept through his body, providing his muscles with a small burst of energy. As the canines continued with their meal, Wade stood up to sniff the air. No birds dotted the sky, and he sensed no vibrations in the earth from sectoids. He fastened his coat around him.

"We need to move."

"What? But it'll be dark soon. Why break camp now?"

"He's right, mister Wade," added the other canine, taking another generous bite of his louse. "We're set for the night. Let's just relax and—"

A wailing noise interrupted his words and grew in volume. The canines froze and stared up at the mountains surrounding them. The scream reached a crescendo...and then gradually died away again.

Wade slowly turned to them, wearing a grin.

"Shall we get going then?"

The wide-eyed canines took a second to compose themselves, and then nodded their heads in agreement.

After packing up the party set off at a brisk walk. However, the joviality that had once existed had been doused along with the campfire's flames. The canines snatched uneasy glances at the slightest movement and at every sound. The rain had finally began to relent, but shadows loomed everywhere with the approach of night.

"You...errr...you ever been this far inland, mister Wade?"

Another scream streaked across the horizon.

The scouts flinched.

"I-I reckon it's just stories like we said..." The scout's voice trailed off as he turned towards the origin of the noise.

Wade made no reply.

Finally, the small group reached the base of a steep summit. At the bottom of the hill stood a tree that forked halfway up its trunk to create a large 'V', as if struck by lightning. The earth around it was as black and hard as coal. A smell like ammonia lingered in the air. Wade pulled out his hip flask from beneath his coat and took another sip of its contents before starting the climb. The two scouts reached the top and hauled their supplies up just as Wade managed to reach its pinnacle. Dragging himself over the summit, the panther fell breathless against the exposed roots of an oak tree. He bowed his head, knowing their final destination was now only a short distance away.

A derelict farmhouse sat amongst stone spires sprouting from the ground: forgotten structures that had been buried by the earth centuries ago. Now, in the last of the evening's light, they looked like they were trying to claw their way out again. The thatched roof of the farmhouse had been stripped clean during its abandonment. A glassless window frame banged an ominous rhythm against the wall in keeping with the wind's tempo. The entrance was now a hole where the door once stood, while part of the east wall had been destroyed, leaving another gaping hole and a few random rocks strewn around the area.

A mixture of feelings swirled in Wade's mind, memories from years past, full of bloodshed and power. They took his breath away and he had to shake his head to regain his focus.

"Is this it?" scoffed a scout when they finally entered the skeletal structure. "All that way for this?"

"We thought there'd at least be a village, mister Wade," added the other canine, glancing up at the roof's rotten beams.

"There was once a village," Wade replied, more to himself.

"Well, clearly there isn't now."

Wade ignored them. After a cursory inspection of the building, he turned to a large chimneybreast built into the center of the northern wall. A detailed set of symbols had been scored into the stone.

"We thought there'd be somewhere to replenish our supplies and get a good night's sleep," huffed the scout. "If this is it, if this is what we've risked our skin for, then—"

"Careful, mate," whispered his friend. "We don't know exactly who he is. He might be a bit, y'know…mad."

"I'll show you blugging mad. You've got two choices, panther, either pay us right now or we're gonna leave you here alone."

Wade blocked out their rambling threats. The more he stood before the symbol, the more detached his mind felt. His body weakened as his thoughts drifted. His head dipped, embracing the intoxication suddenly rushing over him. He dropped to his knees, unable to stem the pressure on his mind. He could hear high-pitched screams, anumals crying out and running for safety as raging fires burned all around. Blood mixed with acrid smoke, burning fur, and flesh. But above all, he heard an infant crying - the one they had searched so long and hard for. Suddenly, its screams began to merge and twist into a guttural yell, the same yell the group had heard earlier that day, growing louder until…

Wade snapped bolt upright. His sudden movement made the scouts jump to attention. They shuffled to the exit, peering in every direction, as the cries drew closer. Wade lifted his head, took a deep breath, and sighed.

The screams stopped.

Wade nodded. "Right on time."

An object suddenly crashed through the skeletal roof, causing brick and brittle wood to pummel into the ground. It slammed against a wooden beam, rebounded into the wall, and then landed with a sickening thud between Wade and the canines.

A body lay in front of them as if it had fallen from heaven...

Yet this was no angel.

Wade nudged it onto its back, revealing the decayed remains of the lead scout. Far from fresh, the cadaver looked aged, as if the life had been sucked from him, wrinkling him like a prune. One of the canines threw up. The other fell back against the wall in a panic. Wade ignored them and muttered one soft word:

"Ghastlings."

As he spoke, a shadowy creature let out an ear-ringing din and came slicing through the air from within the safety of the darkness. Voluminous robes enveloped the creature's frame, but nothing could be seen under the shadow-like folds. It sped at Wade like a rabid creature.

Wade ducked and pulled out his hip flask from under his coat. He rolled to the side and yanked out the stopper before gulping down the remaining liquid in one go. The flask dropped to the ground as a surge of energy primed his muscles. The ghastling turned and came at him again, but Wade snarled and yanked his coat off, whipping it up over the creature's head.

"*Hin xak!*" he yelled.

His claws clouded over with a brilliant metallic red sheen, glowing with an otherworldly power, as he slashed at his attacker. The creature tried to untangle itself from within the long coat, but Wade moved in for the kill. Letting out a roar, his claws tore into the screaming ghastling. A piercing red flash lit up the farmhouse and the monster's robes burst into flame before a shriveled anumal corpse dropped out from beneath them. It hit the ground, exploding into dry, gray powder.

"Look out!" yelled one of the canines.

Another piercing scream blasted through the room while a

second ghastling dove through the hole in the east wall. Wade paused, catching his breath, allowing the dark bundle to advance until the last possible second.

As the creature's talons neared his neck, the panther slammed his fist into the ghastling's hood. Wade began to tremble. Small shivers ran from his shoulder to his hand, and then into the darkness of the cloak. A faint glow grew within the shadowy hood before the ghastling began to shudder. The light intensified. The creature flailed, whipping about under its robes, until Wade finally shouted, "*Shi xak!*" releasing the result of the built-up energy upon the ghastling.

With another flash of red light, Wade yanked his hand away and stepped back. The creature exploded into a ball of light and stinking smoke, leaving the filthy charcoal-gray robes to drop to the ground. The panther paused, waiting to see if any more would attack, but when the silence continued, he relaxed. He picked up his hip flask and carefully replaced it back in his jacket.

The trembling canines leaned against the wall, holding on to one another while staring at Wade. The panther straightened his coat and snarled before shifting his attention back to the symbol on the wall. In front of him, etched into the old stone, was a wide circle of Olde-world animal emblems. A wreath of twisted feathers lined the circumference, circling four larger symbols. The paintwork had begun to fade but it still displayed a blood-red primate handprint, a sky-blue reptile footprint, a silvery hoof-print, and lastly, a sandy-yellow paw mark. Wade lifted his scarred right hand and held it next to the etched paw print. He pulled a knife from under his coat and slid the edge along his palm. Blood slowly dripped down his fingers and onto the ground. The panther quickly tucked the knife away, turned back to the symbol, and concentrated. He pulled from his memory the almost forgotten words of an incantation, and pronouncing them with clarity, triggered the portal.

"*Slath zoohk ti-roemm sharn!*"

As the feline waited, another droplet of blood dripped, but as it fell its descent slowed. Defying gravity, the blood floated lazily back to the paw-print symbol, as if magnetized. More and more spilled blood sprang up from the ground and soaked into the symbol, turning the engraved images a dark maroon. The panther placed his hand against the paw emblem and felt his whole arm go warm.

"Mister Wade...?" One of the canines whispered. "What's going on?"

Again Wade ignored them and sank down into his subconscious mind to block the pain receptors in his arm. The warmth grew in temperature, increasing in intensity until it became a blistering heat. Still, he held his hand firmly in place.

Then the change began.

Underneath his hand the wall felt suddenly mushy like mud. Wade's paw gradually began to disappear into the bricks themselves, as if he was pressing it into quicksand. Inch-by-inch his hand vanished. Lifting his leg, he pushed it into the soft stone, just as he had his hand, and the rest of his body slowly began to follow. The hotter the stone grew, the easier it was for him to slip through. With his body half immersed, he turned to face the canines huddled in the corner.

Through terrified breaths, one of them managed to say, "I...I guess this means we aren't getting paid then, huh, mister Wade?"

Sweat trickled down Wade's fur. He nudged his sunglasses onto his face before reaching into his jacket. Pulling out his knife, he held it close to his face. The blade began to glow red.

"*Na tusta!*" he whispered, as if gifting them with a secret.

He sliced the dagger with quick, precise motions, creating two red-glowing slash marks that rippled and sped off through the air, until they gradually faded. Wade slowly placed the knife back into its sheath. The scouts' eyes had turned glassy. Blood trickled from fresh gashes that had appeared across each of their throats.

"I promised I'd take care of you," answered Wade, sensing their life rapidly ebbing away. "And I take pride in keeping my word."

In the next moment he felt himself completely engulfed within the wall and was sucked through to the hidden lair beyond.

CHAPTER SEVEN

NIGHTMARE.

Wade came to his senses sprawled out at the bottom of a long passage. He groaned, rose to his feet, and wiped the dirt from his coat. The burns and the cut along his palm had disappeared. His wounds had healed.

The panther sniffed the air. Allowing time for his senses to grow accustomed to the lair, he waited patiently and then bellowed a deep roar. The noise reverberated through the darkness and eventually died away. For a few heartbeats there was only silence, until two small flames flickered to life, producing the smell of cold, wintery days.

Light suddenly framed the panther as numerous candles spluttered to life, illuminating a gigantic underground cavern and a narrow, glass walkway for him to tread upon. The path spiraled around the colossal stalactites, which stabbed down into the unfathomable depths, and then wound off into the distance. The panther hobbled along the glass catwalk. He stumbled a few times on his shaky legs yet maintained his vigilance. Eventually, he rounded the curve of a stalactite at the end of the cavern and found himself before a dimly lit altar. A smooth, stone slab lay in an alcove with two items placed upon it. Balanced upright on the center stood a dried, severed monkey arm, its fingers groping upwards as if pleading for mercy. Next to it rested a feline skull that was seared with tribal markings.

Wade sniffed disdainfully at the two items, before lifting his head to face the wall beyond the altar. Ancient, small, large, shattered, bleached white, and gigantic bones of every variety had been fused within the stone surface. Most of the skulls had their jaws open, as if caught mid scream, while in some instances only partial skeletons jutted out. Shadows danced all around the panther, flowing from one pocket of darkness to the next, spreading and multiplying. Wade reached inside his jacket to retrieve his flask, and lifted it to his mouth, but nothing came out. He cleared his throat.

"*Uth tut sahmen ni-toth do klah!*" he announced, his words echoing around the cavern. "I received the call and came as you requested, mistress."

The cavern trembled. Dust sprinkled into its unseen depths. The path of candles suddenly dissipated and the temperature plummeted. Soon Wade's breath clouded in front of his face. The water dripping from the stalactites began to freeze, wrapping every surface in a glistening sheet of black ice. Wade could feel the altar humming with unseen power. Lectric charges buzzed and crackled, throwing sparks back at the grisly wall.

And then he heard a heavy, rasping breathing.

A shadow suddenly sped past him.

Wade whipped his head to the right, but a second shadow also sped to his left. The shadows raced for the altar as the stone shrine emitted a powerful burst of energy, throwing two bolts of blue lectric at the nearest candles. The candles ignited and bathed the room in a stark, azure glow, making the stalactites sparkle with cold beauty.

Wade dropped to one knee and bowed his head.

"It has been too long, mistress."

The panther lifted his head to a large shadow that had swelled into existence on the wall. As he waited, the shadow reared back and began to change, twisting into the shape of a shadowy feline. Two red eyes opened up from within its darkened folds. A shadowy paw protruded from the wall, swiping the air in front of Wade's face and sending an emptiness coursing through his body, before morphing again into the shape of a gigantic snake. A harsh, but velvety, voice slithered through the cavern, as if hundreds of anumals were speaking almost in unison.

"Away!" ordered the voice.

He felt a disturbance on either side of the darkened walkway. Hundreds of ghastlings immediately dispersed into the deeper darkness, fleeing upon her command, while Wade turned to his mistress and rose to his feet.

"They were preparing to ssswarm." The seeress's voice sounded like slowly cracking glass. "A moment longer and they would—"

"Be dead."

The shadow's eyes narrowed. "Maybe."

"Definitely," he replied.

The shadow paused before speaking, as if weighing him up. "It isss comforting to sssee you have sssome fight left in you. I knew you wouldn't sssslip away into obscurity quite so easssily. It hass been many seasons sssince we last met."

Wade maintained his stance. "It feels like an age. And now we live in different times. Yet I have not forgotten my allegiance." He bowed. "As always, I serve you, seeress."

Marama, the Shadow Seeress, paused. Her glowing eyes contracted slyly. "Which isss why you are ssstood here now."

"What is it you require of me, mistress?"

"I believe you already know the anssswer to that."

Wade contemplated his response. "He has returned?"

"Word has reached me sssome time ago about a ssstirring of power to the west. I would not have paid it much heed, had I not felt itsss potent presence once again."

"The west? In Nomica?"

Marama's eyes narrowed in agreement.

"Then there is no choice," continued the panther. "I should return to the Great Plains."

"We could never be ssssure he would not surface again, but now I fear time may be short. The magnitude of the threat we face remainssss unclear, yet I trust you know what musssst be done?"

"I will act swiftly and covertly." Wade paused. "But the Power… Do you think he is ready?"

"He isss. I can ssssense his confusion. He is restlessss. He has finally come of age and isss rotting in that desert cage. He isss ready."

Wade pulled his coat aside and patted his sheathed dagger. "Then I shall travel to Wooburn."

The shadow-snake remained motionless for a moment, before she coiled around herself, sliding in and out of her own slippery form, twisting and changing until she came to rest in the appearance of a komodo dragon. She watched the panther with the same burning red eyes as before, as if peering down into the very bottom of his soul.

"You know they will try to stop you."

Wade looked at the shadow of the komodo and bared his teeth. "If the pact has been broken, they will surely regroup. However, they will not succeed."

"I agree. Strike fast, but do not linger. We now stand on a precipice, Wade, one that we only glimpsed before. Now you shall bear witness to the rebirth…to the creation that has been set in motion."

Wade bowed once more. "And so it shall begin, mistress," he answered, before turning on his heels. He took a step to leave when a sudden thought hit him. He cocked his head. "And what of *him*, mistress? Can I hunt again? Steal his soul? Finally take my revenge?"

"Soon," she replied.

"But he will hinder our every—"

"Your revenge can wait!" snapped the seeress, her voice striking him like the lash of a whip.

Wade spun around to face her, his knife appearing in his hand like magic. The whole of the altar had burst into dazzling blue flames and Marama had transformed into the shadow of a mighty dragon, her magnificent wings stretching wide, embracing the bone-filled wall.

"Wade, my beautiful creature, my blessed servant." The tip of a shadowy claw suddenly passed through his hand holding the knife. Frozen by her touch, the knife clattered uselessly to the ground. "Keep your focus on the task ahead. Your revenge shall come soon enough, but for now we must proceed unchallenged."

Wade tried to move his fingers, yet he could not.

"We must keep focus," she hissed, as the shadow dragon diminished into the distance.

With her departure the light slowly faded. The cold began to dissipate and the temperature started to rise again. Great cracks split the layers of ice smothering the stalactites, and melting water streamed down the walls, dripping again into the unseen chasm. Wade turned for the exit and picked up his knife, but then paused again as the voice of the seeress called out to him from afar.

"For countless seasons you have served me well, Wade, and so you shall again."

Gripping his paralyzed hand, Wade turned and bowed his head. "Till death shall I serve you, seeress. You made me all that I am. I apologize for my foolishness. Old age will do that to you. I will not question you again."

"And so your legend shall rise once more. All, far and wide, will tremble at the sound of your name...your real name."

"Nightmare," sighed the panther, feeling triumph flowering inside his chest. A small smile creased his face. "Failure is not an option, mistress. I shall succeed."

"Good, Nightmare. Good." The seeress turned her shadowy head sideways. Her sharp eyes bored into him. "But do you believe you will be able to achieve your task in your present condition?"

He paused. "Though I am but a mere shadow of my former glory, I am still Nightmare. I shall become the Harbinger, the shadow of destruction, again."

"Then eternity shall be yours."

Before he could react, the seeress snapped out a claw. As it arrowed closer to him it transformed into a shadowy lance that pierced his chest. Wade fell to his knees and arched his back, roaring silently into the darkness.

"Look at you. Aged...brittle...needy." Marama's eyes flared as a pulsating bulge moved along her extended shadow and into the panther's body. "Feel the souls of leaders live within you. Let their power surge through your veins and muscles and flesh." As Marama said the last words, he yelled. His muscles bunched and his jaw tightened, feeling as if his bones might shatter.

As quickly as the lance speared him, it retracted back into the seeress, leaving him gasping. Nightmare fell forward onto his hands, swallowing deep lungfuls of air as the pain receded. He lifted his head and smiled.

"Wade is no more."

The fur between his eyes began to twitch. He cleared his throat and rolled his shoulders, feeling the stiffness of age vanishing, replaced by energy and youth. Strength returned to his arms, and he clenched his fists while pitch-black hair spread along his body, swapping every brittle, gray hair and lifeless follicle with a glossy darkness. Climbing to his feet, Nightmare clicked his neck from one side to the next, gaining vigor and renewed power. He could not keep the smile from his face. "Once again I am risen."

Swishing his coat behind him, he turned to exit the cavern. He took one step along the glass pathway, but stopped, turning one last time to the altar. He glared at the monkey arm and the feline skull.

"You have two of the talismans. But the other three?"

"In time, my faithful servant. In time," laughed Marama, disappearing into the wall, leaving behind two fading red eyes in the socket of a ram's head.

With a curt nod, Nightmare turned away and strolled along the path. His stride grew increasingly confident as he exited.

And his purpose grew deadlier.

CHAPTER EIGHT

<u>SAND PHANTOM.</u>

"The village council has seen fit to release you from the cool-down cages, although I beg to question why," sighed Council Official Farl. "But this is it, Clinton Narfell. This is your last warning."

The small lizard put on his glasses and flicked through a large file on his desk. An Olde-world clock ticked loudly in the background. The walls of his office were adorned with portraits he had commissioned, each depicting the lizard in dramatic poses, such as Farl slaying a kraggon, or Farl conducting Wooburn's courtroom.

All of it was complete fiction.

Council Official Farl cleared his throat. He closed the file and patted it with his hand. "Yes, it appears that you have just about reached the end of the road."

"I haven't done anything wrong, Farl."

The lizard peered over the rim of his glasses as he delicately tapped the brass name plaque on his desk. "I think you'll find that it's 'Council Official Farl', if you please. And regardless of your protestations, the sheer canon of incidents in your file is a clear testament to the contrary. So I am certain this will come as no surprise to you when I say that one more 'mishap' or 'accident' will result in the gravest of measures—"

"But I only tried to help."

"Well, your help has only ever resulted in trouble."

"But—"

"I am tired of your attitude, Narfell, and I am sick of seeing your face in this office. In short, should I hear of any more altercations involving you, I will be forced to act swiftly and decisively. Section three-point-five of village law states: when considering interspecies habitation, no one anumal has the right to dominate another breed based purely on the advantage, or disadvantage, of their given heritage." Farl raised an eyebrow. "Would you dare to try bully me, feline?"

"I didn't bully anyone. And the Sabers are felines too, the same species as me. Anyway, doesn't section one-point-one of Silanian law also state that 'All anumals are created equal'? That none should fear their neighbor, huh? And *that* supersedes village law. Care to remind the Sabers of that, Farl?"

The council official blinked. His small Adam's apple bobbed up and down in his leathery neck. "The Sabers are not the criminals stood before me, are they, Narfell? No. You are." Clinton opened his mouth to speak, but was not given a chance. "And I have reliable information that should you appear in front of Wooburn's officials one more time, the matter will be elevated to a full court hearing. Do you understand?"

Clinton held back a snarl.

"I said do you understand?"

The lion gritted his teeth, but forced himself to remain calm. "Yes…Council Official Farl."

The lizard smiled smugly. He picked up a quill, dipped it in ink and began to scribble some words on the parchment in front of him. After a few seconds he peered over at one of the security guards.

"Well, go on, get him out of here," he snapped.

Clinton was quickly and unceremoniously dumped outside the justice house like a piece of trash. The wind was blowing grains of sand in his face and whipping his hair around. He looked up into the sky. Night had begun its approach, but thick clouds also swirled ominously along the horizon.

"Stay outta trouble, lion!" yelled the guard as he trundled back inside. "If he sees your stinkin' face in front of 'im again then you're in for it! Y'hear me?"

Clinton lifted his hands in surrender and moved away. "Don't worry, I'm going," he said, shaking his head and setting off home. The sooner he forgot about the whole ordeal and got back to Raion, the better. He only hoped that Arkie had been caring for his brother in his absence.

The lion's wounds had dried into crusty scabs, and his bruises ached as he trundled through the market square and into Wooburn's darker side streets. Clinton's stomach rumbled loudly.

Hunger gripped him stronger than ever. It had been days since he had eaten properly. All around him shops and stalls were closing up for the night. Shutters were being slammed over glassless windows while traders threw sheets over their stalls and tethered them to the ground. He knew the prospect of finding food was very slim.

Unless…

He smiled, remembering exactly where he was. Clinton peered around at the buildings and heard a familiar chugging sound in the distance. His spirits lifted as he realized that he and his brother might be eating tonight after all. Rushing off towards Krog's shack, he approached the large, metal fence again. A dim glow radiated from the scrap seller's windows and Clinton could see movement inside. To his relief he heard the familiar sound of snoring.

"Dumb old wegg," he muttered when he spotted Krog's Wife asleep.

As carefully as he could, the lion scaled the fence and leaped from the top before it could buckle under him. Krog's Wife stirred, snorting loudly and chewing her mouth a few times. She arched her back and shifted into a more comfortable position; her legs were stuck up in the air like short, stubby tree stumps. Clinton froze, but with one last chewing huff, the mutt settled herself again and quickly began to snore. The lion let out the smallest of sighs. He tiptoed slowly around her kennel and grabbed on to the sack, but it would not move.

"No! Not now!" he hissed, tugging at the bag. "Don't do this."

He heaved again, and again, and again, until he heard a soft ripping sound…and the bag finally relented.

Krog's Wife snorted.

Clinton froze while the wegg grumbled in her sleep and flicked her ear with a dirty paw. When she settled again, the lion padded over to the fence and swiftly climbed back the way he had come. Just as he swung his leg over the top, he caught sight of a piece of fruit slipping free from the tear in the bag. Clinton lunged out to catch it, but it slipped through his fingers and thudded down inside the yard.

Every muscle in Clinton's body tensed. He gritted his teeth and closed his eyes, waiting for her to spring to life and attack, but Krog's Wife's only action was to continue snoring. He finally relaxed with relief, until he spotted the fallen fruit rolling in the direction of the kennel. Gently, like the softest brush of a feather, it came to rest against the beast, nudging the very tip of her squashed up snout.

Krog's Wife instantly scrabbled to her feet and barked manically, shaking her head from side to side as she showered the yard with globules of sticky saliva. The massive slab of meat pounced up and down as if her toes were on fire and, spotting Clinton, flew at him like a stubbly, pink express train.

Grasping the top of the fence, Clinton saw Krog fling his window wide open.

"What's going on? Who's out there?" hollered the scrap seller, his voice only just audible over his pet's barking.

Clinton threw himself over to the other side of the barrier. He landed in a heap as Krog's Wife rammed her face against the fence, her long teeth chomping into the wire. The lion shuffled backwards, desperate to get away from the crazed wegg as the front door flew open and an old raccoon stood there wielding a stunpike. Its tip was crackling with lectric.

"You again!" he yelled, shouting above his 'wife's' manic howls. "I knew you'd be back, you little scrud. Not enough for you to go beating up innocent anumals? I'm gonna rip off your ears when I get a hold of you! And what've you got there then, huh? Been pilfering from my yard?"

Hearing her master shouting, Krog's Wife attacked the fence with even more fury, pounding her meaty head against the metal.

"I know who you are, lion. Don't think you'll get away with this. You'll see."

Clinton sprinted away, his heart beating only a little faster than his legs were running. As he fled further into Wooburn's back streets the savage barks grew distant and muffled. Holding his bag of treasure as if his life depended on it, the lion sped off for the safety of his home.

* * *

Clinton finally allowed himself to slow down. However, he had not gone far from Krog's house when the wind suddenly picked up. The sky around him had turned even darker, and the ancient, dung-burning streetlights had nearly all blown out, casting the village into an uncomfortable darkness. His cloak flapped wildly in the wind, and sand stung his face like a swarm of sectoids. He bowed his head and set off for the shacks littering the northeastern border of the village when the sound of a warning bell clanged in the distance, setting off a chain reaction.

"Great," he huffed. "A scrudding sandstorm."

The lion turned to look back in the direction he had come from when a cloud of sand nearly swept him from his feet. He shook his head, but the storm continued to batter him, quickly increasing in ferocity. Shielding his face, Clinton bent over and turned his back against the storm. Sand clouded his vision, creating a fuzzy blur in front of him. Soon all he could make out was the indistinct shapes of anumals running for cover. The sound of the clanging bells increased as more joined in with the growing cacophony.

Another gust of wind rocked Clinton sideways, sending him stumbling into the edge of a market stall. Ducking his head, he ran for cover, not knowing which direction he was heading, when his ears pricked up to the sound of crying stock. He rounded the corner of a large building and ran down the street before skidding to a halt. Using his forearm to shield his eyes, he could only just make out the shape of an overturned cart in front of him. Its wheels span in the wind, and rolls of fabric, old furniture, and debris from the dried-up stream were scattered everywhere. Five terrified bovals staggered around in circles, colliding with one another, their small horns making sharp, clashing noises. A figure knelt in front of the cart, oblivious to the mayhem, its features hidden by his wind-whipped cloak.

"Need help?" shouted Clinton, trying to make his voice heard.

52

"Hello…? Do you need help?"

As Clinton approached, the figure let out a deep, snarling sound, followed by a gut-wrenching cough. One of the bovals tried to escape into the night and Clinton reached out to grab it, but it was useless. The dumb creature scuttled around him and screeched even louder before running off.

"Your stock is escaping," hollered Clinton. "You've got to round them up. They won't survive if we don't—"

The wind buffeted the lion back a few paces and his hood blew in front of his face. There was no reply, apart from another fit of coughs. Clinton yanked his hood clear and watched the stranger rise to his feet.

"Good, that's it. Come on. You don't sound well. Leave your stuff and come find shelter with me." He turned to check on the bovals, but every one of them had galloped away. "Your stock's run off and I don't think we'll catch them now. We're gonna have to find somewhere safe."

The stranger took a lurching step.

"That's it." Clinton spun around and scrunched up his eyes as he peered through the storm, trying to find somewhere they could hole up in.

A vice-like hand suddenly gripped his shoulder.

"What the…?" Clinton turned to stare into the darkness of the stranger's hood, when a voice shrieked out of the cowl, sending Clinton stumbling in shock.

"Do not go in there!"

Goosebumps slithered up the lion's spine while his ears rang at the noise.

"Do not go in there!"

A high-pitched warning bell seemed to explode inside Clinton, and pressure built in his head. The lion's legs gave way beneath him and he stumbled back, clutching on to his bag. The strange anumal coughed again and tugged off its hood, following after him.

The face of a rotting badger glared down at Clinton, its features shallow and withdrawn, as if it had been dead for months. The anumal snarled, revealing stained teeth as it pulled back its lips. A foul stench filled the turbulent air. Clumps of his fur were missing, while exposed flesh still stuck to the bones that had long since turned moldy. Sand stung Clinton's eyes, but he could not tear his gaze from him.

"Stay away!" shouted the badger, looming over Clinton while the wind whipped his cloak. "Do not go in there!"

"W-what? Don't go in where?"

"They will find you... They always find you."

"Who? Who will find me? What are you talking about?"

The badger let out a sudden, heart-wrenching wail, and his voice mirrored the strength of the sandstorm. "KEEP AWAY!"

It bent over and grabbed Clinton by the hair, pulling his face close. The lion's stomach heaved at the smell.

"Keep away!" shouted the badger. "KEEP AWAY!"

Clinton cringed. He closed his eyes and tried to push against the abomination's chest, but there were multiple snaps as his hand broke through its rib cage. The badger let go of Clinton and fell away, before glaring back at him through his bottomless eyes. And then his body slowly fell apart. The head crumbled, disintegrating into the wind, before his shoulders, arms, body, and feet followed, turning into dust that was whipped away by the storm.

Unable to catch his breath, Clinton sat in shock as the weather raged all around. After a few seconds, his senses returned. He fought his way to his feet and charged through the whirling eddies, making his way towards the nearest building he could find. Half blind from the storm, and numb to his bones, he practically threw himself against a large, wooden door. He grabbed the handle and tumbled inside.

Jasper's Tavern had never been so welcoming.

CHAPTER NINE

JASPER'S TAVERN.

Clinton forced all of his weight against the tavern door until it finally slammed shut. The noise from outside died down. He pulled back his hood and shook his head, flinging sand from his hair. Every anumal inside stopped what they were doing and turned to fix their eyes on him over their half drunk mugs of grain water, plates of food, and ongoing games of lazarcards. Smoke lingered in the air, infusing the tavern with the cloying scent of burlico-sticks and pipes. Dark booths surrounded the main room, while mismatched tables and chairs were bathed in soft candlelight from the hanging, wooden chandeliers. To one side a thick, oak bar spanned the length of the room, covered with empty mugs and plates. Row upon row of colored bottles containing liquors, spirits, and grain water sat on shelves that towered up to the ceiling.

Picking up a small ceramic pipe, Jasper, the tavern owner, banged it loudly against the bar to empty out the burnt ash. "Wild out there tonight."

Clinton flinched. He turned and saw that Jasper was staring at him through the smoky hue. The canine blew into the end of his pipe. "Bit jumpy, aren't we, lad? It's only a storm."

The lion cleared his throat before finally saying, "I-it's getting worse out there."

"Well, you're welcome to wait it out in here as long as it's not any bother you're wantin'."

He nodded. "I'll be gone as soon as the storm settles."

Jasper huffed, glanced over to the corner of the room, and took his attention back to cleaning his pipe. Clinton slowly sat down at a table and placed the bag by his feet. Patrons continued to stare, yet every time he caught one of their glances they turned away. Behind the bar, Jasper pulled the cork from a bottle and watched a few drops of grain water dribble down the neck.

"Drink?"

The lion shook his head and clasped his hands together, trying to stop them from shaking. The image of the badger flashed through his mind, churning his stomach.

"Suit yourself." Jasper placed the bottle on the bar and slid it towards an old, fat puma, who deftly caught it. The feline looked over at Clinton and snarled. Without a word, he set it on the countertop and trundled off in the direction of the tavern's rear.

"Vincent?" blurted Jasper. "You not drinkin', pal?"

The puma glanced back at the lion. "Not with this company I'm not."

The sound of scraping chair legs suddenly reverberated around the entire room. More anumals followed Vincent's lead and began to exit, clearing the bar for the tavern's back room. Within seconds, the place had almost completely emptied.

Clinton rose to his feet. "I...I don't get it. What's their problem?"

The front door rattled, hit by a gust of wind.

Jasper threw his dirty dishtowel onto the bar and shook his head. "I knew it," he muttered. "Of all the places you had to show up, Narfell. An' 'specially tonight."

A mug slammed against a tabletop in the dimmest corner of the room, followed by an arrogant chuckle. At the sound of the noise Clinton's stomach squeezed into a tight ball.

"Well, well, well. Look what the cat's dragged in," drawled a high-pitched, nasal voice. "Seems like this is a popular refuge tonight, eh, Jasper? I think my luck's beginnin' to change. Lads, if you'd be so kind?"

From out of the corner lumbered two familiar figures. Barn and Graff stepped into the light, Graff chuckling to himself and Barn staring blankly, scratching the side of his head. Slinking out from behind them slid a greasy-looking weasel wearing a spiteful, crack-toothed grin. He squirmed between his two cronies and swaggered ahead, cocking his head to one side.

"'Ello, stranger," he hissed, radiating sadistic delight. "Thank Silania for the storm, huh. Looks like I've finally managed to find you."

Clinton felt his hackles rise. The claws in his fingertips extended involuntarily.

56

"Remember what I said," warned Jasper. "There's to be no trouble in here. You hear me?"

Outside another gust of wind shook the doors and rattled the ceiling.

"Now, now, Jasper." Galront rubbed his hands together and let out a soft chuckle. "What d'you take us for? We is all civilized folk here."

Keeping his gaze fixed on the weasel, Clinton inched closer to the door.

"Not so fast," snapped Galront, scampering forwards on all fours before rising to stand in front of him. The weasel rose onto his tiptoes, now almost face to face with Clinton. "What's the matter, kitty? Thinkin' of leavin'?"

Galront raised an eyebrow. "You wanna know what really tickles me, huh, Narfell?" His whining voice had forsaken all pretenses of pleasantness. "It's that you thought you could pull a fast one on old Galront." He let out a blast of sadistic laughter and his breath smelled of rotting fish and burlico.

Dressed in a shabby, oversized suit, with ripped sleeves and patched trousers, neither the suit nor the weasel gave the impression of having seen clean water in the last few months. The mangled stub of a brown paper burlico-stick hung from his mouth, looking stale and soggy.

"Now why would you ever wanna 'ide from little old me, eh, Clinton? I ain't that bad am I...?" Galront waited, but there was no response from his cohorts. "AM I?"

"Oh, no, Boss, no!" mumbled Barn, swinging a loose chain in his hand.

"Definitely not, Boss. You're practically an angel," grinned Graff.

Galront smiled. "We've missed you at work again, lad, an' now the quotas have fallen short. But what's even more suspicious is that stocks don't appear to be tallying up right. Wouldn't know anythin' about it, would you, lion?"

Clinton's hands felt numb as his grip tightened around his bag.

"Come on," goaded Galront. "I'd have thought an anumal like

you'd know if food was goin' cheap in the village. Always assumed you'd have an eye out for anythin' dodgy, what wi' you in your...*situation* an' all." Galront leaned closer. "Care to enlighten me?"

Clinton sputtered a few incoherent words.

"Now, now, what's the matter? Cat got your tongue? Speak up, lad, we can't 'ear you." He snatched a glance at Barn and Graff to share his joke as they closed in on Clinton. "So where've you been? Tell us."

"N-nowhere."

Galront scowled. "Then why weren't you at work?"

The lion's mouth flopped up and down, but no words escaped.

"You've been dodgin' your duties, Clinton."

"I...I just ran into some trouble."

"I 'eard!" snapped Galront. "Thought you'd 'ave a pop at that big fellow, didn't you? Thought you'd start on the elephant! Why'd you do that then? He 'ave some credits you wanted to steal? Food? What was it?"

"No. You've got it wrong, Galront. I didn't hurt the elephant, it was..." Clinton stopped himself from mentioning the Sabers. He knew all too well the circles that Galront associated with, and the weasel's dealings with the Sabers and Dallas had never been much of a secret.

"Wadda you mean 'I got it wrong'? You callin' me a liar, huh?"

"N-no, I—"

"'Cause I'm no liar. I despise 'em, I do. D'you know what 'appens to liars, eh? Well, I'll tell you: liars tell one too many lies an' finally get caught. An' then guess what?" Galront smacked his fist into the palm of his hand. "Well, let me say that I've got a little friend who doesn't really understand the subtleties of deception. No, all he cares about is rippin' things apart...with 'is teeth."

The weasel looked over to the darkened corner of the room and whistled loudly. "Come 'ere, boy! Come an' say 'ello to the nasty, lyin', cheatin', lion."

Nothing happened.

Barn and Graff looked at each other. The bear scratched his head while the dingo let out a soft, inaudible groan.

"Oi! Come 'ere, boy!" Galront smacked his hand against his thigh. "Come 'ere you dumb wegg! Snarg! Come 'ere, boy!" He kept peering into the shadows, waiting for something to finally emerge. When nothing did, he said, "Barn…where's Snarg?"

Behind him the bear grunted, "Errr…he's outside, Boss. You want me to—"

"WADDA YOU MEAN HE'S OUTSIDE?" yelled Galront, turning to confront him. "You left Snarg out in the storm?"

"But you said—"

"I don't care what I said, just shut your hole an' bring 'im in right now! 'Ave you got any brains in that 'ead of yours, or is it all just kraggon dung? Get outside!"

Barn nodded and trundled off through the back entrance, scattering anumals out of his way as he barged into the next room.

"Listen, Galront," said Clinton. "Please, I can explain."

"You can't explain anythin', thief. I'm not stupid."

"I don't know what you're—"

"Food goes missin' the same time you do, and then a few days later you're kicked out the cool-down cage. Hardly a coincidence is it?"

"So what?" scoffed the lion. "That doesn't mean anything."

The tavern door suddenly burst open, making everyone jump. Gusts of sand blew into the room as the occupants peered out the door.

"There you are, Galront!" wheezed an out of breath voice. "Listen, I've just seen that little scrud again. He was stealin' stuff from my yard and upsetting my little Buttercup."

The door banged shut.

Krog hobbled into the room and his gaze fell upon Clinton. The raccoon's jaw dropped open. "That's him!" he squealed. "That's the scrud. Trespassed on my property and left his nasty tree food behind. My little baby hates tree food, it gives her gas."

Galront grimaced a wicked smile as if relishing the flavor of every word Krog spoke. He turned his head to stare back at the lion. "So he's been snoopin' round your yard, eh? Upsettin' your Wife..." He stumbled over the word. "I mean upsetting your pet. What's her name again? Little errrrr...Buttercup, huh?"

Graff sniggered.

"Shut it, idiot!" snapped Galront.

Krog nodded, showing a squashed piece of fruit to the weasel. "This must've fallen outta that there bag he's holding."

The weasel's face lit up with gleeful energy.

Everyone's eyes slowly came to rest on the bag in Clinton's hands. "An' what do we 'ave here, Narfell? Wouldn't begrudge me from 'aving a small peek inside would you? Just to satisfy curiosity."

"Errr... I'd let you...but... Errr... It isn't mine. I'm just delivering it to someone, earning a few extra credits."

"All I'm askin' for is a little looky-looksee inside. No 'arm in that, eh?" Galront asked, narrowing his eyes.

"Honestly, like I said, Galront, I—"

"Graff!" barked the weasel.

The dingo ripped the bag from Clinton's hands. He threw it to Galront, who immediately shoved his hand inside.

"Explain *this* then," whispered the weasel, revealing a dented piece of dried fruit. "What else you hidin' in here, eh? I bet you've pilfered 'alf me bluggin' stockpile, you..."

Clinton felt Graff grab him round the neck.

"Oh, you're in for it now, scrud," muttered the dingo.

"Give me that back!" Clinton ordered, struggling to free himself.

"An' what do we 'ave here?"

Galront pulled out a fresh palm fruit.

Clinton struggled to break Graff's grip, but it was useless. "Please, Galront, it's not what it looks like."

Galront eyed the palm fruit and grinned. "I'll tell you what I'm gonna do." He squeezed his hand into a tight fist, squelching the fruit to mulch. Seeds and juice splattered onto the floor. "I'm gonna make you wish you never laid eyes on me, lion."

Galront cocked back his fist.

Clinton closed his eyes, ready to take a beating.

"*Now that will do!*" barked a voice.

The lion tentatively opened his eyelids.

Jasper shoved himself between Galront and Clinton, stopping the attack. He peeled back his lips and bared his teeth. "I said there's to be no bother in my tavern, Galront, an' I meant it."

Galront sighed and shook his head. "Graff, shut 'im up."

Letting go of Clinton, the dingo dove for Jasper, and with a single punch, knocked the canine to the floor. As soon as Graff released his grip, Clinton seeing his opportunity, waited until the perfect time...and slammed his boot into the dingo's belly. Graff let out an explosive whoosh and doubled over. Not wasting a second, the lion yanked the bag from Galront's hands and dashed off across the tavern, heading for the long, wooden bar.

"What are you doin', Graff?" wailed Galront. "You've let 'im escape, you thick piece of... Go after 'im!"

Clinton vaulted over the bar, his adrenaline pumping. He threw himself onto his knees and skidded towards the cellar hatch in the floor. After fumbling with the handle, and struggling to lift up the wood, he was confronted with a thick pool of darkness below him. He slid through the hole and into the tavern's cellar.

The lion tumbled down the steps until he rolled to a stop at the bottom. As Clinton's feline eyes quickly adjusted to the minimal light, he noticed the outlines of a long, narrow cavern filled with barrels and boxes. Rickety archways curved over him, supporting the roof. He stumbled through the cellar, vaulting barrels and crates of liquor as the thudding sound of shouting and footsteps increased above. The patter of cobwebs broke against his face, and the air smelled of stale grain water and mold. He reached the end of the cavern and stumbled onto another staircase leading to a second, bigger hatch. Scrambling up the stairs, he reached the top at the same time as light flooded the opposite end of the room.

"No point hidin'," echoed Galront's voice. "We'll find you, lion. You'd better be sure of it."

Clinton forced the hatch open, and the wind immediately pummeled him. He emerged into a compact courtyard at the tavern's rear. Barrels and crates had been blown over by the storm, and smashed glass decorated the gritty sand. A tall, chained gate stood before him with a stack of crates piled in front of it. Clinton quietly lowered the hatch and darted for the nearest stack of crates. He jumped up, intending to climb them, when he heard the sound of yapping, followed by the jingle of a chain.

"Settle down, Snarg!" shouted Barn's voice, above the wind.

Clinton stopped dead. Panic squirmed along his insides. He scanned the area, knowing if he climbed the fence he would be spotted. Running out of options, he jumped back down again and wedged himself into a corner of the courtyard, between another stack of crates and three rusty sheets of corrugated iron. The lion pressed himself into the shadows and waited as his attackers closed in on him from all sides.

This time there was no escape.

CHAPTER TEN

PURSUIT.

"Come out, kitty. We know you're down 'ere. Come out an' face us so we can RIP YOUR LEGS OFF!" Galront swung his fist into one of the barrels, tipping it over and spilling grain water everywhere.

"Owwww!" he yelled, shaking his hand as blood dripped from his split knuckles and onto his boots.

Graff stumbled into the back of him. "You okay, Boss?"

Galront shoved the dingo and wiped the blood down the front of his suit. "Just give me some space." As the weasel passed by a stack of crates, his nose twitched, catching the lion's scent. He followed the smell deeper into the darkness. "This way."

"Y-you're sure we shouldn't just leave it, Boss? Go after him another time perhaps? I don't think he stole too much stuff."

"That ain't the point," Galront snapped, sliding through the room with ease, while Graff stumbled along after him. "You know the value of food. It doesn't just grow on trees."

After a few silent seconds Graff mumbled, "He...he must've been quick to get in an' out of the compound without any of us seein' him."

"Oh, you think?" sneered Galront.

"Maybe we should look at getting better security, eh, Boss?"

Galront stopped dead and slowly turned to face the dingo. "Well, maybe if you did your job properly he'd never 'ave got into the storeroom in the first place. An' where was everyone when he was busy smugglin' goods out of my compound anyway? Just what am I payin' you scruds for?"

The dingo scuttled backwards, nearly tripping over his laceless boots. "Well, Barn was with Snarg... An' the Lurcuss brothers were arguin' again – I've told you about them before. An' I was helping you sort out that...ahh...other business."

"Oh, shut up. I'll 'ear your excuses after we catch 'im. An' when we do, believe me he's gonna regret it." The weasel lashed out with his hand again, hitting it against the wall. "Owww! Look, just get going will you."

The two anumals continued to scour their way through the darkness, fumbling through almost every nook and cranny until they eventually reached the second set of stairs. They paused at the bottom, peering nervously up at the hatch.

"Go on then," snapped Galront.

The dingo shrugged. "What?"

"Get up there."

"You mean me?"

The weasel's eyes twitched. "Who do you think I mean? Get up there an' check it out, you stupid idiot. Do I 'ave to do everythin' myself?"

"No, but... I mean..."

There was a faint scuffling sound beyond the hatch, followed by a muffled thump.

A soft whimper cried out.

Galront and Graff looked at one another.

"What was that?" whispered the dingo.

"I dunno, but you'll be able to tell me once you get your bony butt up there."

Graff turned reluctantly to the hatch, then back to Galront.

"I SAID MOVE IT!" yelled the weasel.

"Okay, okay!"

The dingo carefully scaled the stairs while the weasel inched back behind the safety of a large barrel. As soon as Graff pushed the hatch open an inch, the wind blew a flurry of air through the gap.

"There's nothing here, Boss."

"Well, get outside an' 'ave a better look then."

The dingo took a moment to steady himself. He wiped his hand across his brow for good luck, and pushing against the latch, flung himself out into the courtyard. The cellar suddenly filled with the sound of the storm, before the hatch slammed back into place again.

Galront pulled a small blade from his jacket and waited in the darkness. Uncomfortable minutes dragged along. Above, the wind rattled the trap door. The sound of dripping water began to grate on his nerves. Galront wiped his bleeding hand on his jacket again. Finally, he slithered over to the bottom of the steps and listened for any noises, but could not hear anything over the storm.

"Graff?" he whispered, sneaking up a few stairs, "Graff, you glux, what's going on?"

No one replied.

"Barn...? You there?" he hissed, a little louder. "You two better not be ignorin' me!"

The wind let out a moaning wail that rose to a shriek.

"Come on. I'll let you 'ave a nice grack steak if one of you answers." He smiled for a few moments, hoping someone would finally reply. "Okay...two?"

Still there was only silence.

The smile slowly melted from his face.

Footsteps thudded against the ceiling. Jasper had probably come around from his attack.

Galront snarled. "Oh, why am I forced to do everythin' myself?"

Psyching himself up, he gave the hatch a shove and burst out of the cellar, screaming a manic war cry as he swept his blade out in front of him. However, his cry soon changed into a wail when a shadow unexpectedly reared up and crashed into him like a flying boulder. Before Galront had time to truly register what was happening, a mass of muscle and saliva smashed him back through the hatch and down the cellar steps.

"No, Snarg!" wailed Galront, fighting to keep the beast off him. "SNARG, GET OFF!"

The scavenger's stubby tail wagged excitedly before its nostrils flared. Its huge claws scratched grooves into the wood as it started to chomp its lips together. Totally hairless, the beast had pinprick eyes resting on either side of his gaping, pointy-toothed mouth. Sticky saliva dripped from his green, forked tongue, and clouds of damp breath snorted from the wegg's sniffing nostrils. Locating the blood, Snarg clamped its mouth around the weasel's injured hand and began to yank it from side to side. Galront screamed. He tried to pull away, but Snarg shook his head, merrily tugging and jerking on the weasel's sleeve, ripping the fabric to shreds.

"Gerroff, Snarg! You stupid, bloody... Arggggh!"

Galront struck the beast with his fist, catching the mutt's eye. Snarg yelped and tumbled backwards, hitting its skull on the bottom stair with a loud thunk. The beast shook its head and slowly turned to face Galront with a nasty snarl.

"N-now, boy," cajoled the weasel, creeping backwards. "Good little mutt. You, you, you play nice now..."

The pink scavenger growled and took a step closer.

"SNARG...NO!" Galront commanded, trying to show the wegg some authority. He squirmed further away before bumping up against a large barrel. Galront raised his foot, trying to create some kind of barrier between him and the mutt. "Keep back yeah? Just stay back, you dumb glux."

Snarg did as he was commanded.

Galront sighed.

The scavenger's nose began to twitch. It could smell the weasel's blood on the boot being waved enticingly in front of its nostrils. Snarg slowly licked his quivering lips and reared onto his haunches.

"Oh, frag," Galront mumbled as the creature sprang though the air. It crunched its mouth around the protruding leg in a frenzied rush of excitement as agonized screams rang out from the cellar like a wailing siren.

* * *

Clinton flinched at the sound of the bloodcurdling cries that echoed through the courtyard, until they eventually weakened and died down. With a firm hold of the bag, the lion edged out from his hiding place and glanced around the yard. He yanked off his hood and let it flop back. The storm had begun to ebb, revealing layers of sand that had settled over every surface. Clinton rubbed his eyes and stared at the ground, unable to comprehend what he was seeing.

Before him, Graff lay in the middle of a stack of smashed crates, as if he has been tossed into them by the wind. About ten paces away was Barn sprawled out in a crumpled mess. Identical markings had been drawn in the sand next to their motionless bodies. The lion stared at the markings but could not make head nor tail of the wiggles scratched into the earth. He searched for signs of danger, yet could not find any…until he leaned back and looked up at the rooftops. Like a ghost, a hulking shadow slipped out of view before Clinton could get a proper look. The lion peered around again, wary of coming face to face with the ghastly badger, but he could not see another living soul.

"Who are you? Show yourself. Did you do this?" he shouted, staring up to the rooftop again.

However, the shadow had vanished.

Lifting his hood back over his head, and without so much as a glance, Clinton fled the yard with his bag firmly in hand.

CHAPTER ELEVEN

THOUGHTS OF HOME.

The darker hours of night had well and truly settled in by the time Clinton reached the rickety bridge crossing Wooburn's dried up stream. From there the road dipped sharply, leading away from the village center and towards the slum district. Here the houses changed from wood, brick, and clay structures, to shelters constructed from sheets of corrugated iron and salvaged scrap. Clinton tried to piece together what had happened at the tavern as he walked, but his mind felt like a shattered pane of glass. His imagination painted all sorts of pictures as a result of the bloodcurdling screams he had heard, yet even they paled in comparison to the sight of the badger and what had happened to Barn and Graff.

He slumped against a polelamp and buried his head in his hands, unable to decide whether he was going mad or whether the world was going mad around him. With a sigh, he looked up and realized where he had paused. Only a few feet away was a white fence that reached up to his waist. It marked an unofficial boundary between Wooburn's grander buildings and the start of the impoverished areas that stained the vicinity below. Beyond the fence, its windows twinkling with candlelight, stood a lavish house.

Clinton stared up at the structure. Two flourishing needle-trees stood amidst the well-tended grounds, and an ornate sign hung from a post on the edge of the fence. It creaked as it swung from the last vestiges of the storm. He reached out and caught a hold of it, dusted sand from its cracks, and saw the name Brook Manor painted on the surface. Underneath the paint, however, he knew the property's former name would still be there.

"Well Wood," he muttered. "Home."

He stared at his old house, remembering back to when his father had built it. He had called the house Well Wood after planting the two needle-trees, and then joked that he had created a veritable forest in the desert. Clinton had wondered why Grayorr wanted to grow such ugly plants, but his father had liked that they were survivors, able to withstand anything nature threw at them.

Try as he might, though, Clinton could not stop the darker memories from surfacing. He pictured the sneer on the mayor's face, watching with delight as Clinton and his brother were cast out of their own home and onto the street. Every trace of Clinton's family had been erased from the area, and items deemed as unworthy enough for the mayor to claim had been tossed out into the front yard. By the time the locals had finished plundering his family's possessions there was barely anything left to salvage. Clinton subconsciously touched his ear where it had been pierced by a small tooth all those years ago. He had fought hard to save his lazarball armor from the clutches of a gator called Oran Nree. Snapping at his ear, Oran had pummeled the young cub to the ground before Arkie had arrived in time to save him from the beating. Regardless, Clinton had stood in front of Wooburn's court for the first time the very next day.

Shaking himself out of the past, Clinton ruffled his hair and picked up the bag of food. He turned away from Brook Manor and continued on in the direction of the shabby buildings, where his brother, no doubt, would be waiting for him. As Clinton reached the bottom of the hill and finally entered the heart of the slums, he saw a light twinkling in the window of his shack. His heart lifted with every step, and the pains from his wounds seemed to vanish. Before he knew it he was approaching his dilapidated door.

"Well, guess who's decided to finally show up!"

Clinton dropped the bag and spun around. His claws had protracted in readiness for trouble.

"Whoa there! Just a simple statement, lad. Bit jittery, aren't we?"

Clinton's shoulders slumped and he retracted his claws. "Sorry, Arkie." He picked up the bag and crossed the street. "It's just been one of those, well...weeks, really."

"You don't say," sniffed the old gecko. He continued with his task of sweeping sand from his front porch. "Darned storms. Nothing but a nuisance."

Clinton watched for a moment before Arkie stopped his sweeping to chew on the end of his pipe. "You just gonna stand an' watch? The spell in the cool-down cage make you lazy or crazy, or both, huh?"

"You don't know the half of it," answered Clinton, reaching out to take the broom from Arkie. "Need some help?"

The lizard pulled it out of his reach. "No, just wanted to see if you'd offer. Anyway, I'm fine... And there's no use changing the subject either. What were you in for this time? Fighting or shouting your mouth off?"

Clinton chuckled. "Both, I think."

Arkie chuckled along with him, leaning on the broom for support. "What am I gonna do with you, Clint? You're like a magnet you are, always attracting trouble, finding it where nobody else could ever dream it existed. Reminds me of a fellow I once knew... What was he called again? Always in a bind. Couldn't go a day—"

"Burgess somebody-or-other," Clinton murmured, knowing where this was heading.

"That's it, Burgess! Burgess Jerall. Strange fellow he was. Always kept himself to himself. Met him when I used to teach your dad hunting. Y'know there was this one time when he nearly got his arm taken off by a—"

"You've told me, Arkie," cut in Clinton. "About a hundred times to be precise."

"Less of the backchat!" grumbled the lizard, pursing his lips. He looked Clinton up and down, and then grimaced. "You...errr, you alright, son? You seem a bit vacant."

Clinton cleared his throat. "Arkie, have you ever..." He stopped himself and huffed. "No, never mind."

"Aww, c'mon now, Clint, don't start all that dung with me. Your father used to do that too. Now, 'have I ever' what?"

"Nothing, really. It's just... Well, I..." The lion saw the badger's skeletal face flash in his mind again. "I just keep *seeing* things. It must be because I'm tired and hungry, right?"

Arkie did not reply, but his eyes narrowed as he continued to chew on his pipe.

Clinton decided to change the subject. "Anyway, how is he?"

"Oh, he's fine, he's fine," huffed the gecko with a dismissive wave of the hand. "Hungry as always, but what's new there? I gave him some of my food to keep him going, but sectoids ain't much of a meal for a growing feline to survive on."

Clinton squirmed at the thought of eating sectoids.

"I'm sorry you had to look after him again, Arkie. I really didn't mean to—"

"Oh, I'll be having none of that," interrupted the gecko, resting the broom against the house and grabbing his wooden walking stick. He approached Clinton and looked up at him as if he were a giant. Arkie's head only just reached past the lion's waist.

"Sounds to me like you could do with a break. It ain't good to be seeing 'things' as you say; it can turn an anumal crackers that can." Arkie looked the lion up and down again. "You're not looking too good with that face of yours pounded up like a lump of raw meat either."

Clinton touched the side of his face and winced in pain. "You're right." He pulled up his hood to hide his wounds.

Arkie shook his head and fell back into his rocking chair. "Well, I'm sure that he'll be giving you a good telling off himself, so I'll be shutting up now." He bent over and unscrewed the lid off a tin resting beside his chair. He shook the tin upside down onto his lap, but nothing came out. "Scrud! Ain't even one measly knat for a reptile to chew on."

Clinton smiled. He knelt down to rummage around in the bag and took out half a loaf of rock bread. "Here, take this!"

"What?"

"Take it!" ordered Clinton, before Arkie could protest any further. "I've enough in here for Raion and I, and you need it just as much as we do. I'm only glad I can help you out this time round."

He carefully laid the bread on the gecko's lap.

"How did you get your hands on this? No, wait, you don't have to explain." A mischievous smile crossed the gecko's face and he began to laugh. "Y'know, it's uncanny. You're every bit your father's son."

There was a pause as Clinton let the words sink in.

"Arkie, do you remember the lazarball match against the Thirstland Thunderers?"

Arkie's head shot up, and his face dropped. "Why-why do you ask?"

"It's just I had a run in with Tanner Burnjaw's old man. He mentioned it when I was in the cool-down cage. He said my father didn't—"

"Burnjaw?" huffed Arkie. "That dumb old bear has been two targets short of a lazarball match ever since I've known him. Burnjaw's the type of anumal who shouts at brick walls and pretends he has super powers. My advice? Forget him, Clint. Don't listen to a word he says, 'cause it's dung, the lot of it. "

Clinton smiled uncertainly.

"Trust me, lad, your folks would have been proud of you the way you've grown up." Arkie gently nodded. "I know I certainly am."

Clinton looked back at the aged reptile and smiled. He walked towards his front door. "Proud of some half-crazy lion that has to resort to stealing in order to feed his family? I'm not too sure."

Arkie remained quiet as he nudged his rocking chair back and forth.

Clinton gave the gecko a respectful nod. "I do miss them, Arkie."

Arkie nodded back. "I bet they miss you too, lad," he said in a husky voice. "I bet they miss you too."

CHAPTER TWELVE

GHOSTS FROM THE PAST.

Clinton opened his front door and a small figure bounded towards him, nearly knocking him from his feet. The two brothers hugged until Raion finally released him and moved back to the door.

"So where've you been?"

"I…errr… Well, I got myself into a spot of trouble. Nothing to worry about though." He dropped the bag on top of a rickety table and sat down on one of the two chairs. "It's been an eventful few days, Rai, believe me. Have you been behaving yourself for Arkie?"

Raion fiddled with the door's many bolts and chains. "Uh-huh," he nodded, struggling with the final lock.

"You sure?" asked Clinton. "He'll tell me if you haven't."

"Fine, ask him," huffed the youngster, snapping the lock into place. He sat down at the table with his brother. "So what happened? You were gone ages."

"You know…wrong place, wrong time."

Raion smirked. "Ahhhhh, the usual then?"

"Shut up," smiled Clinton. He reached over the table and ruffled Raion's small, dark mane.

Raion's forehead furrowed. "What happened to your face?"

Clinton stared at his brother for a moment and then sighed. "Don't miss a trick do you?" He pulled down his hood to reveal his injuries. "I didn't walk away when I should have."

"They sent you to the cool-down cage?"

"Yeah." Clinton's shoulders slumped. "I'm sorry I wasn't here, and I'm sorry you were left alone again."

Raion shrugged. "I know."

The brothers sat in silence for a moment.

Clinton bowed his head. "Look, Raion, next time I promise I won't be stupid. I'll ignore any trouble and walk away."

The young lion's green eyes slowly drifted back to the bag on the table. "So how come you got into all this mess if you were supposed to be working?"

"I *was* working, but I thought I'd do a little homework. Y'know, check out the stadium. Make a few plans."

Raion burst into a beaming smile. "You mean you're gonna enter?"

Clinton thought back to Dallas's warning, but Raion's enthusiasm seemed too hard for him to ignore. "I'm not sure yet. We'll just have to see."

However, the young lion had already jumped up from his chair. "This is brilliant! My brother's gonna be in the tournament."

"I said I don't know yet," corrected Clinton, trying to calm him down.

"You're gonna win. I just know you are. You're the best player in the village; there's no one as good as you. We'll show 'em."

"Whoa there, hold on! I said I don't know yet. I just need to think about it."

"You can do it though, Clint, I know you can." Raion sat down again. "Come on, admit it, you could beat them all. It'll be simple. And think of the credits you'll win. You can even wear the armor."

Clinton sighed and sat back. He stared over to a wooden chest in the corner where he kept his prize possession. "It would make her happy."

The room fell silent.

Leaning over the table, he squeezed Raion's shoulder, swallowing a sudden lump in his throat. "You errr... You hungry?"

Raion raised his head and his face lit up. "Are you kidding?"

Reaching over to grab the sack, Clinton emptied the contents onto the table's surface. Fruit, two nearly stale loaves, and scraps of dried meat fell out. Raion's eyes widened as he looked on in disbelief at the scant feast laid before him. He grabbed the nearest piece of fruit and immediately bit into it.

"Where did you get all this from?"

Clinton tossed a piece of dried meat into his mouth. "I... Ahhhh... Well, I got it from the usual place, of course," he said, forcing a smile. "Come on, eat up."

74

However, Raion stopped chewing and lowered the fruit to the table. "You didn't steal it did you?"

"Oh, come off it, Raion. Stealing isn't the right word." By the look on his brother's face, Clinton knew he should try and steer the conversation off the subject as soon as possible. "Anyway, about the tournament, I saw Jed Medinka and that dumb scrud, Keefer Jolt, practicing a few days ago. Broke into the stadium they did, but—"

"You *did* steal it."

Clinton tossed his food on the table. "Okay, I know, I know, stealing's bad and you should never do it, but I had no choice, Rai. If we don't eat, we starve. It's that simple."

Raion frowned. "But you work, don't you? You earn credits?"

"Well..." Clinton grabbed a piece of bread and tore a chunk off. "I did work."

"Did?"

Clinton huffed. "I... Ahhh... I'm kinda fired."

"*Fired*?"

"Well, let's just say I don't think Galront will be welcoming me back with open arms again."

"Why? What happened?"

"Look, it's complicated, Raion." He sighed. "It's just...complicated."

"So tell me."

The brothers stared stubbornly at one another.

"Okay," relented Clinton, finally. "Listen, I risk my life for a pittance."

"Yeah, but at least it's something. At least you're getting paid."

"Well, no, actually. You see the truth is that Galront hasn't paid me for three weeks now. We've nothing left."

"But he can't do that. *Why* would he do that?"

"Because he can, and does, whatever he likes."

Clinton took a weary breath. "Galront made up some excuse about me being constantly late. He said that I was a lazy hunter and I wasn't bringing in my daily quota, which is complete scrud 'cause I'm the best hunter he's got. Most of the time I actually bring in extra. But he's just trying to find ways to keep all the profits to himself." Clinton got up and poured some water from a jug into two wooden cups. He passed one to Raion. "But who could I complain to about it? Even if anyone did believe me, would they have cared enough to do anything about it? Nah, of course not…

"So I saw an opening and I took it, and now Galront wants me roasted alive." He took a sip of his water. "And don't even get me started about…"

Clinton snapped his mouth shut, cutting off his words.

Raion was just about to take a sip too, but he stopped. "Get you started about what?"

"Look, Raion, it's all over, so let's just forget about it." Clinton put his drink down and walked over to the window. He gripped the wooden sill and stared outside. "I didn't mean for any of this to happen, but I had no choice."

The small lion slid quietly off his chair and went to stand by his brother. He rose up onto his tiptoes and followed Clinton's gaze. They both looked up to the top of the steep hill at the lights shining from Brook Manor.

"It's okay, Clinton." Raion patted his brother's hand. "You did what you had to do."

Clinton smiled, but it immediately evaporated again. "Yeah, and look where it's got us."

* * *

Clinton woke up early the next morning. He sneaked out of the house, so as not to wake Raion, and scaled the abandoned lookout post behind their home. He stood gazing across the Plains. A wind blew softly against his skin. The rim of the morning sun was peeking over the horizon, painting the sky with a wash of brilliant oranges and purples. Sand and grit had created a film over every surface from the previous night's storm, yet in the face of such a vast and empty expanse of land, Clinton had never felt so trapped. He sighed, not sure whether he could risk defying the tiger or not.

Last night the sight of Raion had filled him with purpose, a purpose that had been poisoned by Dallas's words. He caught sight of anumals sweeping sand from a narrow path that skirted Wooburn's perimeter fence and ended at the village's burial ground.

Many generations ago it had become a tradition in Wooburn that the strong and able would take their turn for half a moon's cycle to fend off any scavengers such as gracks, silvermoons, leece, boerbeasts, and krimmels, trying to feed on the newly buried corpses - guarding those who had recently taken their final journey into death. Even the mayor had been forced to undertake this duty. Although, when he had participated, the accompanying contingent of security guards, advisors, and hangers-on had turned the practice into more of a gross spectacle.

The sight of the burial ground made Clinton's mind wander. He remembered the time when his father had served as a guardian, and the time he had decided to take Clinton along with him to experience the ritual.

* * *

"What is it, Clinton? What's wrong?" asked Grayorr, his voice muffled by the crackling campfire. Around them spread the emptiness of the Plains, whilst above them hung the star-filled sky.

Clinton hugged his cloak tight against his body and shrugged. "Nothing."

Grayorr ruffled his hair. "It's okay to be scared, son."

Clinton took a fleeting glance out across the Plains and then back at his father. "Has anyone ever been...y'know?"

"What? Attacked? Of course. Happens all the time. Why that fellow we just took over from, he went back to the village with half his leg chewed off. Said a pack of silvermoons got him."

Clinton's face dropped, he peered back out at the Plains again before scooting closer to his father.

Grayorr set off laughing. "I'm kidding. I'm just yanking your chain, son. Believe me, scavengers are few and far between round this area. They know it's guarded. Plus, look at all those bushes and trees over there." Grayorr pointed off to a distant line of scrubs that circled the village perimeter. "They've been planted especially to keep scavengers away. Remember, the leece hates the smell of the lleema tree, and the grack gets puss sores if it touches a dondywolf bush. And if scavengers are so stupid as to try to get through," Grayorr nodded to a large bell hanging two feet away from them, "we ring that and the guards come running."

Clinton nodded, but remained close to Grayorr's side. He looked around at the clay resting-markers pegged into the ground, foot high monuments marking where the dead rested. The fire's shifting flames caused their thin shadows to flicker, continually catching Clinton's attention.

"Dad?" mumbled the smaller lion. "You don't think they mind do you? I heard the ghosts here get angry with anumals hanging around."

"And why would they be angry?"

"Well, aren't we trespassing? Aren't we on their ground?"

"Oh, no, son, you must understand that ground belongs to no one. We might put up fences and build barriers and say that it's our property, but that doesn't mean we ever truly own it."

"But they must get angry with us for digging them up." He pointed out a segment of the graveyard that was in the process of being cleansed.

"No, no, not at all, Clint." Grayorr sat back and pulled out his pipe. "Y'see, Wooburn's graveyard was built long ago on good soil, soil that was rich and easy to dig. Thing is it was filled to capacity and there was nowhere else to bury folk." He packed some burlico into the end of his pipe and lit it. He puffed on it a few times, sending smoke into the air. "So it was decided that we should exhume those longest deceased to make space for newer bodies. Anumals would burn the skeletal remains before grinding what was left to dust. The ashes were then scattered over the Plains, allowing the departed to be at one with the earth again. After that their clay resting-marker was hung in their clan temple so that their spirit would be forever remembered. Now they live on *in the temples, and also in our memories. They're happy, son. So there's no need to be scared."*

"Scared?" barked Clinton, trying to hide his nerves. "I'm not scared."

The fire made a loud crackle. Clinton snapped his head towards it, his eyes wide.

Grayorr chuckled and climbed to his feet, pacing around the fire as he smoked. All Clinton could see of him was a tall, muscular outline. "No, they won't hurt you. Not if you treat them with respect, and especially if you don't fear them. Fear is a strong weapon, and to be fearless is to be—"

"But I'm not—"

"Clinton, you don't ever have to hide your fear. Fear keeps you aware, it keeps you alive and alert and ready to fight. But first you must recognize it, and only then can you face it. If you don't embrace fear, know what it's like to feel that surge of energy, to have your heart beat fast and your muscles quiver, if you don't know how to recognize and control it, you will never defeat it."

Grayorr finally sat down on the other side of the fire, his features completely hidden in shadow.

"But spirits do exist, don't they, dad?"

"Yes, son, they exist," he whispered, loud enough for Clinton to just catch his words. "And sometimes they linger."

"Why? What for?"

"For another chance." Grayorr blew out a long plume of smoke. "A chance to relive their lives, or to complete things they never finished. Some search for revenge, and some to protect loved ones. Others are so full of regret they simply can't rest. They stay for many reasons... Many reasons."

"But you said they wouldn't hurt us."

"And they won't. But there are a few who might try."

"How?"

"They'll try to steal your dreams," whispered Grayorr, leaning in close. "They prey on those desperate to achieve something, those who have dreams yet to be realized. They'll try to steal your hopes."

79

Clinton could only just see the smallest part of Grayorr's eyes twinkling in the firelight. They were shrewd eyes, full of wisdom. The young lion shivered. The air felt cold. He pulled his cloak even tighter, nearly smothering his face in the homely-smelling material. "So how can you get rid of them?"

Grayorr chuckled and walked over to his son. He wrapped his arms around him, pulling Clinton into his chest to shield him. Clinton would never forget the feeling of his father's heart beating against his ear.

"Well, to tell you the truth, I don't know the answer to that, but I do know you can only guard yourself against them by making sure you have no regrets." Grayorr peered down and smiled. "Life's too short to waste, Clint. Never be too scared to take the plunge, or too nervous to follow your heart. If you reach for your dreams and accidentally rock the boat, then who cares? Find your balance and wait for it to settle, because it will. Eventually, everything does. At least then you'll be able to say you tried, even if your dreams don't turn out to be what you expected. You have to live your life knowing full well that when you pass on into the next world, that when the Bone Collector gathers your spirit and Silania welcomes you into the beyond, that you won't linger. You must be able to hold your head up high and say, with honesty, that you gave it a try. Because not dreaming, Clinton, is not living... It's merely existing..."

* * *

It's merely existing.

Clinton snapped out of his daydream and opened his eyes. He peered out into the light of the morning sky, rubbing his cheek and then scratching his messy mane. His father had been right. He had always been right. Everything Clinton stood for was because of his commitment to looking after Raion. And now before him was a chance to prove just how much his brother meant, and also for him to realize his own dreams of leaving Wooburn. A stubborn smile crossed his face. Digging his claws into the lookout's timber, he welcomed the new day with fierce determination.

"Sorry, Dallas," he murmured, "but there are bigger things than you to think about - dreams you'd never understand."

Clinton stood up straight and tall, his body energized.

"And I'm tired of merely existing. It's time I finally started living."

CHAPTER THIRTEEN

A SPECIAL ANNOUNCEMENT.

Two slow weeks had drifted by since Clinton's run in with Galront, and in that time he had hidden away from the village, avoiding contact with everyone apart from Raion and Arkie.

As the sun rose on the morning of the fifteenth day, Clinton crouched, crawling on all fours along the gritty terrain of the Great Plains. A pack of leece grazed on the shimmering horizon. Six powerful legs lined each of their sectoid bodies. They stabbed the ground with their front legs, creating holes in which to insert their long noses and forage for grit lice and moisture. There were five leece in total. The lion's eyes, however, were fixed solely on the elderly scavenger wandering away from the pack. The muscles in Clinton's legs trembled. His claws dug into the ground. The scavenger moved slowly, following a sectoid buzzing past its nose, and its spindly legs tapped against the rocks as it stepped over the ground.

"Easy. Gotta be quick," whispered Clinton, his stomach scraping the dirt. "But...don't...rush."

He knew his voice would not alert the leece to his presence. *They're as deaf as posts, son,* remembered the lion from his father's teachings. *But don't get too cocky; those scrawny legs of theirs can feel the vibrations of a farting knat.* The lion smiled at the memory, yet as he stalked closer his finger nudged a stone. The stone rolled and tapped a rock.

The old scavenger's head shot up. Its nose twitched, sniffing the air before its gaze finally came to rest on Clinton. It skittered away.

"Scrud!" he hissed.

Clinton burst out from his hiding place, behind a low hillock, and set off on all fours at a blistering pace. The leece immediately turned and bolted for the safety of the pack. Bounding over boulders, and skidding around dried bushes, Clinton reached the scavenger within seconds. He could smell its fear. The leece let out a high-pitched warble while banging its legs against the ground, and the four remaining scavengers raised their heads.

Clinton leapt. His front paws reached out and caught his prey's flanks, digging into muscle and hide. It cried out. Blood streamed down his claws. The scavenger's back legs buckled and, as it tumbled, Clinton somersaulted over its body, flipping round to face his prey and position himself between the pack.

"Easy now," he said in a soothing voice. "This'll be quick."

The ground began to rumble.

Behind him the sound of the charging leece thudded in his ears. He grabbed the scavenger's flailing skull in a headlock, but two fangs unfurled from its mouth, trying to bite Clinton's hands. He evaded the fangs, knowing that leece poison could make his muscles seize up as firm as rock - yet another piece of advice imparted from his father.

"From earth to life, and back again. Your sacrifice shall be rewarded," he muttered, before forcing his hand against the scavenger's lower jaw and snapping it shut. With a jerk, he yanked the head sideways, and a sharp crack filled his ears. The beast went limp.

A deep warble suddenly rang out behind him.

Clinton hoisted the old leece over his shoulder and strapped it into a hunting harness on his back. He turned. A leg stabbed at his face. The lion dodged the attack and it smashed into a rock next to him. Debris exploded and he coughed, wafting away the dust as another spindly leg stabbed at his head. Clinton ducked under the swipe, but the leg caught his hair and ripped out a patch. He spun around to flee to his left, but a scavenger was blocking his exit. He turned to the right and another leece scuttled in, barring that pathway too. Clinton felt his panic rising as he desperately searched for an escape. He hunkered down, growling and brandishing his claws as the group slowly circled him. The four leece hissed. Their mouths had stretched wide to bare their dripping fangs.

A young female began to shudder before she shot ahead and reared at him, snapping out a quick bite. Clinton dove to his right, but another scavenger swiped its front leg at his throat. He grunted and twisted away from the attack, evading the blow, yet caught a scratch along his neck. He threw himself to the ground as another charged in from behind, closing their trap on the lion. Snapping his head from left to right he saw the leece had formed a tighter formation. Clinton's hands shook. Try as he might he could not think of a way out, and with every passing second the group were inching in, peppering the air with hisses.

"Get away!" he snarled, slashing his claws in warning.

The leece paused, but then inched closer.

Clinton felt his lip quiver. He slashed, desperate to drive them away, but they continued to tighten their net, stabbing their legs into the ground.

"Please." Clinton pleaded, dropping to one knee. "Please just… I'm sorry… We needed to eat."

"Well, would you look at that?" He could hear his father's voice chuckling in his head, remembering the first time Clinton had been taught how to hunt. *"A pack of scrudding leece, and you turn yellow? I thought better of you, Clint. What did I tell you, huh? You only turn from hunter to prey when you give up the fight…and you ain't a quitter, boy, are you?"*

Clinton growled and shook his head. "I'm no quitter," he hissed. "I'M NOT A SCRUDDING—"

Two leece reared up in front of him.

"GET AWAY!" Clinton yelled. He jumped up, threw out his arms, and protracted his claws. "LEAVE ME ALONE!"

The group stopped dead.

Clinton's voice echoed so loudly across the Plains it sounded like thunder. Inside, he could feel a wave of fear begin to radiate from the scavengers as the four leece scuttled back a few steps. They lifted their legs like they were running across hot coals, snapping at the air in front of them and shaking their heads. As the echo of his yell faded, the leece ceased their movements and remained perfectly still, frozen to the spot.

Silence blanketed the surrounding area, as if the whole Plains were holding its breath in anticipation of his actions.

The lion panted. It took a moment for his heart to stop

pounding, but when it did he heard a rhythmical thud drumming in his ears. He spun around in terror, assuming more scavengers were approaching, but realized the noise was something else.

It was the beating of the scavengers' hearts.

He could taste their fear and feel their muscles primed and ready to bolt. Yet they were rooted to the spot. He inched between the frozen leece, unable to comprehend what was happening, until he came face to face with the young female. Clinton stared into her glassy black eyes, and a word popped into his head.

Go!

Released from their stasis, the scavengers instantly fled, each of them darting away without a backwards glance. As they ran, Clinton's sense of panic began to subside. The thudding of their hearts diminished in his ears. He brushed his hand through his hair and gulped, before glancing over his shoulder at the dead leece still clasped in the hunting harness.

Without another thought, Clinton sped in the opposite direction to the leece and, within moments, the village's perimeter fence inched into view.

* * *

Clinton glanced around the slum sector to double-check no one was watching. He pushed the carcass through Arkie's back window, and wincing as it clattered to the floor, climbed in after.

"Take a good look at that," he said, trying to act cool. "I think birthing season's starting soon."

Arkie turned from his front window and nodded, genuinely impressed. "How'd you get that?"

Clinton pulled off his harness and cloak, and unstrapped his utility belt. "Hunted it."

"What? On your own?"

Clinton shrugged and tried to keep his face neutral. "I…errr… I got lucky, that's all. Anyway, the herds are gathering. This time next month the Plains will be crawling with leece. Just you see."

"Looks like they gave you a run for your credits." Arkie

pointed out the scratch on his neck. "There was only one other fellow I knew who could catch a leece by himself. Most folk are too sensible to try."

"Yes, I know. My dad was just as crazy as me." Clinton could not stop the tension from sneaking into his voice. He looked down at his kill. "Anyway, I'd prefer to be crazy than starving."

The lion looked up to see Arkie and Raion staring solemnly back at him. Clinton's eye twitched, suppressing a wave of dread.

"Oh, no. What's wrong?"

Arkie leaned back in his chair and lit his pipe. A trail of smoke sneaked out the corner of his mouth. "I take it then you didn't see?"

"See what?"

"I think you'd better go look at your home."

Clinton groaned, rushed to the window, and pulled back the tattered curtains. A snarl escaped his lips. The front door had been kicked in and smoke was leaking out from the opening. Mud had been slung at the walls and their kitchen furniture lay smashed on the dirt track in front of the door. He snapped the curtain shut and turned to Arkie and Raion. He picked up the leece and slammed it on the table with a crash.

"Those damned scruds!"

Arkie blew out a cloud of smoke. "What did you expect, Clint? They aren't gonna let it lie, they'll keep looking. Like I said, you can stay here as long as you need. Live here for all I care, I don't mind. I kinda like the company...except for Raion's snoring—'

"Shurrup," muttered Raion, resting his head in his arms.

Clinton sighed. "Arkie, I appreciate the offer, but how long until they start sniffing round here too? It's okay hiding out for a few weeks, but they aren't stupid. It's only a matter of time before they find us. And where will that leave you?"

Arkie leaned forwards and jabbed his pipe at Clinton. "You just let 'em try somethin'. I'll show each and every one of 'em I'm not to be messed with, lad. Believe me."

Clinton pulled up a chair and sat next to Raion, ruffling his hair. The young lion batted Clinton's hand away and moved out of his reach.

"Look, I know you'd have us stay with you, Arkie, but we need to get out of here. I'm telling you, this time next week we're gone."

Raion looked up at his brother, a hopeful smile creeping across his face. "You're gonna beat them all. I just know it."

Clinton grabbed him in a playful headlock and started ruffling his hair again. "You bet I am, bro."

"Whoa! Whoa there, son," cut in Arkie as they wrestled. "You're forgettin' something."

Clinton released the young lion. "Oh, yeah, what's that then?"

"You dumb scrud. Are you telling me you're gonna just stroll through the village, dance up to the registration desk, and then sign your merry self in? You think they're gonna welcome you with open arms and a hearty handshake, huh? Don't wanna burst your bubble, Clint, but it ain't gonna happen anytime soon."

"Ah, you see, Arkie, I've already got that covered." Clinton tapped his finger against the side of his head. "Just gonna need a little bit of your help that's all."

Arkie narrowed his eyes. "Why do I have a bad feeling about this? What are you planning?"

"All in good time." Clinton winked. "Trust me, I'll get us in there, and when I win the credits we'll be joining up with the first travel gang available and be getting out of this skorr hole for good. You included, Arkie."

"What? Me? You need your head testing. I'm too old for all that scrud. You two get on out of here without me and start your lives afresh. I'll be just fine."

Arkie stared at the wall and took another puff of his pipe.

Clinton smiled. "Oh, shut up, old-timer. We're all going and that's it. If I were you two I'd get packing," Clinton thumped the table, "'cause by this time tomorrow, Wooburn will know exactly what the Narfells are made of."

* * *

87

Wooburn's streets were transformed overnight from the dreary village it normally was and into a carnival of color. A lectric atmosphere surged through the village, charging the hordes of anumals as they milled towards the stadium.

With his hood covering his face, Clinton bowed low and shoved his way through the sprawling crowds, heading for the stadium's main entrance. Sweat dripped from his sandy colored brow, and his eyes darted in every direction, taking in his surroundings and looking out for any sign of trouble. As his anxiety grew, so did the noise around him, mingling into a mindless racket. The smell of cooked boval filled the air, tickling Clinton's nose as a stock butcher carved strips of meat from a roasting joint. To his left, another butcher fried chunks of bleater meat, its yellowy-green scales hissing and spitting fat.

Clinton remembered his first ever lazarball tournament. He had walked through the crowd with his dad, mesmerized by the colorful street flags, entertainers, and traders.

"Metal work! Beautiful scrap metal work!" yelled an elderly voice above the noise of the crowd, making Clinton jump.

This struck up a barrage of competing cries.

"Garments! Finest stock-hide garments! Ladies and gents, get your garments!"

"Olde-world antiques. Refurbished mech. All in working order."

As Clinton neared the stadium, the busier the streets became. Loud music pounded near the entrance. Traditional instruments such as the stringed banouki and the slytherfin-skin jug-drums pounded out yet another famed Wooburnian folksong. A towering podium had been erected especially for the event with abundant posters attached to every possible surface. The words, 'VOTE FERRIS! FERRIS LAKOTA!' had been painted above a picture of the mayor. Village guards were dotted amongst the bustling crowds, or stood watching from the rooftops, scanning the crowd for any sign of clan friction or trouble.

A rainbow of clan colors and logos could be seen in every direction. Many of the felines wore their hair platted with interwoven white beads, showing their allegiance to the clan of the Air Spikes. The Crimson Watcher reptiles had also reared their heads for the occasion. Fire-red lines were painted down the sides of their faces from forehead to chin. The machine loving Technals had shown up as well as the mostly despised Humaneers, preaching to the crowds about the end of anumalkind and the resurrection of the extinct race. Most prominent, however, was the sight of a simple rope bracelet tied around many an anumal's wrist, showing their allegiance to the dominant Union Wheel clan.

Clinton stood on his toes to peer over the gatherers and saw a long line of anumals to the left of the podium, waiting to hand in their application forms. In the middle of the line stood a familiar figure. The lion chuckled. He double-checked that his face was still covered by his hood and turned to make his way over to the other side of the stadium, but a fanfare suddenly struck up. A surge of anumals rushed to the podium, trapping Clinton within the bustle. Anumals were shoved to the side while a cluster of security guards and officials paraded past, escorting their employer to the podium's base. Emerging from the protective cocoon, waving regally at his onlookers, mayor Ferris Lakota shuffled up the rickety steps until he reached its pinnacle. Clinton felt his teeth grind at the sight of the pompous little beaver.

Ferris mounted a plinth and pulled out his spectacles and a piece of paper from under his coat. Wearing an immaculate black suit, covered by a thick, red-velvet coat, and accompanied with a ceremonial chain made of aged runes and bones, Ferris had certainly come dressed to impress. He 'harrumphed' loudly, impatiently waiting for the noise to die down.

Slowly, all traces of conversation vanished.

Ferris attempted to look charming, but Clinton thought it looked a little on the smarmy side.

"Ladies and Gentlemen, welcome to Wooburn's Biennial Solo Lazarball Tournament."

The crowd exploded into heartfelt cheers.

Ferris nodded his head and raised his hands in triumph. "Thank you, thank you, loyal citizens. I never expected such a wonderful crowd to gather to hear the humble mutterings of a servant of the people such as I, but…well, here you are."

An old bloodhound advisor visibly sighed behind him.

After a few moments the noise died down again. The lion stared at the mayor's smirking face, remembering that same expression the day he and Raion were cast out of Well Wood.

"Ladies and Gentlemen," the mayor repeated, "as you know, today's tournament is a time held tradition. It is steeped in honor, and those winners often mirror many of Wooburn's ideals. A bit like myself." The mayor nodded and looked at his bloodhound advisor for support, but the advisor merely stared blankly back at him.

A muscle in the beaver's face twitched.

"This year, however," continued Ferris, scowling at his aide, "the tables have turned. The dawn of a new era is upon us, for I have the proud pleasure of announcing that there will be more than just one winner when today's tournament is concluded."

A confused murmur ran through the crowd. Clinton's brow furrowed.

"Yes, my fellow anumals, young and old, this season's prize is both bigger than my love for the village, and grander than my desire to live in harmony. You see, after many years of misery, after years of wandering through a bleak wilderness of depression, Wooburn has decided to recreate its past glory." Grabbing the lapels of his coat, and puffing his chest out, Ferris gazed over the crowd with pride. "Thanks to the recent tax increases and the consideration of my loyal citizens, the village can say that enough is enough! We shall watch Wooburn thrive again, like the good old days when legends such as Kit Medinka, Vall Drukken, and Reymin Farr graced our stadium: bountiful days, like the ones before our last decade of turmoil."

Unhappy mutterings sprang up amongst the crowd. Clinton's hands curled into fists as he heard a name cursed in hushed tones…Grayorr Narfell.

"I know." Ferris raised his hands to pacify the crowd. "I know, and I feel your anger, but rage is like boiling water. At its peak it will burn and scold, but left alone to cool, it becomes palatable and will quench a thirst. Wooburn, the time is upon us to reclaim our status within the Great Plains once more. For today we are proud to announce that the Plains Punishers are to be...reborn."

The words rebounded around Clinton's head and took a few moments to fully sink in. The noise of the crowd slowly rose from shocked silence, to gasps, and then to deafening cheers.

"Yes, that's right," nodded Ferris, fanning the excitement germinating in the crowd, "for today we shall not only be looking for a tournament winner, but we will also be scouting for competitors talented enough to represent Wooburn's lazarball team."

Ferris threw his fists into the air and the crowd erupted into applause. "Now tell me, would Rufus Trumple present such an opportunity to you, huh? I sincerely think not. Don't elect Trumple, re-elect Ferris! Vote Ferris Lakota!"

The band suddenly struck up a celebratory tune, and like a colony of knats, hopeful players surged forwards, even more eager for what had now become a team tryout.

Clinton stood still, welded to the spot. Jostled from all sides as the crowd dispersed around him, he could not keep his mouth from floundering. He wanted to rush off to see Raion, to tell him the news, but he waited, letting all the implications sink in. He lifted his head and looked up at the bright morning sky. His father had once led this village to prosperity. The Narfell name was a part of Wooburn's lazarball history, along with the other legends that Ferris had mentioned, and yet Clinton now wondered whether this was a chance to make the name soar again. The Plains Punishers were about to rise from the ashes...and with it, so too could the Narfells.

On his podium, Ferris yanked a chord behind him and a curtain fell, revealing the Plains Punishers' new team logo. The light beamed on a tribal-looking black and white hand grasping up at a black sun.

A dormant sense of pride suddenly bloomed within Clinton, and he smiled underneath his hood.

CHAPTER FOURTEEN

THE PLAN.

Nightmare rolled his neck, flexing his muscles. The panther reached the summit of the shallow canyon and crouched down to gather a fistful of sand. He lifted it to his nose and inhaled the brassy aroma. His senses tingled. Other leece blood had been spilt here too, killed about a day ago. He dusted off the sand and lifted his head towards the watercolor sky smeared above the Great Plains.

Something powerful had been in the area.

He sighed and set off again, leaving behind the bones and shredded flesh of four adult leece at the bottom of the canyon. Crimson stains splashed the rocks and sand like grisly artwork, evidence of the panther's recent butchery.

* * *

Since the mayor's speech, a bomb of enthusiasm had exploded amongst the Wooburnians. The line to register for the tournament had now swelled to include anyone and everyone. A current of lectric-like chatter pulsed up and down the line, with anumals of all ages, species, and clans waiting to hand in their application forms and take their shot at the grand prize.

Having waited for over an hour, Arkie's eyes were slowly drooping. Surrounded by younger and fitter players, he blocked out their jabbering and slowly began to drift off. The gecko found he could sleep practically anywhere, especially when the sun was beating down on him. He was leaning heavily against his stick when a hand tapped him on the shoulder.

"Yo, lizard, you're up," snorted a muscular pig.

Arkie smiled in reply, rubbed his eyes, and pulled out his pipe from his pocket. "Much obliged, son," he muttered, and moved forward, approaching the desk where an old gator sat. Towering piles of paper surrounded her and she brandished her pen as if it was a deadly weapon. Arkie took one look at the gator, blanched, and murmured, "Oh, great."

"Application form!" she snapped, declining to look up from her paperwork.

"Shoulda known you'd be involved in this, Edna Grellik." Arkie struck a match and lit his pipe. "Always in the thick of it, ain't you?"

Edna's head whipped up. Her beady eyes nearly popped out of her head, and her mouth went slack. "Well, as I live and breathe," she whispered. "Arkie Kaweka. I thought you were dead."

"*Hoped* more like." Arkie grinned, blowing out smoke. "Ain't gonna get rid of me that easily, though, I'll tell you."

Edna cracked a rebellious smile, causing the wrinkles in her hide to deepen like the canyons in the Plains. "Well, if you've finally come to apologize, you'll see I'm far too busy for the likes of you." She wafted him away like a bad smell. "I haven't the time for beggars, and I've got more important things to do than listen to sad excuses…excuses more than twenty years too late."

"Oh, I ain't here to apologize, darlin'. I mean, what a fool I was to stand up such a pretty young thing back then, but by the looks of you now, seems I made the right decision." Arkie burst out laughing, until it spluttered into a dry cough.

Edna's eyes narrowed into a glare.

"No, no, gorgeous," Arkie slapped the application form into her hand, "do me a favor and sign me up for the tournament will you?"

"What…?" An uncertain glimmer twinkled in Edna's eyes. "You?"

"That's right." He sniffed. "I'm entering the tournament."

Edna leaned back for a moment and then carefully put her scholastic weapon down. "Well, I thought I'd seen it all. You do know what they do with anumals like you, don't you? Send 'em out to those camps in the Plains until they get their heads straight again."

"And what's that supposed to mean?"

"It means you must be a bit…" Edna whistled and circled her finger next to her temple. "Wrong in the head. Not all there. A few bovals short of a farm. Understand?"

"What? A bit like the anumal who married you?"

Edna jolted forward, ready to yell, but then managed to stop herself. She took a deep breath and folded her arms. "Look here, Arkie Kaweka, you couldn't even stand up in a suit of lazarball armor, let alone prance about like the young 'uns do." The pig behind Arkie chortled with laughter, until the gecko spun around and shot him a look that would have shriveled a bodando berry. Edna carried on regardless. "Face it, you're no spring chockeral anymore."

"I'm gonna choose to ignore that comment, thank you very much," harrumphed the gecko.

"Oh, sweet Silania! Arkie, you need to start growing up. Then again," her smile twisted into a scowl, "you needed to do that a long time ago."

Arkie leaned forwards on his stick. "Now you listen, leather face. I'm here to enter the competition, so stop your moaning and let's get this over with."

Edna blinked. "Errr... What did you just call me?"

The lizard moved closer. "Oh, sorry, hard of hearing too are we? Well, I sure hope you hear this, 'cause you might like sitting there pretending to be something of a big shot, but you forget the youngsters in this line have no idea who you *really* are. Now, I'm more than sure you wouldn't want any of your past...indiscretions...slipping out, would you, huh, Mrs. Grellik? Certainly not that issue of the stolen grain water, or that time Majj Dribbledown found you crawling home after the summer solstice festival?"

"You wouldn't dare," whispered Edna in a deadly tone.

Arkie smirked. "Oh, I certainly would. Now, you know I got a loud mouth, my dear, an' I don't know how long I can keep these lips of mine quiet, so you either accept my application into the tournament pretty quick, or the gums start flapping. Understand?"

Edna snarled.

Arkie reached out to take his player's number from the table but the gator slammed her hand down atop the pile before he could get a hold of it. "Not. So. Fast."

"Look, just give it to me."

A smile crept across her face again as she scanned the paper. She slid his application form from the table and held it in her hands, raising an eyebrow. "And who, might I ask, is Burgess Jerall?"

"That's...errrr... That's my 'player' name. You know...'Bad Burgess Jerall'... It's for the crowd." He snapped his fingers in a jaunty manner. "Pretty fancy, huh?"

A distant mutt barked. A sectoid buzzed past Arkie's face. Edna blinked slowly as she continued to stare.

Arkie's eyes narrowed. "Look, just sign me up."

He reached out to snatch his form back again, but Edna was too quick and whipped it away. "You really do need dragging off to one of those camps." She puckered her lips and wafted the player number in front of his face. "Anyway, you can talk, because your past ain't so squeaky clean either. I've got the dirt on you. And believe me, *Bad Burgess*, I can be just as loose lipped as the next lizard. So tell me. What makes you think I'm gonna just hand it over to you, huh? What little game are you up to?"

Arkie closed his mouth and stood there mute, unable to come up with anything to say. "Ahh stop messin' around, will you, Eddie. Can't you see there's folk watching?"

He reached for the paper, but she snapped it away again. Her teasing smile grew predatory. "Let them watch, bug eyes, because if I do help you out, what do I get in return, huh?"

Arkie was just about to start shouting when he noticed a seductive twinkle under her mass of wrinkles. Edna clambered to her feet. Numerous vertebrae in her back popped. "So...?"

Arkie's face screwed up. "Oh, come off it...leather lips."

"Pipsqueak," she murmured.

"Handbag."

She leaned in closer. "Flakey."

Arkie took a deep breath. "Crossbreed."

Both anumals were now so close their noses were almost touching. He gazed into her eyes and gulped. Edna stared back.

"Tomorrow night?" he whispered. "Eight o'clock?"

"Tonight. Nine." She held the paper just above his hand. "And you're paying."

Arkie snatched his player number from her and turned to hobble off. "You'll be the death of me, Edna Grellik."

As he trundled back into the crowd, Edna cackled and called out, "Oh, and, *Bad Burgess*...you're going the wrong way." She pointed behind her. "The changing rooms are that way you old fool."

With an audible huff - and a rude hand gesture - the gecko ignored her shouts and continued to walk in the same direction as before. Guards approached to tell him he was going the wrong way, but the gecko merely swiped at them with his stick if they came too close.

"Oh, leave him be," shouted Edna, in despair.

The gecko looked back at her and the gator's face had once again dropped to its usual scowl as she dealt with the next applicant. His stomach churned, unsure whether it was from nerves or indigestion. "By skorr, Clint, you owe me big time for this, son. You owe me huge."

CHAPTER FIFTEEN

THE SOLO LAZARBALL TOURNAMENT.

"Clinton? Clinton are you there?"

"Arkie? Is that you?"

The gecko tutted loudly as he hobbled into the backstreet. "Who else would it be, numbskull? Where are you?"

Clinton leaped from the top of an abandoned market stall and landed next to the gecko. Arkie stumbled back a few paces, nearly jumping out of his skin. "Don't do that, you dumb glux! I swear you're gonna be the death of me."

Clinton shrugged. "So did you get it? Am I in?"

"You're in, son." He pulled out a piece of paper. "Player fifty-eight."

The lion looked down at the entry form and frowned. "But it says Burgess Jerall on it?"

"Well, I was hardly gonna give 'em my own name, was I? Or yours for that matter. Yeah, my name's Clinton Narfell. You might've heard of me?" Arkie shook his head. "Anyway, just be thankful you even have it in the first place."

"Why? What happened?"

"I don't want to talk about it." Arkie shivered. His green skin seemed to turn a bit gray. He blinked and then jabbed his stick at Clinton. "But don't you ever say I never do anythin' for you."

Clinton stared at the paper in his hands as if it was a priceless object. "Arkie, you don't know how much this—"

"Oh, yes I do. I know all too well."

"How can I ever thank you?"

The gecko grinned fondly and winked at the lion. "You can start by getting out there and winning that blugging tournament. I'm sick of the sight of you two brothers, I am. Just get to that stadium, win the prize, and leave me in peace. You hear?"

"Yeah, right. When I win those credits Raion and I are gonna tie you up and drag you along with us. And that's a promise." Clinton ran to his friend, picked him up, and swung him around. "You don't get rid of the Narfells that easily, old-timer."

"Bloomin' rascal! Let go of me! Gerroff, you scrud!" cussed the lizard.

Clinton put him down and grabbed his backpack. He moved to the entrance to check the coast was clear. "Right, let's do this," he muttered, more to himself than to Arkie.

"Haven't you forgotten something?" asked the gecko. "Your face. You can't wear your cloak during the tournament, Clint. Here, you'd better take this." Reaching around his neck, he untied an old, red hanky, and held it out to Clinton. "My throat's gonna be freezin', but hey, you need it more than me."

Clinton folded the hanky and tied it around his face, covering his nose and mouth, before pulling his hood back over his head.

"Now get going!" snapped the gecko. "And don't come troublin' me again, you hear?"

The lion started to leave, but then faltered. He turned back to the gecko.

"Is he still angry with me?"

Arkie nodded. "Yup, but he's also smart enough to know why you made him stay home."

Clinton smiled. "Take care of him will you."

"Don't worry, son. He'll be fine. Just don't come back a loser."

"I'm more concerned about the credits myself. The next time you guys see me, I'm gonna be Wooburn's top lazarball player. Just you wait and see." Clinton looked over his shoulder as he headed for the stadium's entrance. "Get the celebrations ready."

* * *

It seemed that Wooburn's stadium was just as busy on the inside as it was on the out. The bleachers had filled with spectators while the newly appointed lazarball officials busied themselves, checking to see that everything was working in tip-top condition. Another band played a merry tune for the waiting anumals as stock-meat sellers hollered loudly, selling bags of Fangton's Gristle and Bone Drops or Gilder's Gillet Bits, throwing them to customers sitting deep inside the crowded bleachers. The gamefield floor had been polished especially for the event so that it gleamed under the light of the desert sun. Wooburn's stadium had truly been resurrected for this special day. The giant had been awoken from its sleep. Yet the fun and frivolity around the gamefield seemed a world away from the atmosphere inside the stadium's underbelly.

"Move it, Keefer, your equipment is spread out everywhere," grumbled Jed Medinka, barging the wolf out of the way. He swept his arm along the locker room bench, forcing Keefer's lazarball armor aside. "You're taking up too much space."

"What you doin', you stupid pig?" growled the wolf. He kicked Jed's helmet and it spun off across the floor. "Go get changed over there if you don't like it. And while you're at it, maybe you should think about gettin' a shower."

"What? Stop talking scavenger spit." Jed threw his filthy towel at Keefer. It brushed past the wolf's shoulder and landed in the far corner, away from all the players.

Clinton lifted his head from his hands to see that the towel had landed near his feet. He had decided to sit away from the others to avoid any possible conflict, yet as the tension between the competitors grew, he knew it was becoming increasingly unlikely. With his face still masked by Arkie's hanky, Clinton fiddled with the piece of clan-rope around his wrist and studied his surroundings.

A flickering bulb swung from a wire above. Two speakers attached to the wall hissed occasionally as if eager to burst into life. Line upon line of battered lockers ran down the room's center like a formation of soldiers, and benches ran in between them as well as skirting the perimeter of the room.

Clinton stared again at the wall next to him. Etched into it were countless clan symbols, player names, and team logos from previous competitors. Many anumals had graced the room with their presence at one time or another, and he knew his father must have been one of them. He could picture the lion getting kitted up, strapping on his armor while bantering with his teammates. He ran a finger along the etchings, but resisted the urge to carve his name there too. Now was not the time…not yet.

"You're like a child, Jed, throwing stuff around," bickered Keefer, drawing Clinton from his daydream. "What's wrong with you?"

"I'll tell you what's wrong with me. *You're* what's wrong with me," huffed Jed, "lording it around the place, looking at the rest of us like we're dirt."

"Yeah, well in some cases, that'd be about right."

"I'm gonna wipe the floor with you if you don't shut it."

Clinton buried his face in his hands again and took a calming breath. As long as his disguise remained intact then everything would be fine. He just had to go out there and do what he knew best…what his father had taught him. He picked up his bag and checked his equipment for what must have been the fifth time that day. Carefully opening his backpack, he pulled out a sleek pair of catch-gloves with gold, parallel wires connected to perfectly aligned shooters. Next he revealed a blue-gold skin suit, on to which his breastplate, elbow, and kneepads would be attached. Finally, he took out a pair of boots, polished to such a sheen that the reflecting light was dazzling.

The other players wore tattered suits, cobbled together catch-gloves with wires sticking out, wonky shooters, and breastplates battered back into shape again. Clinton knew the armor made by his mother sat in a totally different class to everyone else, and every time he wore it, he could not help but feel unstoppable.

* * *

The hustle and bustle of the locker room gradually increased in volume as the participants grew impatient to get the tournament started. Now, fully dressed, Clinton tried to remain inconspicuous, but his armor had already received more than a few jealous glances. The din was thankfully interrupted when the speakers squealed to life.

"Attention competitors, please note that in the first rounds the player numbers will be drawn at random, deciding who and when entrants play. Each match will be a sandglass of time, and the loser, eliminated. Size and species allowances will not be considered."

"Let's just hope I'm up against you then," snorted Jed, looking at Keefer.

The announcer continued. "Please exit the gamefield as soon as your time has expired. Thank you for your assistance...and good luck."

With a final squeal the speaker's hiss died away, replaced by excited banter whipping around the locker room.

"Hey, Jed," blurted Keefer. "I've heard there's a few rodents in the other room hoping to play an easy round. Maybe they might get lucky and draw your name?"

"Don't be a complete glux."

"Oh, I do apologize," sniggered the wolf.

"Will you two just shut it!" yelled an ox from the other side of the room. "Or else I'll come 'round there and shut you both up for good."

Clinton clenched his fists and tried to control his breathing. He knew that the competitors' nerves would soon manifest into trouble. Taking a deep breath, he quietly slipped from his bench and exited into the corridor...just as something banged against the door behind him, followed by the yelps of a wolf.

The lion shuffled past anumals making their way up and down the passageway. Above him he could hear the rumble of the crowd in the bleachers. Dust drifted from cracks in the ceiling, and the stadium's wooden supports creaked from the sheer volume of anumals they held. Bowing his head, he paced down a dark side passage when he heard some recognizable voices. He stopped dead in his tracks.

"Leave it alone, Clint," he warned.

Yet the voices were growing louder.

With a deep breath, he sidled against the wall and peeked around the corner. Four feline outlines were swaggering in his direction.

"So if I were you, I'd count yourself lucky," continued Gizi, coming into view as he threw his arm around the shoulder of a young feline. "The Ocelot Master wants all the Sabers to attend the meeting tomorrow, an' that includes you too."

Kayn meandered behind them, fingering the point of his knife. "Oh, I smell big things for you, bro, big things."

"Anyway, enough of that, we shouldn't be speaking of this in the open."

Clinton's eyes narrowed.

"Scared someone might overhear, Gizi?" chuckled Kayn. "You've been nothing but tense ever since that Narfell bust you up good and proper."

Clinton's ears pricked up at the sound of his name.

The younger Saber looked from Kayn to Gizi in confusion. "But Gizi told me *he* beat Narfell up?"

"I did," snapped Gizi. "Look, just shut your trap, Kayn. Besides, word is that Dallas actually saw him hangin' around the stadium this morning. The stupid glux is even dumber than I thought."

Jakz began to laugh. "He will never get past that old gator battleaxe. She scares the life out of me. Someone needs to teach her a lesson one of these days."

Gizi stopped at a door and grabbed the handle. "Look, let's just keep focus and show Treeg here how we Sabers roll, eh?" Gizi pointed to each of the Sabers as he spoke. "Just remember, we ain't here to win it for ourselves, we're doing it for feline supremacy. The Punishers will be our way forward. Now, you all ready?"

"Sure am, bro," winked Kayn.

"Me too," nodded Jakz.

All three Sabers turned to the youngster, who nodded anxiously back.

"We'll make a Saber outta you yet, I just know it." Gizi opened the door. "Now let's give the master something to smile about shall we?"

They entered the room and slammed the door behind them.

Clinton rested his head against the wall. He closed his eyes and thought about the upcoming Saber meeting, dreading to think what propaganda they would be spouting. And as for the Plains

Punishers… He tried to not even think about that. He knew he should try to focus on winning the credits, but the more he thought about the team, the more something stirred within him. At the back of his mind he could not help but acknowledge the fact that the competition had evolved from winning mere credits to a chance for him to lift his father's name from out of the gutter.

An announcement suddenly rang through the corridor and the sound of cheering shook the building to its foundations.

"Ladies and gentlemen, calling to the gamefield player number thirty-five and player number sixty-two. I repeat, number thirty-five and number sixty-two. Thank you."

Clinton scampered out of the way as the door the Sabers had entered smashed open and nearly flew off its hinges. A hulking, eight-foot brown bear lumbered out and strode off down the corridor, the number sixty-two stuck haphazardly to the back of his battered armor. He huffed, pounding his huge fist into his palm after every few steps.

"Go get 'em, Tanner. You Burnjaws can beat 'em all," cried a voice from the room.

The bear snorted and trundled off down the passage. After a few seconds the crowd exploded into deafening cheers. As Tanner Burnjaw entered the gamefield, a shadow slowly crept along the corridor behind Clinton. A small, white, female rabbit passed by, grasping on to her player number with shaking hands. Her lower lip was trembling. Clinton watched her head onto the gamefield before muffled laughter erupted from the spectators and the whine of the lazar generator filled the air.

* * *

The tournament steadily progressed into the afternoon, and the constant stream of contenders disappearing from the locker room meant that numbers rapidly began to dwindle. Clinton paced back and forth in the darkened corridor. The thought that his life could finally change grew with every competitor that was summoned to the gamefield. He did not know what lay beyond the Great Plains, or even past Wooburn, but he remained hopeful nonetheless. Outside the village he would have no history. He would be just another face in the pack.

He sat down against the wall, and trying to block out any thoughts of what could be, felt a strange sensation sweep over him. Clinton's hands turned cold and clammy, and then they began to shake. His head spun. A sudden surge of adrenaline coursed through him, soaking into his muscles and pumping blood through his veins in rapid pulses. Clinton shook his head. His vision blurred. Focusing hard on his breathing he squeezed his eyes shut and tried to concentrate. His father's face suddenly flashed in his mind. Like a flicker of light it vanished, leaving behind only a blurred imprint. He blinked and stared down the darkened corridor for a moment.

"Focus, Clint." He gritted his teeth. "Keep it together."

The powerful surge subsided. The pounding in his ears began to settle and, after a moment, his body ceased its trembling.

"Player fifty-eight!" shouted the announcer's voice over the speakers. "This is the final call for player fifty-eight! Please make your way to the gamefield immediately."

"Scrud!" cursed Clinton, stumbled to his feet. Sweat was matting his fur. He picked up his helmet and staggered off to the player's tunnel where numerous officials, no doubt, were anxiously waiting for him.

CHAPTER SIXTEEN

TRUE COLORS.

The sun reflected off the sunken, bowl-shaped gamefield, making Clinton squint. He lingered within the security of the player's tunnel, listening to the crowd's roars and the stamping of their feet. Supporters waved banners painted with names and clan symbols. Others blew horns and sirens. Clinton frowned, unable to explain what had just happened to him in the corridor, but the final vestiges of the incident were lingering, causing his hands to shake. He clenched his fists, determined to take back control of his body again, and studied the crowd.

Faces seemed to spring out at him: anumals from his old school house, stony-faced guards, and village officials. In the middle of the bleachers, underneath a canopy, lounged the mayor on a throne-like chair. His wife occupied the smaller throne next to him, looking as bored as usual, while gathered behind the regal pair stood the mayor's officials and his retinue of security guards.

"C'mon, Clinton, you can do this," muttered the lion, under his disguise. He swung his arms back and forth, trying to relax. "Just play and win. That's all you have to do... Play and win."

Up in the commentary box an aardvark spoke into a microphone, his long snout swaying from side to side. "And now, Wooburn, please give a generous cheer for our next contender, player number fifty-eight."

The commentator's words echoed in Clinton's head. He took a deep breath and closed his eyes, bracing himself to enter.

"Fifty-eight, you're on. Go! Go! Go!" shouted a high-pitched voice before someone shoved him onto the gamefield.

As soon as the crowd saw him emerge, they cheered even louder. Not knowing where to look, his senses felt assaulted by the barrage of noise. Clinton's heart pounded like a caged scavenger in his chest. Adrenaline coursed through his body.

"And now, ladies and gentlemen, it gives me great pleasure to introduce our next competitor," yelled the aardvark into the microphone. "Please put your hands together for the mayor's son, player number two, Harris Lakota."

As the noise intensified, a short beaver burst out of the opposing entrance.

"Frag it!" cursed Clinton.

Harris Lakota raised his arms in an all too similar fashion to his father, acknowledging the village and lapping up their adoration with a smug grin. He paraded across the gamefield, heading straight for the lion. The two players met in the center.

"Acknowledge the mayor," ordered an official from the rim of the gamefield.

Both contenders turned to face the main stand. Harris banged his fist twice against his chest with conviction, but Clinton hardly bothered.

"Challengers, take your starting positions!" barked another official, behind them.

Clinton and Harris faced one another and crouched down on one knee. They stared into each other's eyes as the crowd clapped, eager for the action to commence.

Harris checked the shooter on his glove.

"So what is with the hanky? Got an ugly face, huh?" He chuckled. "Or maybe I should be worried about catching something?"

Clinton almost took the bait, but stopped himself at the last second and shook his head. Harris scowled. He eyed the lion's superior armor and his forehead creased.

"So are...errr... Are you actually any good, or is this going to be a walk in the park for me?"

Clinton glared silently at the beaver, staring right into his eyes.

Harris blinked and forced a smile. "Look," he murmured, so that only Clinton could hear. "I don't know who you are, but you can have two hundred."

"What?"

"Two hundred nugs. Just throw the match, let me win, and it is all yours." Harris winked and held his hand out for a deal. "Oh, and...ah...make it convincing."

Clinton stared at the outstretched hand. Two hundred nugs

would be enough to secure him, Raion, and Arkie a place in a caravan and out of the village. But as he peered around the stadium, hearing the buzz and hum of the spectators, Clinton knew the tournament was now offering him far more than just credits.

"Not a chance."

Harris's face turned an unhealthy shade of red. "Why you ungrateful scavenger."

"Prime the generator," wailed the speakers.

"Believe me, you'll regret that," snarled Harris. "There's only one central attack position in the Punishers, and it has my name on it."

"Really?" laughed Clinton. "Has daddy pulled a few strings?"

"Shut...your...mouth."

Harris snapped the helmet visor down.

Black smoke puffed out of the lazar generator's exhaust as officials wound the crank handle. A familiar whine sailed across the gamefield.

"Lazar to be fired in... Three... Two... One..."

As soon as the machine juddered, the official slammed the release button and shouted, "Fire!"

A lazar blasted from the generator and streaked up to the crystal. The machine's noise dwindled away as the lazar disappeared into the dangling jewel and was redirected out of a new facet, heading straight for Harris.

"And we're off on another whirlwind ride, ladies and gents," announced the aardvark. "Now let's see these two warriors do battle."

Clinton burst into action.

Harris caught the lazar and his glove lit up a dazzling purple, showing he was in possession. No sooner had the beaver landed, though, than Clinton slid across the floor, straight at him. The lion slipped past the beaver's defenses and clipped Harris's glove, easily stealing possession. Clinton's glove shone sky blue. Jumping into a forward roll, he sprang to his feet and barged Harris out of the way before sprinting off, leaving the beaver to eat his dust.

"What a cunning challenge there from player fifty-eight, Burgess Jerall. And look at him go! He's tearing down the gamefield like a gibbet with its butt on fire." The crowd screamed with delight. "But Harris Lakota is now hot on his heels."

Clinton snatched a glance over his shoulder as Harris lunged at his legs. The lion somehow evaded the move and left Harris sprawled facedown, punching the floor. Moments later, he approached the beaver's scoring zone - a semicircular line etched into the floor that continued up the smooth, sloping walls, and around the target alcove.

"Foul!" cried Harris. "He threw me to the ground."

"And he's going for a shot, Wooburn…"

Clinton raised his glowing glove. Knowing he only had seconds before the lazar would automatically be ejected, he aimed for the ten-point moving target at the back of the alcove. Clenching his fist, his fingers tapped the firing switch in the palm of his hand. The lazar whooshed out the shooter. The light in his glove faded. A shower of sparks lit up the alcove as the lazar crashed into the target.

"And that's a scooooooore!" yelled the announcer.

Clinton threw his arms into the air and roared. He looked up at the mayor's section. Ferris had grabbed the collar of one of his officials and was shouting profusely. The mayoress merely sighed and continued to file her claws. Clinton could not help but laugh.

"Can you believe it, ladies and gentlemen? An effortless ten-point target there from fifty-eight. Will Harris Lakota be able to battle back from this disappointing start?"

"I let you have that one," hissed Harris as the two met in the center. "Thought I would…errr. Thought I would give the crowd some excitement."

Clinton shrugged. "Whatever you say."

Harris smacked his visor closed and assumed his start position. His eyes narrowed. "Who are you anyway? Do I know you from somewhere?"

Clinton reached up to check his disguise was still in place. "Just an out of towner," he replied.

Harris's head tilted to the side. "Oh? Where from?" The whir of the lazar generator suddenly caught the beaver's attention. "Well, get ready, because this is where it gets serious. After I am finished, gutter scum, you are going to be leaving this village and running back to whatever crappy little clan you belong to, thoroughly—"

"Gutter scum?" Clinton showed him the clan rope around his wrist. "We're in the same clan."

Harris scowled. "Which is where the similarity ends."

"Yeah, thankfully."

"Why, you—"

"Lazar in three," yelled the commentator. "Two. One. Fire!"

With a whoosh, the lazar sped from the generator, rebounded from the crystal, and was redirected towards the beaver once more. Harris snarled and leapt for it.

"And look at this, ladies and gentlemen, the mayor's son is first off the mark."

Harris headed the lazar. It streaked off to the other side of the gamefield before hitting the wall and rebounding back. Clinton moved in to tackle Harris, but the beaver ducked and rolled. Flipping to his feet, he caught it on his breastplate. The lion lunged to steal the lazar from him, but Harris covered himself in time to keep possession. He charged away with Clinton hot on his tail. Trying to intercept, Clinton forced the beaver to transfer the lazar from his glove to his chest, and then back to his glove again.

"Number fifty-eight is closing Harris down," shouted the commentator. "The mayor's son is going to have to take drastic action soon, before… And what's this?" The crowd gasped. "He's fired it back at the crystal."

The lazar shot over their heads.

Clinton dashed back to the center as the lazar slammed into the crystal and was redirected, this time aimed only a few feet in front of him. Wasting no more opportunities, the lion stretched out his hand to collect it.

Harris suddenly slid between his legs.

Batting the lion's arm aside, he stole possession before Clinton could get anywhere near it. The beaver slammed his powerful tail against the floor and flipped back onto his feet, speeding off for Clinton's scoring zone.

"And Harris is hurtling down the left side of the stadium...but fifty-eight is giving pursuit. Oh, this is too close to call, Wooburn, it's just too close to call."

Clinton snapped out his glove, trying to steal the lazar, but Harris saw it coming and sprung at the nearby wall. He rebounded off the surface, leaping through the air, before landing on Clinton's shoulders. Using him as a platform, Harris launched himself higher, and spinning in mid air, flung open his arms at the very last possible moment. He aimed his glowing glove at Clinton's targets.

In the next second the lazar soared off like a bullet, streaking past the one-point targets and clipping the five-point target like a miniature firework. Again alarms blared to life and lights flashed while the aardvark tried to compete with the deafening noise.

"Wow! What can I say?" he yelled, sounding impressed. "An incredible display from Harris Lakota there, and I have to say the best play I've seen all day. The score now stands at ten points to five with player fifty-eight maintaining the lead."

Another lazar fired into the stadium. This time it headed in Clinton's direction and he caught it on his chest. Harris closed in on him, but the lion turned on the spot and raced for the scoring zone, dribbling the lazar around his body. He passed it from his chest to his gloves, to his boot, and back again, each piece of armor glowing upon contact. Sensing Harris gaining, though, Clinton upped his pace.

"And now there's a race between the competitors. But who will be the victor? Player fifty-eight is in the dominant position, but Harris isn't giving up without a fight. The winner takes all, ladies and gents. The winner takes all!"

High above, the stadium's sand-clock displayed the final seconds rapidly trickling away. Clinton charged on, knowing that he only had to hold out for the next few seconds in order to sail through to the next round. Every shred of energy powered him towards the target zone.

Harris suddenly began to shout.

Something sparked inside Clinton. An urge ignited that seized his muscles, forcing him to make an involuntary stop. Against his better instincts, the lion stumbled to a halt. In the very next moment the player's entrance burst open and three security guards surged onto the gamefield. Clinton could not quite believe his eyes as they pounded over to the scoring zone, spreading their arms wide to create a barricade. All around him the crowd erupted into shouts of disbelief, jumping to their feet in outrage. Harris, however, too intent on catching up with Clinton, sped straight past the shocked lion and plowed into the guards himself, bouncing off them and sprawling flat on the floor.

Everything around Clinton began to swirl and lose focus. He heard one of the guards shout, "D'you think Harris forgot the plan?"

"So…ah…wadda we do now?" replied another guard, his voice growing faint.

A thudding pulse overwhelmed Clinton's senses. Rooted to the spot, warmth tingled over his body, bristling the fur beneath his armor in an overwhelming wave of power. A smell alerted his senses…the smell of sweat, and blood, and fur…before the heat completely engulfed him. The lion relaxed, allowing whatever was occurring to take over. His hand shook so he raised it skyward, and with a sudden flick of his fingers, squeezed the button on his palm. His glove shuddered as the lazar burst from it. With his eyes closed he lost all visibility, but that did not matter, he instinctively knew where the lazar had gone. He pictured it shooting skyward, heard the lazar crackling as it raced through the air. Feeling as though he was locked in slow motion, he lowered his hand and tensed his muscles. Once the lazar reached its pinnacle, it began to fall again, and the hum of its descent grew with its approach. Clinton threw himself into a back flip. His leg snapped out, kicking as hard as it could, nudging something against his boot. He thudded onto the floor. A collective gasp swirled all around. For a few seconds after there was only silence, before the crowd erupted into screams and cheers.

"What the…" yelled the commentator. "What can I say about that, huh?"

Clinton felt his muscles twitch, and the warmth that had engulfed him dissipated. His body relaxed and his mind sharpened, as if emerging from warm water.

"Let's take a look at the replay," shouted the commentator.

Clinton's eyes snapped open and he was greeted with the sight of Wooburn's stadium again. Ancient screens, perched high above the crowd, suddenly flickered into life. He rubbed his eyes. The veins in his head pounded a beat against his skull. His vision swirled as he stared at the screen.

He had shot the lazar skywards before twisting, flipping over, and snapping out a fierce bicycle kick that sent the falling lazar shooting between the dumbstruck guards and into the ten-point target.

The lion's heart raced. It took him a few moments to realize what had occurred. His mind whirled, knowing he had just won the match…even though he had not been in control of his own body.

"Can you believe it? Can…you…believe it? Now there's a move I haven't seen in over a decade!"

Clinton stumbled to his feet. He took a shocked breath, trying to understand what had just happened as the crowd went wild.

"Give it up for player fifty-eight!"

The lion glanced up at the sand-clock and realized that only a few seconds of the game remained. Lifting his head high, he turned to make his way off the gamefield and, as he exited, the sirens blared into life, signaling the end of the match.

"That's it, folks. With a score of twenty points to five, our winner is number fifty-eight, a truly remarkable player called…Burgess Jerall!"

Clinton looked over his shoulder at Harris. The beaver stood rigid with shock, surrounded by his dour-faced guards. High above, in his box, mayor Ferris was busy shouting at various match officials.

Ripping off his helmet, Harris threw it across the gamefield at Clinton, followed by his gloves, and then a boot. "You filthy cheat," he wailed, storming over to the lion. "I don't know how you managed it, but I won't let you get away with this."

Clinton's hand twitched. He felt an urge to tear off the hanky and show Harris exactly who had bested him, but he forced himself to remain calm and leave it intact.

"You won't win. I'll see to it," Harris yelled. "The Punishers are *my* team, do you hear? Without me they're nothing. They won't even—"

But before the beaver could finish, the guards dragged him, kicking and screaming, back towards his private dressing room.

Clinton smiled in triumph, but then gathered his wits together and headed off for the player's tunnel. He knew he might have survived the first battle, but today there was a whole war to be won.

CHAPTER SEVENTEEN

BURGESS?

"Did you see it, huh? Burgess Jerall, now *he's* a player that could drag this village from out of the dung," jabbered a raccoon, tossing a handful of sand nuts into his mouth. "I mean, I ain't seen a maneuver like that—"

"Since Grayorr Narfell, yeah, I know, you've told me like a hundred times now." The hog barged the raccoon out of the way to take his seat. "And for Silania's sake will you please give it a break?"

Dallas watched the two anumals from within the comfort of the shade, leaning against a wooden lighting tower at the rear of the stadium. Villagers scurried around like sectoids in front of him, scrambling over one another to get to and from their seats. Yet one topic of conversation continually fell from their tongues. He growled, exposing the tips of his fangs, and scraped his claws along the beam. With a huff, he turned to leave.

"Ah...excuse me, Master D-Dallas, sir," stuttered a match official.

Dallas spun around to face him. "Did you finally find the replay footage I wanted?"

The official wrung his hands together, gibbering on the spot. "I-I'm afraid the replay...became corrupted. The, the, the tape of the Burgess match is unwatchable. Please, I assure you we are trying to find out w-why."

"And what of Narfell?"

"He was seen last this, this, this morning, sir, loitering in the crowds, but n-no one has spotted him since. We're continuing to—"

Dallas grabbed the official by the scruff of his neck and shoved him into a thick, support beam. His head bounced off the wood with a dull thud.

"Look harder."

The tiger dropped the unconscious official to the ground, casually stepped over him, and walked out the stadium's exit.

* * *

"Clear off, you little runts!" hollered Edna, jumping up from behind her desk. The crowd of infants who had been busy shouting abuse at her ran away, giggling and swearing. Edna huffed as she hunched back over her work again.

Dallas would normally have found such interactions humorous, but as he approached the old gator he found the situation irksome. He could see her desk covered with mounds of player registration forms, many with red crosses stamped on them, identifying the entrants who had been eliminated from the competition. Edna busily filed the papers before tying them into neat bundles. The tiger stalked up behind her, purposefully casting a shadow over her work.

Edna dug her stubby claws into the current pile she was filing. "You know what? I'm sick to the teeth of this. Can't an anumal be left alone for one measly second without harassment?" She started to turn around. "Now clear off you ignorant little..."

Her words died a sudden death. The color of Edna's hide turned even duller as an uncomfortable smile ebbed along her gummy mouth. Dallas slowly circled her until he came to a stop at the front of the desk.

"Ignorant little what?"

"M-Master Dallas, w-what a lovely surprise," she blurted. Jumping to her feet, she practically curtsied. "What could I possibly do for you this fine day?"

Dallas popped one of his claws and grabbed the nearest bundle of forms. There was a short 'pinging' sound as the tiger slipped his claw under the string and sliced it apart, carelessly sifting through the registration forms. "I require information."

"Information?" she asked, through clenched teeth. The wrinkles around her eyes puckered as she watched the casual destruction of her hard work.

Dallas tossed the pile aside and grabbed another stack.

Edna cringed. "Anything I can...help you with?"

115

He paused for a second to inspect her. "Hmm…perhaps there is. Did you register every player here today?"

"Ah, yes, I did. And I promise you that everything was filed correctly despite what that old sow, Majj Dribbledown, might have—"

"Player fifty-eight!" he snapped. "Who was it? What did he look like?"

"P-player fifty-eight?" she gulped. "I'll have to check the records for that…"

The tiger's eyebrow lifted.

Edna immediately jumped to it. She flicked through the papers on her desk with seasoned practice and thumbed through the surviving bundles. Dallas drummed his claws on the table and occasionally glanced at the milling villagers. They would meet his gaze for only a fraction of a second before scurrying away.

Edna suddenly jumped up with a form in her hand. "Ah…fifty-eight!" She looked at the name on the form and her jaw clenched. "That…little…scrud. What trouble has he got me into now? You know, whatever stunt he's played is probably just some kind of a joke."

"So you remember the entrant?"

"Remember him? You bet I do. That little glux owes me dinner."

"Little?"

"Why, yes, Master Dallas. He's a midget of an anumal. However, he sure makes up for it with that big mouth of his. But let me tell you his wallet is definitely gonna be a whole lot lighter after tonight," she cackled.

The tiger merely stared at her, stone faced.

Edna cleared her throat. "Anyway, I told him he was too old, but he wouldn't have any of it. Wouldn't listen to a single word I had to say. And talk about rude. He's a few fangs short of a full set a teeth, if you get my meaning, Master Dallas." The gator leaned around the tiger to grab her player roster from him. "I'd just forget all about him if I were you. He's nothing but a silly nuisance. This is probably all just a big mistake."

Dallas slowly held out his hand.

Edna blinked, but reluctantly held up the clipboard and roster for him to take. "Here you go."

Dallas snatched it out of her hands, examined the players' names, and muttered, "Burgess Jerall...?"

"See...like I said, nothing to worry about. Just ignore him."

Dallas took a deep breath, sighed, and then turned to leave.

"Stupid fake name..." muttered Edna.

The tiger's head whipped around. He locked his gaze on her, making her squirm. "Fake name?" His lip curled back to reveal a fang. "Why is his real name not written down?"

Edna blanched. "Well, he wanted to impress the crowd..."

Dallas took a step closer. "And what, pray tell, is his real name then?"

"Oh, ummmm..." She lowered her head. "It's... Ummmm... Arkie...Kaweka."

Dallas lowered the clipboard as the name clearly registered in his head. He pictured the small lizard, not the lizard as he currently looked, but rather the seasoned hunter who had assisted Grayorr Narfell in dragging the young Dallas back to Wooburn all those years ago. The tiger felt a growl rumble at the back of his throat. A long dormant memory surfaced, one where the mayor had hauled him away from the clutches of Grayorr and his friends. He glared down at Edna, making sure she had a full view of his fangs. "This Burgess, where did he go?"

"G-go?"

"Yes. Where did he go after he signed up?"

"Oh...I'm not sure."

The tiger growled and Edna immediately jabbed a stumpy finger away from the stadium. Dallas turned his head to follow the direction she was pointing.

"I tried to tell him he was going—"

"Fool!" he smashed his fist against the tabletop, sending paper flying in every direction.

Edna yelped and cowered back from him.

"Insolent fool!" he fumed, ignoring the forms fluttering around his head.

"Is, errr…is there something wrong, Master Dallas?"

The tiger stared coldly at her. "Tidy up this mess." He turned and walked away. However, before entering the stadium again, he paused to peer sideways into a shadowy alcove. "Did you hear?"

Four silhouettes – Gizi, Jakz, Kayn, and Treeg – skulked into the daylight and nodded their heads. Dallas turned back to watch Edna as she began the task of rebinding the loose papers.

"Then you know what to do."

The Sabers smiled.

Dallas strode back inside the stadium.

CHAPTER EIGHTEEN

THE LOCKER ROOM.

The tournament grew steadily difficult for Clinton as he progressed through each subsequent round. After his first match he was forced to play another five competitors. Three of them proved to be no trouble at all. The first, a zebra called Gille Zawaani, he beat sixteen points to five. The second, a lizard he only knew as Gague, he virtually annihilated thirty-one points to three. The third competitor seemed trickier at first, until Clinton discovered a weakness in the bobcat's defensive tactics and then dominated the game from then on. The final challengers, however, had turned out to be a completely different kettle of krig.

His match against the village guards' favorite, a buffalo affectionately called Titch, had seen the mountain of an anumal trample Clinton's right leg. His fellow security guards had cheered him on, pounding their batons against the floor, and Clinton had barely managed to secure the victory before limping off to the locker room. In the next round Clinton's luck went from bad to worse when he was forced to compete against Tanner Burnjaw. During the match Tanner took every opportunity to exploit Clinton's injured leg, leaving him to barely scrape through with a two-point lead.

Now Clinton sat on a bench in the empty locker room. He untied his disguise and ran his hands through his mane-like hair. Sweaty grime dripped from his fingers.

The speaker crackled to life.

"This is a ten minute warning for competitors one and fifty-eight. You have ten minutes to kit up and prepare for the final. Ten minutes."

Clinton picked up his helmet and grinned at his reflection in the polished metal. "I did it. Just one more match to go."

A tap dripped steadily at the back of the room. The sweat-tinged air felt humid. Clinton sighed and rested his head against the wall. He tried to concentrate on the match at hand and visualize who his competitor might be so he could formulate some kind of game plan, yet he remained completely ignorant.

"So much for laying low," he huffed, listening to the dull echo of the empty room. "You've laid so blugging low you don't even get to know who you're facing. Dumb scrud."

An odd sensation distracted him; a tremor ran down his spine. He snapped his head to the side and stared at the door. Only moments ago he had heard anumals in the corridor, officials scurrying about, preparing for the final match, yet the clamor had abruptly disappeared. Clinton sat motionless, listening for any sound of movement, before a feeling of dread swallowed him whole. He rose to his feet as the door handle slowly turned. The lion flinched and snatched up Arkie's hanky as the door gently swung in and tapped against the wall. Sneakily, one by one, three shadows slipped into the room. A fourth followed, strolling in with all the confidence in the world. Clinton scrabbled to cover his face, but Kayn stepped into the light, smiling whilst appraising the lion.

"Well, well, well, bro. Why am I not surprised?"

Kayn turned away from the lion and signaled Treeg. The youngster leaned into the corridor and whispered, "Y-you were right, sir. He's in here."

The Sabers parted, slinking to each side of the doorway as a new figure stepped into view. Everything seemed to melt away to nothing as Dallas entered, his cold gaze boring into the lion.

"Door," he commanded.

Behind him, Gizi slammed it shut.

Clinton and Dallas stared at one another. Everything in Clinton begged him to take flight, to slip past them and make a run for it, but he was not stupid, he knew it would be pointless.

Dallas slowly looked him up and down, the snarl on his face revealing his displeasure. "So...Burgess. Having fun are we?"

Clinton took a deep breath. "I...I said I'd enter."

"Yet you were *told* to stay away."

Clinton watched the Sabers slowly spread out, forming a circle around him. "Well, it's too late now," he snapped. "So whatever it is you're here for, just get it over—"

"Oh, please," chuckled Dallas. "We are not in the playground anymore, Clinton. I have a reputation to maintain."

"Yeah, I know all about—"

"Clinton!" Dallas raised his hand to silence him. "Drop the act. Cocky little street urchin is so last season."

The Sabers cackled.

Dallas shrugged, his gaze glued to his victim. "You seriously need to get a grip. Besides," he placed a hand on Gizi's shoulder, "why should I bark when I have dogs to do that for me?"

The Sabers' grins faltered, but Dallas clicked his fingers, making them jump to his bidding. Clinton felt someone grab his hair and yank him back. His head hit the floor with a thunk. His vision swirled. A boot appeared out of nowhere and kicked him in the stomach, expelling the breath from his body. Again, the Sabers cackled like an evil chorus.

Dallas turned and clasped his hands behind his back. "I warned you not to enter, yet still you wormed your way in, making fools of us all with this…pathetic masquerade."

"Coward!" coughed Clinton as he scuttled away, half crawling and half limping, in the direction of the washroom.

"Please, Narfell, I am talking," glared the tiger. "As I was saying, your foolish actions have come at a very awkward time within the village. With unrest growing in the outer sections, the reformation of the Plain Punishers is to act as a symbol of unity - a common bond of passion to be shared amongst the classes. After all, content vermin tend to refrain from unsettling the dung piles. So, as such, the council has decided to, shall I say, take a 'hard stance' against any aggressor deemed as a threat to their goal. And if any such act should be discovered, then they are to be thwarted and dealt with in an…appropriate manner."

Clinton tasted blood trickle from a cut in his mouth. "And you think this is appropriate?" He tried to climb to his feet, but Jakz shoved him back down again.

"You will stand only when I tell you to stand," sighed the tiger. "Now, please, listen."

"No, Dallas, I won't listen to a word—"

"Well, that is unfortunate. I wonder, however, if that brother of yours will be more receptive to my—"

"You even dare—"

"Tell me, Clinton, have you ever heard someone you love scream in agony? Seen their face filled with terror and be powerless to stop it?"

"Leave him out of this! He hasn't done anything wrong. Stay away from him!"

Dallas sauntered closer. "Maybe he is innocent now, but who is to say what his crimes will be in the future? He is burdened with the name of Narfell, after all, and his current role model is hardly, shall we say, inspiring. Maybe I will be doing Wooburn a vast service by enforcing the natural order onto him too? Remind him exactly who he should be respecting and the consequences of disobeying rules?"

Clinton tried to get up, but Gizi stopped him with his foot. Dallas waited a few seconds until he eventually said, "He is allowed to stand."

Clinton slowly rose to his feet and stumbled closer to the tiger. His muscles twitched; his anger urged him to take down his foe. He wanted nothing more than to lash out, but he knew he could not. Dallas would make good his threat and Raion would be the one made to pay for his crimes. Standing nose to nose, he stared into the tiger's brown eyes and gritted his teeth.

"I'll pull out," he conceded, bowing his head. "Just don't hurt him. I'm the one to blame. It was me, not him. I'll forfeit the match."

Dallas practically oozed with smugness. "Oh, it is too late for that, Narfell."

"What do you mean?"

The tiger started to laugh. "Clinton—"

"If you so much as—"

"You *dare* to threaten me?"

The Sabers took an involuntary step back. An ill silence descended over the room.

Clinton tensed, readying himself. "I'll do more than threaten you if you touch my brother."

Dallas stared at Clinton for a long beat before baring his fangs. "I am sorry, but that was the wrong answer."

The tiger attacked.

Dallas swiped his claws at Clinton's face, but Clinton sidestepped the blow and stumbled out of range.

"I mean it, Dallas." The lion's hands were shaking. "I'll stop you, whatever it takes."

Dallas made another lunge, but the lion dove under his arms and ran for the exit. The Sabers, though, anticipated his move and surged around him. Grabbing him by his armor, they thrust him back at the tiger. Clinton stumbled awkwardly into Dallas's swinging fist. His head jolted back and he fell into the sinks.

"Oh, this is pathetic," taunted the tiger, casually following him. "Stop scampering around like a rodent and at least try to make this a tiny bit exciting."

Dallas leapt at him with another swipe, but Clinton dodged the blow and hurled himself sideways. He heard the scrape of claws against stone as Dallas's hand swiped through the space he had just been occupying.

"I wonder whether your brother will put up a better fight?"

Clinton snapped. He roared and dove at Dallas, bringing his hand crashing down against his enemy's face. The two felines toppled. Twisted and entwined together, Clinton struggled to break free as they scuffled. Finally, he managed to shove the tiger away and roll to freedom. Breathing heavily, they clambered to their feet.

Dallas touched the side of his cheek. From his forehead to his cheekbone glared three open claw-wounds over his left eye. Blood trickled from the gashes, dribbling down his skin. He looked up from his stained fingers and stared at Clinton in shock. A burning fire ignited behind his eyes. He pitched his head back, and throwing his arms out, vented a roar of undiluted rage.

"Get him!" he ordered.

The four felines attacked Clinton without hesitation and, in reply, he thrashed around, not caring what or who he hit, before he was finally overpowered. Kayn punched him in the ribs. Treeg giggled manically, trying to get in on the action, while Jakz attempted to grab Clinton's legs. The lion grunted and kicked out, slamming Jakz back through the air. The chubby Saber crashed into the locker room speaker. Smashing it to bits, he lay crumpled in an unconscious heap, dragging the loose wires along with him.

Kayn and Gizi threw themselves on Clinton, restraining him under their combined weight, before Dallas slowly loomed into view, right eye already swelling. Blood coated his face and clothes. Clinton struggled against their hold, but his captors would not relent. With bloody hands, Dallas leaned over and grabbed a clump of Clinton's hair, yanking his head from the ground before ramming it into the floor.

The Sabers cackled.

"*Silence!*" he ordered.

Clinton's vision spun.

"So you think you are ready to take me on? You want to be the big hero?" Dallas gently touched his wounds. After inspecting the blood on his fingers, he casually flicked it away and wrapped his fingers around the lion's neck. "You need to learn some respect."

"Show me someone worth respecting and I will."

Dallas wiped a rogue dribble of blood from his face and glared down at his victim. His gaze finally settled on the lion's injured leg.

"So be it."

With a wet, tearing slash, Dallas swung his claws into Clinton's thigh, cutting through the skin armor and tearing into muscle. Blood squirted. Clinton wailed. Wearing a satisfied smile, Dallas inspected his work, and then decided to punch the wound for good luck. Blood splattered across his face.

"Do you respect me now, lion?"

Clinton jerked back and forth, babbling incoherently from the pain. Sweat trickled down his face.

"Come on, Narfell, answer me." He punched the wound again. "Come on! Do you respect me now, huh?"

Clinton desperately tried to stifle his screams. A cloud of blackness threatened to embrace him and steal away the pain, but

124

the teasing relief remained elusive.

"You will respect me, Narfell." Dallas casually punched the wound over and over, as if he was possessed. "You. Will. Respect. Me."

The tiger's delight seemed to grow with every strike, almost feeding off the pain. Even the Sabers released their hold on Clinton and backed away.

"YOU WILL RES—"

The locker room door burst open.

All eyes turned towards the intrusion.

Through his blurry vision, Clinton saw a small figure shuffle inside. With her head bowed, and her long, white ears drooping, he only just recognized the rabbit that had competed against Tanner Burnjaw in the opening rounds. She trundled over to a lonely backpack, before sniffing the air in confusion. Her head snapped up and she peered over to the washroom area.

"Get her!" whispered Dallas.

Wasting no time, she dropped her bag and pelted for the door, disappearing at speed with the Sabers in chase. Dallas watched as the door gently creaked shut behind them.

"This is not over, Clinton," he promised, leaning in close. He turned and approached Jakz and, giving him a slap around the jaw, roused him from unconsciousness.

"Dallas…?" mumbled the Saber.

"Get out of my sight!"

Jakz crawled to his feet before slipping from the room with his tail tucked between his legs.

Dallas turned back to the lion. "Okay, so here is the deal, Narfell." He knelt over and patted the lion's cheek. "You want to compete, so go on… Compete. But let us make the situation a little more interesting."

Clinton could only groan as he rolled around in agony.

"If, by whatever chance, you end up winning today, then I promise to overlook your defiance. However, if you fail…" He grabbed Clinton's leg and held his claws next to the wounds. "If you fail, then I will make true my threat regarding your brother."

"No. I'd never—"

"Excellent." He patted Clinton's cheek again, leaving a smudge of blood. "I just knew the idea would appeal to you."

The tiger stood up and grabbed a towel. He carefully wiped the mess from his hands and face and then tossed it into the far corner of the room. The towel knocked against the remains of the speaker and snagged against the dangling wires.

Dallas departed without another word.

Clinton's head spun. He could hear the speaker wires crackling as he tried to follow after the tiger and stop him, but it was all too much for his body to handle. The lion slid back down against the floor and quickly sank into darkness.

* * *

Pain lanced through Clinton's thigh. It was like a hot poker was being jabbed into it. He opened his eyes, and using every ounce of his strength, forced himself up onto his feet.

"Dallas!" he shouted, before his words turned into another cough. "Dallas!"

He stumbled for the door, but his leg gave way and he fell to the side.

"Please!"

He rolled onto his back and gripped his thigh while blood slowly trickled through the cracks in his fingers. Clinton spotted his cloak next to his backpack, and shuffling along the floor, ripped off a strip along the cloak's hem to bind his injury. He sat back and closed his eyes, trying to muster as much energy as he could. However, a smell suddenly tickled his nose. His eyes widened when he saw a thin wisp of smoke trailing from the wire-snagged towel.

"Scrud," he hissed.

The locker room door burst open and, reacting instantly, Clinton covered his face with the hanky. A flustered official ran into the room and grabbed him by the arm.

"We've been calling you," he panted. "They're waiting for the final to start."

The speaker wires crackled.

"But—"

"You're late!"

Clinton yanked his arm away. "Get off a—"

"Guards!" shouted the official.

Two guards stormed into the room, flanking the smaller official on either side. They took out their batons. One of the guards grunted, "They're waitin' for you."

"Move it!" added the other, shoving Clinton's helmet into his hands.

The official winced when he saw the blood seeping through the cloth on Clinton's thigh. "We can patch up your scratch by the side of the gamefield. However, we need to get you there as soon as possible."

A huge hand seized the lion by the arm and yanked him into the corridor. He limped along the passage with his custodians, staring ahead at the player's entrance. He could see the lights and hear the noise of the crowd while the lazarball official ran off to get some bandages for Clinton's 'scratch'. As he approached the gamefield, he knew he had been left with no other choice but to compete for his brother's safekeeping, or suffer the consequences.

CHAPTER NINETEEN

BACK TO WELL WOOD.

"Citizens of Wooburn, on behalf of Mayor Ferris Lakota it gives me great pleasure to introduce the tournament's final match," shouted the aardvark into his microphone. His words struck a fuse in the audience, causing the crowd's frenzy to surge to an explosive level.

Clinton's guards grasped his shoulders in a vice-like grip, unwilling to let him go for even a split second. He looked up at the crowd from the edge of the player's tunnel and his gaze settled on the mayor. The sight of Ferris lapping up the adoration forced his resolve to harden.

"Silence, please!" said the aardvark. There was a sound of shuffling papers. "I have a quick announcement to make."

The noise quelled to an expectant murmur.

"Ladies and gentlemen, I'm sure you will acknowledge that today we have witnessed some of the finest lazarball players of our generation." The crowd yelled their agreement. "Who knows, maybe some of them may grow to be as famous as Garrick 'The Wiz' Kranner, Bucky 'Nin' Nitts, Leesha Longtooth, or even Grayorr Nar—"

The crowd hissed.

"Erm... Anyway, the lucky competitors who have impressed us today will soon learn whether they have been recruited into the Plains Punishers."

Ferris waved and nodded in agreement from his high vantage.

"On another note," continued the announcer, "Mayor Ferris would like to remind you all that any donations for the team would be greatly welcomed. Remember, a pledge to the team is a symbol of loyalty to the village, and generous displays of charity will be—"

"Shut up and get on with it!" hollered a voice.

"Start the final!" yelled someone else, over the jeers.

"Yeah! We wanna see some action."

"If...if you could just remain quiet," begged the aardvark,

battling to finish his speech, "the mayor would like to ask... Oh, scrud it! Without further ado, let's get the final going."

All at once, chanting, foot stamping, and clapping spewed forth from the crowd.

"And here he is the mystery man, the ace from another place, the masked crusader himself. Ladies and gentlemen, put your hands together for the one...the only...player fifty-eight. BURGESS JERALL!"

Clinton heard the clamor of noise, but it did not truly saturate into his consciousness. He wanted nothing better than to feel pride in his achievements, but none of it mattered any more, not the credits, his pride, nor the adoration from the villagers. He cursed turning down Harris Lakota's earlier offer and stared at the lazar crystal glistening in the cloudless sky. Like the crystal, the freedom that he had been so close to grasping was dangling out his of reach yet again.

"Raion," he muttered.

"What?" grunted a guard.

Clinton shook his head. "Nothing."

"Well what are you waiting for? Get going."

The guard shoved him out of the tunnel. Clinton stumbled onto the gamefield, but stopped and turned back to face the guard.

"You touch me again and I'll have your hand off."

The two locked gazes, but the lion finally relented and limped away. Deafening screams pummeled his ears, yet they could have been screams of terror for all he cared. He ignored the noise and kept his head down, heading for the center. The pain in his injured leg was as evident as his bloodstained armor and his lattice-scratched arms. The crowd eventually began to quiet down.

"Thank you, Wooburn," echoed the announcer's voice. "And now, speaking on behalf of the village, I am very proud to welcome to the gamefield the second of our mighty finalists, the pride of Wooburn itself, everybody's number one hero: Dallas!"

Every seat in the stadium emptied as the crowd jumped to their feet.

Clinton growled. He should have known, yet the tiger's name

still bounced in his head like a grenade, ready to detonate at any moment.

The opposing player's entrance swung open. Out of the darkness emerged the tiger, stepping onto the gamefield with long, self-assured strides. His armor looked as fierce as his glare, forged from black metal - with fire-red linings that matched the glower in his eye. The openings of his gloves and boots tapered into points that led up his shins and forearms. Small points also protruded from each shoulder and kneepad. Having wrapped a bandage around his head wound, Dallas arrowed for the center, pushing his helmet down onto his head. It too was adorned with spiky nubs and a shiny, metallic grille that stretched across the front, sculpted to appear like fangs. The tiger clicked his neck when he came to a halt before Clinton.

"Surprise!"

"Competitors shake hands," ordered the announcer.

Neither anumal moved.

Dallas grinned. "I knew you would not disappoint."

"Let's just get this over with."

The tiger smiled as he looked down at Clinton's injured leg. "Insolent to the very end. But you will lose nevertheless."

"Maybe so, but have you ever stopped to think about what *you* could lose today? The great Dallas outclassed in front of the entire village? You're taking a great risk."

Dallas shrugged. "I see no risk, only certainty. You do not stand a chance against me."

Clinton tried to put some pressure on his injured leg, but a sickening fire burned along his thigh. "Yes, and you certainly saw to that, didn't you?" He reached behind his head and yanked Arkie's hanky tight, securing it around his face.

"If you only knew, Clinton. If you only knew."

"Competitors, please shake hands," ordered the announcer again.

Dallas smirked. "Shall we?" He held out his hand. "We do not want the villagers to think us unsporting."

"Just tell them to start the game. The sooner I'm out of here the better."

The tiger chuckled. "Really?" He lowered his outstretched hand. However, the amusement in his voice remained. "Oh, yes… Raion. Sorry about all that. You have my deepest sympathies."

The breath stalled in Clinton's throat. "What do you mean?"

"Why, your brother, of course. Such as shame—"

"Stop it!"

"Those Sabers, they never listen to what I tell them. I said to wait until the *end* of the match, but off they went."

"What have you done, Dallas?"

"Me? Nothing. But the last I heard the Sabers said they had business to attend to in the slum sector." Mock surprise crowned Dallas's face. "I think somewhere near your humble abode."

"Enough!"

Clinton turned to leave. Dallas, however, lunged for lion's shoulder and yanked him back again. The crowd cheered with delight at the drama on the gamefield, but the blaze inside Clinton suddenly swelled into an inferno that fired his every muscle. It was as if a bolt of energy struck him. The lion's back suddenly arched and he collapsed to his knees while Dallas maintained his grip. A piercing ache stabbed along Clinton's forehead. With his teeth and eyes clamped tight, he gripped the side of his head and tugged at his hair.

"What is happening?" blurted Dallas.

Clinton opened his eyes, trying to focus on anything through the pain, but it was no use. Dallas's cries swirled out of existence. Underneath the war-like drum of his pulse, he heard a building cacophony of coarse whispers - hundreds of voices fighting for his attention - calling to him in different pitches, somehow drowning out the deafening crowd. The lion peered from side to side, drunkenly searching for the anumals, but no matter how hard he tried he could not find them. All he could see was the tiger slowly being replaced by another vision. After a few more seconds Clinton finally stopped resisting and fell away into the current of a long forgotten memory.

*　*　*

Wooburn...

Well Wood's interior swam into focus. The candlelit living room, where Clinton's mother worked hard on the finishing touches of her son's lazarball armor, looked cozy.

Standing on a small stool with his arms spread, Clinton wore the sky-blue skin suit that Loretta had made for him. Scattered across the floor spread the remaining pieces of his detachable armor, waiting to be fastened into the holding slots attached to the skin suit.

Loretta stood back and gazed at her son.

Clinton also looked down at himself, and smiled. "I can't believe it's nearly finished. It's taken ages."

"Excuse me, young lion," she chided, chuckling while tugging at the suit to check the stitching. "Now it may be a bit big for a while, but you'll grow into it in no time."

"I think it's amazing." Clinton admired himself again. "I don't know what to say, mom."

Loretta hugged him tightly. "This is all the thanks I need."

Fast asleep in a comfy-looking chair by the fireplace, Raion snorted and murmured. Clinton remembered the cubling had driven his mother to exhaustion asking when he would have his own armor too, until the toddler had been pacified with an old cooking pan for a helmet and a pair of Grayorr's hunting gloves.

"Do you think he'll be jealous when he sees it's finished? You know what he gets like."

"Raion will get his own armor in time." Loretta stroked the younger lion's head. "He'd grow out of it by next season if I made some for him now."

The wind outside howled, making the windowpanes rattle. Clinton's smile faltered.

"Is dad going to be back late again? He spends more time at the justice house than he does here."

"Well, a great many anumals look to your father for guidance, much to the annoyance of some, may I add."

132

"You mean Ferris?"

"Mayor *Ferris is in charge of this village, and we should respect him... However, yes, he can be a little...aggravating at times. Now stand still while I adjust this sleeve."*

The house dipped into silence. Loretta hummed a gentle tune as she worked. Clinton caught a glimpse of her looking at him and spotted the warmth in her eyes. A feeling of security told Clinton he would always be safe with her. Every time he looked into her eyes he just knew everything in the world was perfect. The burning wood crackled and the flames suddenly danced in the fire. As Loretta turned to see what the noise was, the candles in the room began to flicker and shrivel, leaving behind smoking wicks. The fire died abruptly as if it had been smothered.

Clinton stood rigid, not daring to move from atop his stool. "W-what's going on?"

"Wait there."

Loretta checked Raion, but the cubling had slept through the incident. She cautiously approached the fire. Picking up a wick to relight the candles, her ears pricked. The lioness turned to the window.

A deafening crash boomed through the front room as the windows blew in, showering glass everywhere. Raion jumped out of his sleep and wailed as his mother scooped the cubling up into her arms. Pulling Clinton off the stool, she dragged them over to the far wall and away from the danger. An unnerving howl screeched from the fireplace. Gusts of wind seemed to be sucked up the chimney. Slowly, the stool Clinton had been standing on was pulled along the floor, followed by chairs, cabinets, and ornaments. Then, with another violent gust, flames blew from the fireplace and a volley of red-hot wood chips exploded everywhere like bullets. Loretta hunched over Clinton and Raion as the chips shattered into embers and rained down on her.

"Mom! What's happening?" *cried Clinton.*

"Stay by the doorway." *Loretta headed across the room.* "Just try and keep calm. And look after your brother."

He nodded and grabbed Raion's hand as she padded out into

the hall.

The front door slammed shut.

Clinton could hear his mother run to it and struggle with the handle. She desperately tried to force it open, while outside the wind intensified, whistling and shaking Well Wood to its foundations.

Clinton put his arms round Raion and hugged him tight. "D-don't worry. She'll be back soon."

Raion sobbed into Clinton's belly. Around them the air grew heavy, weighing them down. Clinton's small, flyaway hair fluttered in the breeze, whipping against his eyes as he tried to maintain his nerve. A snarling cry piggybacked on the wind and snaked through the house. In the hallway Loretta's footsteps pounded against the wooden floor, running in the direction of the kitchen. Clinton turned to Raion. Without a word the brothers scuttled after her. Snarling cries met them as they raced through the darkness. Gusts shook the house, rattling the walls and shelves.

"Stay there!" Loretta shouted, her shoes crunching through the debris as she grabbed the kitchen door. "Don't move."

Clinton ignored her orders and scrabbled into the room. Moonlight flooded through the window, bouncing off his armor as he ran to her side. Raion, however, did as instructed and waited in the hallway. Loretta pushed against the back door, trying to force it open. Shadows flickered. The noise intensified. She rammed her foot against it again, and it finally crashed open. A blast of wind engulfed her. Without pause, she ran outside.

The door slammed shut behind her.

Raion scampered next to Clinton.

"What's happening?"

Clinton shoved his brother aside and rushed for the door. "Stay there, Rai. I need to help—"

"But—"

Clinton grasped the handle and slammed his shoulder against the wood. "I SAID STAY!"

The door flew open, presenting him with a sight that caused his world to grind to a halt. Outside, in the howling wind, Grayorr roared, his teeth bared and his claws extended, guarding the doorway. Hovering in front of him, beating its featherless wings and creating giant gusts of wind, loomed the skeleton of a huge dragon. Clouds of sand enveloped the monster, dampening the moon's glow. The dragon's head alone was as big as Grayorr and each of its talons twice the size of his hands. It reared its head and screeched into the sky, the spine-piercing cry echoing out into the Plains and beyond.

"Loretta!" yelled Grayorr, dodging a blow. Deep gashes lined the lion's back and arms, and the moonlight in his eyes glinted a deep green. "Get them back!"

Them?

Clinton turned to see Raion shivering next to him.

Loretta swung around, her face a mask of terror. "Get inside now!" Falling to all fours, she positioned herself between the flying monster and her children. "Clinton, Raion, get inside! Run!"

However, Clinton's feet were glued to the spot.

The dragon lunged at Grayorr, talons slashing through the air. Ducking low, his father slipped away from the strike. Loretta burst into action. Diving at the beast, she wrapped herself around the monster's leg, yanking at its giant bones. The dragon shrieked. It snapped its foot out, flinging the lioness high into the air and making Clinton's father roar louder than he had ever heard him before.

Loretta slammed into the dirt.

"GET INSIDE!" she screamed, turning to her children as the dragon forced its giant bone-wings earthwards and arched its body back.

It shot upwards, hovering briefly in midair, before whipping around on itself and hurtling back down again, diving in for the kill.

CHAPTER TWENTY

<u>**PLAY AND WIN.**</u>

Clinton felt himself torn from his memory. As his disorientation cleared and the whispers in his head subsided, he broke through the surface of his trance to heave a breath of air. The stadium slowly slid into focus.

"Mom…Dad?"

He rubbed his temples, trying to anchor the images, but they dissipated, becoming fractured memories once more.

"I don't understand." He pounded his fist into the ground, and then his gaze fell on Dallas. "What did you do to me?"

Clinton's words echoed in the silence.

Dallas forced himself from his knees to a standing position, staring at his hand in shock. Small trails of smoke spiraled from his fingers. "I-I have no idea."

"Yes, you do. What happened?"

"I said I do not—"

"Liar!" Clinton stumbled to his feet. He reached out for Dallas, but stopped himself, fearful of the reaction occurring again.

"Listen, Narfell, I am not sure what stunt you are trying to pull here, but it will not accomplish—"

"Just tell me what you did."

"I did nothing." Dallas blew away the last bit of smoke from his fingers. "You must have had a type of seizure. Oh, wait, I should have guessed you would try to pull something clever like this, some ploy to get you eliminated. However, your plan backfired, Burgess Jerall, or rather…Clinton Narfell. Seems like you have truly let the cat out of the bag…all by yourself."

"What do you…?" The lion slowly reached up to touch his face. Feeling only skin beneath his fingers, he looked down at the floor to see an innocent-looking handkerchief lying by his feet.

"No!"

"Now this is where it really gets interesting," chuckled Dallas, folding his arms.

The whole stadium seemed to close in on the lion. A wall of

twisted scowls glared at him from the bleachers. A murmur of unrest began to ripple amongst the crowd, cutting through the shocked stillness. Clinton could hear his family name uttered in low tones.

"It can't be!"

"It is! It's the Narfell boy."

As the crowd's disbelief fermented, Clinton realized that he was standing in the epicenter of an expanding ring of hate. In every direction familiar anumals seemed to be appearing out of nowhere. To his left Galront's hunters were storming towards the gamefield, stumbling over one another in their haste to get to him. To his right a group of guards were plowing through the crowd, their spears and clubs drawn in readiness. The stadium spun around Clinton, becoming confining, until it felt like he could hardly move.

"Let me out of here, Dallas. Please, I'm begging you."

The tiger's eyes twinkled. "But I thought you were desperate to compete in the competition?"

"Scrud this!"

Clinton made a dash for the player's entrance, but the doors burst open at his approach. A stream of guards waded onto the gamefield, surging at him like a wave of muscle. He turned back to Dallas and saw more guards also filing out of the opposing player's entrance.

"Coward!" he yelled.

Dallas shrugged.

"Is there gonna be a final or what?" shouted a spectator.

"Yeah! Smash that Narfell scum!" hollered another.

Clinton ignored the comments and locked his gaze on the tiger. "Let me go, Dallas."

"You know the deal, Narfell."

"I will destroy you and everyone in this place if you don't let me out of here right now!"

The crowd gasped.

"You seem upset, Clinton. Having a bad day?"

Every impulse the lion felt demanded he crush the tiger where he stood, but all he could picture was Raion face to face with the

Sabers. "If your friends touch one hair on—"

"Oh, be quiet and turn around."

"What?"

"I said turn around!"

Clinton took a fleeting glance over his shoulder and saw Gizi, stood by the side of the gamefield, running his thumb down the blade of a knife. Behind him loitered three more Sabers.

"See, your brother is fine for the time being. Now stop your pathetic whining."

The sight of the Sabers almost brought Clinton to his knees. "Then why'd you—"

"Would you have played if I had not?"

"You're real scum, you know that?"

"Scum?" whispered Dallas. "You think I am scum?"

The tiger leaned back and roared as loud as he could. In an instant the stadium came to a standstill. Even the mayor stared in shock.

A tingle ran along the lion's spine.

"Tell me. Can scum do that?"

"Just let me go."

"You defied me. Furthermore, you not only deceived the council, but you deceived the villagers too. You think your punishment is avoidable? I do not. Why would you even dream of crossing me? Was it the credits? The glory? Or maybe it was the hope of regaining the tiniest morsel of dignity back for your cursed family?"

Clinton lowered his head.

"Ahhh." Dallas smiled. "But do you not see where your dignity has led you now?"

Clinton's head snapped up again. "It led me to the final, didn't it? It got me here, right now. But you were so scared of losing, you had to—"

"Shut your mouth!" hissed the tiger. He pointed to the bandage around his head. Tiny red dots of blood spotted the white cloth. "This makes us even, Narfell. This levels the gamefield."

Clinton surveyed the guards, knowing there was no way out of the encounter. "So what now? You get your lapdogs to drag me to the cool down cage again?"

"Oh, no. The wager remains unchanged. The Sabers will act on my command unless—"

"I beat you."

Clinton turned to scan the bleachers and only disgusted stares met his view. "Fine. Let's get it over with."

Dallas smiled and leaned in close. "Good pet," he muttered. "It will be a glorious sight for the scavengers of this village to see me finally trounce the Narfell name for good."

Dallas threw his arms out as if to embrace the whole stadium. "Citizens of Wooburn. It seems you have been served a great injustice this day, an injustice that I intend to rectify. For when defeat is upon this anumal, when he realizes that shame is his only friend, then maybe the general public will finally come to accept that the Narfell name will never threaten us with grief, or darken our future, again. For today, as we witness the rebirth of the Punishers, so too will we witness the destruction of the vermin who cast this village into the very skorr in which we now exist."

Cheers, yells, and roars of approval met the tiger's words. High in the official's box, Ferris clapped with vigor. Dallas basked in his praise before slowly dropping his arms and facing Clinton. Forced to assume his starting position, only inches from the tiger, the lion slid on his helmet while the lazar generator was primed.

"How can I ever thank you?" smirked Dallas. "The crowd is finally going to have their revenge on your cursed family."

"Lazar to be fired in... Three..."

Clinton felt his claws scrape against the floor.

"Two..."

"As I said, Clinton." The tiger's smile dropped into a malicious snarl. "You *will* respect me."

"One..."

Burning with rage, Clinton roared, but Dallas immediately returned the gesture.

"Fire!"

The lazar blasted into the stadium, only to be reflected back over Clinton's head. He glanced at the tiger, and readying himself for the worst, shouldered his opponent aside with all his might. To Clinton's surprise no weird reaction occurred. No whispers, no swirling memories, just him and the tiger…and a lazar heading over them both. Ignoring his injuries, Clinton leaped into the air, but the pressure tore at his wound. Snarling in pain, he headed the lazar upfield and landed again on all fours. Using his strength and pure stubbornness, he propelled himself forwards, hurtling past Dallas.

"This is it, ladies and gents, the final has officially begun."

Like lightning, Dallas set off after Clinton on all fours too. The felines raced along the gamefield as the speeding lazar ricocheted off the far wall and hurtled back at them. Clinton dove to intercept. He stretched out his hand…

"Down you go," hollered Dallas.

Another searing pain exploded along Clinton's leg as he felt the tiger swipe it. The lion tumbled while Dallas leapt over him, flipping at the last moment to land on both feet. He caught the lazar in the center of his chest. Clinton slammed his fist against the floor. Wasting no time, he rolled to his feet and gave chase, but as the two closed in on the scoring zone, Dallas took aim. The lion barreled forwards, smacking into the tiger's outstretched glove just as the lazar was fired from the shooter. The lazar sped towards the scoring zone and only just managed to clip a one-point target before fizzling away to nothing. Sirens burst into life. The crowd erupted.

"And it's a point to Dallas!" bellowed the announcer over the riotous blare. "The village hero has immediately taken the lead."

Once again the generator screamed and a lazar soared into the sky before streaking back down in Clinton's direction. The lion raised his glove to catch it…when something rammed into his stomach. The crowd erupted into unruly cheers. He fell back to see Dallas lowering his foot. Dallas punched the air. Turning his back on Clinton, he completely ignored the lazar as it streaked off towards his own scoring zone. Clinton snarled. As soon as Dallas turned to face him again, he lunged, slamming his shoulder into the tiger's gut. Grappling the back of his thighs, he flipped Dallas onto his back. Clinton staggered to his feet in time to see the lazar's rapid approach. Using Dallas as a step, he somersaulted forwards and slammed his chest against the hurtling projectile. It soaked into his breastplate, lighting it up a dazzling blue and, in the blink of an eye, he set off for the targets. The taste of the tiger's scent on the air told him Dallas was already in pursuit.

Clinton tapped his breastplate and transferred the lazar to his glove before firing it at the end wall. Readying himself for the rebound, he glanced over his shoulder to see a hand powering towards him. The lion was jerked sideways as Dallas dragged him down by the helmet, slamming his head against the gamefield surface. Clinton ignored his dizziness, though, and swept Dallas's foot out from under him, sending the tiger crashing to the ground by his side. The lazar shot over both felines, bounced off the wall, hit the floor, and rebounded out of the stadium's open roof. Once outside, it lost its consistency and fizzled away with a soft pop.

A loud klaxon cut through the crowd's cheers and brought a halt to the match. Two flustered officials appeared on the gamefield and helped Dallas to his feet. One of the officials blew on a large silver whistle and waved his arms animatedly.

"We have a foul, ladies and gentlemen!" yelled the aardvark. "We have a foul!"

The stadium went wild.

Clinton staggered to his feet and automatically made his way to the penalty spot, ready to accept a lazar.

"And stepping up to take his penalty is...Dallas," shouted the announcer.

The crowd cheered as the tiger strolled up to the penalty line, his glove already glowing red, charged with a fresh lazar.

"What? He fouled me," shouted Clinton, grabbing an official by the shoulder. "Are you blind?"

"Touch me again, Narfell, and I'll have you disqualified," snarled the official, shoving the lion away.

Dallas took his time to take the shot. He followed the ten-point moving target with his glove, and was just about to fire...when he cocked his head and smiled at Clinton. The trigger mechanism clicked. His glove's crimson light dimmed as the lazar snaked through its circuits.

A ball of light burst from the shooter and streaked off towards the target zone. It smashed against the target in a hail of light, scoring a direct hit. Yet Dallas never once shifted his gaze from Clinton. Despite the blaring sirens, the lights, and the crowd, Dallas simply stared, soaking up the sight of his defeat.

When the half-time buzzer finally sounded, Clinton felt relief flood through him. Four more times the lazar had been fired into play, but despite his efforts nothing had wielded him any results. Dallas had blocked his every attempt using any means possible...be it legal or not. With aching and bruised limbs, he stumbled off to his exit...but a barricade of guards blocked his path. Clinton stared along the line of muscle at their steely faces and yanked off his helmet.

"You have to be kidding me?"

The guards, however, would not move.

He tossed his helmet aside and slumped against the side of the wall. After a few seconds, he peered up at the mayor's section to see Ferris staring down at him. Clinton let out a deep snarl before hanging his head low, forced to spend the half time listening to a torrent of insults from the raucous crowd.

CHAPTER TWENTY-ONE

A LAST DITCH ATTEMPT.

The sun's gradual descent through the desert sky promised yet another stunning sunset across the Great Plains. Nightmare stooped outside the village perimeter fence and studied the abandoned lookout post. He let out a soft rumble of a growl as a tide of emotions flowed through him.

"Wooburn, oh, how I have missed you."

Straightening his coat, he shook off the temptation to recall the past and sniffed the perimeter. No guards were near. Popping out the claw on his index finger, he knelt down. The panther scraped two lines into the dirt, a symbol similar to the shape of an egg timer, before he added a few smaller lines to it. He stood up and lifted his finger to his eye, touching his eyeball. When he pulled his finger away, a small teardrop clung to the end of his fingertip. Nightmare sighed and gritted his teeth at performing the longwinded Floor magic. Conjuring up the types of cantrip that any village priest or street magician could perform was beneath him, but he knew he had no choice. Wielding something as powerful as Weaver magic would alert others to his presence, and he knew stealth was the only option at this juncture. After rubbing the tear into the dirt symbol, he stood up and slammed his foot on top of the charm, and shot off through the air.

The panther arced upwards, his long coat flapping behind like giant, black wings, until he landed on the roof of the lookout post. His lips twisted into a satisfied grin.

Deeper in the heart of the village he could hear the sound of muffled cries, cheers, and screams coming from the stadium, while below spread what could only be called a shanty town. Taking a deep breath, he could practically taste the desperation and rage in the village, charging the very air itself. He stepped off the lookout roof and dropped to the ground on the other side of the wall.

"Welcome back," he muttered.

He dusted down his coat and strolled off through the deserted slum sector.

"Lazar to be fired in three… Two… One… Fire!"

After what seemed like hours of waiting, the second half finally got underway, yet Clinton could not get past Dallas's defenses. The more he tried, the more Dallas beat him back. It was only by pure chance he succeeded in scoring three one-point targets, but by then the majority of time had slipped away, until only a few minutes of play remained.

"The score stands at eleven to three, with Dallas in the lead," informed the announcer. "Yet it looks like Narfell has got some fire left in him, and a ten-point target could still steal the match from Dallas."

The lazar shot into the stadium.

"And we're off."

The ball of light took a trajectory towards Dallas, but Clinton lunged to intercept. Dallas snarled and swung his elbow into the lion's visor with such force it crunched against his nose. Clinton stumbled back, his eyes pooling, while hot blood splattered across his face. Just as Clinton hit the floor, he felt his glove being tapped as Dallas stole possession. Clinton sprung to his feet and set off after the tiger, ignoring his ringing ears and the pain in his leg. Within seconds he caught up to his opponent near the scoring zone.

"Well, folks, there's only sixty seconds left in the final match, but it isn't over just yet, not if Narfell has anything to do with it."

The lion hollered a determined roar. He slid alongside the tiger and stretched his arm out to steal the lazar. Seeing the tiger dodge away from the maneuver, Clinton dropped and swept the tiger's feet from under him. Dallas stumbled forwards just as Clinton's glove clipped his breastplate to reclaim the lazar.

"An excellent tackle by fifty-eight… And what's this? Narfell has an open run ahead of him," screamed the aardvark.

Clinton flipped back onto his feet and sprinted off for the target zone. He gasped for air, his throat burning almost as much as his leg, and raised his shaking hand, aiming it at the targets.

He focused...

Just one shot. Just one ten-point target! That's all.

He gritted his teeth. "C'mon, Clint! C'MON!"

A ferocious roar echoed from behind as something slammed into his back. Clinton felt a fist beat against his helmet before the tiger dug his claws into the gaps between his armor. Gasps and cheers stirred the crowd to their feet. Clinton and Dallas fell in a heap of flailing limbs, and the lion felt blood trickling from fresh claw wounds. The tiger rolled to his side and kicked his foot out, smashing the sole of his boot against Clinton's face before the lion could get away.

"That's enough now!" shouted a voice from the crowd.

"Yes, give it up! Leave Narfell alone," added another.

"Go on, Dallas. Finish him!"

Clinton lay on his back in the center of the stadium, waiting for the whistle to blow, when a shadow moved over him. The tiger dropped to his knees and pinned Clinton's injured leg down.

"What are you doing?" The lion tried to yank his leg away. "Get off me!"

Dallas pulled off his helmet and threw it aside, revealing a sadistic smile. He tore off Clinton's leg armor before opening his jaws and sinking his fangs into Clinton's bloody thigh.

"What the...?" yelled the commentator as the microphone squealed and went dead.

Clinton's wail rang out while anumals gasped or covered their faces. The lion kicked out at Dallas with his free leg and tried to swing punches at him, but still he could not break free from the tiger. Finally, after what felt like an eternity of pain, he felt Dallas's grip release. Waves of dizziness tempted him again with the promise of a painless rest, but still he resisted. Gritting his teeth while fighting the nausea, he waited for the alarms to blare to life, to signal that a foul had been committed, and the chance for him to take a penalty.

However, the alarms never rang.

Dallas stumbled to his feet and towered over Clinton. He smiled, showing his bloodstained teeth. Lying on his side, clutching his bleeding leg, Clinton strained to see inside the official's section. Ferris stared back down, while his son, Harris, stormed from the box in horror, pushing guards out of his way as he departed. Up in the announcer's box a village guard snatched the microphone from the commentator's grasp, while the match officials remained in stunned silence.

Clinton tried to get up from the floor, but the pain crippled him. He slowly pried open his misshapen visor to see Dallas laughing.

"Do you understand now, Narfell?" Dallas bent over to show his red-pulsing glove, clearly in possession of a lazar. Calmly, he straightened up and raised his arms. "I will never allow anyone to better me. I am the victor."

A spatter of applause trickled from the crowd.

The smile on the tiger's face twisted into a scowl. He roared so loud that a flock of wefrings took flight from the rafters. "I AM THE VICTOR!"

Wooburn sprung to its feet. Like an infection, a chant for Dallas spread through the crowd. Lapping up the adoration, the tiger turned to the scoring zone and pointed his glove at the distant ten-point target. The crowd immediately hushed, waiting for the shot to be fired.

"It all ends here, Narfell. With one simple action, your name, your family, and your life, will forever be—"

"Stop!" yelled a shaking voice from across the gamefield.

A commotion struck up within the player's tunnel.

Clinton turned to see a small, white rabbit, slip past the crowd of guards and onto the floor. Unable to speak, she pointed back at the player's entrance. "F-f—"

"C'mon, let's have you," said one of the guards, attempting to grab her.

She stumbled out of his reach.

"F-f-fire," she quivered. "The, the, the stadium… It's on fire."

Every anumal turned to the player's entrance, only to be greeted by gushing black smoke, condensing with every passing second. It took a few moments for Clinton to truly comprehend just what he was witnessing.

"Fire in the locker room," blurted the rabbit again. "Fire!"

The seed was sown.

Panic erupted. As one, every anumal bolted to their feet and surged for the stadium's exits like the surf crashing against the shore. Guards and officials scrabbled up the walls of the gamefield. The mayor's eyes widened and his mouth fell slack. Dallas lowered his hand and backed away, towards the safety of the opposing player's entrance.

Clinton remained on the floor, frozen with shock.

Wooburn's stadium, the city's pride and joy, was on fire.

CHAPTER TWENTY-TWO

THE TRIAL OF WOOBURN'S WORST.

"Could the court of Wooburn please rise!" hollered the security elephant, banging the end of his spear against the floor. The packed courtroom rose to their feet.

"Bring in prisoner four-three-seven!" the elephant barked.

Safety locks clanked and catches screeched as the latches were released. All heads turned to the end of the central aisle as the two metal doors slowly swung open. With his hands and ankles bound by shackles, Clinton limped out of the darkness, nudged ahead by two guards, keeping him at spear point. Stripped of his armor and dressed in bloodstained rags, the lion squinted his eyes until they adjusted to the light. He stumbled up a flight of steps to an elevated, circular dais in the center of the room.

The courtroom loomed before him. Upon its highly polished wooden floor, carved benches and railings separated the horseshoe-shaped viewing galleries from the officials' section. An enormous circular stained-glass window took pride of place within the grand room, casting rainbow-colored hues upon a large desk, behind that sat the esteemed Giraffe Council.

Clinton looked up at the regal giraffes before him, yet their presence churned his stomach. His teacher, Mrs. McCarbe, had taught Clinton years ago that for centuries giraffes had been considered 'the eyes of the land'. Receiving the name due to their role as lookout during the Dawn of Sentience, early communities depended on them to watch out for signs of danger. And being one of the most perceptive species, the giraffe usually saw things as logically as their long necks allowed them visually.

Ferris Lakota sneered at Clinton from behind a large, marble-topped desk in front of the Giraffe Council.

"Humble citizens of Wooburn, I thank you for your attendance today," said one of the council, a somber, elderly male called Kordo. "Since Silania herself laid down the very laws of society, we have demanded that all anumals be treated fairly and live free from danger. The Dawn of Sentience taught us to oppress our most feral of instincts, and instead adopt peace, consideration, and understanding. We live in these huge villages and cities to protect ourselves from the mindless scavengers, and to live in them you must follow their laws. Yet there are those who willfully choose to break these laws and let their baser instincts drive their actions. It is a rare occurrence that calls for the attention of the full Giraffe Council, but today such attention has been deemed appropriate. Please, Wooburn, be seated."

The courtroom took their seats. Ferris slouched down on his chair and picked up a quill, ready to begin.

"Every so often a crime so heinous is committed that the mayor and his officials must be provided with suitable wisdom and guidance," explained Kordo, nudging some papers in front of him. "It is therefore decreed in village law that at such times the Giraffe Council shall convene and oversee proceedings. Mayor Ferris, if you would be so kind?"

Ferris put his quill down and strode towards the giraffes' desk. Pulling on a cord, he unraveled a long piece of black cloth with a gruesome portrait of Clinton painted on it. It hung down from the edge of the desk so the whole room could clearly see it.

"And so, on this day, we shall commence the trial of prisoner four-three-seven, an anumal of the feline species. Family name: Narfell. First name: Clinton. Clan: The Union Wheel."

Kordo peered up from his papers and over the rim of his spectacles to study the lion.

The mayor banged his gavel against the desk. "Council members, you are asked to begin today's proceedings by informing the accused of his crimes."

Councilor Kordo nodded curtly back at Ferris. "Prisoner four-three-seven, you are here today accused of the destruction of public property and endangering the lives of your fellow villagers. Are you aware Wooburn's stadium has been destroyed?"

Clinton's throat felt raw. "Yes," he croaked, holding his head high despite his matted hair and stinking clothes.

"And what do you have to say on this matter, son of Grayorr?" asked an elderly female giraffe, sitting to Kordo's right. "Do you comprehend the impact this tragedy will have on the village? Not only have we lost a stadium, we have set back our chances of rebuilding our wealth within the Plains."

Clinton eyed the courtroom and saw nothing but hate aimed in his direction. "I...I ask the council...if I could please see my brother."

"We are not here to discuss your visitation rights," snapped Councilor Kordo. "We are here to discuss the alleged arson—"

"But is he alive? Is he safe at least?"

The council muttered amongst themselves and turned to look questioningly at the mayor.

"Just answer the question, Narfell," Ferris snapped.

Clinton growled at the beaver. "Okay, I'm innocent. I haven't done anything wrong. On my honor."

"That's a lie!" Ferris shouted, thumping the table with his fist. "What does this creature know of honor?"

"Mister Mayor!" cut in a young, male giraffe to Kordo's left. "*We* are the judges in this courtroom, not you. Control yourself."

"Well, it's obvious he did it, Councilor Blare."

"KEEP...your opinions to yourself, Mayor Lakota. Now, please be seated."

Ferris huffed theatrically and plunked himself back onto his seat.

Returning his attention to Clinton, Councilor Blare sighed before continuing. "Just to clarify, Clinton Narfell, you are telling the council that you were in no way responsible for the fire that resulted in the stadium's destruction? That you, more importantly, did not put thousands of innocent lives at risk?"

"As I said...I am innocent."

Blare looked over at the elderly female giraffe for a second, his face unreadable. "Then could you kindly explain how it was that the fire originated from inside your own changing room?"

"Yes, explain that one," snapped Ferris.

A couple of eager onlookers leaned forwards in their seats.

"Your honors, I was attacked just before the final match could begin. I-I remember a speaker was smashed in the fight, but the guards wouldn't listen to me...and I was dragged off to the gamefield." Clinton bowed his head. "After that I wasn't allowed back inside the room. I didn't see the fire until everyone else did."

"Oh, come on!" blasted Ferris. "You expect us to believe that dung? Who were these so-called attackers then, huh? Give us names, Narfell. Or are they just another part of your warped fantasies?"

Clinton tried to shut out the beaver's taunts. Taking a deep breath, he looked up at the council. "Your honors, I was attacked by Dallas and four Sabers."

Nobody moved until Ferris forced out a laugh. The room tentatively joined in. Even a couple of the giraffes chuckled. Clinton felt like shouting, telling them to shut up, but he knew it would land him back inside a cell again.

Seated at the far left of the Giraffe Council, next to Councilor Blare, a middle-aged, female giraffe narrowed her eyes. "Silence!" she ordered. "I will not tolerate such behavior in my courtroom, not from anyone."

As she spoke the last words she gave scolding glances at her fellow giraffes, raising her head and neck higher to signify her control. She stared back at Clinton, her glare tinged with remorse. "I would also like to ask the members of this courtroom why they find this statement humorous? Is what the accused said such a wild allegation to hear? After all, I am informed the tiger's actions during the final match were far from noble. Who is to say that Clinton Narfell is not, in actuality, telling the truth?"

The council responded to her with neutral stares.

Ferris turned to the giraffe. "My dear, Councilor Barla, I am sorry to contradict your fair self on this matter, but the very idea of our beloved Dallas ever lowering himself to the standards of this...criminal is out of the question. Why, as I know Dallas in such a close and personal manner, being the one who opened my home and heart to him when no one else would, I can personally vouch that even if he did pay this thug a visit, he must have had the village's best interests at heart. And I can confirm that Dallas was also charged with protecting the village, and the tournament, from any threat that conspired to sabotage it. You have to understand, councilor, when considering Clinton Narfell, we are talking about an accomplished liar and a heartless criminal. He hails from a family of charlatans. Why, this thug deceived his way into the tournament. He had no business being in the stadium in the first place, and now he's obviously trying to cover his tracks."

A low murmur of agreement circulated the audience.

Clinton resisted the urge to bite back.

"This cursed anumal," continued Ferris, his voice gaining volume. He thumbed through a large pile of papers. "This deceitful anumal must logically be the culprit. Why, taking his past record into account clearly shows that burning down our most prized possession is nothing out of the ordinary for him."

"The matter of the lion's past misdemeanors and his actions regarding his enrollment in the tournament is not the subject on trial here," informed Barla.

"But surely these incidents go to highlight the level of deceit he will stoop to?"

"Mayor Lakota, I can hardly liken the act of bending some rules to enter a competition, to willfully destroying a public building filled with thousands of anumals. The two are simply incomparable. Besides, it still does not dismiss the fact that this *beloved hero* of yours could also have been near the locker room before the final match began. Do you not think that this is enough of a motive to at least consider what the lion has to say, or are you so blinkered into making the accused confess that you will disregard any other lines of inquiry?"

"Oh, please, Councilor Barla," scoffed Ferris, "I know that Dallas would never dream of doing such a thing. And I resent your remarks regarding my questioning."

"And I resent you trying to influence the council's decisions today."

Ferris flinched, unable to find his words. "B-but…well, I… Please, your honor, I, I have no idea what you are referring to. A-anyway, if you want an opinion on the tiger, then all you have to do is ask the general public. I'm sure they will be more than pleased to give you their impression of what kind of a citizen he is."

"Can we please keep the conversation on track," asked Councilor Blare. "I am not here to listen to opinions. I am here to judge facts and facts alone."

Ferris bowed his head and returned quietly to his desk. "My apologies."

A young female giraffe, sitting between Councilor Kordo and the elderly female, spoke up for the first time that day. "The fact, as I see it, is that there are no witnesses to say whether your claims regarding the tiger are reality or fiction," she said in a brusque, clipped manner. Most of the giraffes nodded as she paused to scrutinize the lion. "In fact, there was no one, apart from you, Narfell, disguised or not, seen near the locker room for the entire match. Unless you can think of anyone to verify your claim?"

Clinton immediately thought of the female rabbit.

"No he can't," cut in Ferris. He folded his arms and smiled. "And that is because he didn't see *hide nor hare* of any other anumal anywhere near the locker room that day."

Clinton realized that the mayor had already dealt with that particular nuisance; she would never confess to seeing Dallas in the room…if she were even alive, that is.

Onlookers shuffled impatiently in their seats.

Clinton shook his head and looked up at the council. "I…I don't know anyone else."

The younger female giraffe leaned forward. "Clinton, if you wish to confess to the crime now, we will see that your punishment is more lenient."

"But I have nothing to confess," he protested. "I didn't do it. Please believe me."

"Ha! Believe you?" Ferris jumped to his feet again. "A thieving cheat? Everything points towards you, Narfell. You even said in the competition final that you would destroy the stadium and everyone in it if you didn't see your brother. The whole stadium heard you. This is just another example of the type of behavior expected from an anumal who has been in this very courtroom pleading innocence more times than I care to remember."

"That isn't true."

"So you were not stood before one of my officials a few weeks ago accused of attacking an elephant? Who, I might add, has not been seen nor heard of since."

The crowd whispered to each other and glared at Clinton.

Ferris grabbed the papers from his desk. "It's all here in black and white, Narfell, every…last…detail."

"But it wasn't me, it was…"

"Who, Narfell?" Ferris slammed the papers down. "Enlighten us."

The lion had second thoughts again. The truth about the Sabers terrorizing the elephant would make him appear to be an even bigger liar than he already looked.

"No one… It's nothing."

Strolling out from behind his desk, Ferris approached the raised dais. "Nothing? Narfell says it's 'nothing', ladies and gentlemen." Ferris shook his head in disgust. "As you can see, my fellow Wooburnians, the lion's words are, at best…unreliable. However, I am going to say this: I, for one, am tired of having to put up with his reign of terror. It simply has to stop. We need a new start - a new beginning. One without…" Ferris searched for the right word, "brutes like this, bullying the populace. We need to locate this kind of thorn and pluck it from the village once and for all, so we can create a safer society in which our children can prosper."

Clinton glared at the beaver.

"So what course of action are you suggesting, Mayor?" croaked Councilor Kordo.

"Yes, just what are you suggesting?" blurted Clinton, his voice shaking.

"What I am suggesting," smiled Ferris, ignoring the lion's outburst, "is that we exile this hazard once and for all."

The sentence took a moment to cement itself in Clinton's head. "Exile?" he gasped. "B-but you, you can't do that."

"Oh, but I can." Ferris turned to address the giraffes. "Honored council members, I feel that exile is the only practical solution. Will the citizens of Wooburn ever feel truly safe with this criminal lurking in the shadows? Remember that this lion has terrorized innocent citizens his entire adult life, thieved food during the shortage, yet more importantly, he has singlehandedly destroyed Wooburn's beloved stadium."

"How many times do I have to tell you I didn't burn it down? How can I be exiled when I haven't done anything wrong?"

"Wrong?" hollered the mayor. "Haven't done anything wrong? Is every word you utter a complete lie?"

"I'm not lying. Now let me go, I need to see my brother."

Ferris turned around so quickly he almost spun on the spot. "I believe you have no right to tell me to do anything, slum trash."

"Mayor Ferris!" snapped Councilor Blare.

"I'm sorry, Councilor, but the cursed Narfells are all the same. Just like his parents destroyed his chances in life, he is trying to destroy my-our village."

"Don't you dare talk about my parents like that!" roared Clinton, lunging at Ferris.

Guards instantly yanked on Clinton's shackles and others rushed to surround him with their spears drawn and ready. Ferris shrieked and jumped back. The whole courtroom fidgeted as the remaining guards moved into a tight formation around the prisoner.

"Silence!" shouted Councilor Kordo. "Silence, or we shall adjourn. I must have order within the room."

Clinton panted, his fangs bared. He paced back and forth on the dais. Ferris reappeared from behind a security guard, wearing a satisfied grin.

"Continue, mayor," ordered Councilor Kordo. "But this is your last warning." He swept his spectacled gaze around the room. "And that means all of you."

"Thank you," whispered Ferris, bowing and rubbing his hands together. "Well, I'm sure that you can all see this lion is clearly…unstable."

Clinton continued to pace and growl, scolding himself for falling for the taunts.

"Narfell is even so violent that he will try and attack me, the mayor of Wooburn, in broad daylight. Isn't that proof enough of the twisted psyche the creature hides?" Ferris looked out into the audience and pointed an accusing finger at Clinton. "He simply has to go!"

The crowd burst into applause.

Ferris placed his hands behind his back and turned to stare at Clinton. "I hereby plead that the council motion for the punishment of exile by gorespine. And may his face never darken our fair village again."

"No!" Clinton gasped.

"A gorespine exile is the most serious of punishments," interjected Councilor Kordo, ignoring the lion. "Surely a few seasons in the junk mines would be more suitable?"

Ferris sighed. "I am afraid an anumal can always return from the junk mines, however decayed and decrepit the air down there turns them. And I feel that a threat like Narfell needs to be completely cauterized from Wooburnian society."

"Well, you will have to draw up the intended proposals, and have the appropriate documents completed before we can make a decision as drastic as that."

With a theatrical swish, Ferris stepped behind the small desk and picked up a handful of papers. "They're right here, all signed and ready for your inspection, your honors."

"You can't do this!" roared Clinton, yanking at his chains.

The council looked at one another, a few blinking in surprise, and then signaled to a nearby guard. Seeing the signal, the rhino took a few steps forward and bellowed, "The Giraffe Council will now discuss the case. Guards, remove the prisoner!"

Without delay, the two guards dragged Clinton back to his holding cell.

CHAPTER TWENTY-THREE

A SAVING GRACE.

Clinton paced his cell and kicked at the filthy straw covering the ground. The rhino standing guard hit his baton against the metal bars.

"I won't tell you again. Sit down and stop fidgetin'!"

Clinton sighed, leaned his back against the wall, and slowly slid to the ground. He prayed that the council would see past the web of lies, discover the truth, and refuse the mayor's application for exile. However, a cold feeing told him not to hope too hard.

Light suddenly spilled into his cell as the door swept open. Two burly shadows blocked the entrance, chains in one hand and batons in the other. His heart racing, his hands shaking, Clinton rose to a crouch as the guards stomped into his cell.

"It's time."

* * *

Flanked on either side, Clinton entered the courtroom and took up his position on the dais. He did not know how long he had been waiting, but the sun's rays were beginning to wane. The crowd's mutterings died a swift death upon sight of the prisoner, yet their stares spoke volumes. Looking intently at the six giraffes, Clinton saw them dart him an occasional glance. From time to time, Councilor Barla would stare in his direction too, her eyes kind, but full of distress, before she would sort through her papers.

Clearing his throat, Kordo silenced the whispers before he began to speak. "I see that the accused is with us once again. Prisoner four-three-seven, Clinton Narfell."

"That he is," Ferris replied, resuming his seat behind his smaller desk.

"Good. Then I can confirm that on this day, the twenty-sixth day of the denning season, the Giraffe Council has convened and a verdict has been found." Kordo looked to his right and left, at which the other councilors nodded their agreement. Barla ignored

Clinton and peered at the brightly colored window. "It has been decided, by a majority of four votes to two, that prisoner four-three-seven is to be perceived as a threat to the general interests of Wooburn."

Ferris grinned.

"After much deliberation, it can only be deemed that a creature of questionable characteristics could, in all likelihood, be the cause of the heinous destruction of Wooburn's stadium. However sparse the evidence may be, the consideration of his past misdemeanors and obvious temperament signify that the anumal standing before us, prisoner four-three-seven, is the most likely cause of this egregious crime. Prisoner four-three-seven…"

Clinton closed his eyes, waiting for the words.

"It has been decided that you represent an increasing threat to Wooburn and to the safety of its citizens. As such we must put the wellbeing of the general populace into consideration and remove that said threat from the village…permanently." The crowd began to stir as the mayor's grin increased. "So it is with the power entrusted to us that we, the Giraffe Council, keepers of the scales of justice, sentence you, Clinton, son of Loretta and Grayorr Narfell, to the punishment of exile by gorespine."

Clinton could not move.

"From this moment on your rights and citizenship are null and void. You will no longer be offered protection from our village." Councilor Kordo looked up from his paper. "Clinton Narfell, you are to be cast out of Wooburn …alone."

Unable to fully grasp the extent of his ruling, the last word eventually made some sense in Clinton's head. He pulled against his chains before the guards could react. "You can't do this. What about Raion? What will happen to him? You won't even tell me if he's okay." He wrenched at the shackles, causing the metal to scrape his skin. "I have to see him. TAKE ME TO HIM!"

The guards charged up the dais steps and grabbed the lion by the forearms. Clinton struggled to break free from their grip.

"Please…anyone! You can't do this." He looked along the council members before he noticed Councilor Barla bowing her head. "Councilor Barla? Please!"

The guards began to drag Clinton down the aisle towards the tunnel, but he resisted. One of them raised their baton to strike him. Barla closed her eyes, as if to prevent the onset of tears, before she raised her head high.

"Stop!" she shouted. "Let the prisoner go."

The guards reluctantly released their grip on Clinton.

"What is the meaning of this?" Ferris barked.

"Clinton, please calm down," urged Barla above the ruckus. "I truly understand your pain, but you must listen to what I say."

Ferris jumped to his feet, intending to protest, but the councilor swung her gaze in his direction. "And you," she snapped, her words echoing loudly. "You have had your chance to speak today, so sit down and do not interrupt me."

Ferris blinked at her orders, but did as he was told.

Barla swung her head back to the lion. "Clinton, I fear that not just one, but two, acts of injustice have been implemented in this courtroom today."

Kordo gasped at her words. "Councilor Barla, this is most inappropriate."

"No, Councilor Kordo, I will have my say." She ignored the shocked glances from her fellow councilors. "I believe that Clinton Narfell is innocent—"

"I beg your pardon," interrupted Councilor Kordo, "but you are seriously undermining the council's authority with this behavior."

"I am well aware of what I am doing, councilor, and as I have said, I truly believe Clinton Narfell is—"

"Must I remind your honor that the council has already voted and the verdict has been passed? Your opinion no longer matters, Barla."

"That is my entire point, Councilor Kordo. My opinion never mattered in the first place," she hissed, practically spitting out the words. "My views regarding this whole trial have been ignored and brushed aside by the village's enthusiasm to pin the guilt on a scapegoat. Never before has the verdict of exile taken such a short amount of time to be decided, especially when the welfare of two citizens hangs in the balance. Our ancestors would be appalled and shocked today. After the great wars with the humans, we pledged that we, the descendants of the Armies of the Ark, would forever treat anumalkind with equality. We promised never to become the mindless weapons we were bred to be. We made an entire species extinct because of those promises, and from it, we evolved. We learned to settle problems diplomatically and without savagery. Yet within these walls today, I cannot help but feel our evolution has regressed into the murky origins from which we were created. The council has acted with nothing short of savagery."

The courtroom burst into gasps.

Barla cast her glare upon every anumal before her.

"W-well, Councilor Barla," Kordo cleared his throat. "I do concede that you are entitled to your opinions on this matter, however exaggerated they may be, but I must insist that you keep them to yourself. The council's majority vote was for exile, and to reverse the decision or call for a retrial is out of the question."

"Yes, Councilor Kordo, and however much I am loath to say this, I am aware that the verdict is irreversible." Barla glanced back at the lion. "I am sorry, Clinton, but I have no choice. I cannot change the way we hold our trials; these procedures have been in place for hundreds of years. And as much as I would like to, I simply cannot."

Councilor Barla lowered her head, but then immediately elevated it again, raising it higher while giving the room a slow, commanding look. "However, I do believe that due to your impending exile from this village, a second injustice has been served to your sibling." Clinton went rigid at the mention of his brother. "As a result of this unfair verdict, Raion Narfell will not only lose a brother and mentor, but possibly one of the only friends he has."

A rebellious tear trickled down Clinton's cheek.

"Yet," Barla's voice turned stone cold, "I am pleased to say that this is one matter I am far from powerless to act upon. I, Barla of the Wooburn Giraffe Council, pronounce that from this day forth, I will be acting as full guardian to Raion Narfell, son of

Grayorr and Loretta Narfell."

The crowd tried to stifle their gasps as the remaining council turned to her in astonishment.

"So Raion's not hurt then?" Clinton's heart lifted. "Please tell me he's okay. Let me know that at least."

"Why, he's fine. The authorities took him as soon as you were apprehended at the stadium. Why would you think otherwise?" Clinton snuck a glance at the mayor, and Barla followed his gaze. "I see... Then let it be known that your brother, Raion Narfell, shall remain in my protection until the time comes when he is old enough to leave the village of his own free will."

"But Councilor Barla, this is unheard of!" interrupted the younger female. "It is preposterous, do you hear me? Tradition forbids it."

"And today has shown us that tradition is fallible, Councilor Cair," snapped Barla. "Disbar me and remove me from the council if you will, but I will not alter my actions."

"This is rocky ground you are treading, Barla," warned Kordo.

"Yes, it may be rocky, councilor, but my eyes are not blinkered. I know what justice is, and today I have not seen a trace of it. Today our honorable system, like most things in this village, has been tainted."

"I agree!" added a new male voice.

Barla turned to look at the spectacled giraffe sitting two places from her. This giraffe had remained silent throughout the whole trial, but now he lifted his gaze from his papers. "This is not right. The verdict, I mean. The way it was reached was...wrong."

"Thank you, Councilor Neeve," said Barla. "It gives me some hope that at least two of the council can see when a mockery is being made."

Neeve nodded gently before looking back down at his papers again.

"The councils' behavior today is intolerable," croaked Kordo.

"That is the wisest thing you have said all day," retorted Barla.

The female giraffe locked her gaze with her fellow members. Councilors Kordo and Cair stared the longest, but then finally looked away. Barla, however, turned to the lion and smiled remorsefully. "I know this is not much of a condolence, Clinton, but I assure you that Raion will be in the safest of care. I promise."

Clinton looked at her with an empty heart and tried to mutter the words *thank you*, but his pain prevented it.

Mayor Ferris gathered his papers from his desk and muttered under his breath.

"And you, mister mayor," snapped Barla, making the whole room jump. "I take it you are not impressed with my proposal?"

"Oh, but I am. Indeed, I am. Now, with you subsidizing him, the youngster will not be a burden to the taxpayers. Why, the last thing the village needs is another Narfell bleeding the coffers dry." He bowed theatrically. "It is a bold step, Councilor Barla, and I commend your...noble actions."

Barla narrowed her eyes. "Well, Mayor Ferris, I would like nothing better than to commend you on your actions today, but, regrettably, the council are not pleased with you in the slightest." She glared upon the squat beaver from above. "Yet seeing as you are in such strong favor of my idea to raise the child, I decree that you shall also spend at least one of your rest days every week taking him under your wing. Your attitude has shown me that you need to remember the anumals on trial here are not mere names and numbers. They have feelings, and emotions, and families."

"I am all too aware of the Narfell family," snorted Ferris. "And I would also like to make a point of reminding you, your honor, that I am the mayor, not a common child minder. I simply do not have the time for such—"

"Make the time! Believe me, Ferris, I am not asking you to do this, I am ordering you! As you were so very quick to blame and convict prisoner four-three-seven, your actions have orphaned an innocent—"

"B-but, your honors," he whined. "Members of the council. It is beneath my station to play nursemaid to every waif and stray abandoned in the village. I simply—"

"If memory serves me correctly, this would not be the first time you have done such a thing, or should we listen to gossip and presume your motive concerning a certain abandoned tiger was really just a publicity stunt during your election campaign? Now, mayor, I am ordering you to spend time with the child so that you can experience, first hand, what your actions have accomplished."

Ferris inhaled, intending to retaliate.

"Do not press me on this matter, beaver. You shall do as I say or you shall find yourself standing before the council with the closet of your past flung wide open, skeletons hanging for all to see."

Some of the council members bowed their heads and shuffled their papers. Ferris shut his mouth with an audible snap. Barla lowered her head so that she was looking as close to the beaver as she possibly could.

"Do you have anything else to say, mayor?"

"N-no, thank you, councilor," he mumbled. "I understand."

"Does anyone else have any objections?" she asked, looking at the giraffes.

"We will talk later," repeated Kordo, before practically whispering his final words to the crowd. "We, the Giraffe Council, have reached our final decision today. The case is now closed."

The council quickly exited the room in single file before the mayor had a chance to complain.

Still numb from the verdict, Clinton felt a thick, heavy cloth shoved over his head. Struggling to break free from the guard's grip, his legs were swept from beneath him and a baton struck him from behind. As his vision swam, Clinton felt the guards dragging him from the courtroom and out into the unknown.

CHAPTER TWENTY-FOUR

GORESPINE.

"Make it tight. I don't want him breaking free," ordered a deep voice.

"You just worry 'bout them feet of his, Boll, an' I'll worry 'bout his hands," snapped a gruffer voice.

Clinton's eyes felt like they had been welded shut as he gradually forced them open. Greeted with deep, orange rays peeking over the rim of the horizon, the early evening sun had all but set. A strong smell of dung hit his nose. Surrounded by large, wooden pens and stables, Clinton's ears pricked to the sound of numerous stock bleating and grunting. Farmers busily guided the herd back through the village's main gates and to safety, away from the nightly scavengers that would roam the perimeter. Metal troughs were emptied of their precious water and grain, while farmhands loaded bails of straw, tools, and feed onto wagons. A chilly breeze blew across the landscape.

"Are we set?"

"Nearly. Keep your hide on, Boll, the gorespine's still bein' watered."

Gorespine.

The memory of the giraffe's verdict pricked his thoughts like a poisonous thorn. He felt his stomach churn. The trial seemed like an age ago now, a time lost in a nightmare, but in reality his exile had been decided only hours before. His muscles felt tenderized and his joints stiff. Dried blood matted his fur and a metallic tang hung at the back of his mouth. Clinton remained deadly still for fear of yet another beating, until he felt the figures wandering away. As soon as they were out of sight, he tried to yank his hands apart, but they had been lashed to a wooden pole behind him. The same had been done to his feet. He paused, letting his eyes adjust to the fading light.

A group of officials stood close to the village gates, sifting through paperwork and adding their signatures.

The air suddenly swelled with a deafening groan. The ground

beneath him rattled and shook. He looked down to see that the pole he was tied to had been erected in the middle of a wooden cart.

"Gorespine's watered," shouted someone from the front of the cart.

"About time," snapped Boll, rushing to help wheel a huge container away. Not a drop of water had been left in it. "The old girl is just itching to get away."

"Hang on, hang on," called an approaching guard. "We're still waitin' for the driver, then you can get him out of here."

"No! Please...let me...go." Clinton's head dropped against his chest, too weak to hold it up. "Not...gorespine... Please..."

Clinton turned just enough to glimpse the gigantic beast attached to the front of the wooden cart. It shook its head from side to side, dripping precious water over the sand. Clinton had often marveled at a gorespine's size. Resembling a giant hippo from the Olde-world, the gorespine was bigger than four elephants combined, yet evolution had not been so kind to its shape. Its tiny brown scales reflected the setting sun, and its muscular legs twitched, ready to get going. Black talons on the end of each foot scraped into the rough terrain of the Plains. Its two small eyes were dwarfed by large nostrils at the end of its snout and an even bigger mouth with two skyward pointing tusks. A bridle with reins had been attached to the bit in its mouth, carved out of a tree trunk. Beneath it hung the beast's sagging stomachs, used to store gallons of water.

The lion felt the cart rock as a small figure jumped up into the driver's seat. "She had enough to drink?"

"Enough to satisfy her for a week or so, I reckon," replied Boll.

The driver turned and whistled back to the other two guards. "Right, then. Ready when you are."

"About scruddin' time too," snapped Boll.

One of the guards clambered onto the cart next to the driver before he turned back to his partner and snatched a piece of paper from his hands. He examined it and said. "Four barrels of Fire Mead? Twelve bags of grack steak? Twenty-three lengths of yanlin silk? Are you taking the—"

"Shut your complaining," replied the other guard. "Oh, and if you swing by Crank Head, be sure to look up my sister, she'll sort you out with—"

Boll shook the cart. "Look, can we go? I'm getting bored."

"So am I," replied a fourth voice, one that made Clinton burn inside. "I hoped he would have already departed."

"Y-yes...of course, Master Dallas, sir... She's on her way now," said Boll, indicating the gorespine.

The lion looked up through the crowd of stable workers and only just managed to catch Dallas's face before the cart jerked into motion, rattling away from the village. Clinton tried to call out, but his voice broke in his parched throat.

"Hah, look, Narfell's awake," laughed Boll. "Lucky you, huh? You got to see Wooburn one last time."

The sound of a cracking whip echoed as it struck the gorespine's backside. The massive creature grunted and picked up its pace.

"Back to sleep, Narfell," said Boll, giving a sarcastic wave in the lion's face. "Don't worry, you'll have a safe journey. Nighty, night."

With that, the guard brought down his baton on Clinton's head.

* * *

The chilly air blew against Clinton's body, biting through his thin robes. His eyelids peeled open and a starlit sky swirled into focus. He groaned, waiting for his senses to stir, before rolling over and pushing himself to his knees. The Great Plains spread out before him in its vast entirety, its rocky terrain resembling an alligator's back: a barren wasteland of jagged hills. He rubbed his hands against the bump on his head. All he could remember was fragmented memories. Unwilling tears welled in his eyes, but he blinked them away and rose to his feet. Rolling his sore neck, he noticed a small backpack lying in the sand next to him. He leaned over and scooped it up. It contained a small water-flask made from stock skins, fruit, some sour smelling meat, a piece of rock bread, a

166

small blanket, and a few clean bandages.

"Scrud!"

He flung the pack aside and bent down to inspect the sand, trying to find any tracks, but the evening's wind had erased all evidence of the gorespine's passage. Other than wandering aimlessly, Clinton knew that his only hope was to cross paths with a caravan of traders or a random traveling party. However, the migrate season had ended and the amount of anumals traveling the desert paths would be paltry now. His only other chance was to make it to the border of the Great Plains within a couple of days. If not…well, he preferred not to think about the alternative. Clinton ran his hand through his hair and stared across the expanse of land, desperate to see any sign of life, but as expected there was nothing.

"Right, c'mon, Clint. Think!"

Staring up at the sky he searched for the end of the constellation called the Pan and Handle. He counted two stars to the left of one that shone the brightest. "The Pole Star," he nodded, remembering his father's lessons. "The hunter's guide to the north."

Clinton quickly bent down and picked up a handful of sand. A mixture of grit and rock fell through his fingers, with the occasional tuft of short, dry grass.

"Okay." He picked up a nearby stone. "Let's figure this out."

The lion began to scratch a map of the Plains in the sand. "So, the most arid section is a huge band that spreads from north to south," he mumbled. "If I am facing north, then all that lies to the west is…"

He turned westwards, knowing that the land would become rockier as it transformed into the Gap Tooth mountain range.

"West to death, east to feast," he chanted, repeating the words his father had forced him to memorize. "North and south is an empty mouth. It's west to death and east to feast."

He turned to face the opposite direction.

"So that means…"

Narrowing his eyes, he just managed to see a lonesome brittlebush swaying in the breeze. Pockets of dried grass smeared the land like blemishes. Clinton knew more shrubs would replace the rough terrain, and then further east would be grassland. He looked up to the stars once more.

"So, if you taught me right, old man, that foliage over there leads to the eastern border of the Plains." His forehead furrowed as he assumed a stubborn look. "No point hanging around."

He lifted the small backpack over his shoulder and, with a huff, set off walking.

"See, dad, I finally did remember something you taught me... Ten years too late though."

* * *

The night grew steadily colder as Clinton's journey wore on. Fishing out the small blanket from his pack, he tied it around himself. His head drooped as he stumbled through the barren landscape. He yearned to see his brother one last time, even if it was only to explain what had happened and to say goodbye properly. However, the council had not even allowed him that. Councilor Barla had been right: he had been turned into a scapegoat.

Time dwindled away slower than a rust slug's pace. Stopping only for short breaks, he would occasionally sip his water to keep his strength up and sit in the shade to rest his feet and legs. For a full day and night he trundled on, loath to stop and waste precious time, but by the following morning every muscle in his body screamed for a moment's respite. He persisted onwards until midday when the sun was at its hottest. Barely able to stand, he found a small outcropping under which to take shelter. Dropping to his knees, he slumped to the ground and rested his head on his backpack. Seconds later his eyes closed as he slipped into sleep's tender grasp.

* * *

"Oh, 'ere, Boll, get ready. They're back," grunted a guard, flicking

168

his burlico stick away and climbing to his feet.

Boll yawned and scratched his head. "'Bout bloody time too."

Night had settled over Wooburn, and thick clouds covered the moon. A light mist clung to the air. The smell of charred dung hit Dallas's nostrils as he perched high upon a rooftop overlooking the perimeter fence. His eyes narrowed when the gorespine came into view. However much he wanted to feel triumph at the sight of the empty cart, an expanding emptiness inside him pushed against his senses. The sound of clattering wheels and tired voices rushed to meet the waiting tiger.

"So how far did you take him then?" asked Boll, grabbing the gorespine's reins to bring the beast to a halt.

"You know the pits over by Crank Head?" replied the driver. "Past there and then northwards, towards the Steppes."

Boll inhaled. "Scrud! That far, huh?"

"As requested."

Dallas lifted his head and peered out over the Great Plains. He scanned the dark horizon, knowing Clinton was out there somewhere, by now gasping for water and ravished by hunger. Yet Dallas felt an unusual urge welling inside. Something at the back of his mind niggled at him to slip down from the roof and plow into the Plains after the lion. He shook his head. *Stop being so stupid,* he thought, and turned to exit…when the conversation made him pause.

"Anyway, Boll, you might be able to answer this," said the driver, jumping from the cart. "It's been annoying me since Crank Town. You remember the forty-one lazarball season?"

"Do I ever. One of the best, my friend."

"Well who scored the winning target in the quarterfinal match with the Marshland Maulers, huh?"

The cart rocked as the guard accompanying the driver jumped off. Two lengths of hide swung from his pocket - strips that had bound Clinton's hands and feet. "I said it was Reymin Farr," he started packing his pipe with burlico, "but that dumb glux over there won't agree with me."

"I'm tellin' you Farr had retired by then. It was either Medinka

169

or Trollet."

"Nah...I'll tell you who it was." Boll rubbed his wobbly chin for a moment. "It was Narfell."

Dallas's head slowly swiveled to look back down at the anumals again.

"Ohhh, now there's a thought," nodded the driver, unstrapping the gorespine from its reins. "Y'know, it might just have been him. A young Narfell, though. And I don't care what any of you say and what happened, Grayorr Narfell had skill."

"Yeah, I know. I hate to admit it, but you're right." The guard rested his bulk against the side of the cart and lit his pipe. He took a few puffs and the smoke drifted up towards Dallas. "Just imagine what life would be like now if he hadn't done a runner, eh? Sponsors, tourists, the lot. Damned waste of talent if you ask me."

Boll could not help but chuckle. "Ironic, eh? The son pays for the guilt of the father. Well, I'm telling you this, I saw Clinton Narfell play with my own eyes—"

"As did we all, Boll. We all was watching the tournament," cut in the cart driver.

"Yeah, well, as much as it pains me to say it, he looked every bit as good as his dad out there. And Clinton was only what? Seventeen?"

"Eighteen," corrected the guard, blowing out a stream of smoke. "Eighteen years old and skill like that? Just imagine if him and his dad were playing for the Punishers now, eh? Now *that* would be a sight. It's a shame. The youngster had the world at his feet."

Boll shrugged. "What a waste. For scrud's sake he nearly beat *Dallas*. If the tiger hadn't...y'know...fouled him, then who knows what might have happened?"

Dallas stepped closer to the edge. A fire ignited inside him. His claws slipped out from the ends of his fingers.

"Yup," sighed the guard. "The Narfells might have been wastrels, but they knew their lazarball like the backs of their hands. Had Clinton not messed up, he could have become one of the greatest players this village ever knew. Forget the rest of 'em.

Even Dallas. With what I saw, it was Narfell who'd have saved this place. Could've been a real hero."

Dallas grabbed the sides of his head and yanked at his fur to try and block out what he had just heard.

No! No! No! No! No!

He snarled, before slamming his fist against the roof.

"Here, what was that?" whispered Boll.

The three anumals glanced up to see what the thud was.

"I don't know. Probably a wefring or something," commented the guard.

Dallas slinked deeper into the shadows. A growl rumbled at the back of his throat. Inside, he prayed that Clinton had already perished, but deep down knew he would not have given up so easily without a fight.

We will see, he thought, exhaling while composing himself again. *We will see, Clinton Narfell.*

* * *

Clinton woke just as the sun had started to rise. His leg pounded from overuse, and the scabs from his wound had begun to leak blood and pus, emitting the sour smell of infection. The lion cleaned the wounds as best as he could and wrapped a fresh bandage around them. Dragging himself to his feet, he looked up at the sky. Unable to fathom what day it was, he limped off through the Plains again with a whole night of traveling to look forward to.

A few hours into his trek, his stomach began to growl with hunger. He carefully opened his backpack and pulled out some meat he had saved, but his nose twitched from the bitter scent filtering from it.

"Oh, scrud!" he dropped it to the ground as maggots fell from the rotting meat and rolled across the sand. Clinton stepped back in disgust. "Fantastic. Just…fantastic."

He flipped the pack open and tipped out its contents to see if anything was still edible inside. However, the maggots had not only been dining on the meat, but on most of food in there. Only a solitary piece of fruit remained unscathed. Clinton fell to his knees and punched the sand repeatedly until he ran out of breath. Falling onto his back, he looked up at the stars.

"I give in." He closed his eyes. "You win."

Clinton did not know how long he laid there, but after what seemed like hours, his eyes fluttered open.

"Scrud," he sat up, realizing he had fallen asleep. His attention, however, drifted towards a tickling sensation on his leg. He looked down to see that some maggots were crawling over his thigh, squirming towards his rotting wound.

"Get off!" Clinton went to swipe them away, but then stopped himself at the last second. Watching the white creatures, he realized what they could do for him.

Picking up more maggots from the food, he carefully unwrapped his bandage and placed them on his cuts. The small creatures wriggled around at first, and then almost immediately set to work, eating away at the infected flesh. Stopping himself from throwing up, he quickly bandaged up his leg again and forced himself to his feet. The way the maggots were helping to cleanse his wound struck a chord in Clinton. Some creatures did anything to survive. They adapted and changed, taking any chance possible just to live that extra day. A seed of strength blossomed inside him, and a determined smile crossed his face.

"If you can survive, then so can I." He shook his head and sighed. "Would you look at me, I'm speaking to scrudding sectoids now."

Picking up his backpack, he set off limping through the desert, focus set firmly on the destination ahead.

CHAPTER TWENTY-FIVE

A NEW ARRIVAL.

"An' when I say I want payment today, I don't mean tomorrow or in two bluggin' week's time, I want it now!"

Gizi's voice hollered along the passageway, followed by the sound of smashing glass and breaking wood. "Now, Dallas is waitin' outside, so if the next words that come out of your mouth aren't *here's what we owe you, mister Gizi,* then your throat'll be coming out instead."

The tiger leaned against the alley wall and sighed. Standing in a pool of shade to keep out of the blistering sun, the noise of hammering and sawing echoed through the village. Another cart loaded with planks and salvaged metal trundled by the end of the alley, heading for the stadium's construction site.

Dallas sniffed.

"Pathetic. They might as well try polishing a dung heap."

"You say something?" asked Gizi, stepping out of the Olde-world antique shoppe. Jakz and Kayn followed behind. Gizi dropped his bulging sack, and the distinct sound of credits and metal could be heard clanging inside.

"It is nothing." Dallas shook his head and eyed the Sabers with disdain. "I take it that they paid?"

"Every last credit, sir," Kayn replied, taking out a cloth to meticulously clean the blood from the end of his bat. "I must say, though, having you along sure makes this debt collecting a whole lot easier. Mention your name and anumals practically *throw* credits at us."

"Yeah, I wish you could tag along with us every time we do this," Jakz agreed, sliding his knife back into a sheath on his belt. He scratched his protruding belly. "So how come you decided to come? Not that we don't appreciate you being here, of course."

Dallas growled and turned away from them. Like the carts passing by the exit, life seemed to just trundle ahead, rolling ever onwards. He existed in a village of nobodies going nowhere. The tiger raised his hand and traced his fingers along the three scars running over his eye. "I...I just wanted to take my mind off things."

For many nights now Dallas had roamed the village. Sleep had evaded him more than a blum fly evaded the sugar-sting vine, and every time he closed his eyes a face sprang to the forefront of his mind. He felt empty inside. His purpose seemed hollow and lost, and nothing he could think of was able to fill the void. So he walked Wooburn's streets, searching for something, anything, to alleviate his listlessness. Tagging along with the Sabers had been just one more effort to distract his mind from his frustration.

"'Ere, listen up, you wanna hear something funny?" asked Gizi, as the group exited the passage. "So I was passin' Rhanna's Tavern last night when these two dumb Horn Heads were talking outside, an' you'll never guess what one of 'em said?"

"I'm not sure, bro," chuckled Kayn. "That you only have one brain cell in that head of yours?"

"Shut yer mouth!" snapped Gizi. "No, one of 'em was blabberin' on about a friend who was sure he'd seen a feral Narfell wanderin' the perimeter fence, trying to claw his way back inside the village."

The Sabers laughed, yet Dallas remained silent.

"I heard something similar," Jakz added. "Treeg said that his younger brother, who gets taught by old McCarbe in the school house, swears that the daft old flyer has only gone and started threatening the kids, telling them they'll be exiled like Narfell if they don't start behaving in her lessons."

"Dumb old owl'll spout any type of dung to get her own way," sneered Gizi. "Always hated her."

A bubble of stillness seemed to follow the group's journey as they sauntered along the market streets. The passersby shied away, and traders eyed them warily while muting their calls. An air of obedience emanated from every anumal. Wooburnian life seemed to grudgingly carry on, albeit with its head hanging low and its tail tucked firmly between its legs.

"Well, long may it continue," sniffed Jakz. "Just look at them. Folk are scared stiff to put a foot wrong."

174

"Which is exactly what the mayor intended," mumbled Dallas, watching Jakz nod in agreement. "A sacrificial bleater is the most efficient method of displaying the sharpness of the blade."

"So Narfell was just an example?" asked Jakz.

"Nah." Gizi shook his head. "He's guilty. He totally set fire to the stadium."

The group stopped to stare at him, making Gizi scowl under their collective disdain.

"Your stupidity knows no bounds," sighed Dallas, watching as the scraggly Saber lowered his head in shame. "I am this close to giving up on you."

Dallas stepped away from the group and slipped into the crowded market place. As he walked, anumals backed out of his path like he was a magnet repelling his polar opposites, and a clear walkway was made available to him every time he changed direction. The tiger growled. Jakz had been correct. Narfell's exile had created a considerable reduction in offences within the village. Criminals had taken note that disobedience was not going to be tolerated any longer, and they had crawled back under whatever rocks they used as shelter and were behaving themselves.

Making his way through the square, the tiger passed the end of the long street that led to the lazarball stadium. For all the activity that seemed to be occurring, progress on the new construction looked to be painfully slow. A large presence of guards had been ordered to oversee the work. The official reason for this was to keep back any anumals whose wish was to hamper the construction, yet Dallas knew the real reason for the guards' presence. Had the abundance of primates not deserted the village over the last few months, the current work situation would have been very different.

As the tiger finally approached the justice house, two guards snapped to attention and immediately stepped aside to let him pass. The sound of a child could be heard, shouting and yelling in protest, followed by the distraught calmings of a frazzled voice. Making his way up to the mayor's office, Dallas slowly opened the door to find Ferris staring out of his large window.

The mayor shivered.

"Cold are we?" asked Dallas, his voice velvety smooth.

Ferris turned to see the tiger lingering in the doorway. "Oh, Dallas! I...I didn't hear you arrive." The beaver's voice sounded sickly sweet. "How are you today?"

Dallas ignored the question and strolled in. "Your secretary is going crazy down there."

Ferris raised an eyebrow.

The tiger sighed. "Am I right in saying that you are supposed to be looking after the Narfell orphan yourself, instead of dumping him with her all day?"

"Well, I...errr..."

"It sounds as if the brat is acting up."

The beaver let out a hearty sigh, pretending to find the news bothersome.

Dallas shook his head. "What am I talking about? Dealing with temper tantrums should be second nature to you by now. And talking of brats... How is that son of yours?"

Ferris plastered on a fake smile. "Ahhh, Harris? He is fine. Totally wonderful."

"Really?" Dallas smirked. "Have you even seen him since the tournament?"

"Yes, of course I have... It's just that he's out in the Plains. He...errrr...joined with a band of Union Wheel missionaries to...help the less fortunate. You know what Harris is like."

"Unfortunately, Ferris, I do, so you can drop the act. That Journey Tale might be something that will work on the villagers, but it is insulting to even try and use it on me."

Ferris's shoulders drooped. "Sorry, Dallas, you're right." The beaver banged his hand against the chair arm. "How utterly selfish of him to run off. That little scrud better crawl back within a week and beg for forgiveness. He knows how much public opinion matters in the run up to a re-election."

Ferris bent over, opened a drawer in the desk, and lifted out an expensive glass bottle. He poured two crystal clear glasses of water and offered one to Dallas. He downed his drink in one. Downstairs,

Raion began to shout again, followed by the sound of something toppling over.

The tiger took a small sip before gazing out the window. "Can you not shut him up or something? Stuff a gag down his throat perhaps? Or make use of some shackles?"

"Of course, of course." The mayor poured himself another shot of water before realizing what he had just agreed to. "Oh, I didn't mean... I couldn't possibly..." The flustered beaver shuffled off in the direction of the door. "Ever such a tiresome child. Always causing a commotion. Just like his brother."

The empty well inside Dallas expanded at the mention of Clinton. He took another sip.

"Fredrik? Fredrik, I need you!" Ferris shouted, leaning out of the doorway to get his bloodhound assistant's attention.

Dallas carefully put down his glass and turned to study the streets below. "I can see the stadium's reconstruction is falling behind."

"Yes, it's getting harder to find the workforce these days."

"So I see. More fool you for putting your trust in the few primates we have left."

"Well, it's cheap labor isn't it?"

"Cheap? I saw your guards practically treating them like slaves."

"Oh, come now, Dallas. I've merely restricted a few of their breaks and given them a little more...motivation to work."

"Yes, I heard the cracking whips. Are you even paying them for this?"

"Of course I am." The beaver cleared his throat. "Eventually."

"You had better make sure you keep this under wraps. Silanian law dictates—"

"Who cares about silly monkeys? They're barely anumals the lot of them. And it's not my fault we don't have villagers willing to help with the construction. Drastic measures needed to be taken."

"Vermin," muttered the tiger only just loud enough for Ferris to hear.

The beaver shuffled closer to Dallas. "I beg your pardon?"

"I said vermin."

"The monkeys?"

"No," snorted Dallas. "The villagers."

Ferris's cheek twitched. "I don't understand."

"Oh, come now, Ferris. You completely understand."

"Well, I agree they may not be the most...ah...gracious of sorts, but they're what makes this village—"

"Rich?" cut in Dallas. "Or should I say, makes *you* rich. Just how much are those fools going to be stung for the new construction anyway? More precisely, is there even a point to it?"

"Of course there's a point. The point is they're building it for you, Dallas. It will be your stadium. As captain of the Punishers, you will be making history—"

"They are building it for *me*? A rundown stadium in this hovel of a village? How embarrassing. No self-respecting anumal—"

"Embarrassing?"

"Yes. I despair at why I continue to allow myself to be trapped in this krig pen."

Ferris's mouth flapped open. "But Wooburn is your home, Dallas, your life. When I rescued you from—"

"From what?" asked the tiger, slowly.

"Oh, not this again." Ferris walked back to his desk and slumped onto his scavenger skin chair. "I've explained it time and again. I don't know why you still question me. If I hadn't found you in the justice house when you were young, and rescued you when I did, then who knows what might have happened. Someone like Grayorr Narfell could have discovered you instead. And then where would you be? He'd have sold you for sure. Or even worse..."

Dallas leaned over the desk. "So you keep telling me."

"Oh, come on, Dallas, this is absurd! I took you in, sheltered and educated you. I've given you everything you've ever needed - expensive clothes, luxurious foods. *Everything.*"

"And if I force your dear assistant, Fredrik, to recall my origins right now, are you positive he will give me the same story? The only anumal who conveniently knows anything about my past seems to be you."

Ferris smiled. Opening his arms he said, "Look, Dallas, you're just tired. You have many burdens to bear, and you only ever bring this up when you're in a bad mood. No wonder you question your origins. I mean, who wouldn't?" Ferris patted the tiger's hand. "I promise we'll find out who you are one day, until then, be happy just being you."

Dallas picked up a finely drawn sketch from Ferris's desk. It depicted Ferris, his wife, and Harris and Dallas as youngsters. Ferris nervously sipped his water.

"Why me?" murmured the tiger.

"Sorry?"

Dallas placed the frame back on the desk and turned to the door. "I...I cannot do this anymore. I need to get out."

Ferris gasped at his words and scampered after him with his arms outstretched in mercy. "What are you saying? You can't leave. The village needs you. They don't have anyone to lead them. They're desperate. This isn't like you. You haven't been the same since Clin..." Ferris stopped himself. "Please, Dallas, we'll give you whatever you want."

"That is just it!" Dallas grabbed the sides of his head. "Do you not understand? I do not know what I want."

Ferris floundered. "Well, you... Dallas, you should just remain calm, okay? Don't do anything rash. I'll think of something for you, yes? You know you can depend on—"

Ferris's words were cut short as Dallas grabbed him by his coat. The mayor's eyes swelled as he was yanked closer.

"No, Ferris, it is you who depends on me." His voice rumbled only just above the level of a growl. "Who will be there to keep the officials off your back, huh? Who will keep the villagers in line while you blunder your way through another term of office? You are losing control."

"Dallas, no, listen to me for one second, you don't know what you're—"

"And the whole business with the lion was just..." He released Ferris and hunched over the desk, taking a deep breath.

"But Dallas, how was I supposed to know he'd trick us and enter the competition? Disguises and all, it's so...childish. So predictable."

"I would hardly call it predictable. You did not see it coming."

"Ah, yes, well he has gone now, hasn't he? Granted, taxes will have to be raised again, fixing three guilty verdicts from the giraffe council out of six wasn't bad, but we managed to get rid of him."

"That is just it!" Dallas swiped his hand across the desk, smashing the framed sketch to kindling. "Do you not understand he will never be gone? However much you try to fight it, the Narfell name will never be expunged from this village."

The tiger tapped the side of his head. "He is there, fixed in the mind of every inhabitant. His legacy will linger like a virus."

"Trust me, Dallas, the memory of him will disappear with time."

"Trust you?" gasped the tiger. "You were so caught up in your own self-importance that it was left to me to discover Narfell's trickery."

"I had duties to attend to. I couldn't possibly have noticed—"

"That in front of your very eyes a masked anumal was playing to the standard of the great Grayorr Narfell? Are you that blind? Because, believe me, it looks like others spotted it." Dallas scowled as he touched his itching scars. "Look at what he did to me, Ferris. He left his mark. You may think he is gone, but every time I see my reflection I will see him on my face."

"I know, but it wasn't like he would have beat you."

The room sank into silence. "No." He stood straighter and dusted down his coat. "And he never will. Narfell will never beat me. No one beats me, Ferris, no one."

"I agree, especially now he's gone." Ferris took a moment to collect his thoughts. "There is no way he could have made it to safety. Not with the provisions we gave him, or the distance the gorespine took him into the Plains. He will never be a threat to us again, and his name shall truly fade. And... And eventually, when you look on those scars, they will remind you of his defeat; they are battle wounds from which you have emerged the victor."

Trying to smile, Ferris maintained a nervous look that grew close to becoming a pained grimace. "Dallas, it would take a miracle for him to have survived."

"Yet we know how slippery he can be. Nothing is ever certain with him, Ferris. Do you have any witnesses of his death? Any proof? If I only knew for certain—"

"Well, of course I don't have any witnesses. I wasn't going to have him execut—"

"Which is why I intervened."

The beaver blinked. "I'm sorry?"

"Do you not think Narfell will be using every shred of energy to return here for his brother? Of course he will! Which is why I took some precautions."

"Precautions? What are you talking about?"

Dallas turned to face a large map of the Plains hanging from the wall. "Tell me. What do you think the odds are of Clinton finding help in the desert? I would say they are very slim. However, I would definitely put credits on him running into a few obstacles along his way."

"What obstacles?"

"You will find out soon enough, Ferris."

The mayor winced. "No, honestly, Dallas, what have you done?"

Bending down so that their eyes were level, the tiger scowled. "In time, mayor."

The sound of Raion's voice could be heard downstairs, picking up in volume. Dallas broke the stalemate.

"He is still shouting, Ferris. Go and shut…him…up."

"Y-yes, of course. Yes, I'll shut him up straight away." The beaver scuttled over to the door and bellowed, "Fredrik! Fredrik…FREDRIK!"

However, there was no reply.

"Dumb, lazy canine," muttered the mayor. "Not to worry. I'll deal with the problem myself. I'll only be a moment."

Without waiting, Ferris scuttled out of the room.

Dallas gazed back out the window as lingering thoughts of

Narfell snuck up on him. He shivered. An ice-cold ripple coursed along his spine.

The door slammed shut.

"That was quick." He slowly turned to face the mayor. "Do not tell me you actually gagged…"

No one was there.

Dallas turned back to the window, thinking he really was starting to go crazy, when he caught sight of movement in the reflection. His fists clenched. Behind him a tall figure swept across the room like a ghost. Another tremble wracked his body. Remaining deadly calm, he continued to stare, waiting to see what move the intruder would make, even though his instincts knew the stranger was here for one thing…

Trouble.

CHAPTER TWENTY-SIX

FAMILIAR VOICES.

The days dragged by in a haze of agony. Like a machine, Clinton persisted with his endless journey, focused solely on his path across the stark terrain. The horizon wobbled with the shimmering heat, and the sun baked his head. Now, though, deeper canyons surrounded the lion, providing him with much-needed respite from the rays. A tree would occasionally display a hint of foliage within its skeletal branches, but such sights remained few and far between.

After pushing himself as far as he could, extreme hunger and thirst nearly beat Clinton to submission, until his salvation came in the form of a small pack of zilers. Trying to find refuge in a cave for the evening, the rodent-like scuttlers had defended their territory, flying at him with their clawed wings. After beating them away, Clinton had managed to catch one of the creatures before fleeing the fight. Carefully gutting it, the ziler had provided him with enough of its stringy meat to sustain him for a few more days, wrapping the food in the creature's leathery wing membrane to preserve it.

By the sixth day of travel the sky had finally released its wet fury on him. Holding his water pouch up, trying to collect as much rain water as possible, he had rolled the ziler's wing into a cone and attached it to the lip of his pouch, creating a makeshift water funnel. He also removed his clothes and wrung out the water from the fabric into his mouth in an effort to preserve the precious liquid. Eventually the downpour stopped as the sun began its ascent through the morning sky.

Shading himself from the midday heat, the path he walked descended into a shadowy gorge with rocky slopes on either side. After a quick search, Clinton found a niche nestled amongst two large boulders, tucked away from the blistering heat. He sat down and took out the water pouch from his backpack. Yanking out the stopper, he took a long, refreshing gulp. The water cooled his barren tongue for a few seconds, quenching his throat, but all too soon his thirst returned, nagging at him for more. He stoppered the pouch and lolled his head against a rock.

"C'mon, Clint. Get up. Keep going. Don't give up."

As the lion sat propped against the shaded rock, staring off into the distant sky, his eyelids grew heavy. Within minutes he had fallen fast asleep.

* * *

A sound startled Clinton from his slumber. His eyes snapped open and he sat bolt upright. Taking a breath, he tested the air and dragged himself to his feet. He rubbed his bleary eyes and padded out from between the two boulders.

Something smashed into him from the right, knocking him to the ground. He tried to scrabble to his feet again, but a heavy weight pressed down on the center of his back. Squirming underneath the pressure, he attempted to flip himself over when a thick boot slammed into his jaw. The left side of his face exploded with pain and bright colors burst to life behind his eyelids. Over the ringing in his ears he could just make out the sound of voices...all too familiar voices.

"You want me keep hittin' him, huh? How 'bout stamp his head in?"

"Jus' keep 'im down, will you. Don't let 'im get up whatever you do, Barn."

"He won't run. Look at his leg. It's rotten." There was the sound of deep inhalation. "Stinks real bad."

Clinton tried to rub the dust from his eyes, but a sloppy nose touched his ear. A wet sniffing sensation zeroed in on his face. Clinton's eyes widened. Right in front of him loomed Snarg, with saliva dribbling through the gaps in his fangs. The monster's nostrils swelled as it savored another hungry sniff of the lion, tasting his aroma.

"Keep Snarg away, will you. The boss'll kill us if he gets 'im."

"Maybe we should let him have a leg of lion? Won't run away then," proposed the bear.

"Just... Just quit it with your ideas, Barn. Thinking ain't good for you."

Barn stomped away, trudging along the dirt path as if he was trying to flatten it, while dragging Snarg after him. The creature yelped as its choke chain tightened around its neck. Clinton tried to push himself to his feet, but only managed to get to his knees before another kick caught him in the ribs, downing him again.

"He's tryin' to stand up, Barn. I told you to keep an eye on 'im," yelled Graff. He turned to Clinton. "That was just a little taste of what you'll be feelin' today, lion. So you can thank that big friend o' yours for what he did to us back at Jasper's. And believe me, when we find 'im he's gonna be kraggon meat too."

The dingo smacked his fist into the palm of his hand.

Snarg barked excitedly, but Barn gave the chain another tug to shut him up.

"What...are you...talking about?" gasped Clinton.

The dingo lifted his foot. "Do you want another taste of this?"

Clinton closed his eyes and waited for the blow, but nothing connected.

"Good. Now shut your mouth and stop askin' stupid bluggin' questions." Graff turned to the bear. "Barn, get 'im up."

The bear let go of Snarg's chain and the scavenger immediately arrowed in for the lion. Barn snarled at the pet, and Snarg cringed and scuttled away in fear. With a grip like iron, the bear grabbed Clinton's forearms and yanked him to his feet. Snarg took a sniff of the air, yelped, and started to shiver with excitement. As fast as he could he ran up the path and around the bend, dragging his chain along after him. After a moment's silence the slobbering pet started to yap, and then he reappeared, frantically wagging his stub of a tail.

Graff could not keep the excitement from his voice and rubbed his hands with barely controlled glee. "They're here, Barn, they're here." He looked Clinton straight in the face. "Oh, you're in for it now, you filthy scrud."

Barn yanked Clinton around to face a group of anumals trundling towards them. At first the lion could only see wavering outlines distorted by the rising heat, but with every step they took, the approaching figures sharpened into focus. Each of them carried hunter's tools. Some gripped wrackers in their hands, some held ground-pounders, while others wielded lethal looking stunpikes, their tips crackling with sparks of lectric. Each was powerful enough to disable a grack. Clinton gulped. Every one of the hunters possessed a roguish wildness about them, a streak of selfishness that accommodated any ambition as long as it was for the right price. And all of them fell under the employment of one particular individual.

As the group drew near they parted, allowing their vengeful leader to emerge from within their midst.

"Well, hello again, Clinton," hissed Galront. "Bet you'd thought you'd seen the last of me, huh?"

CHAPTER TWENTY-SEVEN

NOWHERE TO RUN.

Galront hobbled closer, a gnarled crutch wedged under his arm, helping him to walk. A grimy-looking bandage had been wrapped around the stump where his foot and calf had once been, before Snarg had chewed them off.

"You don't know how much I've dreamed of this moment," he panted, masking his snarl. The mob muttered their agreement. Their stunpikes crackled and hummed, promising Clinton a world of pain. "Thought your troubles vanished when you escaped Wooburn, huh? Thought you'd skip happily away, free of your crimes?"

Galront jabbed his finger in Clinton's chest. "Well, how's it lookin' now, eh?"

Clinton tried to think of something to say, but nothing came to mind. The fear that had sprouted inside him had fully drained, leaving only a void. The whole ordeal of his exile, losing Raion, and nearly perishing in the Plains made Galront's threats seem insignificant. *You can't beat a beaten anumal*, Clinton thought: another piece of advice from his dad.

He stared up at the sky. "You know, Galront, I've had better days."

Galront flinched and shuffled even closer. "What d'you say? You think this is some kind of joke, eh? HAVE YOU SEEN THE MESS YOU'VE MADE OF ME?" he screamed, swinging his stump. "YOU SEE IT?"

"Look, it wasn't me."

"Oh…*it wasn't me! It wasn't me!*" mocked the weasel. He reached out and grabbed Clinton by his jaw. "Look at what I lost! I'm a scruddin' freak. You turned me into a laughin' stock. They'll be draggin' me into the Plains next and leaving me to rot here too. Well, I've news for you, lad. We ain't in Wooburn no more. This is lawless country, Narfell. No rules, no guards. It's survival of the fittest. An' you, well, you ain't looking so fit anymore are you?"

Galront reached down and pulled out his blade. He swiped it in front of Clinton's face, but Clinton did not bat an eyelid.

"Come on," Galront hissed. "Not even gonna try an' stop me?"

Clinton shrugged, his stare unmoving. Some of the gang shifted their weight from foot to foot and glanced at one another.

Galront grabbed Clinton by the scruff of the neck. "Look, Narfell, I ain't fraggin' around. I'm thinkin' maybe an eye for an eye is too generous for you, yeah? It should be more like a leg for a leg."

"What about hacking 'em both off, Boss?" asked Graff. "Let's see how far he can crawl without no legs on him at all?"

"That's one idea, Graff, but then again, I've got an even better plan for our little *Burgess* here." The gang began to chuckle. "I want him to go through exactly what I went through. Only he needs to suffer much, much worse."

Galront pointed his knife at Clinton's throat.

"Now what do you think of that, lion?"

Clinton shrugged again. "You know what, Galront, do whatever you want."

Galront's smile trickled from his face as his eyelid twitched. "Oh, come off it, Narfell, you're ruining this for me. I can't tell Dallas you didn't scream at least once."

Graff's fist landed a punch in Clinton's belly. "Show the boss some fear. Stop ruining his fun."

Barn let go of Clinton and laughed when the lion dropped to the ground.

The weasel's shoulders slumped. "You ever thought about what it's like to watch a scavenger take your leg off, eh? Well, I can tell you it's worse than you'd imagine. Sharp teeth crunchin' your bones, searing hot pain as your muscles an' tendons are ripped apart. I screamed so loudly I hacked up blood." Dribble clung from Galront's chin as he talked. He took his rancid burlico-stick from behind his ear and put it in his mouth. "An' when I came round, all I could think about was one thing. D'you know what it was, huh? It was how much pleasure I'd get from watchin' you go through the same ordeal."

Clinton stared up at Galront, muscles tense. "Why did you just mention Dallas's name?"

"Ohhh, now look at this, lads, Narfell is suddenly interested. You still scared of him, eh, boy?"

"He sent you out here to kill me, didn't he?" Clinton closed his eyes, picturing Dallas's face. "So who's it going to be then, huh? Graff? Barn? Maybe just Snarg?"

"Oh no, no, no," hissed Galront, "not Snarg. He's changed 'is ways, that little scrud's gonna be vegetarian from now on. No, we've got somethin' special for you, lad, somethin' a bit more…theatrical." The weasel stuck two fingers in his mouth and whistled. The high-pitched noise echoed along the incline of the sloping walls. "Spared no expense did Dallas. Told me to do whatever was needed. Oh, and believe me, never let it be said I do things by half."

Galront stroked Clinton's hair before grabbing a clump of it. He signaled to Barn. "Get him to his feet."

Barn yanked Clinton off the ground, and a perimeter of anumals sprang up around the lion. The gang raised their stunpikes and a hum filled the air as the settings were boosted to high. Clinton's eyes darted everywhere, desperate for any escape routes. He tried to back away, but Barn stopped his retreat.

"What's the matter, lion?" asked Galront, hopping gleefully around his prey. "Finally getting a little scared are we?" Galront turned in Clinton's direction and stepped aside to give the lion a clear view of the surrounding canyons. "This is just a little somethin' to bring me some closure. I do hope you enjoy all the effort."

* * *

Silhouettes emerged along the top of the inclines, stunpikes in hand, struggling to control the scavengers by their sides. The air suddenly filled with yapping as the tethered beasts thrashed wildly.

Clinton went deadly cold. "Galront, what are y—"

The lion fell forwards as a boot shoved him in the back.

"Shut it!" shouted Graff, spitting on the ground next to

Clinton's head.

Galront knelt down, leaning on his wooden crutch. "Oh, I'm not gonna do anythin', lad." He giggled as he put his mangled burlico-stick carefully in his jacket pocket. "No, I'm just gonna have a right lovely time standin' back an' watchin'. Oh, but I forgot, there's still one more little thing left to do."

Before Clinton knew it, Galront ran his blade across the lion's wounded thigh, creating a cut that trickled blood down his leg. The crazed weasel clambered onto his remaining foot, and Graff shoved a stunpike into his hand.

Galront slid his tongue across his teeth as he turned to inspect the yapping scavengers. "Can you 'ear 'em, eh? EH? They're just dyin' to meet you, Clinton. I bet they can't wait to 'ave a closer look at that bleedin' leg of yours."

Galront cackled and hopped away until he was at a safe distance. He shoved his fingers in his mouth and whistled a high-pitched note. "Come on, boys! Come get your fill! Tonight it's lion on the menu!"

* * *

At Galront's command the scavengers were let loose from their chains. The hunters jabbed a few of the creatures with their stunpikes, causing them to charge at top speed down the incline like a cascade of savage flesh. The remainder of Galront's crew assumed their battle positions - weapons ready for any beast that tried to deviate. The scavengers filled the canyon with their howls and terse barks.

As the raucous cries hit Clinton's ears, he cringed and whispered, "Impalers."

His father's lessons flooded his memory. So called because of their wicked set of front fangs, impalers would inject acid into their prey before tearing out the tenderized flesh with their fishhook-like claws. The closest Clinton had ever come to a live impaler was when his father had once stumbled upon a lone female wandering Wooburn's perimeter. The bitch had lunged for Grayorr's leg, before Grayorr had forced her back. Shaped like miniature, nightmarish wolves, and as quick as gibbets, in small numbers impalers were manageable, but when they attacked in a swarm they left nothing behind, not even a cleanly picked carcass.

Clinton struggled to rise to his feet.

Touching the small of his back, a stunpike sent a lectric shock coursing through his weakened frame. The lion's spine arched as every muscle snapped taut. Then, as quickly as the shock gushed through him, it ended. He collapsed to the ground and jolted spasmodically as everyone around him laughed. Clinton's jaws snapped open into a silent scream, and spittle spattered from his mouth.

The lion eventually found himself lying on his back, staring up the sky.

"Stay right where you are, Narfell," goaded Galront, hopping up and down, slamming his wooden crutch into the dust with glee. The approaching noise rumbled around the canyon. "There's no point tryin' to escape. They're comin' just for you."

The weasel snapped his head towards the oncoming tsunami of monsters before backing away, fleeing with great hops behind his barricade of hunters. Within seconds, not an anumal remained anywhere near the injured lion.

Clinton felt the paralysis from the stunpike slowly wearing off. He could feel a tingle in his hands and feet again. He raised his head, pleading with his body to obey him, but his legs just flopped around like a dying gillet. Looking down at the wound, he knew his blood had become a magnet that would undoubtedly drive the impalers crazy. The sound of yapping intensified with the impalers' rapid approach. He tried to lift himself up, and managed to get to his elbows, but collapsed again when his muscles shook with uncontrollable spasms. Tears welled in his eyes, but he bit them back.

"Rai, I'm... I'm so sorry."

The lion closed his eyes and reached inside himself. He made his brother a promise. He would guide and protect him however it was possible after he died. Clinton knew there would be no burial

191

for him, no clay marker to hang up in the village temple, no ritual to scatter his ashes, but whatever happened, he would defy everything to protect the ones he loved. In his final moments, with death rearing over him in its dire guise, his own determination made him smile. He turned to Galront.

"You won't beat me!" he yelled.

Galront stopped laughing and tilted his head. "You what?"

"I won't scream, Galront, not like you did!"

"Shut 'im up. SHUT 'IM UP!" ordered the weasel, spinning to face Graff.

"Tell Dallas whatever you want! Tell him I cried my eyes out, I DON'T CARE! Because *you'll* know, Galront. You'll live the rest of your stinking life knowing that I spent my final moments laughing at you, instead of fearing anything about you. You pathetic little scrud!"

"I'm gonna kill 'im!" Galront hollered. "I'M GONNA KILL 'IM!"

But it was too late.

Clinton raised his head one last time to see the impalers almost upon him, now less than three hundred feet away. Betraying his satisfied smile, his heart pounded, his body ached, and his mind screamed. The rumbling sound of death mixed with Galront's muffled rants. As Clinton finally felt his limbs coming back under his control again, he turned and grinned at the weasel one last time, making sure Galront saw his defiance. In his final seconds, he scrunched up into a ball and waited for the scavengers to feast on his flesh.

CHAPTER TWENTY-EIGHT

ATTACK!

Clinton coiled into a tight fetal position. He could sense the impalers bearing down on him. He anticipated the first bite, the sting of venom injecting his body, slowly reducing his muscles to pulp. Yet as he tried to block the images, his senses detected another noise. At first it sounded like a whisper, like a sectoid buzzing around his ears, but the patter of words swelled in volume to reach a crescendo of high-pitched shrieks. The tortured chorus slowly overwhelmed the rumble of the stampede. The barrage of voices ricocheted off the rocks, smothering every nook and cranny.

"What the...?" Clinton eyes opened a fraction to see a black cloud sweeping through the canyon.

At first the words sounded jumbled, their echoes adding to the mayhem, but as the cloud approached, four words became synchronized. The words pummeled Clinton's ears from every direction, making his vision swirl.

"Kham-sham ni darr... Kham-sham ni darr... Kham-sham ni darr..."

The rumble of the scavengers' charge suddenly died. Each impaler slowed to a tentative walk. Clinton peered at the nearest female. She bared her fangs and scuttled back. Shaking her head, she raised it skywards, twitching her nose and whimpering in confusion. A sharp, bitter scent stung Clinton's nose. The female lost control of her bladder and let loose a stream of urine across the sand. Around her, countless impalers reared up on their hind legs, swiping at the air, while others started to spin on the spot, snapping and growling at anything nearby. Clinton shook his head. During his life he had sensed the fear of many scavengers just before swiping his claws across their throats, but he had never experienced anything like this. He took life to preserve life, and in a scavenger's dying seconds a peace usually filled their eyes, as if they understood the natural order. Today that peace had become extinct, wiped clear by a feeling of pure terror.

An odd warble reached his ears. Scavenger after scavenger

whimpered, each one cowering before him, forcing their trembling bodies flat against the ground. Then, as one, two, ten, all of their heads whipped to the north, Clinton pushed himself to his elbows and followed their gaze. The ominous black cloud had almost covered the sky, looming over the canyon like a blanket of death. The lion gulped. His mane-like hair wafted in the breeze. As if reaching out, tendrils of the approaching blackness erased the light, raging towards the hunters, and spurting over the landscape. The scavengers increased their howling, digging their hooked claws into the ground to grapple themselves in place.

Hunters started to turn tail, fleeing from the gathering tempest. The breeze quickly turned into a gust, blowing grit in Clinton's face and making him squint. Like the scavengers, he dug his claws into the ground, readying himself for the onslaught. A powerful gust suddenly slammed against him, shoving him back. He scrabbled to find something to hold on to, and managed to grab a rock jutting out of the ground. He curled himself around it and held on tight.

"Turn them bleedin' things 'round!" ordered Galront, his voice muffled under the howling gale and scavengers' yelps. The weasel held on to a tree stump, bracing himself against the wind. "Make 'em attack! Shock 'em again if you have to, but get 'em turned 'round!"

"What?" yelled Graff, reaching out to grip on to Barn. "Are you kiddin'? In this?"

Even the huge bear was struggling to keep his footing. "Boss, not sure 'bout this," he rumbled.

"I SAID TURN 'EM 'ROUND!" screamed the weasel. "I want him dead, you 'ear me? DEAD!"

"Boss, I'm not gonna wait 'round and let you get killed just to watch some two-bit glux eaten alive. Scrud! I don't even think they will eat him. Look at the state of 'em." Graff pointed to the cowering scavengers. "I say we get out of here. Let the storm finish him off."

"NOOO!" Galront wailed, his voice carried by the wind. He locked stares with Clinton. "I'm orderin' you to make 'em eat him.

D'you 'ear me?" The weasel's front lip curled, showing a mouthful of rotten teeth. "'Cause if you think Dallas'll be upset, that ain't nothing to what I'll—"

"But, Boss, we really need to—"

"DEAD!" The weasel struggled to keep a hold of the tree as he whipped out his knife. "KILL 'IM, GRAFF! KILL THAT PIECE OF DUNG RIGHT NOW!"

Graff flinched. He drew his knife and squinted at the weakened lion, then turned back to Galront and shook his head. "Nah, this is madness. We're getting you to safety," he yelled, turning to the group. "Barn, give the order to flee. I'm not risking the boss for that piece of—"

The dingo's eyes bulged as if he had been told a secret.

A thin stream of blood slowly snaked out of his mouth and blew across his fur. He stumbled and dropped to his knees before falling face first against the ground, a knife sticking out of his back. Galront clung to the dingo and yanked out the knife. Forced back by the wind, he grabbed onto the tree stump again before wiping his blade against the lapel of his suit.

"So," he yelled, "anyone else wanna disobey me?"

No one replied. Everyone stared in shock.

Galront took a shaky breath and pointed the knife at them. "Good. Now forget that fraggin' breeze, an' make the pack finish off what we started, you 'ear me?"

Without any arguments, Galront's hunters let go of what they were holding and charged at the scavengers. The smallest of the hunters lost their footing and were blown back, but the bigger anumals staggered ahead as if wading through syrup, grasping their stunpikes and turning up the voltage.

Clinton's gaze swept over Graff's dead body. The dingo's lifeless eyes continued to stare, his leaking blood blowing across the sand like a crimson cobweb. Clinton started to crawl away, desperate to escape, but shuffled back again when a dark figure loomed over him. His heart jumped. Losing his grip on the rock, the wind pushed him back before he managed to steady himself.

"You!" he gasped.

A ghastly hand grabbed Clinton's shoulder and forced him to the ground. "Stay down. Don't move!" The decaying badger stood before him, unmoved by the howling winds. Rotting lumps of flesh fell from his face. "You hear? Don't move."

The whites of his eyes widened, revealing a crazed emptiness. Saliva dripped from his cracked teeth. "They're coming." He looked up to where the storm clouds were swelling. "Ghastlings… They're here."

Clinton froze rigid. Before his eyes, the badger stepped back and began to disintegrate, his body falling like sand, every grain torn away by the wind. The lion squinted back at the horizon to where the badger had indicated. Dark shapes stirred within the clouds, gliding through the torrent of raging air. At first they looked like a flock of ragged flyers, twisting and weaving amongst each other, but then the temperature dropped. An uncomfortable chill embraced him, like someone had thrown a pail of ice water over his head, smothering him in despair.

As the wind reached its extreme, dozens of black shapes exploded from the cloud like bullets. They arched through the air, letting out high-pitched screeches, before targeting the group of hunters. Every impaler scrabbled to their feet and fled in Clinton's direction. The ground rumbled. Masses of tattered cloaks sped in front of the churning darkness as if they were dragging the cloudy maelstrom behind them, threatening to consume everything in its way. Scores of ghastlings swooped closer to the ground and tore through the canyon, towards the fleeing group. The smaller ghastlings bounded from rock to rock, while larger ghastlings smashed into any obstacle in their path.

Clinton, however, did exactly as the badger had commanded and remained fixed to the spot.

* * *

The swarm of ghastlings screamed so loud Clinton felt bile rise in his throat. Galront's hunters scattered, fleeing in every direction, shoving past one another and running into the stampede of scavengers. The badger's words rang in Clinton's mind.

Stay down. Don't move!

He gritted his teeth and lifted his head to take another look at the destruction around him. A female coyote vaulted over him and charged past a stray impaler. A ghostly black mass trailed behind her, its huge frame lumbering over Clinton as though he was invisible. She looked over her shoulder and cranked up the power setting of her stunpike before turning and ramming its end into the ghastling's hood. Thrown back by the force of the impact, streaks of azure lectric erupted from the cloak, causing the creature to wail in pain. The ghastling's bear-like teeth snapped together so hard they shattered. Black smoke billowed from its hood before the robes burst into flame. The burning cloth dispersed like the remnants of an exploded firework. The coyote turned to look at Clinton, her face a mask of horror.

"Makuzi's killed one!" shouted a hog as he skidded to a stop next to her, struggling to stay upright in the wind. "Stun 'em in the face! GET THEIR FACES!"

The hog ran off with Makuzi in tow, both charging back into the melee. A flurry of shapes flashed past Clinton in pursuit.

Everything whipped around him like a blur. He caught sight of a ghastling swooping over a fleeing scavenger. It threw its arms around the impaler's waist and, skidding next to the lion, spun it around. The impaler yelped, bucking its legs and gnashing at the ghastling, trying to break free. In one swift movement the ghastling snatched the impaler's jaw and rammed its elongated hand into the creature's mouth, forcing it down the scavenger's throat.

Clinton fought against his urge to be sick.

A gurgling growl escaped the impaler's mouth, before the ghastling tugged its hand back. As if an explosion had been detonated inside the scavenger, an eruption of blood and guts spilled out the scavenger's mouth as the ghastling pulled its hand free. The impaler's insides sizzled on its palm, creating an acrid smell that was stolen by the wind. The impaler's skin and muscle burnt away from its skeleton in dull, smoking embers.

Within seconds the canyon had turned into a battleground of

blood and dirt. Ghastlings attacked anything that got in their way, reducing their victims to ash. In their insanity, some of the impalers attacked one another, while others turned against the anumals. Caught between escape and the prospect of fresh meat, the foamy-mouthed scavengers gorged on their prey, making themselves easy pickings for the roaming ghastlings. Anumals tried to beat off attackers with their stunpikes and ground-pounders, hammering them away, or shocking them with jolts of lectric.

The cloying air made it hard to for Clinton to breathe. Sand nipped his skin while he remained frozen, watching hunters avoid scavengers, only to face the wrath of the ghastlings. Time after time a hunter would run past, swinging their weapon at anything within striking distance, while behind them pounced ghastlings.

Something grabbed Clinton's hair. Before he could react, the lion felt himself being dragged across the ground. He kicked out, trying to force off the hand, but the grip was like iron.

"Got 'im!" boomed Barn's voice, tossing Clinton closer to Galront. Chunks of the lion's hair were torn out, like trophies of war, left behind in the bear's grasp.

The lion thudded next to Graff's fresh corpse. Galront's sneering face came into view.

"Think some flyin' freaks are gonna get in the way of my revenge?" The weasel wiped his forearm across his jaw, holding firmly to his stunpike for support. The sound of guttural cries and snarling struck up behind him. "Well, think again, Narfell. Not even Silania herself could stop me this time."

The lion slowly backed away from the weasel, digging his claws into the sand to brace himself from the wind. Galront took a step closer, but a sudden gust slammed into him, making him yelp. The weasel fought against the gale, shoving his stunpike into the ground for support.

"BARN!" he hollered. "BARN, GET 'ERE NOW!"

No one replied.

"BARN! Are you bluggin' deaf?" He turned to see where he was. "Get over 'ere right—"

His words lodged in his throat.

Clinton craned his neck to see what the problem was, but all he could see of Barn was a pile of smoking ash on the ground in the form of a bear.

"Barn?" Galront gasped in horror. "Is that…?"

Particles of the bear blew away in the wind, before a ghastling suddenly burst through the mess and wrapped its hands around Galront's neck.

"Arrrrgh! Get off!" screamed the weasel. He rammed his stunpike into the ghastling's chest and released a bolt of lectric, causing the monster to shriek. The ghastling fell onto all fours and shuddered. As the ghastling burst into flames, another attacker swooped in from the side, knocking Galront to his knees. Shuffling back, he grasped his stunpike and triggered the crackling energy. "Come on you fraggin' freak. Just try and get a piece of me."

The ghastling snarled, revealing a mouth full of fangs – but still it did not attack. Rather, it snapped its head to the side.

"What? Scared, huh?" yelled the weasel.

Ignoring him, the ghastling leaped for Graff's dead body. It grabbed the dingo's jaws, and with a sharp crack, yanked them wide.

"What the… WHAT YOU DOIN'?" wailed the horrified Galront.

The ghastling glanced back at the weasel, before it shoved its fist down Graff's throat.

Clinton remained totally still, terrified of alerting the creature to his presence. He could see the ghastling's boney hand make ridges along the dingo's swelling neck. Instead of pulling its hand free in an explosion of gore though, the ghastling shuddered as something slid along its arm, through its fingers, and into Graff's body. In the next moment, the creature's tattered cloak blew away, its skeleton breaking apart like parched mud. The cloak snagged against Graff's boot buckle and whipped around in the wind.

Galront stared in shock, and carefully hoisted himself to his feet. Another impaler whipped past as the weasel edged closer.

"Hey!" he bellowed.

The cloak whipped in the air over the dingo's corpse.

Galront reached out to push the cloak aside...

Graff's hand snapped out and snatched Galront's ankle, yanking him onto the ground. The weasel tumbled into a heap and his stunpike skittered across the sand, out of his reach. A red fire glowed in Graff's glazed eyes. His nose scrunched into a horrific snarl, and green bile dripped from his mouth. Galront thrashed and wailed, hitting the dingo's face and chest with his crutch, but Graff ignored the blows and continued to pull Galront closer.

"N-Narfell!" screeched the weasel, pressing his back into the ground and lashing out with his leg. There was a thud followed by a snapping sound. Galront heard the sickening noise, retched, and threw up. "Help me!"

Clinton looked up to see that Galront had kicked Graff's head so hard it had twisted around and was now flopping against the dingo's shoulder. As he watched, he saw Graff scrabble unnaturally fast across the ground, before pouncing on the downed weasel.

"GET OFF ME!" wailed Galront, as claws dug into his chest, pinning him against the sand.

The possessed dingo jerked his body forwards, flopping his broken head just above Galront's face. The weasel screamed again as he struggled in the dingo's grasp, lashing out, snapping his teeth, and rolling through the vomit he had just created. Ignoring the blows, Graff leaned closer to take a bite out of the greasy weasel's neck.

"Narfell! Help me! HELP ME!"

Out of nowhere a terrified impaler slammed into the zombie's back, its shoulder shattering the cadaver like a hammer against chalk. In the next second a nightmarishly thin creature streaked out of the dingo's body, ripping free of the husk in a flurry of gore. The dingo collapsed as the last wispy trails of the ghastling soared off into the air with a shriek.

Galront scrabbled onto his leg and hopped off towards a gap in the rocks. "Y-you tell anyone you saw that and I'll kill you," threatened Galront, seeing the lion staring.

"You've already tried and failed."

Dithering on the spot, Galront pulled out his knife, but hesitated. "You ain't worth it. I hope you get what's coming to you, and I hope it's painful. So frag you."

The weasel turned tail and hobbled off while Clinton remained motionless, flat against the ground. As more ghastlings swooped overhead, the lion thought he would surely have to fight, to beat them away as he had seen so many of the hunters do, yet for some reason he was ignored. Despair rolled over him, washing away his determination. The temperature continued to plummet. His skin felt like it was matted with ice. Waves of pressure pounded against him, making it almost too much to bear. But still he did not give up. He opened his mouth and yelled, trying to drown out the sound of death, but still he could not escape the ghastlings' wails.

"*Uth tut rrah-mune!*" commanded another set of voices.

A sucking sound reverberated off the rocks. Clinton's ears popped. The air pressure switched and the temperature slowly started to rise. The raging wind suddenly dispersed and the whirling sand settled. In mere seconds the turbulence ceased, like it had been switched off or siphoned away. Clinton opened his eyes. He tried to move, but could barely twitch his little finger. And then a thought hit him - a powerful thought that seemed to feed his muscles and limbs with warmth.

Raion.

As if he had been bathed in sunlight, he snapped out of the paralysis and sat up, dislodging the sand that dusted his body. His eyes took a while to accept that everything around him was not a twisted nightmare, but a frightening reality. Huge streaks of blood splattered the rocks and sand. Bones, corpses, and tattered cloaks lay flapping in heaps, along with charred carcasses. Weapons were strewn randomly, now silent with no one to operate them, while tufts of anumal fur drifted around like tumbleweed. He trembled. His mind tried to grasp what had just happened, but it seemed too crazy. He ruffled his hair and sand sprinkled everywhere.

There was a loud slurping noise.

Clinton turned his head in the direction of the noise and

realized that it was coming from the other side of the rocks. He stumbled to his feet, staggering like a newborn cubling, as the noise increased. Nothing stirred. He doubted anything could have survived the attack, unless…

"The badger."

He limped nearer to the boulders.

"H-hello?" he croaked. "Is… Is that you?"

Clinton braced himself, but his eyes widened when he caught a glimpse of a pink, hairless creature, its stubby tail wagging with delight, snarling and making munching noises. Squeezed into a crevice between the rocks, Snarg was contentedly gorging himself on something. Clinton's hackles rose as the wegg paused and raised his head to sniff the air. Blood smeared the mutt's mouth like a twisted clown's smile had been painted across its lips, and a grubby hand protruded from the beast's maw. Galront's foot, and a snapped crutch, was also poking out from underneath the feasting pet.

The lion inched back and clapped his hand over his mouth. Slipping silently from the scene, he spied his water pouch, backpack, and a stunpike. Picking them all up, he fled the carnage, limping for the horizon and as far away from the desert massacre as he could possibly get.

CHAPTER TWENTY-NINE

THE PANTHER'S PROPOSAL.

Dallas continued to stare at the refection in the window. His fists were clenched tight, waiting for something to happen. Fighting the impulse to greet the intruder with bloodshed, he instead took a calming breath.

"I hope you have a good view of whatever you find so captivating. However, I believe it is impolite to stare."

"As if you have the slightest notion of manners, tiger," replied a smooth, calculating voice from the far corner of the room.

Dallas's lip curled.

"Easy now," continued the voice. "Your heart is pounding. No need to be scared."

"It is you who should be scared."

The tiger lengthened his claws as he let out a deep, resonant growl. He spun around to face the stranger, but his anger quickly dispersed. A jet-black panther, wearing dark glasses and a long leather coat, emerged from the depths of the shadows. Dallas sensed an aura of maturity, wisdom, and death emanating from him, as if he was inspecting some kind of relic, similar to when he had visited the ancient temples on the Steppes. He held his ground as the panther slowly approached. After four strides the felines came face to face. Dallas stared at the glasses covering the panther's eyes, but could not see through the darkened glass. His claws twitched. An unknown feeling surfaced, one that urged him to lower his stance and yield to the newcomer, yet his heart told him different. It pumped anger through his veins, anger that seemed to take control of his actions. The tiger gritted his teeth. His hand shot out to grab the panther's neck, but as soon as his arm moved, the stranger reacted. Instead of blocking the tiger, though, the panther allowed Dallas to seize him, and in the space of a heartbeat, both anumals stood grasping the other by the throat.

The panther smirked. "Quite the predicament we have."

"What do you want?" gasped Dallas. "Who are you?"

"Let go and I'll explain."

"Do not take me for a fool."

"Yet you are certainly acting like one. Now let go."

Dallas squeezed tighter. "I will crush your windpipe. You do not know with whom you are dealing."

The panther's smirk changed into a knowing smile. "No, Dallas. I know exactly who you are." The panther pulled him closer as he uttered some low, guttural words.

"*Tu-un athay!*"

Dallas's hold on the panther suddenly weakened. His eyes widened and his breath caught at the back of his throat. As he fought for air, his orange fur began to fade to a dull rust color while his muscles slackened, their toned contours wasting away like rotten fruit. Dallas's knees buckled. His once rigid whiskers drooped as his cheeks sunk inward, tightening around his skull. Fur molted from his body in clumps. Yet with every second that Dallas weakened, Nightmare's grip strengthened.

Dallas tried to speak, but all he could manage was a splintered moan. He flopped helplessly in the panther's grip, and his thoughts grew sluggish as his vision clouded over. He felt the yearning to let go, to give up the pain and the fight and just slip into a peaceful rest...

No more hurt, or lies, just sleep.

However, something anchored the tiger to reality.

A roar echoed in his head that grew in power. His pulse pounded. The very sound seemed to prime his muscles. From the depths of his soul, he felt the pressure build and snake up from a hidden well, until he threw back his head and roared so loud his throat felt like it would burst.

A bolt of energy shot up his frame and spat out of his chest, smashing into the panther and causing his black coat to flare out. Dallas's eyes snapped open just in time to see the panther smash into the far wall. The wooden paneling shattered into splinters as the feline toppled behind the mayor's desk. Dallas felt energy flood back into his emaciated frame. The color surged into his fur and his muscles filled out again. He let out another defiant roar and charged forwards, bounding over the mayor's desk, smashing ornaments and scattering papers.

But no one was there when he landed.

"Well, that was interesting," commented the panther, now standing behind him.

The tiger instantly swung around to see the stranger waiting as if nothing had happened. The panther smiled. With one finger, he drew a triangular shape in the air and slashed it diagonally. The shape glowed a deep crimson color.

"*Zick zik!*" hissed the panther

Sparks dazzled in front of Dallas's eyes as he crashed back into the wall. It felt like a boulder had been slammed into his stomach. He shook his head and tried to regain his focus.

"What did you do?" he yelled.

The panther swaggered forwards and pushed his glasses into place, ignoring the question. Dallas swiped at the panther's face, but he easily parried the attack before grabbing Dallas by the neck again. He forced the tiger so hard against the wall that the mayor's pictures jostled on their hooks. The panther's grip tightened and he raised his free hand. Like a bullet it shot forward, streaking so fast at the tiger's face he felt the air waft his fur. Dallas shut his eyes, waiting for the blow, when a sudden whisper skittered through the room.

Snapping his eyes open again, the tiger saw a fist only a fingernail away from his nose. The panther was stood like a statue with his head cocked to the side. After a few seconds, the panther released the tiger and lowered his hand. Dallas fought to catch his breath as he tried to decipher the whispers, but they seemed to be in an unknown language.

"Yes…I understand, mistress," answered the stranger. He turned to Dallas and took a step back.

"What's going on? What did you do to me?"

The whispers continued.

Nightmare nodded to the corner of the room and raised his hands. "Yes, you have my word, he will be delivered unharmed."

"Who are you talking to?"

Nightmare nodded again. "You suggest I show him then?"

"Stop this!" shouted Dallas, itching to strike. "Get out!"

"Okay, as always, mistress, I obey." He turned back to Dallas and pressed his thumb against the tiger's forehead.

"*Xkorth!*" he mumbled.

Dallas stumbled back into the wall again, grasping his forehead. "What have you—"

And then it hit him.

As effective as a striking fist, a clouded memory jolted the tiger's mind. Vague flashes of his past gushed before his eyes in an unstoppable current. He tried to sift through the images, attempting to figure out just how he knew the stranger. He saw himself as he was growing up, his upbringing in the desert village, his wealth, his power, and his increasing dominance. As the tiger carried out the mayor's demands, he saw Ferris's nods of approval slowly turning from satisfaction, to wariness, to growing fear. Faces of his victims flashed by, faces he had bullied and harassed, and lately even killed. He saw it all apart from the one image he was searching for.

Then all at once he fell into a forgotten memory.

Dallas felt a burning heat on his face. Rain matted his fur as he watched from his small basket. He could not see much around him, but the sky was filled with smoke and screams echoed over the clang of weapons. He caught sight of the dark figure holding on to the basket he was being carried in. The figure was running at great speed, gulping in air and pushing himself faster and faster, keeping the cubling tiger from the nearby figures. Then the stranger looked down and peered at him. The stranger's high collar framed his head as he examined Dallas, before turning away and picking up his pace again.

Dallas snapped out of the memory as if he had awoken from a deep sleep. He gasped and pressed himself against the wall. "You!" he said. "I-I have seen you before."

"You remember?" asked the newcomer, his face set like stone.

The tiger nodded. "What did you do to me?"

"All will be explained in due time."

"You will tell me now!" growled Dallas.

"I advise you to remain calm. You seek answers that I am not at liberty to give. It would be wise, at this moment, to simply listen and follow."

"Tell me! Who are you, panther?"

"I am fear."

"Answer my question!"

The stranger smiled. "I have been known by many guises. Yet there are a few who know my true name, fewer still who are alive to speak it. For now I am what most anumals fear to be, what most anumals fear to see. I am known as Nightmare."

Dallas's eyes narrowed.

"I trust you have heard of me?"

"Nightmare? *The* Nightmare?" A bulge of discomfort fluttered in his chest. He forced out a laugh. "You are telling me you are the taker of souls? The destroyer of villages? The shadow of death? It seems you have listened to too many Journey Tales. You are not the Nightmare."

"Yet inside that brain on yours you know I am telling the truth. Unless you would prefer for me to prove it to you?"

Dallas stepped back. "No...I-I think I believe you. But Brangthorne? Gilderville? The Smoke Depot? They were all villages you slaughtered."

"I prefer not to concern myself with the past, rather, I embrace the present. And the reason for me being here is not to reduce your village to dust, but for another purpose entirely."

"So what is it then?"

"I've already told you that I'm not at liberty to speak of such things."

"Not at liberty? Or you do not want to?"

Nightmare smirked. "Both."

"Stop toying with me. You may call yourself Nightmare, but you do not scare me, panther."

The stranger's smile remained firmly in place. "And yet the reek of fear tells me a very different story. At this moment, Dallas, your world has been rocked. The scales of power have been tipped. You are more concerned for your life than ever before, but believe me, this is only the beginning."

"Enough! Tell me why I should not just kill you right now?"

"Because you can't. The only reason you are alive right now is because I choose not to kill you. On top of that you should consider that I know someone who will answer all those niggling questions you've suddenly discovered in your life, and give reasons why the emptiness refuses to dissipate."

"I seek no answers. I need no one. I—"

"Why are you so unfocused? Why do you feel hollow, impatient, and isolated?"

The tiger refused to answer.

"Most of all, Dallas, I know that without me you will never know who you really are."

The tiger straightened his coat. "What is this idiocy? I know who I am."

"Yet your discussion with the mayor indicates otherwise. You question who you are. You know not where you come from. Add to that the fact that you shot lightning from your body and hurled me across the room. I'd say the questions were quickly mounting up, wouldn't you?" Dallas did not reply, so the panther pressed his point. "Have you never wondered how an abandoned cubling could have made the impact you have upon this village? Or do you think it was just a simple coincidence?"

"Well…" Dallas looked at the floor as an uncomfortable silence stretched out. "I made good publicity for the mayor. I was just a means to gain more votes, a public display of his generosity."

Nightmare chuckled.

"What?" snapped Dallas, gritting his teeth. "Why are you laughing?"

"To say you want to kill me, you're certainly eager to divulge your deepest thoughts. How many others have told that secret to?"

"What are the others to me? Not one single anumal in this village is worth my confidence."

"And that makes you happy?"

Dallas began to say yes, but stopped when he realized he would be lying. He turned to the panther like a knat staring up at an ancient oak tree. "So-so what are you offering me?"

"My associate has all the answers you desire. She will be able to tell you why the lion stalks your dreams, why rage burns so bright within you. But it is your choice. You can learn with us, or you can work against us, either way the wheels have been set in motion."

Dallas stared at the panther for a long time. His head was a jumble of thoughts.

"Okay," he finally relented, breaking the silence. "Take me to this person you speak of. But let me tell you one thing..." He pointed at the panther's throat. "Y-you even *think* about betraying me and I will gut you from your neck to your feet, Nightmare or not."

"Good boy." Nightmare smiled, but in the blink of an eye the panther's hand moved and a knife appeared in it. The distance between the two disappeared as he touched the edge of the blade against the tiger's neck. "But, please, cease with the threats. There are only so many I am willing to take in one day."

Dallas eyed the intricate carvings along the blade and the black handle, spotting the silver signature of an anumal's skull near its rear bolster. He stepped back and, looking uncomfortable, raised his hands. "Okay...fine. Lead the way."

Nightmare lowered the weapon and nodded. "Follow me." Striding past him, Nightmare headed soundlessly for the door. He stepped from the room, into the hall, and out of sight.

Dallas paused and took in the scene of the mayor's office. He did not know why, but something cried out in him, telling him that this might be the last time he would ever see the room again, or the justice house...or even Wooburn. He felt like he was teetering on the edge of a storm of change.

He growled but followed after the panther.

The two anumals stalked along the halls, entered a passage, and slipped down the side stairs that led to the main courtroom. Descending the gloomy, circular steps, the figures vanished into the clutches of the waiting darkness.

CHAPTER THIRTY

<u>**SALVATION.**</u>

Clinton woke up with a groan. The sun had begun to peek over the horizon, lighting up the clear blue sky and promising another hot day. He did not know how long he had been lying in the sand, but rocks stuck painfully in his side and his face throbbed. A sectoid scuttled across his chest. The yellow bug stopped to rub its numerous antennae together and as Clinton sat up, it took flight, buzzing off into the distance.

Pained screams echoed in his head. He clamped his eyes shut, but still it all came rushing back. The memory of blood and the smell of death bombarded him. The line between reality and dream had been blurred in a confusing nightmare. He dug his fingers into the sand, fighting away the images, until he found some semblance of normality again. He remembered running, his lungs aching, trying to create some distance between him and the horrific ordeal. By the time his body had finally surrendered, however, his injured leg burned with pain and his walk had been reduced to a limping stumble. The last thing he could recall was reaching out for the shimmering horizon, before crashing into unconsciousness.

Clinton pressed his palms against his temples to try clear his mind.

"What the…"

The lion felt moisture on his forehead.

He dropped his hands to see that wet sand coated his palms and fingertips. With great effort, he pushed himself to his feet to survey the area. He remembered he had collapsed in between a collection of rocks clumped along the bottom of a gentle slope. Shielding his eyes, he squinted up into the sky, but not a single cloud lingered. He bent down and dug his hands into the sand, only to discover more moisture beneath the surface. The lion's jaw dropped. He turned to scramble up the slope before realizing his injured leg was no longer thudding with pain. Stopping to study the wound, he saw a clean bandage had been applied and the sour smell of infection no longer stung his nose. He sat down and, unraveling the dressing, inspected the injury.

The maggots he had used to strip away the infected flesh had disappeared, replaced by a clean, healing laceration.

"This is mad," he muttered, shaking his head in bewilderment.

He quickly rewrapped the bandage and stared at the surrounding vista, checking for signs of life. Not a scavenger, scuttler, ayvid, or sectoid could be seen. Exhaling, he grabbed his stolen stunpike and continued up the slope until he reached the top...when the breath caught in the back of his throat.

In the distance he could make out a section of the ground where the gritty earth gave way to sparse patches of grass. Instead of jagged rock faces on the horizon, high mountains reached into the sky while tiny trees and bushes swayed in the morning breeze, urging him onwards. Relief washed over him. He sank to his knees and let out an uncontrollable sob. Only a short walk would take him to the border of the Great Plains and to the sanctuary of the Idlefields. Somehow, by some miracle, he had made it to safety.

* * *

Clinton set off for the grasslands. The thought of food made his stomach rumble, especially now he knew he would soon be greeted with clean water and fruit-filled trees. As the morning wore on, his pace quickened. The sun rose high, and before he knew it, the Great Plains had slowly morphed into clumps of dew-soaked grass. Throwing himself onto the ground, he felt the cool grass press against his skin, and he finally released a weighted sigh. After a few minutes of rest, he decided to search for food, water, and shelter. Clinton managed to find all the food that he needed from the karla trees dotting the landscape, and felt much better after eating its tough, but sweet-tasting, fruit. Small hidden vein-like streams ran underneath clumps of grass, providing the life-giving water to the Idlefields. To the west he could make out the rough terrain of the Great Plains, while to the north, as far as he could see, spread the glorious sight of the lush Idlefields. Beyond that, to the northeast, sticking up like giant, jagged teeth, sat the peaks of the Ridgeback Mountains. Clinton smiled broadly as he stared in relief.

Then something caught his eye.

He could just make out the shape of a structure about half way up the distant mountainside. Trees hid part of it from view, but its existence told him that some kind of settlement had to be nearby. Gathering as much fruit as he could, he filled his backpack before heading for his new discovery, stunpike in hand.

By mid afternoon he had stumbled upon the remains of an old road strewn with toppled clan statues. Roofs of abandoned buildings began to peep up along the horizon with increasing regularity, until he found himself entering what had once been a small village. Made from old stone, the derelict structures were now merely lifeless shells. Walls had collapsed, and thatched roofs had long since blown away, leaving nothing but weatherworn beams. Tasting the air, Clinton could discern no signs of life within the vicinity. No fires burned and no anumal aromas wafted on the breeze. The village had been abandoned for quite some time, yet there were no signs of fighting, or raids, or mass migration.

Walking through a fragile-looking archway, Clinton found himself at the bottom of the great cliff leading up to the mountain building. More shattered statues decorated the grassy base and steep stairs had been carved into the rock, creating a path that led upwards, now worn away by centuries of wind and rain. About halfway up the stairs disappeared, partly smashed, partly crumbled, and only handholds remained in their place. The lion glanced back over his shoulder at the desolate village, before looking up to the building again, assessing the route up to it. He did not know why, but he felt drawn in its direction, as if the towering climb would offer no more of a challenge to him than Wooburn's backstreets.

Okay, he thought, studying the route and rubbing his hands together. *Okay, let's do this.*

He mounted the stairs before fumbling his way up the cliff's side, using whatever holes he could force his clawed fingers into. Yet the higher he climbed, the thinner and colder the air grew. He stopped to rest on ledges or outcroppings whenever he could, massaging the blood in his aching fingers to keep them mobile. He wrapped his blanket around his torso to warm his body, and smiled - there was no way he would curse the cold, not after he had been forced to endure the heat of the Plains for all those days.

After a few more hours climbing an end finally came in sight. With one last push, Clinton hauled himself over the edge of a summit and on to flat, grassy land. A deep ravine separated him from the building, but an ancient rope bridge had been erected, creating a single pathway across the expanse. As he crossed the bridge he gaped in awe.

Before him loomed the biggest lazarball stadium he had ever seen. More than three times the size of Wooburn's stadium, it had been carved into the rock itself, dominating the skyline, gazing out over the miles of land without obstruction. Clinton turned and soaked up the breathtaking view, taking in the spectacle of the red-orange sky as the evening slowly settled in. He turned and began to wander the perimeter.

The stadium's stone turrets had toppled, and its once intricate engravings had been warped into mindless markings. Thick decorative columns, tipped with carvings of budding karla flowers, thrust high into the air, dividing walls full of doorways and countless empty windows. After searching the area, Clinton came across a stone archway, its pillars only just managing to maintain the weight of its heavy burden. Two rusty, iron gates lay tangled amongst the grass, keeping company with a corroded metal sign. Clinton bent down and picked up the sign, rubbing away the dirt and rust. He tilted it up to catch the last of the dying light, and blew. The sign read:

SAMANOSKI STADIUM

"It can't be!" gasped Clinton. He dropped the sign and turned to gape at the structure.

Unable to keep the smile from creeping across his face, he ran into the darkened entrance, looking upon his surroundings with his feline vision. Standing in the open archway he could make out a room with doors and tunnels leading off in different directions. He picked the largest tunnel and ploughed ahead into the darkness, through the passage, and onto the biggest gamefield he had ever seen. Two stone towers sat at either end of the field, and stone seats circled the ground, climbing into the air. The first of the early evening stars twinkled above the open roof, but clouds lingered in front of the rising moon, masking its silvery light.

Clinton could not help but think about his old teacher, Mrs. McCarbe, and her history lessons about lazarball and the legendary Samanoski Stadium. Her clipped tone echoed in his ears as he recalled how this very stadium had become pivotal to the success of lazarball as a worldwide sport. Clinton pictured the anumals of old, marching onto the field, ready for battle. Their rudimentary armor and helmets would have been cobbled together from scavenged leftovers, stripped from long-dead human bodies.

"On this day," a clan representative would have shouted from the bleachers, pointing his finger skywards, "we will see peace settled between the Short Claw Clan and the Rose Quartz Masons Clan."

Clinton had been taught that territorial disputes created a storm of bloodshed between anumalkind after the humans had been eradicated. Within decades of their domination, the new anumal rulers had proceeded to wipe themselves out, species killing species, all in the name of acquiring land and technology...until Silania's presence graced the Earth and a new means of settling disputes had arisen.

"Warriors, prepare for battle... Make ready to fire."

The clicking sound of rifles would have echoed as they were raised in readiness. Mankind's leftover weapons – fully functional lazar rifles – would let loose a volley of lethal red energy-balls into the stadium.

A cry of "ATTACK!" would have blared.

As one, both sides would have stormed towards the other as the deadly spheres zipped through the air around them. Lazars would ricochet off armor or slice into exposed flesh, hacking anumals down in the midst of play. Clan leaders would stand upon their stone pillars, risking life to see their warriors succeed. They knew their deaths could meet them in the form of a well-placed shot, but the territorial rewards were too much to ignore, especially when they offered so much power.

After the colony crusades ended, most of the stadiums had been destroyed. Mrs. McCarbe had told her class that Samanoski had managed to avoid demolition, and from what Clinton had seen of the precarious route up to the stadium, he now understood why.

Jumping over enormous stone boulders, he made his way into the middle of the gamefield. In the very center stood a mighty tree, its old trunk knotted together into a giant, wooden weave. Thick roots anchored it firmly into the ground. He reached out to touch the relic in an awed silence, when a thought hit him... Perhaps he was the only anumal to have entered this stadium in decades? He sat down and rested his back against the trunk for a few seconds when his reflections turned sour. His body tensed as he caught sight of a moonlit boulder. What appeared to be the remains of a foot poked up from the grassy undergrowth.

Clinton scrabbled to his knees.

"Well played, Clint, you dumb, stupid glux."

He protracted his claws and swept his gaze around the towering bleachers. Rising to his feet, he carefully padded over to the boulder, when he spotted a skeleton in the grass. He stopped dead, resisting the urge to run, and took a moment to examine the remains.

Upon first sight the skeleton looked to be canine, but it had been dead for years. All traces of flesh had been long since picked clean, leaving behind only stark, yellow bones. Clinton bit on his lower lip, wincing at the large fracture running along the length of its skull. The ribcage had been shattered and the spinal column broken in two. He huffed and shook his head.

"Okay. Pull yourself together."

The lion turned back to the tree, but the clouds parted, allowing a sliver of moonlight to fully illuminate the gamefield.

He froze.

A few paces in front of him lay another pile of bones.

"What the...?"

As he studied the ground he noticed countless skeletal mounds dotting the area. Scattered haphazardly, they created a trail of bones that led to a section of the bleachers that had collapsed over the cliff edge and into the abyss below. Clinton's muscles primed. Adrenalin fueled his body, increasing his heart rate and warning him to flee. However, he stalked closer, drawn to the sight of the massacre. With every step, he passed rib cages, skulls, and shattered hips. A tinge of rot clung to the air. After a couple more reluctant footsteps, he slowed to a stop.

The snapping of a twig echoed behind him, and the tree ruffled. Letting out a snarl, Clinton spun around ready for an attack and caught sight of an anumal's tail high amongst the branches. A second later it whipped away, disappearing into the dense foliage. With dawning recognition, the lion realized he had not been alone for a single moment since entering Samanoski stadium.

CHAPTER THIRTY-ONE

A BALANCE OF POWER.

As the two figures slipped into the main courtroom, Nightmare paused and nodded his head. "Yes," he said, indicating the central dais. "They completed it."

"What?"

The panther ignored the question and approached the raised platform, lifting his hand for silence. Dallas gritted his teeth, but obeyed, quietly following behind. For a few moments the panther sniffed the air and listened.

"Excellent," he eventually muttered.

"What are you talking about?"

The panther gave Dallas a hint of a smile and then turned away to climb the dais steps, shifting his focus to the dominant stained-glass window. "That."

The multi-colored glass had been intricately arranged to depict a wreath of feathers circling a reptile's footprint, a paw-mark, a hoof-print, and a primate's handprint.

"The window?" Dallas shrugged and followed him up the stairs. "Big deal. I hardly even notice it anymore."

"Do you have any idea what the symbol means?" asked Nightmare. "What it represents?"

"Did you really bring—"

"Humor me and take a good look at it."

Dallas sighed and stared at the window. He shrugged. "Like I said, it lets light in and..." His words stalled as a puzzled expression crossed his face. "To be honest I have never truly studied it. The design is...unusual." After a few heartbeats, he turned back to the panther. "Are we done now?"

"And therein lies your problem. You only see the obvious and never take the time to truly observe beyond that. No wonder you grow bored."

Dallas's fingers twitched and his claws extended from the ends of his fingertips.

"Put them away," sighed Nightmare. "Or would you like me to

give you another example of what I can do?"

Dallas stared defiantly into the panther's cold face before he finally backed down and retracted his claws.

"Good, tiger, you're catching on. Power comes from more than just the physical. Look beyond that and see with more than your eyes. After all, eyes can be fooled." The panther lifted his hand, holding it so that it was in front of the paw-mark symbol on the window, blocking it from view. "When you understand how to see things differently, you will discover that everyday objects can possess...unexpected qualities."

"So now what? Are you going to put what you preach to practice, or are we just going to stand here all day?"

The panther threw back his head and inhaled a lungful of air. Opening his jaws, he let out an eerie, high-pitched howl that made the tiger's ears itch.

A banging noise crashed through the courtroom, followed by another and then another. Dallas whirled around, trying to identify the noises, and saw that all the doors had slammed shut and locked themselves tight. The daylight beaming through the window was clouding over like a brewing storm. In quick succession, every candle fixed to the large, wooden chandelier popped to life, burning with a dim, blue flame. Tiny shadows flickered along the walls and floor, appearing and disappearing in the blink of an eye. Dallas glanced to his side and saw beads of sweat dripping down Nightmare's temples. The veins in the panther's hand bulged, and smoke drifted off the ends of his fingers.

"What is happening?"

"Patience, Dallas. It is not wise to interrupt the process when she—"

"I said tell me!"

"And I said patience."

Dallas tried to curb his mounting frustration, but his annoyance was itching at him. Something creaked behind the tiger. Snapping his head in the direction of the noise, he saw the walls tremble. He gasped as the whole surface was suddenly dragged away from reality, sucked off to the edges of his awareness.

"I am losing my mind," he gasped, rubbing his thumb over his brow to ward away evil.

"The sensation will pass when she arrives."

"Who? When who arrives? What is—"

"A little longer and you'll see for yourself."

The feather emblems on the window fluttered and twitched, before they too began to move and writhe around one another. Intense shafts of light showered Dallas in a myriad of hued rays, before an unexpected pulse shot out from the surface, half blinding him and leaving blurred splotches imprinted behind his eyelids. The tiger stumbled back a step. He rubbed his eyes, trying to clear his vision, when he heard a scraping noise followed closely by a hiss. A soft draught tickled his skin. He blinked away his tears to catch a glimpse of movement near the window. The glass and the symbol had completely vanished, replaced by a glowing void and a shadow of a gigantic Olde-world cobra swaying before it. Thin eyes observed him from the shadow's depths, their crimson light radiating with power.

Dallas rumbled a soft growl.

Opening its mouth, the cobra let out an ear-splitting hiss, its shadowy forked-tongue flicking in and out. The room fell into a berated silence. Dallas found himself submitting to the creature's gaze and gradually lowered his head to stare at his feet. The panther standing next to him had likewise averted his head.

"What... Who a-are you?" stuttered Dallas. The shadow simply swayed, hypnotic in its movement, but gave no reply. Dallas pointed at the panther. "He said you wanted to see me. That you had answers."

The shadow-snake reared higher, dominating the room, yet still it did not speak

"The panther promised you would help me," he continued. "Or... Or was he lying?"

"Would you invessst blind faith in a creature as notorious as the Harbinger?" hissed the shadow, finally puncturing her silence. Her tone was harsh, but hypnotic, with hundreds of whispering voices echoing and preceding every spoken word. "The Nightmare has lured many a fool to their death by this method. Who is to say you are not another victim?"

Dallas's memory of being a cub in a basket, staring up at the panther, sprang to mind. "Because I...just know. Besides," he clenched his fists, "if this was a trap, I would be left with no other option but to retaliate."

A rasping chuckle escaped the shadow's mouth. Her eyes narrowed. "My dear, Dallasss Sunaaki. Sssso proud. Sssso defiant. You are everything I expected and more."

"S-Sunaaki?" he commented, lifting an eyebrow. "What does that mean?"

"Is it not your name?"

"No, it is just Dallas. I have no family name."

The shadow-snake slithered from one side of the void to the other. "We shall see, tiger, we shall ssssee."

Dallas turned to Nightmare. "What is it talking about?"

"My mistress may not think you are ready, or deserving, of all the answers yet," he replied, keeping his gaze averted. "They will be disclosed to you at a time of her choosing."

"If I was not ready then I would not be standing here, would I? And by everything that is sane I should not be." He faced the shadow again. "Is this all just a bizarre dream, or have I lost my mind? Have I finally—"

"Thisss is reality."

"But it cannot be!" Dallas yelled, glancing around the distorted room. "It must be a figment of my imagination."

The shadow leaned in close to him, as if peeling herself from the wall. "Then you certainly have a vivid mind."

"Tell me what is happening! Please!"

The shadow swayed from side to side, saying nothing, while her eyes glowed like miniature suns.

"This is absurd. You know nothing." The tiger turned to go. "I should never have come."

The wooden floorboards began to rumble. Every candle in the room burst into jets of blue flame. Dallas stumbled as the floor rocked. He lunged for the exit, but Nightmare appeared before him, as if he had sprung up out of the ground.

"He is not to leave, Wade," ordered the voice.

With one finger, the panther propelled Dallas back. The tiger thudded onto the dais floor.

"My mistress has not finished with you."

"Okay!" he shouted, scrabbling to his feet. "So what do you want?"

The candles settled down to flickering flames.

"A fighter to the end," laughed the shadow-cobra, her voice echoing around the room. "You certainly have confidence in yourssself."

"Is that a crime?"

"No, but sssome would call it impudent."

The shadow halted her movements to regard him through her slit-like eyes. And then she started to change.

Turning in on herself, her form melded into a completely different outline. The silhouette wriggled and squirmed until it had transformed into that of a huge lizard, standing on two legs. Nightmare let out an ominous growl.

"So you wish to know the truth?" she asked, her voice lower in pitch. "Then know that once it is revealed to you, there is no going back. Are you prepared to take that step, Dallas? Are you truly ready to leave all of what you think you know behind?"

Dallas straightened his spine. All that he believed and understood in life had already changed, yet he found he did not care. To merely exist in Wooburn, to be the largest fish in a muddy little puddle would slowly turn him crazy. He pictured the mayor's face, he pictured the village advisors, he pictured the scuttlers and sectoids that foraged about the village pretending to be anumals, daring to class themselves the same as him. He took a relieved breath, and nodded. "I have been ready for this all my life."

"I agree," laughed the shadow. "Then, so be it, Dallas Sunaaki… So be it."

* * *

As soon as the words were spoken, Dallas felt a tremble underneath his feet as the room began to shake. The walls cracked and the floor splintered, ripped apart like a giant had punched through the boards. The chandelier swung back and forth, and pictures fell from the walls, smashing to the floor before the shards sped away, sucked into the blackness that had swelled from the giant shadow. Everything around Dallas crumbled, dropping into the void, until all that remained was a stark pillar of light shooting up from the dais floor. Then even the darkness made a tearing noise, cracking open to create long fractures in midair, opening rifts in the seams of reality itself.

Standing in a pocket of space, Dallas was suddenly engulfed in a vast emptiness. The tiger's thoughts whirled as his fear reached a boiling point. For the first time in his life he felt rooted to the spot, his fight or flight instinct abandoning him, replaced by sheer terror. He glanced to his rear. Nightmare stood next to his shoulder, his features as unfazed as ever. The shadowy creature had disappeared, soaked up into the depths of the void. Dallas searched for her and finally spotted two red slits floating high above his head. As if by magic, pinpoints of light sparkled into existence all around and, before he knew it, he realized he was standing on the dais, suspended in midair, above Earth.

"The facts of creation are known in many temples and by those who study the Great Mother, but only a few know the truth - the truth of life and death, and of creation," began the shadow in her rumbling voice.

Dallas steeled himself, desperate to retain some of his dignity. "We live. We die." He shrugged. "Some gloriously and some hitched to the back of a gorespine. I am more than aware of how we meet our demise. What is your point?"

"My point is that the way in which you anumals are created will ultimately determine the way in which you will perish." The shadow-reptile's eyes widened. "Yet if you change the way an anumal is created, you will change the way their destiny snakes forward. Do you know how anumalkind was born, Dallas?"

"We are all descendants of the Armies of the Ark. Everyone

knows this." When the shadow entity did not reply, the tiger continued with, "And to be more specific, we are born from our mothers."

The shadow's eyes slowly started to circle the dais, blotting out the light from the stars as she moved in front of the felines. "However, the mother is merely the carrier and not the life giver. When a sentient creature is created, it requires a vessel in which to house the soul. These vessels were once made in the image of man, but now they are made in the form of anumalkind. However, only now, since the evolution and the Armies of the Ark triumphed, did your minds progress further than those of the beasts you were spawned from. Only now do you truly look past primal instincts and acknowledge the existence of another power, that of the soul.

"Since learning you are all descendents of the ancient armies there have been many debates as to how the humans actually created you...what gave you the spark of life. But these answers disappeared in the years of bloodshed and violence that swept the planet during the colony crusades. Now there remain only a few who know the truth, Dallas Sunaaki, those such as I."

"That name—"

"Yet I digress. Before a child is born, their soul circles the Earth's atmosphere looking for a suitable vessel in which to bond, and thus, complete the symbiosis. This is called the *joining*, where the body and spirit become one true being."

The tiger's eyes ached as a distant light burst to life. Shooting into focus across the sky swooped clusters of comet-like shapes. As they hurtled past his head, Dallas realized that these were the very souls the shadow was describing.

"Once a vessel has been created, a compatible soul will dive to Earth and merge with the vessel. And from there the newborn being will slowly grow, learning and developing characteristics, its likes and dislikes, to become a whole, complete being."

Around the dais the comet-like souls plummeted in different directions to combine with their chosen vessels - babies who had just been newly born and separated from their mothers.

"Beliefs differ as to how and why this happens, and many

deities have been hailed in order to provide theories, but in truth the Joining simply is. Before anumalkind, before humankind, from the very dawn of time...this is how it has been. Yet, as we all know, Dallas, life is far from consistent. Anomalies sometimes occur."

"What anomalies?"

"Not every soul will have a simple Joining. Souls are fragile entities, as fragile as the strands of a cobweb, requiring the most delicate of touches. Sometimes more than one soul may discover a suitable vessel, and when this happens, the compatible souls will race to join the vessel before it can be stolen away. Then again it might so happen that some souls, those of immense power, will be so determined to capture a vessel that they will dive so fast and for so long, they eventually merge and...Entwine."

The shadow paused for a moment while the sky around her altered to represent her explanation. As Dallas stared, he could see two souls plummeting towards the ground, growing closer, binding together and becoming one entity.

"Then what?" he whispered, unable to tear his gaze from the spectacle.

"Then nothing," she answered, her words barely audible. "When an Entwined soul tries to merge with a living vessel, it will be rejected. An organic vessel such as an anumal could not possibly house such an immense power. It would perish; the vessel would warp and die. Therefore, the Entwined soul must create their own vessel to occupy, for without one they will have no chance of survival. And as the years pass they will grow in strength, defying the limits of time and age, illness and injury, and slowly learn to control and master the powers they possess."

Dallas listened to her, absorbing every detail. "And let me guess," he finally said. "You are one of these Entwined spirits? Two souls that have joined together?"

The shadow's words seemed to pierce Dallas's mind, sweeping through his body, causing his fur to bristle. "My dear, Dallas Sunaaki." She let out a rasping laugh. "I, Marama, the Shadow Seeress, am not merely two souls... I am hundreds!"

CHAPTER THIRTY-TWO

INTRUDER.

Clinton seemed almost stuck to the spot. The pounding of his pulse mingled with the rustling of the tree's leaves. He was certain his mind was not playing tricks on him, that he had seen something move in the branches, yet he could not say for sure what it was. His feline pupils expanded, helping him to see more clearly in the dark, and he took a step closer.

A nimble shadow slipped through the foliage, swinging from branch to branch. Clinton's hackles rose and his shoulders hunched, but as soon as he moved, the shadow disappeared, vanishing before he could catch another glimpse of it.

"Who are you?" he hollered.

A snapping noise came from the other side of the giant tree trunk. Clinton sprang forward like a flash, circling the circumference to catch the culprit, but only fluttering leaves and a swaying branch greeted him.

"Come out and tell me what you want!" he growled. "Who are you?"

High up in the bleachers a wefring darted off into the night. Clinton slipped around the trunk again, straining to hear any other sounds, yet before he knew it he had arrived back at the start.

"Look, I'm going," he shouted. "Do you hear me? I don't want any trouble. I'm just gonna get out of here and leave you be."

He turned to make for the player's tunnel, intending to put as much distance between himself and the stranger, when the lion tripped over a jutting object. With lightning fast reactions he rolled forward and sprung back to his feet, throwing his clawed hands out defensively.

"I told you I don't want any trouble," he snapped, his voice echoing around the bleachers.

A small flock of zilers took off, followed by another couple of wefrings. Clinton watched them speed away into the night sky, but when he lowered his head he caught sight of what had made him stumble.

A cloth bag had been left on the ground.

He surveyed his surroundings before finally nudging the bag with his toes.

Nothing happened.

Dragging it over to a patch of moonlight, he tentatively pulled open its drawstrings and tipped its contents onto the ground. Objects fell onto the grass with metallic clangs. Clinton gasped as a lump formed in his throat. His shoulders slumped and all fear ebbed from him. He dropped to his knees and reached out to touch the fallen objects, but yanked his hand back at the last possible moment, fearful that it was still somehow a trap.

"Is-is this a game? Are you playing with me?" He reached out and nudged the lazarball armor. "I don't understand."

From the moment the gorespine had started its journey into the deep desert Clinton had assumed that all of his belongings would forever be lost to him, yet here he held in his hands his most cherished possessions. He shook his head, unable to fathom what was going on. A spark of warmth ignited in him.

The tree made another rustling sound.

He glanced up, placing the armor back by his feet. "Did you do this?" He stepped forward, peering up into the leafy canopy. "Who are you?"

The seconds slowly slipped away.

"Well, if you're not gonna come down, then I'm going to have to come up," he shouted, kicking off his boots and lengthening his clawed toes.

Launching himself into the tree, Clinton caught hold of a lower branch. His claws dug into the bark and he pulled himself up, rising to his feet. He curled his toes around the wood to stabilize himself. "I'm not going to harm you," he promised. "I just want to know how you got my armor."

He shuffled along the branches, scrambling from one limb to another. Twigs flicked against his face. He clawed through a thick patch of leaves, and pushed aside the foliage to reveal a crouching shadow leaning against the tree's trunk. A face stared back at him with two piercing eyes, a mouth full of pointed teeth, and a large, yellow forked tongue. A deep hiss rumbled from the creature's throat.

Clinton let out a startled yelp. Stumbling back, he slipped and plummeted through the weave of branches beneath him. The lion flipped onto his front...and slammed into the ground, forcing the breath from him. A flurry of leaves and twigs rained all around as he scrabbled away from the tree, craning to peer up through the hole he had created. He turned to grab his armor, but stopped dead in his tracks again. Perched atop of a large boulder sat the creature quietly staring at him.

* * *

Both anumals stood unmoving, intently watching each other as if frozen solid. The moon shone above the boulder as Clinton eyed the monster balanced on its top. The stranger lifted its hairless head. A snout protruded from its face the same color as the clouds - a shade of dirty gray. It assessed Clinton with a stony glare before it started to move. Carefully climbing down the boulder on all fours, it stalked closer, hugging the ground.

Clinton edged away. The creature crept after him, gradually eating away the distance between them until the lion could make it out in a bit more detail. It was a reptile, but one of such a size that Clinton had never seen before. The moon's rays caught the shape of its long, forked tongue whipping in and out of its mouth. Slowly the lizard raised itself up onto its two back legs, revealing a hefty looking tail. Its height and build completely dwarfed the lion, and he felt as if he was staring up at a giant. Clinton took another tentative step away, but stumbled back into the tree trunk. "I-if you're here to kill me then you're gonna have a fight on your hands."

The creature made no reply.

Clinton peered into the monster's bottomless eyes. "Do you hear me, lizard? I'll—"

"Lizard?" cut in the reptile, tilting his head. "Well, it may not be the worst name I have been called. However, I do resent the generalization...feline."

"What?" Clinton gasped, taken aback by the smooth voice. He found himself staring even harder, yet try as he might, he could not make out its features. "Well...stop hiding like a thief. Reveal yourself fully so I can identify you."

The lizard sniffed and then took a few sidesteps, slowly circling him. "First you call me a lizard, and now I am a thief?"

"Well...you tell me what you are. I'm not the one hiding in treetops, spying on folk."

The lizard chuckled under his breath. "I was not spying. I am merely a traveler, a servant if you will. But a thief? No, no, no." The creature stopped and stepped fully into the moonlight. "Most of all, though, I would like nothing better than to be called a friend."

Immersed in the moon's glow, Clinton could see the stranger in full detail. A powerful tail swung from side to side as his dark, reptilian eyes reflected the moon. His gray-green scaled arms ended in huge hands tipped with deadly looking black claws, and around his neck hung a necklace strung with bones and shells. The only clothing he wore was a pair of brown leather shorts and a few leather straps, while around his waist hung a belt attached with numerous pockets and pouches. Intricate and bold tattoos ran along the length of his arms, legs, across his chest, around his eyes and ear holes, and down his neck.

Clinton could not take his eyes off of them.

"Have you seen enough to settle your nerves?" asked the lizard, lifting his arms high so that he could be fully inspected. "Granted, I may not appear to be what you would class as normal in my appearance, yet I am confident you will be able to deduce that I am no mere thief."

"Then what are you?"

"A komodo," smiled the reptile with a slight nod.

"What? But...how?"

"Because that is what I am."

Clinton shook his head and simply stared. After a few seconds of silence, the komodo said, "Well, after that uncomfortable pause,

I think that it would be prudent to introduce myself." He bowed. "In these lands, friend, I am known as Hagen. Hagen of the Hand."

"You're a *komodo*?" Clinton finally gasped, standing up straight to get a better look at the creature. "But komodos are extinct. You were wiped out centuries ago."

Hagen grinned. "Were we? In that case I apologize. I seem to be breaking the rules…yet again. I must remember to tell my tribe the news that we no longer exist when I finally get the opportunity to speak to them."

Clinton's forehead furrowed. "S-so why has no one ever seen any of you then?"

"We have been seen, although granted not as frequently as in times past." Hagen inspected the ground. "The planet changed, and so too did our way of life. We chose to remain separated from anumalkind."

"All apart from you," Clinton noted.

"You could say that, yes. The faith of my Order, and the ways of the tribes, do not allow us komodos to wander the world at will. Like a spider in its web we walk along certain strands, down individual paths only permitted to us at birth. Nevertheless, you will have seen us, but you anumals do not truly look and so you never truly see."

"Well, I'm pretty sure I'd spot someone like you in a crowd," exclaimed Clinton. "I'd have to be blind not to."

"Well, unfortunately, Clinton, most anumals are blind in one respect or another."

"Wait!" snapped the lion, his eyes narrowing. "How do you know my name? And where did you get my armor from?"

Hagen folded his arms and leaned back, resting his weight against his tail. "I admit that I was watching you, yes."

"So you *were* spying!"

"I would not go as far as calling it spying."

"You can call it whatever you like as long as you tell me why you were doing it."

The komodo let out a strange rasping noise, and Clinton realized he was laughing.

"I was merely waiting for an opportunity to introduce myself, and to deliver your armor to you. That is all."

"But...why?"

Hagen cocked his head to the side. "It is a treasure of yours. I thought you would want it?"

"But how'd you...? And where...? And what about...?" A barrage of questions detonated in Clinton's head. However, one essential question remained at the forefront of them all. "Raion! Have you seen him? Is he okay? Is he upset or—"

Hagen held up a hand.

"Please, Clinton, your brother is fine. Yes, of course he is upset and desperate to see you again, but—"

"You saw him then? You spoke to him?"

"Not exactly, no. However, I have been informed that he is being cared for. You do have friends, lion, even if they cannot let their allegiance be seen in the light of day."

A weight seemed to lift from Clinton's chest, but at the same time another sank in his stomach. "So these friends, who are they? What are they doing? If they're—"

"Something we shall speak of later," interrupted the komodo. "There is much to discuss first and so little safe time in which to do it."

"Safe?"

"You will understand soon."

"But...But how did you know I'd even be here tonight? I stumbled across this place by accident."

"I knew you would be here because I have been following you. Even though I was out of sight, I have been present, watching and helping you, for a long time. Believe me, I am no newcomer to your perils."

The lion studied him for a moment. "Hey, wait! It was you, wasn't it, outside Jasper's Tavern? During the sandstorm with Graff and Barn?"

"Those two were merely setbacks, troubles you were not supposed to face."

"And my leg? You healed it, didn't you?"

Hagen grinned, and his harsh, reptilian features warmed.

"So why didn't you reveal yourself? Why'd you keep hiding from me?"

Hagen's smile vanished. He scanned the bleachers before looking back at Clinton. "I followed you across the Plains, giving a helping hand whenever I could...but I could not linger in the open for too long. It was of paramount importance that I kept my presence undetected until it was safe enough to reveal myself."

"And what about the sandstorm then? And Galront's attack? Did you make all those creatures appear?"

Hagen's face tightened as distress shaded his eyes. His tongue darted in and out of his mouth. "The ghastlings? No, that was not I. That was something else. Unfortunately from that one incident I was able to discern that events have been moving quicker than even I could have anticipated." His voice dropped. "They have not wasted any time at all."

"Who? Who hasn't wasted—"

"It is complicated, Clinton."

"Tell me what isn't complicated in my life. An extinct komodo turns up at a random location telling me he can't be seen by anyone, and that others haven't been wasting their time in doing whatever skorr knows what. It's all totally scrudding crystal clear to me. It really is." Clinton kicked a rock through the long grass and ran his hand through his hair. "I just don't understand how you knew I'd be here. I only decided to come today."

"Oh, no," Hagen chuckled. "Tonight was decided centuries ago for you. There may have been many paths that led you here, but get here you would...eventually."

The lion stared at him, unsure whether the lizard was laughing at his expense.

Hagen's hairless eyebrows lifted in thought. "I can see that I may need to elucidate.

"Many years ago while meditating on my home island of Orakomo, my mind was touched by the strands of fate." He turned to peer up at the moon while recalling his story. "I was searching, you see, as my ancestors had done since the dawning of the age of the anumal. However, that day I finally found it, and within seconds, my life was irrevocably changed.

"I was yanked through time and space, shown something we Sensors had all been desperate to see: clues to the whereabouts of a Soul of Power – one that was locked in torture." Hagen lowered his gaze to peer at the lion stood before him. "It was a soul with the ability to save and protect...it was your soul I saw that day, Clinton. You."

"*What?*"

Hagen adjusted his belt, making his pouches rustle. "I will explain more about that later, but for now be settled with the fact that you have arrived here safe and sound, right where you needed to be."

"A special soul? That's insane," he laughed, the whole situation becoming too much for him to take seriously. "This is me you're talking about. I'm here by accident. It was just bad luck—"

"Or so you think." Hagen pushed against his tail and rose up to his full height. The glow of the moon highlighted his muscular physique. "But like it or not, you must know the facts in order to be prepared. Like I said, they have already begun."

"Who? What are you talking about?"

"To go into the world ignorant would only bring about our destruction."

Clinton stepped forward. "*Our* destruction?"

"Yes, for while you are blissfully unaware you possess immeasurable power within you...others are not."

Clinton shook his head. "Thanks, but this is ridiculous. Look, I don't know who you're looking for, but trust me, I'm no scrudding super soul or whatever it was you said."

"Appearances can be deceptive."

"Not this time."

"Clinton, you can only ever discover the real anumal by probing beneath the surface."

"Yeah, but you don't know me or what I've been through, because if you did, well, you wouldn't be saying any of this scavenger spit. I'm a nobody! Look at me, I'm nothing."

"If you were nothing then I would not be able to see or hear you, lion, you simply would not be there. And since I *can* see you standing in front of me, maybe you should start believing that you are indeed – how would you say it – a somebody."

"Listen, don't get me wrong, Hagen, and I appreciate you trying and everything, but I really do think you've got the wrong lion."

"I do not think, I know I have the right one. Test me if you wish, or should I mention your recent troubles brought about by smuggling food from Galront's compound? Or the time Raion trapped himself in the slum's flood pipes? Or how you overcame your fear of the dark to rescue him? Funny how it took that little adventure for you to realize you could see shapes in the dark with your feline vision.

"You like boval milk and Fangton's snacks, but you find leece meat a tad stringy. And however much you pretend to Raion that you like his oatmeal, you still think it tastes like grack dung. Teya Farnik was your first love. However, she was too interested in that Burnjaw child so she never noticed you in class. She eventually moved to Gelderfield, but you still think of her at times.

"You had a collection of oddly shaped scavenger bones that reminded you of some village members. You kept those under your bed. Raion lost most of them, while the others were destroyed in the fire. Oh, and what about the initials you carved on the back of one of the needle-trees at Brook Manor? Or should I call it Well Wood? Mayor Ferris was never able to get rid of them." Hagen smiled a lopsided grin. "Oh, yes, it is small things like that which are most effective."

Clinton gaped.

"Would you like me to continue? I have many more examples I could relate…although some are a tad embarrassing."

Clinton stood there, his jaw sagging, and shook his head.

"Good, because I need you to trust me, Clinton. The day that you were forced out from behind the security of Wooburn's high fence was when the gamefield changed. Yet it was inevitable. I know that life there was tough, but believe me when I say

233

Wooburn was the only thing that kept you protected. Things could have been a lot worse... A lot worse. To our enemies, anumals are nothing but pawns, but you, Clinton, you are different."

The lion swallowed, trying to think of something to say. He watched Hagen, and the sight of the komodo felt like a weird dream coming to life.

"I need to know whether you are ready for the responsibility? Are you prepared to know your true path in life?"

Looking at the sky, Clinton realized that tonight he was about to embark on an adventure he had not even been aware existed until that very moment. Yet he felt as certain as he had ever been. He nodded his head.

"Tell me. I want to know everything."

CHAPTER THIRTY-THREE

WHEN TWO SOULS COLLIDE.

"I am one of the last remaining Entwined to inhabit the planet."

Marama's words sank in as Dallas let her voice wash over him, feeling its power. Common sense told him he had no reason to doubt her words - she knew things about him, things that no one else did, and she undoubtedly knew more. He looked into her ruby eyes and came to realize that however much he wanted to dismiss her story, he truly did believe her. The scene around Dallas slowly began to fade away into a gray void. The only thing that could be seen was the shape of the shadow-lizard and its pinprick eyes.

"This planet is lacking ambition," she said, snatching Dallas away from his thoughts. Nightmare, as always, remained motionless by the tiger's side. "The ruling powers know nothing of advancement. Each day is merely endured until the next one dawns, where the cycle begins afresh. They wallow in their insignificance, never looking for a new horizon."

Ferris Lakota popped into Dallas's mind.

"Yet there were once those who strived to change this, Entwined who searched to ensure order and prosperity. We clung on to existence by the barest of threads, unable to stay for long within an organic vessel before it became tainted, driven mad, or twisted with the vast power we possess. We inhabited thousands of bodies, yet none of us could survive the vessels for very long."

A chorus of shrieks filled the gray void. From behind Marama's shadow shot countless floating forms, whipping in and out of one another in a wild ecstasy. They swooped high like a vortex, before turning in the air and arrowing back at Dallas, their decaying fingers reaching out for his living flesh...

The void suddenly burst into an inferno.

Dallas stepped back as intense flames erupted all around. The ghastling nearest to the tiger exploded in a rage of fire. It thrashed and flailed in midair before its cloak disintegrated. Charred bones disappeared into the wall of flames as the other ghastlings swooped back to their mistress, taking refuge in her shadowy form again.

Dallas shielded his face out of reflex, but realized that he felt no heat. He tentatively moved his fingers closer to the blaze and raised an eyebrow when not even the slightest singe or burn appeared.

"What the…"

His words, however, were stolen away when he turned back to face Marama. The richly textured shadow of a dragon now snaked in and out of the flames, its red eyes blazing with obvious desire.

"Fixated on their quest for power," she continued, "the Entwined dwindled. Time and again an Entwined spirit would lose their sanity within their fragile vessel and turn against those around them. Yet I was different. Unlike the others, I would not allow my knowledge to be lost to time, damning us to remain in this state forever. And so I waited, longing for a power to be delivered back to Earth." She paused to hoist her head up, gazing into the burning chaos of the flames. "As predicted, the cosmos finally bestowed upon us another of its celestial ploys. It sent unto us a being of purity, a beautiful power like none before, a power so great that to harness it would mean domination."

"A weapon?" Dallas asked.

Marama leaned forward. Her shadowy head pressed through the blaze, looming only a few arm spans from him. "Oh, no. This is much more than that. Picture many souls, pure souls aware of the true order of life, and merged like an Entwined spirit. Now imagine the consequences if this spirit fractured and separated in two pieces again."

"Split? But how?"

"Within all of you exists a multitude of instincts, some primal, harking back from your animal heritage, and others more akin to your human predecessors. Yet one set of these instincts are relative to both races…the instinct of fight or flight.

"These urges ignited within the Entwined spirit as it rushed to Earth, causing it to fracture into two components. One half sought safety to ensure survival, but the other wanted so badly to inhabit a vessel that it continued…thus defining the way it split."

"So one half fled while the other remained to take the vessel?"

Dallas asked, rubbing his chin. "Why run away? It should have stayed, taken the spoils and grown in power."

"If only it were that simple," muttered Nightmare.

"Wade is correct," agreed Marama.

The tiger glanced over his shoulder, realizing the seeress was referring to the panther as Wade. After a second, the tiger said, "So what became of the souls?"

"The fracture was more traumatic than either half expected. They needed time to recoup. In search of sanctuary, the two fractures traveled the cosmos, where they remained for centuries before finally finding their way back to this planet. Understand exactly what I am telling you, Dallas. These pure souls became one Entwined spirit, and then split apart again, slicing the raw energy into two different forms. They achieved everything an Entwined had ever craved: the ability to occupy a living vessel without consuming them with their power. So, in this one instance, evolution did not so much as step boldly forwards, it stumbled. You see an Entwined spirit had the ability to Join with the living…and survive the process."

"And this affects me how?"

The shadow-dragon studied Dallas closer. Her burning eyes were as narrow as dagger slashes. "The Crystal Soul, as it is called, remained for an age in flux, deliberating what, and whom, the perfect vessel should be. This soul clung to its need to survive, to protect and provide, and gained strength from its willpower and abstinence. While the opposing half, the Shadow Soul, consumed with a desire to grow and flourish, had a more rapid recovery. Plunging to Earth, it spent centuries searching for the right vessel, one less susceptible to fault or physical weakness. It tested many vessels before one finally emerged that could retain its power and harness its full potential. And from then onwards it grew mightier than I could have ever wished."

"So this Shadow Soul, it killed other vessels? Other anumals?"

"Infants, adults, even the old. It tested hundreds. Yet such is the price for finding perfection. You see, Dallas, for many years I searched for this being, *we* searched this planet, relentless in our quest for its discovery."

"And once we found it, we waited for the time when it could emerge and assume its rightful position within the world." Marama spread her wings in a breathtaking display of power. "And the time for his ascension has finally arrived, for that anumal, Dallas, that Shadow Soul, is in you."

The flames blasted with such ferocity that the tiger flinched back. He stared vacantly into the conflagration, trying to comprehend the enormity of the secret he had just been told. His mind grew clouded by reason, insisting it could only be nonsense, but wedged within that pillar of doubt existed the tiniest shard of belief. He had always known there was something more to him.

"I have waited an age for the birth of the Souls of Power, Dallas, and planned for a future that can now be made real. To unite these souls again, to fuse them back into one entity, would create the greatest being of all time. It would be a creature with such power that its very existence could throw the evolution of anumalkind back into the fires of skorr."

Dallas's mouth felt bone dry, but he remained focused as he listened.

"I am referring to the legend that is the Primarian Beast," she purred.

"The...Primarian Beast? I have never heard of it."

Marama's gaze fixed on him, examining the tiger through the fire. "Legend foretells that the creation of the Primarian Beast will be the result of the merging of two powerful souls, two Entwined souls that were primarily one. It is said that the beast will rise and usher in a new dawn of existence...the next stage in evolution."

Dallas swallowed, finally allowing himself to wet his throat. He turned to regard the panther, before slowly turning back to her blood red eyes again. "I-I do not understand."

"Do you ever feel the whisperings of power trickle through you when you're near pain? Or feel empowered by your anger? These emotions are like a fuel for you. You control others, and this gives you a sense of peace. But when an anumal disregards your natural order..."

Clinton's face sprang up in the tiger's mind, immediately stirring his anger. "I can think of a perfect example."

"Yet I recall a time in your childhood when your sense of order was challenged. It was a time you showed a spark of your potential. It was because of the mayor's son if I remember correctly? You never liked him, did you, that Harris boy? And even though you resided with their family, you were nothing more than a decoration to improve the mayor's public persona."

"I do not see what this has got to do with anything," he snapped, folding his arms.

"Oh, but it has. You see, my spies informed me of a certain evening when you lost your temper and told the Lakota family exactly what you thought of them. And then you became angry."

Marama's eyes held a hungry glimmer to them. "It might have taken the mayor and a few of his guards to finally wrestle you to your room, but by that point you were beyond reconciliation." Her huge neck coiled coquettishly. "So what was it that you did again?"

Dallas grimaced. "I-I smashed through the window," he shrugged. "I would not be held captive, so I jumped into the backyard. What has this to do with anything?"

"You jumped from the second story, and though you broke your elbow you still refused to make a sound, even when you realized you landed in the pen."

"The pen? Reky's pen? I do not—"

"You landed in the pen," Marama repeated. "And the mayor's finest racing beast attacked you."

Dallas forehead furrowed. He tried his hardest to recall that night, but was met with nothing but blurred images. He shook his head. "I... No..."

"It had you cornered. Your life was in danger, and so you took action."

The tiger had a vague recollection of the Lakota's cruzer - a sleek reptilian-like scavenger, with powerful hind legs and huge arching horns that provided the rider with a means of steering it. Dallas knew he could not have possibly stood a chance if the cruzer had started to buck or attack him within its enclosure, but he shrugged off the humiliation. "Well...well, there is nothing shameful about a child fleeing from a scavenger pen."

"Oh, no, Dallas. You didn't run and hide." Her eyes glowed with motherly pride. "You reacted. Reacted with every ounce of bitterness and hatred that you were feeling. And when the mayor heard the screams in his backyard, he found you sitting amongst the remains of his finest racing beast, covered head to toe in blood."

Dallas shook his head, irritated that he could not recall anything of what she was describing. He turned to peer at Nightmare, but the panther merely raised an eyebrow.

"You did not just kill it, Dallas, you tore it to pieces. Is that not right, Wade?" The panther nodded in reply. "And as the Lakotas stared at you with dawning horror, you gazed back at them through fresh eyes."

Vague flashes of memory resurfaced in the tiger's mind: blood-soaked stable walls and the sound of a cruzer's horn being snapped in two with his bare hands. He felt the anger and the loneliness still lingering inside him even after all these years, but more than anything he felt the longing to simply destroy.

"You single-handedly killed a cruzer."

"And what if I did?" he shrugged. "It should not have attacked me."

"One of the scavengers responsible for more domestic deaths than any other—"

"I had to!"

"DALLAS!" Marama's yell stirred the fire into a rage again. "Dallas, my dear tiger, you were only seven years old."

Dallas blinked. What the Seeress was saying was correct; what she had said all along was completely true. Everything. He could feel a power inside of him, something that had always hidden just out of his reach, like a wick waiting for a spark. But now, now he was aware of what that spark was. Like a scab ready to be torn off, he knew he could discard his old life to discover his true potential.

"That night," Dallas said, as more images flicked through his memory. "I ran away. Where did I go?"

"That is of no consequence. What is important is that you were found and taken back to safety." Marama's voice had sharpened with unease. "And from that moment on, life in Wooburn became very different for you. They feared you, Dallas, and thus your ascension began."

A smile grew on his face. "Ferris never questioned or shouted at me again. And the guards, his advisors, all of them, reluctantly obeyed my orders."

"And would this have happened if they thought you were just a normal anumal? Or do you think they saw a glimmer of the hidden Dallas, the *real* power within you?"

Dallas nodded, feeling the missing pieces finally slotting into place. "Yes...you are right."

"Then you should be aware that to merge with the other fractured soul would mean even more power being directed into your own vessel. The power you feel now would be nothing in comparison to what you would wield as the Primarian Beast."

Dallas took in the sight of the inferno, Marama's sinuous dragon form, and Nightmare still anchored behind him. Yet there remained one question.

"So what is the catch?"

"There is no catch," Nightmare answered. "You have grown and come of age. However, there is much to be done."

The dragon's head drooped. "The manipulation of the soul can only be performed by beings of immense power, beings with the knowledge of the ritual involved. This burden will be mine, of course. Ultimately, though, it will be your responsibility to claim your own birthright and the glories that accompany it."

"And what will you gain from it all? There must be something in it for you."

"What will I gain?" she laughed. "My dear, Dallas, I shall see my planet become what it always should have been. I shall see peace as a new world rises."

Dallas waited for more, but Marama did not elaborate.

"And this Crystal Soul?" he asked, slowly. "What will it gain?"

"The ritual demands a price, and only one vessel, the strongest vessel, can survive the merging. That is the reason why the Shadow Soul tested so many."

"So one anumal will die? The anumal who does not host both souls will be expended?"

"Correct. But Dallas, you are strong of body and of will. We shall prepare you so the Crystal Soul will surrender long before you do. You must rise in power, both within yourself and across the planet. Your power, your domination, will feed the soul inside and make it strong…stronger than its polar opposite, ensuring its survival when merged."

Dallas mulled over her words. "But will I be altered when the Crystal Soul is a part of me? Will I even feel like me afterwards?"

"You shall find yourself enhanced in ways you could never imagine," she hissed. "The Primarian Beast will be flawless. You will be the perfection of evolution, and the father of a master race. You will command all and be worshiped by the whole planet."

The tiger's frown morphed into a hungry smile. He chuckled as if he was drunk on the mere possibility of what he could achieve. His chuckle turned into a laugh, and the more he laughed, the more her proposal seemed likely to become reality. "You say we alone will control this power?" he asked, almost out of breath. "That we will rule everything? That I will be the dominant… The alpha?"

"Correct."

All at once he stopped laughing. His smile vanished and he glared at Marama with pure, insatiable greed.

"Then give it to me!"

In the next moment the fire abruptly vanished. Like time had been spun in reverse the justice house walls, floor, and ceiling reformed with breathtaking speed, attaching themselves back to reality before his very eyes. Piece by piece, wooden panel by wooden panel the room rebuilt. In the space of a few seconds, Dallas found himself standing in the darkened courtroom again, staring at a dim light glimmering around the stained glass window. Crawling along the surface of the glass scuttled the shadow seeress in the form of a giant spider.

Night had fallen. The moon's rays shone through the glass, lighting up the room as yet another of the chandelier's blue flames extinguished with a dull pop. He realized he must have been in there for hours.

"So be it!" she answered, her multi-voice acquiring an alien clicking resonance.

The tiger took a hesitant step next to the rim of the dais, unsure whether the walls or floor were stable yet. "What happens now then? Where do we begin?"

"Begin?" She let out a short laugh. "This began long before you were even born. The pieces have been in place for years. You are entering the game in its final stages. Training your power is tantamount for now, but when you are stronger you must achieve one thing: locate the Crystal Soul and bring it to me."

Unprompted, as if he had been waiting for a signal, Nightmare stepped up next to Dallas's shoulder. His voice remained flat. "You say he is to find the Crystal Soul, but what of the guardian, mistress? Have you received word of the armies?"

The window's unnatural light faded away.

"I have searched, Wade, but no word has yet reached me of his whereabouts, or of the Sensors. My servants have reported no news of their camps, yet we must not assume they are ignorant to current events."

"This is a war fought on many fronts. I shall prepare for any eventuality, mistress."

"Be ready to strike at the first hint of movement," answered the spider, her silhouette gradually fading as she vanished into the depths of the glass surface. "They will act with deadly precision if they know the pact has been broken. They will unite the tribes. Yet I have made contact with the east, and soon the great armies will be ready for your command. With such power even the united strength of the Sensors will be rendered meaningless. And with the pact broken, they will retaliate. But that should be no great burden for you to bear, should it, Nightmare?"

The panther finally cracked a smile.

An unsettling feeling washed over Dallas. "What Sensors?

What guardian? What are you not telling me?"

"It is of little importance. Merely safeguards to ensure your protection."

"Protection?" he scoffed. "I need no one's protection."

Nightmare raised an eyebrow. "Really."

Dallas sneered back at him. "You talk of power and protection and broken pacts, yet you have still failed to tell me one thing. This Crystal Soul... Who is it?"

The whispery voice filtered through the rafters of the courtroom, only just managing to reach his ears. "Come, come, Dallas. Do you really need me to answer that?"

After a couple of heartbeats, Dallas sighed. "So he is still alive."

"Only just...had I not intervened and brought an end to your ambush."

"Then there would have been no Primarian Beast," he observed. "So what happened to the hunters I sent?"

"Do they matter?"

Dallas let out a short bark of a laugh. "No."

With that, Marama vanished, leaving the two felines to contemplate her words. Everything in Wooburn was normal again...apart from Dallas.

Nightmare's low voice rumbled next to him like the promise of thunder. "Savor this moment, youngster. Today you start your life anew."

Dallas stared at the panther before making his way down the dais stairs. "So...Wade," he smiled. "I guess we have work to do."

CHAPTER THIRTY-FOUR

CLINTON'S QUEST.

Above the Idlefields at Samanoski Stadium, the wind gently blew Clinton's straw-colored hair. His eyes had glazed over, staring open mouthed at the cross-legged komodo sitting atop the boulder.

"So this Crystal Soul," he finally managed to say. "You're certain it's me?"

"That is correct."

The large tree in the center of the stadium swayed in the breeze. Its leaves rustled. Clinton carefully walked over to where he had slung his boots and the backpack full of newly acquired karla fruit, trying to grasp the full extent of Hagen's tale. "So do you mean that Dallas is my brother?"

"Well...yes and no." The komodo pondered his reply. "You are both part of the same Entwined being, yet you remain two separate physical entities. But spiritually...? Well, that is another matter entirely."

"So is he...a copy of me? Like we're the same anumal underneath our skin?"

"No, Clinton, you are not the same anumal. However, you are linked. You are both independent, but polarized, spirits - opposites of each other. His power is drawn from his initial need to covet, dominate, and control. You, on the other hand, find your strength from different virtues like honor, courage, and hope."

"Courage?" huffed Clinton. "But you're telling me that my natural instinct is to be a coward." He sat down on a rock to pull a boot on. "I run away, Hagen. That's what the Crystal Soul does, and it's what I've done best all my life."

"Yet it means so much more than that. To take flight is not to be cowardly. To take flight is to preserve and protect, to weigh all the options, to use one's wisdom and to guard those you care for. You will come to understand it in time. Seeing another anumal beaten does not to boost your powers."

"Unlike Dallas, you mean." The lion pulled on his remaining boot. "Anyway, this so-called mighty force you say is inside me, why have I never felt it? Why hasn't it emerged to help me when I was in trouble?"

"But it has," nodded Hagen, slowly.

Clinton jumped to his feet. "I'm sure I'd know if something had happened to me. And, trust me, there've been no bolts of lightning shooting out of my backside recently…" The lion stopped speaking as memories popped into his head: the tournament, the flashback, the feeling of time slowing, the odd behavior of the leece, and the way he had scored against Harris Lakota. "No…that was just…"

"And yet you question it."

"Or it could have been exhaustion. Besides, I can't remember any other times it's happened. And if it did, then I've obviously—"

"Forgotten," finished Hagen. "Yet I can remember an instance when your power surfaced. It was a time when you actually saved Dallas's life."

"What?" Clinton wanted to deny Hagen's claims, but he was quickly learning to accept the komodo's facts as truth. "I saved Dallas? But we've always hated one another for as long as I can remember."

"Yet, even so, he owes you his life. You see, Clinton, when Dallas was still a cub he accidentally discovered he was very different from most others. The night I am referring to was when Dallas savagely killed the mayor's pet and then fled into the Plains. He took to the dessert, cold, alone, and confused. And do you know why?"

"I've…no idea."

"In his distress, the Shadow Soul subconsciously searched for you while you were out hunting. You became like a beacon to him, and he was drawn to you. After you discovered him in the desert, Grayorr took him back to Well Wood where Loretta nursed and fed him - your mother was quite the healer."

Clinton nodded in agreement.

"Your parents had no idea what had happened to him, yet they never questioned the situation. They saw an anumal in need, and they helped. They let Dallas sleep in the bed next to your own while Grayorr went to inform the mayor."

"This is all news to me," huffed Clinton. "I remember being in the Plains with my father and Arkie - I've got the proof of that on my ribs…but I don't remember anything of Dallas."

Hagen nodded. "When the mayor came with his guards, he did not see how unnaturally fast the tiger was healing, or how your own ribs had improved. Ferris demanded the tiger be taken back to his home. He said your father was attempting to steal him away, accusing Grayorr of kidnapping the cub for his own political gain."

"But he only ever tried to help."

"Yes, and if it had not been for you and your family, Dallas may well never have survived. Yet, from that night onwards, life began to change for the Narfell family. Within days of the incident, the memory was wiped clear from your mind. And your parents—"

"Disappeared." Clinton bowed his head. "Do you think Dallas remembers any of this?"

"That I very much doubt." Hagen carefully toyed with a shell pendant around his neck. "These things were deemed best forgotten…for everyone's benefit. However, I am digressing. Needless to say, Dallas was raised to detest the Narfell name, and I'm sure you know how the rest goes."

"But I was always told everyone hated us because my father caused Wooburn's downfall."

"Unfortunately, they were led to believe that was so, but that does not make it true. No one player can cause the collapse of a team. No, Grayorr did not cause the slump, but even so, it gave Dallas a purpose - it gave him a reason to justify his anger and frustration."

Clinton sat on a boulder and buried his head in his hands. A floodgate of questions and answers had been unlocked. Memories begun to surface, happier times when all seemed well with the world. The mention of his past bought one question to his mind though. He took a deep breath and looked up at Hagen.

"You seem to know everything about my life, so tell me, what exactly happened to my parents?"

Hagen peered off into the sky, his eyes glistening. "It took a great power to be able to steal them from you. It was a terrible loss…" His voice trailed away before he looked back at the lion with renewed determination.

"But?" asked Clinton.

"But the truth remains unclear, at least to me. However, I do know that dark forces have resurfaced, and they will use you for their own ends. That is why I am here, to protect you from them."

Clinton slowly meandered off in the direction of the tree, swiping at the grass with his feet. In the distance, through the crumbling walls of Samanoski Stadium, he could see the first signs of morning beginning to stir along the horizon.

"So what am I supposed to do now then?" he asked, leaning against the giant trunk.

Hagen jumped down from the boulder. "What it is you feel you must do."

"Well, I don't want to be alone anymore." His voice showed the burden of isolation that Raion and he had endured for most of their lives. "I just want to be happy again, like I was when my parents were alive. Also a wagonload of credits wouldn't go amiss." He chuckled, before his face dropped. "But…but most of all I want Raion. Above all things I want my brother back."

Hagen nodded in understanding.

Clinton peered up at the bleachers, seemingly searching the stone seats for an answer. "I just want to see him again. I never got to say goodbye properly. I know you told me he's safe, but I won't truly believe it until he's by my side again."

"Well, your life belongs to you. It always has. If you say you want Raion, then we will make it happen."

The lion gasped.

"Clinton?" The komodo's eyes narrowed. "Is everything alright?"

He did not respond.

"Clinton?"

The lion's stomach knotted with dread. A surge of panic swept through his body, making his palms clammy.

Hagen's tongue snaked out to taste the air for danger. "What is the matter?"

"I don't know," he whispered, peering up at the bleachers again. "But something's definitely wrong."

"What?" Hagen spun around to scan the seats. "What do you see?"

Clinton's focus remained fixed. His eyes widened as he watched the ghostly figure of a badger glide amongst the uppermost rows. From where Clinton stood, the spectral form appeared as the size of a knat, and its appearance could mean only one thing...

"I think we're in trouble."

"Why? What is it?"

The lion opened his mouth to speak, but stopped again.

"Clinton, as long as I am here, then nothing will harm you. Maybe fatigue is playing tricks with your eyes?"

"But I can still see the badger, and every time I see him, bad things happen."

"Badger?" gasped Hagen, his head whipping back to the bleachers again. "Where?"

The ground made a slight rumble before the lion had a chance to reply. Yet as quickly as the sound resonated, it ceased again, leaving Clinton wondering whether he had heard anything at all. He glanced back at Hagen and saw him frozen with tension. A flurry of leaves drifted down from the tree when some wefrings took flight.

"Are you sure it was a badger?"

The lion's face dropped. "Why? What's going on?"

The komodo remained silently scanning the bleachers.

"Hagen, what is it?"

The komodo raised his hand, signaling for silence. He sniffed the air, his yellow tongue flickering in and out while turning in a circle, surveying the entire structure. Clinton could only stare as Hagen's hairless head darted from left to right, up and down, trying to detect the slightest trace of danger. For a brief moment the tattoos and markings over the komodo's body shimmered with blue light. Stillness settled all around. And then, all at once, the ground shook beneath their feet.

"What *is* that?" demanded Clinton, feeling the rhythmic shaking. "They're like huge—"

"Footsteps."

"But whose?"

Hagen raised his hand again for silence.

"I knew it!" snapped Clinton. "Stuff like this happens every time I see that scrudding badger."

"Gather your things," ordered the komodo, ushering him over to the pile of armor and his backpack. "We need to leave immediately."

The tremors grew increasingly more defined.

Clinton emptied the karla fruit from the backpack and stuffed his armor inside. "Why? What can you smell? It's not those ghastling things is it? Don't tell me they're—"

"No, this is something different."

"Then what?"

"I think that we are about to find out..." Hagen repositioned himself between the lion and the stadium's far wall. "Ready yourself."

"For what?"

A silence blanketed them so thick it was almost palpable, before a high-pitched shriek blasted through the stadium. The tremors intensified.

"I just realized why there are so many bones here," muttered Hagen, his eyes widening with recognition.

A deafening sound of collapsing stone made them jump back in shock. A section of the far stadium exploded into a pile of rubble, spitting boulders down upon the gamefield. Again a thunderous scream erupted into the morning air and a cloud of dust billowed outwards. What remained of the wall toppled, revealing a cave that led deep into the mountainside.

"We have a visitor," observed Hagen. He grabbed the lion's forearm and pulled him in the direction of the player's tunnel. "Run, Clinton! We have to run!"

Even though the komodo appeared calm, the lion could detect

fear in his voice.

"What *is* it, Hagen?"

"Kraggon."

That one word made Clinton snap back to his senses. An unparalleled fear primed his every muscle. He stared at the other end of the stadium and finally caught sight of movement from within the cave. Emerging through the waves of cascading dust, with another ear-tickling shriek, pounded a fully-grown kraggon.

CHAPTER THIRTY-FIVE

THE END AND THE BEGINNING.

Clinton gasped at the sheer size of the creature emerging before him.

"Run, Clinton. Run!" hollered Hagen.

The kraggon began to pound after them, swinging its pincer-like arms in front of its giant body, smashing everything out of its way. Even bigger than a gorespine, its head was an ugly collection of sweeping spikes, with two rows of oversized teeth lining its jaws. An ebony exoskeleton of hard, steel-like bones protected the creature from the outside, hiding its vulnerable internal organs. Down the back of its head and along the ridge of its burgundy-black scaled spine, ran thousands of tiny needle-like spikes, decreasing in size until they ended at the tip of its thick, swaying tail. Six spindly legs propelled the creature forward at an awesome speed as its pincer-like feet plowed into the grass, tearing up patches of turf with every step. The kraggon trumpeted a sharp cry and increased its speed.

An immense cracking noise filled the stadium as the kraggon smashed into the ancient tree. There was a long whooshing sound and a tremendous crash as the trunk slammed into the ground. Thick roots catapulted into the air, showering mud, leaves, and sectoids in every direction.

Clinton snatched another glance over his shoulder, transfixed by the monster, before picking up his pace. If he was indeed the Crystal Soul, the soul of flight, then he was doing a great job of it that morning. He had never run so fast.

As they approached the player's tunnel the kraggon sprang at them, lengthening its front arms and spreading its pincers wide in anticipation.

"JUMP!" hollered the komodo.

Hagen shoved the lion ahead, his claws digging into his skin and nearly drawing blood. Unable to stop his momentum, Clinton tumbled into the tunnel like a rag doll. He fell into a forward roll before scrabbling even deeper into the opening. Hagen followed, flying over the lion's head. Diving into a roll, he sprang to his feet without pause.

The light in the tunnel suddenly dimmed, followed by a colossal crash. The kraggon smacked into the entrance and rebounded onto its back with a scream of fury. It thrashed around for a second, but flipped onto its feet and rammed against the opening, attempting to widen the hole. The frantic creature shoved a pincer through the entrance and swiped it through the air, attempting to capture its prey. When that did not work it rammed its head inside the tunnel again, snapping its jaws in a frenzy. Clinton and Hagen moved back, neither daring to take their eyes off the enraged monster. With a frustrated whimper, the scavenger shouldered the entrance again and scratched at the walls like a mutt eager for a bone.

"Clinton, we should go."

As soon as the scavenger heard the komodo speak it went wild. The creature butted its head against the entrance with increased force, making the ceiling shake.

"You said it was prophesized I'd end up here, right?" snapped Clinton, setting his armor by his feet to catch his breath. "Then couldn't they have warned us it was going to be a scrudding kraggon's nest?"

Hagen's head cocked to the side. "Well, I must admit it would have been helpful."

The komodo chuckled, and Clinton joined in.

Hagen glanced up at the roof and his smile vanished.

"Watch out!"

He dove at Clinton, ramming into the lion and forcing him aside as a boulder slammed into the ground. The tip of the kraggon's pincers pierced through the ceiling, bringing down even more stones. Spindly kraggon arms swiped in front of them as they swerved and darted through the chaos. The scavenger flailed manically, blindly searching for them, and forcing Clinton to slide under a pincer and graze his chest. Hagen, however, did not break his stride. He ran up the wall and flipped past the kraggon, soaring off to safer ground. Both anumals continued to run, spinning past falling debris and ducking below sliding rocks, as the creature smashed through the stones above. And then a thought suddenly struck Clinton, causing him to skid to a stop.

"My armor!" he yelled, looking back along the passageway. "I left my armor."

"Keep running!"

"No, I won't leave it again."

Hagen blocked his path. "Do not worry, Clinton, I will retrieve it for you."

Before the lion could protest, Hagen sped off.

In a blur of movement the komodo glided over the rocks and boulders like a ghost, never stopping, always running, until he reached the backpack. Snatching up the bag, he hoisted it over his shoulder and turned back to make his escape. There was a groaning sound above and, bit-by-bit, the ceiling started to collapse around him.

"LOOK OUT!" yelled Clinton.

A deafening crash filled the tunnel. A cloud of dust surged out, obscuring his sight. He covered his eyes with his arm, coughing all the while.

"Hagen?" he managed to shout. "Hagen, are you hurt?"

The whole tunnel had caved in.

"Hagen!" He wanted to run into the chaos and clear the stones. "Hagen…? Answer me!"

More rocks fell, promising to also block Clinton's escape, as the scavenger's cries turned frantic.

"Hang on!" Clinton yelled. "I'm coming."

Something thudded above, and a large figure crashed through the ceiling to land behind him. He span around to see Hagen rising to his feet. With one hand he wiped dirt from his shoulders, and with the other he held Clinton's bag of armor.

"Hagen!"

The komodo shrugged. "Well, that was certainly interesting."

Clinton glanced up at the hole. "What happened?"

"Let us say that the kraggon is not having a particularly good day."

Clinton opened his mouth to speak when the scavenger rammed its head through the opening. Three vicious claw marks had been scored into its skull. The monster snapped a savage bite before slipping a long arm through another hole behind the komodo. Without warning, its pincer snapped around the hand holding the bag, and Hagen was jerked back.

"HAGEN!"

A triumphant bellow echoed along the confines of the tunnel. The kraggon yanked its head free from the hole and pulled the komodo after it.

"No!" yelled Clinton, running up the pile of rubble as the komodo was hoisted off towards the bleachers. He grabbed on to the komodo's feet. Hagen glanced down. Their eyes locked.

"Do something!" hollered the lion. "Fight back!"

"Let go of my leg, Clinton. Trust me."

"But—"

"Let go and cover your ears. Cover them now."

Clinton could not understand the komodo's logic, but as he saw him close his eyes in concentration, the lion knew he had better do as instructed. He let go of Hagen and dropped to the ground, clamping his hands firmly over his ears. Hagen turned to the kraggon and hissed, teeth bared, while his long tongue flickered. With his index finger, he tapped a sequence of tattoos around his mouth...and they began to glow a cyan color, illuminating the lower part of his head. Clinton watched, unable to comprehend what he was seeing, as a sound exploded from the komodo like a hundred voices screaming at the scavenger all at once.

At first the kraggon roared back defiantly, but Hagen's cries grew louder and louder, increasing until they reached an almost deafening pitch. All Clinton could do was keep his hands over his ears when the noise started leaking through his fingers. As the volume grew, the kraggon increasingly thrashed around. Hagen touched some more tattoos around his ear holes, and they too began to glow. He clenched his fist and, with a huge swing, struck the kraggon in the face. The shocked scavenger reeled back and released its grip. Hagen dropped to the ground. He lay on his back, breathing deeply, as Clinton ran to see if he was hurt.

"Tougher even than they appear," Hagen groaned, rubbing his hand. Clinton opened his mouth to speak, but the komodo raised a finger to prevent any questions. "Later."

Above them the kraggon continued to blink and shake its head. Blood trickled from its stump-like ears, running down its cheeks in small, sticky rivulets. It gulped a deep breath…and let out a bestial scream before pounding its head against the stone in fury.

"Come on!" shouted Hagen, and set off down a side passage.

Within moments they burst into a large auditorium flanked by two sweeping staircases. They sped across the cracked, tiled floor that had been hijacked by weeds and grass. The sun had only just begun to peek through the row of high windows, and the light flickered as they dashed through the many rays. They were moving so fast they practically launched themselves through the stadium's main archway and out into the open, before bounding across the grass, heading for the rope bridge.

A thunderous noise erupted behind them. Chancing a look over his shoulder, Clinton saw the archway explode, toppling to the ground and smash to pieces. The kraggon spun in a circle, searching for its prey as they skidded to a stop on the other side of the rope bridge. Slipping free his claws, Clinton swung them against the dense rope tied around an ornate anchor stone.

"Help me cut them!"

Hagen threw the bag down and slashed his long, black claws against the other set of ropes. After a few hacks, the ropes started to fray.

The kraggon let out a trumpeting wail.

"Quickly, it's coming!" warned the lion.

He swiped with all his might, and felt the rope ping and then release. The bridge swayed. The entire right side swung loose from its bindings. A second later Hagen's side did the same. On the far edge of the ravine the kraggon slid to an ungainly stop, teetering on the lip as the rope-bridge dropped, swinging down in an arc and smashing against the rock face. Shards of splintered wood fell silently into the cloudy abyss. Ramming its pincer-like feet against the ground, the kraggon howled and snorted like an Olde-world bull about to charge.

The lion sunk to his knees in the grass, trying to catch his breath. "Thank Silania! We did it," he panted.

"Yes," murmured the komodo, frowning again.

"What's wrong?"

"I do not know, but the kraggon is acting strangely."

Across the chasm, the scavenger continued to pound its feet. Its neck began to throb and undulate, as if it was choking on something.

"Hagen…what's it doing?"

The komodo took a step closer to the edge. "I am not sure. I cannot say for certain as I have ever seen such actions before."

"Is it hurt?"

"No, I do not think that is the problem, but…"

"What?"

The kraggon lurched forwards and a wretched, gagging sound spewed from its maw. Again its neck bulged, and then its whole body tensed. Lumps of flesh rippled all along its stomach, swelling through the gaps in its exoskeleton.

Hagen's face dropped. "Oh my! I think I know what may be the problem." He turned to face Clinton, stepping away from the precipice. "It appears that it…is a *she*…and she is—"

"Pregnant," finished Clinton, climbing to his feet.

"And in the final stages, I presume. How did you know?"

"She's territorial and hungry." Clinton shrugged. "I don't know. I can just tell."

Hagen turned to the lion. "She is defending herself to protect her young."

Clinton was about to reply, when he suddenly understood what Hagen was getting at. "Okay, okay. Flight isn't just about running away to save yourself, it's about protecting others, and being wise, and not being selfish. Right?"

Hagen placed his hand on the lion's shoulder. "Exactly."

"But I'd hardly say that we're a threat to her."

"In our eyes maybe, but to her anything is a threat at the

moment." They stared out across the drop, watching as the kraggon continued to retch and heave. "Just as she remains a threat to us."

Clinton huffed. "Yeah, but what's she going to do, grow wings and fly over the drop? I wasn't aware kraggons could do that."

"She will not need to," replied Hagen, stepping back even further. "Prepare yourself, Clinton."

"What for?"

Hagen, however, did not have time to reply. With one final retch, the kraggon craned her neck back and opened her jaws as wide as they would possibly go. Her spiked tail whipped up high. Her eyes glazed over, almost bulging out of their sockets, then the monstrous scavenger snapped her head forwards. Two thick jets of steel-like webbing catapulted from the glands in the kraggon's mouth and slammed into the rocks below them. Both anumals jumped back as tiny fragments of the hardening substance shattered like glass, sprinkling shards into the air. On the other side, the scavenger quickly raised her legs and detached the congealing strands from her mouth. Using her pincers, she bent them over at the end, creating hooks, and rammed them into the ground. Carefully lifting each of her legs onto the two tightropes, she teetered along the parallel threads, closing in on her trapped prey.

Clinton began to panic. "What do we do?"

Hagen hurried to the far side of the plateau and looked down over the drop.

"You think we can make it?" asked the lion. "I climbed up that way…"

Hagen shook his head. "It would be suicide. Kraggons are agile climbers. She would pick us off in moments."

"Can't you shout at it again like you did in the tunnel?"

"No. I already burst her eardrums." He scanned the ground. "Although…I think I might have an idea."

"Well, whatever it is, do it now."

The kraggon stepped off the makeshift bridge and on to the grass, and began her attack without pause, swinging her arms in a frenzied rage.

Hagen swerved, and shouted, "Clinton!" as another of her pincers whooshed straight at the lion.

Clinton launched himself out of the way in time to avoid the strike, but his momentum sent him reeling towards the lip. The ground suddenly vanished beneath him. With lightning reflexes, he thrust out his hand and clutched on to a jutting rock. His clawed fingertips gouged into the stone to prevent him from plummeting, while he swung back and forth in mid-air. Supporting his whole body, he could feel his claws slowly slipping, their tips losing what little purchase they had.

"Clinton, up here!"

The lion lifted his head to see Hagen reaching for him, and with a quick yank, hoisted him up to the lip. Scrabbling his feet against the cliff side, Clinton finally got his elbows onto the plateau and back to safety again. The lion looked up...and gaped. Behind Hagen the kraggon had reared up onto her hind legs and was ready to strike.

"Look out!"

Hagen's eyes went wide as he jumped aside, narrowly evading the attack. The kraggon thrust her fangs at Clinton and hissed in his face, revealing the emerald green lining of her mouth. Hot spittle and shards of hardened web blasted against him while he slipped back over the precipice once more.

"Hagen!"

"Hold on!"

Clinton heaved himself up and managed to get one arm over the ledge again. Desperately grasping on to anything that would hold his weight, he saw Hagen snatch up a large rock. The komodo hurled it at the scavenger's head, hitting the kraggon straight in the eye. She immediately stopped hissing at Clinton and snapped her attention back to her attacker, growled, and sprang at him. Hagen dropped to all fours. Slipping between the beast's legs, he emerged at her rear. The kraggon, however, would not be stopped. Blasting a frustrated wail, she started circling around on herself to finish him off.

Wasting no time, the komodo knelt down and lowered his face

259

to the ground. Pressing various tattoos around his mouth, he murmured words under his breath as if he was talking to the earth. As the giant monster slowly got him in her sights again, Hagen's mouth glowed a neon blue color. He lifted a clenched fist into the air and, without a moment to spare, punched a hole deep into the soil. After a second, he yanked his hand free and retreated in anticipation. His tattoos pulsed as he concentrated on the hole, the muscles in his neck bunching from the strain.

"Hagen?" gasped Clinton. The lion grabbed onto a rock, dragging his upper body over the ledge again. "What are you...?"

A single knat suddenly appeared out of the hole the lizard had created. It scurried over the churned up grass and headed in the direction of the kraggon's leg. Clinton frowned, until he spotted another tiny sectoid, and then a third...

Swarms of sectoids were emerging from the ground. Hundreds quickly turned into thousands as the earth erupted into a mass of buzzing and scuttling creatures, like black lava gushing from a miniature volcano.

As Clinton dragged his legs over the ledge, a bugling screech made him flinch. He snapped his attention back to the kraggon as the swarm scurried up her front legs. She reared back and whipped her body from side to side, flicking tiny bugs in all directions. Nonetheless, the faster she rid herself of them, the more took their place, trickling up her rear. The kraggon slammed back down on her front legs again with a gigantic crash. Her eyes bulged as she flung her head about, biting and screaming. And then her crazed eyes locked on the motionless komodo.

"HAGEN!"

The kraggon stabbed out at the komodo's face, and with a crack, struck his forehead. The lizard's tattoos flared like a flash of lightning...and then snapped out. Hagen toppled to the ground, blood running down his scalp.

As if released from a spell, the sectoids began to disperse, scuttling away from the kraggon in rippling waves. They covered the grass like an oil slick, and in seconds, surged over Hagen while moving towards Clinton. The lion shuffled back to the edge again, his heels teetering over the lip.

"Oh no!" he hissed, as the tide scurried over him.

He fell forwards, batting the bugs, desperately trying to swat them from his body. They scampered along his fur, into his hair, and through the gaps in his clothing. Some swept across his face, crawling into his mouth. He could feel them squirming along his gums and wiggling under his tongue. He gagged, but as soon as his throat relaxed, they wriggled down his gullet. A knat scurried over his eyelids and he snapped them shut. A suffocating panic overwhelmed him. The kraggon's wails slowly turned into muffled cries as bugs slipped into the lion's ears. His heart beat frantically. He could feel the patter of bugs all over him, joined with the needle-like nip of bites. Trying to cover his face, he leaned forwards, gritting his teeth and resting his head against the grass. He felt invaded, covered in itches that could drive an anumal to insanity. He swiped at the sectoids over and over again, before he slowly began to relax into submission.

He could no longer fight them off.

A strange blanket of power settled over him, a feeling familiar to that which he had felt in the Plains when the leece attacked, yet this time he chose to embrace it. He allowed his mind to open up, and the more he relaxed, the more it felt like badly needed sleep was wrapping him in its comfort. All sounds swirled and trailed away into oblivion. Nothing seemed to matter any more. He sighed, submerged in peace.

Something tickled against his senses.

He felt disconnected, like he was not within himself anymore. Even though his eyes were closed, tiny strands of color popped into life before him, leaving blurred trails in their wake. At the center of each color shone a tiny light, brighter than its surroundings. Clinton fixed his attention onto one of the lights. Feelings of confusion, anger, and hunger suddenly swept over him - a basic collection of emotions, primitive beyond recognition.

Who are you? Clinton thought. *What are you?*

The dot of light pulsed. As the surrounding lights squirmed, the dot fixed its attention back on him, as if ready to do his bidding.

Clinton felt the power inside him connect with it, and he instinctively knew what to do. Three words formed in his mind.

Leave me alone.

Sectoids exploded off of Clinton in all directions. They spewed out of his mouth in a tide of bile, and fell from his hair like rain. He snapped open his eyes and locked onto the being he had connected with. A tiny sectoid stood motionless within the sprawling mass. He could sense what it sensed and feel what it was feeling. As if he was trapped in a dream, he stared at the shining spark and pointed at the kraggon.

Attack!

The pinprick obeyed.

The singular sectoid clicked a reply that was immediately echoed by others. It turned back to the kraggon as more and more started to follow it. The tiny mind he had connected with intensified. Clinton felt another, then another, and then another mind all enter his consciousness, joining and building at an unstoppable rate, all receiving the message to attack the kraggon. The power was immense. A bright light suddenly pulsed in Clinton's mind, making him gasp. The multiplied emotions became too much to bear. He was not strong enough. He sank to the ground, gripping his head.

Again the kraggon wailed. Clinton opened his eyes to see the swarm had overrun the scavenger and covered her monstrous body from head to pincer. Her screams sounded delirious. Her eyes rolled in their sockets as she took savage bites at the sectoids, yet her attacks only helped to damage her own exoskeleton. They quickly crawled through the gaps in her body armor, burrowing under her skin. She thrashed around, swaying from left to right, desperate to stop the pain, but Clinton knew her efforts were in vain.

The kraggon collapsed onto her side.

He stared openmouthed at the terrified scavenger struggling for her life. His heart lurched with pangs of guilt and sorrow, yet all he could do was watch as the giant predator tried to rid herself of the bugs. Out of nowhere, Hagen burst into action. He darted forwards on all fours and slammed into her side with his shoulder. He grunted as he heaved the monster up and over the side of the precipice, panting as the air filled with a high-pitched cry that rose and fell in a terrifying undulation. The kraggon tumbled over the side and dropped out of sight.

"Clever," sighed Hagen, rushing to the edge.

Covered from head to foot in bites, a long trickle of blood ran from his scalp. He looked down to where she had fallen, and then gazed out across the horizon, as if searching for something. Clinton spat more dead sectoids from his mouth and stumbled to his feet.

"Are you okay?"

Hagen turned to him with a sad smile on his face. "Always thinking of others."

"Well, those little scruds bite like skorr." The lion picked the final dead bug from his mouth. "But what—"

Hagen raised a hand. "Before you ask, we need to get moving as soon as possible."

"What? Why?"

"At most we will have a day before more arrive, and trust me, they will be coming."

"More?" Clinton followed his gaze to the fallen scavenger. "Kraggons?"

Hagen nodded, turned to Clinton, and placed a hand on his shoulder. "She just called out to all the herd fathers in the area. They will have heard the wail and will set off immediately. We must get moving."

* * *

Hagen and Clinton were slumped on a ledge half way down the cliff, resting their backs against the stone to regain their energy. The komodo moved his finger over the dried blood and dirt on his skin, scraping away the filth to try improve his appearance. A bandage had been wrapped around his injured head.

Clinton looked at the bedraggled komodo, suspecting his own appearance was not much better. He sighed. Everything seemed to be moving way too fast. His life over the past few weeks had sped out of control. He had lived through so much that he had finally given up trying to make sense of it all. Yet only in the aftermath of each occasion did he sit back and realize just how close to dying he had actually come. He just prayed his luck kept holding out in the future.

He peered over the edge, seeing they still had a fair way to go until they reached the bottom. A sudden sadness washed over him. "You don't think they're dead, do you, Hagen? The babies."

"They will be fine," replied the komodo, closing his eyes and leaning his head against the rock. "Her swollen web-glands should have protected them from the impact."

"So she might still be alive then?"

Hagen shook his head. "No, I doubt that she will have survived such a fall. Her young, however, should have."

Clinton shifted uncomfortably.

"You should not feel any guilt, Clinton. Female kraggons die during childbirth, after the babies tear their way out of their mother's stomach - another raw deal that the Great Mother can bestow. Besides," Hagen rolled his neck, "the sectoids knew not to harm the youngsters."

"But how?"

Hagen opened an eye. "Because I told them so. Just like you told them to attack."

Clinton gulped. "What happened up there, Hagen? What exactly did I do?"

Hagen chuckled. "Well, that, Clinton, could be called the start of your training. I had not thought it possible yet, but your display of power has shown me you are indeed ready."

A few seconds passed. Clinton sighed again. However much he had tried to dismiss it, he now knew for definite that he possessed powers, and the episode with the kraggon had only cemented it. Eventually, he peered over the ledge again. "And you're *certain* they weren't harmed?"

Hagen groaned and sat up.

"You are not going to let this lie are you?"

"I just wish I knew for sure. It wasn't her babies' fault, and I hate to think that they suffered."

"Very well, I will check for you."

"Check? But how?"

The komodo crossed his legs. He touched a tattoo between his eyes and then another on the top of his head. Slowly lowering his hands, he rested them on his lap.

Clinton waited for something to happen in the silence.

A few more seconds passed.

"Hagen? Are you okay?"

The tattoos Hagen had touched started to glow, and his skin turned pale and dull, like the vibrancy had all but drained from it. Clinton dare not move for fear of interrupting whatever it was the komodo was up to, so he sat and watched. After a minute the tattoos flared and then dulled again. Hagen opened his eyes as color flooded back to his skin.

"The kraggon's pups did indeed survive, but they have fled. There were three in total, but one turned on the runt and managed to injure it. Judging by the amount of blood the runt lost, I find it unlikely that it will survive. Doubtless all three will go into hiding until the herd fathers arrive and lay claim, and by that time we had best be long gone. It will be like a war zone around here tomorrow."

Clinton shook his head, not knowing whether to laugh or cry.

"What is wrong?" asked Hagen, tilting his head.

"Everything," Clinton answered, not missing a beat. "Those *things* you did back there: the screaming, the sectoids, and now this… How?"

Hagen smiled his lopsided grin. "It is merely a different type of defense to what you are used to, that is all. Plus I can push my senses to more extremes than others."

"Well, I certainly wish I could have you around the next time I'm fighting any monsters off my back."

There was a slight pause before Hagen spoke.

"But you will, Clinton."

The lion looked back at him. "Will what?"

"You will have me fighting by your side."

Clinton chuckled and climbed to his feet. He wiped his hand across his face and looked down at himself. He was indeed full of cuts and grazes. "So what do you intend to do then? Follow me around for the rest of my life?"

"Pretty much," remarked Hagen as he also rose to his feet. "My *lifequest* has just begun, and you, Clinton, are it. I am the Crystal Soul Guardian, and you are the Crystal Soul. Therefore, I will protect you until the time the bone collector gathers your soul for the final Journey."

"Guardian? But...why?"

"From this moment forward, forces will try to claim you for themselves." Placing his large hand on Clinton's shoulder, Hagen of the Hand smiled warmly. "So like a shadow I shall become, never leaving your side until your quest has ended. Like it or not, Clinton, I am with you."

The lion looked into Hagen's reptilian eyes, and saw no way of dissuading him. Whether he was against having a companion or not, Clinton knew that from now on he had company. An idea snuck to the forefront of his mind, and his face lit up. "Why don't we both head back to Wooburn then? The village guards won't stand a chance if you're with me. You can do those things you do and clear the way to Raion—"

"The enemy will have Wooburn covered by now. It will be expected for you to head back for your brother, and they will be waiting for your return. The rules have changed. The pact has been broken."

"What pact?"

"Please trust me, Clinton. You are no longer safe anywhere, Wooburn least of all."

"So they'll have taken over the village?"

"Wooburn will be watched. I suspect you would not get within a day's travel without ghastlings or something worse discovering you."

Clinton's fist clenched. He looked out over the Great Plains, feeling his heart being pulled towards a village he could no longer call home.

"If I think he's in any kind of danger then I'm going back for him, Hagen, and nobody will stop me."

"I know. And I promise that he will be protected. Contingencies were put in place. To journey back now would only throw him into danger, and I am certain that is not an outcome you would wish for him." Clinton nodded his head. "I promise you there will be other ways of being reunited with your brother, but first we must think of a means to successfully achieve your goals."

"My goals?"

"A power threatens to consume and eradicate all we are, Clinton. You were born for a purpose, one you shall soon find anumalkind begging you to fulfill."

The lion contemplated his words.

"Okay," he finally said. "So if I can't return home, then where do we go now? What should I do?"

Hagen cleared his throat and looked at the mountains. "I suggest we head north."

Clinton turned to peer across the landscape. "And what lies for us there then?"

"My tribe and other sensors," he answered. "They will guide us to the best course of action to see your brother again. And, of course, begin your training."

A few wefrings flew over their heads and settled in a nest within the rocks. The lion watched as the female set about feeding her youngsters. Only a few weeks ago Clinton had been doing much the same thing, scavenging for food so that he could feed Raion. Yet back then he had wished for nothing more than to escape that life. As the morning sun gradually rose, so did a fresh feeling of purpose within the lion. Inside him he knew he had to become *someone*... An anumal to respect.

A leader.

And be it in a season, a year, or even two, he would return to collect Raion. That, he promised himself, was what he would work for more than anything else in the world.

Hagen cleared his throat. "Are you ready?"

"Yes, I think I am."

With renewed vigor the two continued their descent down the rock face and towards the steps carved into the base of the mountain. Once they reached the bottom, they turned north and set off for the mountains, bathed in the light of the morning sun.

* * *

High above the Idlefields, in front of Samanoski's ruined entrance, the ghostly badger paced back and forth, watching them trek northwards. His face twisted in anger and his bottomless eyes narrowed to slits. He shook with a rage that had festered and eaten at him for years. Angry words built inside him until he could not hold himself back any longer.

"Don't trust him!" he hissed, his decayed teeth chattering together as he spoke. "He's not what he seems. Don't trust any of them!"

Outside the deserted stadium, the badger's words echoed, causing the scuttlers hidden within the crevices to scamper away in fright.

"He's not what he seems... No one are what they seem!" whispered the ghostly anumal one final time.

With a grunt, he turned back to the stadium's entrance and slowly wandered off amongst the newly made ruins. As he departed, he gradually began to meld into the deeper shadows and, after a few more seconds, completely disappeared from view.

- - -

END OF BOOK ONE

- - -

Read more in

BOOK TWO

ANUMAL EMPIRE: ALPHA

Darren and David would like to say thank you to:
Edwina, Aliesha, Phil, Odele, Luke, Isabelle, Anne, and Chris for
your love and support.

Paul Burston, Paulo Kadow, Alastair Macaulay,
Emma Ruthven, Azucena Durán, Emma Burton,
Charles Hinkle, Dan Worth, Jenny Jenson,
and Damien Stirk for your honest words,
kindness, and talent.

Ben Wilkinson for the wonderful cover art.

Dedicated to Michael Ayres (the big man upstairs)
and Martin Oakley (the best ever English teacher),
and to all the people who gave us advice and encouragement.

Follow us on Facebook – Anumal Empire
anumalempire.com
darrenjacobs.com

@DavidAyres01
@darrenjcbs

Made in the USA
San Bernardino, CA
05 September 2016